Happy Ever After

For Megan
S.W.

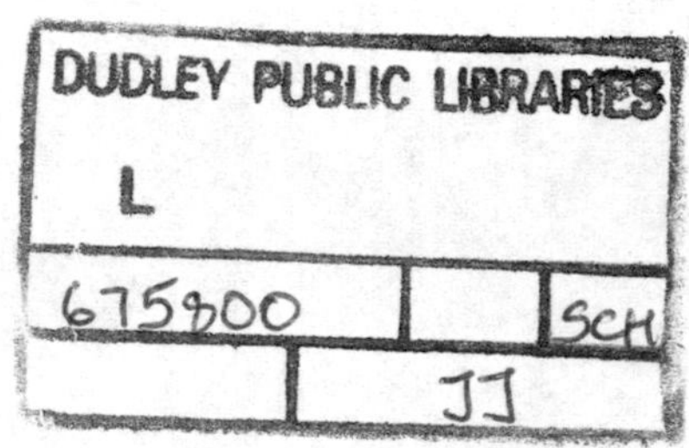

ORCHARD BOOKS
338 Euston Road, London NW1 3BH
Orchard Books Australia
Hachette Children's Books
Level 17/207, Kent Street, Sydney, NSW 2000

ISBN 1 84362 529 6 (hardback)
ISBN 1 84362 537 7 (paperback)
First published in Great Britain in 2006
First paperback publication in 2006

 A CIP catalogue record for this book is available from the British Library.

1 3 5 7 9 10 8 6 4 2 (hardback)
1 3 5 7 9 10 8 6 4 2 (paperback)
Printed in Great Britain

Tony Bradman

Happy Ever After

THE FAIRY GODMOTHER TAKES A BREAK

Illustrated by Sarah Warburton

ORCHARD BOOKS

Deep in the forest there stands a little cottage, and in that cottage is a cosy bedroom, where somebody's alarm clock is about to go off...

BEEP-BEEP-BEEP! BEEP-BEEP-BEEP! BEEP-BEEP-BEEP!

"Oh no!" groaned the Fairy Godmother. "It can't possibly be time to get up already. I feel like I've only just gone to bed."

"Sorry, dear," said her husband, Mr Fairy Godmother. "I, er... set the alarm for a bit earlier than usual. I think it could be a very busy day."

“Huh, so what’s new?” muttered the Fairy Godmother. She pulled the duvet over her head. “Busy, busy, busy. I never get a second to myself...”

“Oh well, never mind,” said Mr FG. “I’ll go and put the kettle on.”

The Fairy Godmother kept muttering under the duvet.

She muttered in the shower, too, and while she got dressed, and she was still muttering when she sat down at the kitchen table. Mr FG put a nice cup of tea in front of her.

"Nobody ever thanks me, either," she said.

"Take Cinderella, for instance. I spent a whole week running around for her, putting spells on rats and mice and pumpkins and sorting out her life. And have I heard from her since?"

"Well, dear," said Mr FG, "that's probably because..."

"I'm tired of granting wishes," the Fairy Godmother muttered, interrupting him. "Anyway, where will I be waving my wand today?"

"I'll find out," said Mr FG. "I just need to switch on the computer."

Soon Mr FG was sitting before a large, glowing screen. He worked as his wife's personal assistant, and he had a special, magic computer that only accepted one kind of message - wish-mails.

Whenever someone in the forest made a wish, it instantly arrived on the screen with a...PING!

Mr FG tapped the keyboard, and the wish-mails started to come in. PING! PING! PING! PING! PING! PING! PING! PING! PING!...

There were far more than usual, and the screen quickly filled up.

"Right, that's it," said the Fairy Godmother. "I've had enough. I quit. I resign."

"And just to make it absolutely official..."

She held up her magic wand...and snapped it in half. Mr FG winced.

"Oh well," said Mr FG. "Er...would you like another cup of tea, dear?"

"No thanks," said the Fairy Godmother. "I'd rather have...a holiday!"

Mr FG sighed again...but he called Fairy Tale Holidays and arranged everything.

The next morning they flew out of Forest Airport, and a few hours later they arrived at Club Enchantment, their holiday destination.

"Ah, this is the life," said the Fairy Godmother as Mr FG unpacked their suitcases. "Sun, sea and sand - I can feel myself relaxing already..."

Mr and Mrs FG spent the day swimming and sunbathing (always remembering to put on sun cream) and reading their books.

In the evening they had dinner at The Magic Spoon, Club Enchantment's best restaurant.

The band was really cool, and the food was a thousand times better than Mr FG's cooking.

But the Fairy Godmother didn't seem too happy.

"Those dwarves over there are staring at me," she whispered.

"Oh no, I don't think they are, dear," murmured Mr FG, who was tucking into his dinner. "This lobster is terrific. You really should try some."

"They *are* staring at me, and I don't like it," the Fairy Godmother said. "And I'm NOT going to put up with it, either. Come on, we're leaving!"

"B-b-but..." Mr FG spluttered. Then he sighed, paid the bill, and followed his wife, looking longingly at the lovely lobster he was leaving behind.

The next morning they went to the beach again. Mr FG had just got to a good part of his book when the Fairy Godmother poked him in the ribs.

"Psst!" she hissed at him. "Somebody else is staring at me now."

"Calm down, dear," said Mr FG, looking up. "I don't think anyone... Actually, you're right. He is staring at you, isn't he? How strange."

A young troll in swimming trunks couldn't take his eyes off the Fairy Godmother.

And as they watched him, he smiled shyly, and waved. Then he said something to a family of elves nearby, and pointed at her. Soon they were smiling at her too and so was everyone else on the beach.

"You realise what this means, don't you?" the Fairy Godmother hissed to Mr FG from the corner of her mouth. *"They all know who I am!"*

"Oh, of course!" said Mr FG. "But that's no surprise. You've helped so many people, dear. There are bound to be some here who recognise you."

"They'll be asking me to grant wishes, next," she said. "And you know I won't get a word of thanks. Come on, we're leaving!"

"Yes, dear," murmured Mr FG, closing his book with a deep sigh.

That evening they didn't go to The Magic Spoon, but to another restaurant instead. It wasn't as good.

The Fairy Godmother wore dark glasses and a headscarf, and didn't take them off even when she was eating. But people still stared at her, and smiled and waved.

Then, the next day on the beach, the Fairy Godmother suddenly froze.

"Oh no," she whispered to Mr FG, panic in her voice. "Don't look now, but I think that princess is coming over to talk to me. Come on, we're..."

“I know, I know,” muttered Mr FG. “We’re leaving.”

The Fairy Godmother strode off, and Mr FG hurried behind her carrying their bags, with the princess in hot pursuit.

In the end, the Fairy Godmother and Mr FG were practically running, but the princess caught up with them.

"Please, wait!" she called out. "I'm sorry, but I simply had to make sure it was you. I would never, ever forgive myself if I missed this chance to..."

"Sorry! Can't stop!" said the Fairy Godmother. "Come along, dear!"

"...say a huge thank you for everything you did for me," said the princess.

"Er...I'm Cinderella, in case you'd forgotten. You totally changed my life."

"Did I really?" said the Fairy Godmother, peering at the princess for a second, then smiling. "Yes, I remember you now. Well, how are things?"

Cinderella told the Fairy Godmother all about her new life with Prince Charming. Cinders also said she would have thanked her before, but didn't have any way of getting in touch with her.

As they talked, lots more people came up to the Fairy Godmother and said exactly the same thing.

"Anyway, enjoy the rest of your holiday," said Cinders at last. The Fairy Godmother beamed at her.

"Although I bet you can't wait to go home and start helping people again. How wonderful to have a job like yours... Bye!"

The Fairy Godmother's smile vanished, and suddenly she looked upset. And by the time she and Mr FG were back in their room, she was in tears.

"Cinderella is right," she moaned. "It is a wonderful job, and I've thrown it away. Why didn't you tell me no one knows how to send me any thanks?"

“Er...I did try,” said Mr FG. “Anyway, I’m sure that’s a problem I can solve. You need to get out a bit more too, maybe do some follow-up visits.”

"Follow-ups to what?" she wailed. "I won't be able to grant wishes any more. I broke my wand, remember? Although now I *so* wish that I hadn't..."

"Well...your wish is granted," said Mr FG, smiling. He opened one of their suitcases and pulled out...her wand. "Sort of, anyway. I mended it before we left home. And though I say so myself, it's, er...almost as good as new."

The Fairy Godmother looked at it in amazement...and hugged him.

They enjoyed the rest of their holiday. And even though there were loads of wish-mails waiting for them when they got home, the Fairy Godmother didn't mind.

In fact, she was keen to get back to work now that she felt more appreciated. Mr FG rather liked having the cottage to himself too...

So the Fairy Godmother and Mr FG and just about everyone in the forest who made a wish lived...

HAPPILY EVER AFTER!

Written by Tony Bradman
Illustrated by Sarah Warburton

Mr Wolf Bounces Back	1 84362 523 7	£8.99
Jack's Bean Snacks	1 84362 524 5	£8.99
Rapunzel Cuts Loose	1 84362 525 3	£8.99
Cinderella and the Mean Queen	1 84362 526 1	£8.99
The Frog Prince Hops to It	1 84362 527 X	£8.99
Red Riding Hood Takes Charge	1 84362 528 8	£8.99
Fairy Godmother Takes a Break	1 84362 529 6	£8.99
Goldilocks and the Just Right Club	1 84362 530 X	£8.99

GEORG DOX

DIE RUSSISCHE SOWJETLITERATUR

GEORG DOX

DIE RUSSISCHE SOWJETLITERATUR

Namen, Daten, Werke

WALTER DE GRUYTER & CO.

vormals G. J. Göschen'sche Verlagshandlung · J. Guttentag Verlagsbuchhandlung · Georg Reimer · Karl J. Trübner · Veit & Comp.

BERLIN 1961

Archiv-Nr. 440761

Satz und Druck:
Deutsche Zentraldruckerei AG, Berlin SW 61

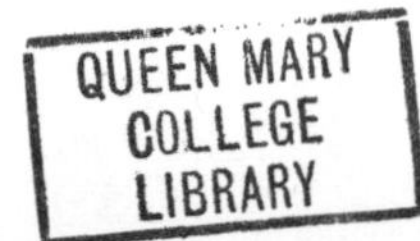

VORWORT

Die vorliegende „Russische Sowjetliteratur" gibt in alphabetischer Reihenfolge Auskunft über das Leben und Schaffen der bekanntesten russischen Sowjetschriftsteller. Unter russischen Sowjetschriftstellern werden solche Schriftsteller verstanden, welche in der Sowjetunion leben oder wenigstens eine gewisse Zeit dort gelebt haben und vor allem in der Zeit nach 1917 literarisch tätig waren und ihre Werke in russischer Sprache verfaßten bzw. verfassen. Entscheidend aber ist, daß sich die betreffenden Schriftsteller selber zum russischen Kulturkreis zählen. In dieser Hinsicht jedoch eine verläßliche Grenze zu ziehen, ist nicht immer durchführbar. Die sowjetische Literaturforschung, wie auch die Große Sowjetenzyklopädie, teilt die sowjetischen Dichter in drei Gruppen ein, nämlich in „russische", „russisch-sowjetische" und „sowjetische". Dabei spielt aber auch das nationale, historische und politische Moment eine nicht geringe Rolle. Für unsere Zwecke genügt jedoch die von uns getroffene Einteilung. Freilich werden zu den russischen Sowjetschriftstellern manchmal auch solche gezählt, welche ihrer Abstammung nach zwar nicht russischer Nationalität sind, aber im russischen Kulturkreis wirken (z. B. Šaginjan, Erenburg).

Der Leser möge berücksichtigen, daß das vorliegende Buch eine noch nicht erstarrte Materie behandelt, daß manche Urteile revidiert werden müssen, daß manches noch nicht bekannt ist und manches aus der Perspektive einer späteren Forschung wahrscheinlich anders aussehen wird, als es die Zeitgenossen sehen. So erhebt zum Beispiel die jeweils angeführte Bibliographie keinen Anspruch auf Vollkommenheit, da nur die bekanntesten und wichtigsten Werke der Autoren berücksichtigt werden konnten. Die Titel der Werke wurden (nach Möglichkeit mit Angabe des Erscheinungsjahres) ins Deutsche übersetzt. Insofern die deutschen Titel der Werke nicht bereits durch erschienene Übersetzungen allgemein bekannt sind (z. B. „Der stille Don"), erheben sie keinen Anspruch auf „Endgültigkeit", da der Verfasser nur bemüht war, ihren Sinn genau wiederzugeben. Eigennamen und geographische Begriffe wurden nicht übersetzt.

Eine subjektive Bewertung der Autoren wurde vermieden. Nur hie und da wurden — unter Hinweis auf die Quellen — allgemein gültige und besonders typische Charakterisierungen bekannter Autoren angeführt. Das Buch ist im großen und ganzen das Ergebnis jahrelanger Studien. Die herangezogenen literarhistorischen Standardwerke werden in einem besonderen Verzeichnis angeführt.

Als wesentlicher Anhang wurde ein Verzeichnis gebräuchlicher sowjetischer literarischer Begriffe meist in sowjetischer Diktion beigefügt.

Besonderer Dank sei an dieser Stelle auch meinen zwei Mitarbeitern ausgesprochen, nämlich Frau Margarete Fuchs, Research Associate an der Fordham University in New York, für ihre mühevolle Mitarbeit in der Qellenforschung, und Herrn Franz Templ für seine gewissenhaften Korrekturarbeiten.

Linz/Donau, im Jahre 1960 *Der Verfasser*

INHALT

TRANSLITERATIONSTABELLE

А а	=	A	И и	=	I	Р р	=	R	Ш ш	=	Š
Б б	=	B	Й й	=	J	С с	=	S	Щ щ	=	ŠČ
В в	=	V	К к	=	K	Т т	=	T	Ъ ъ	=	–
Г г	=	G	Л л	=	L	У у	=	U	Ы ы	=	Y
Д д	=	D	М м	=	M	Ф ф	=	F	Ь ь	=	'
Е е	=	E[1]	Н н	=	N	Х х	=	Ch	Э э	=	E
Ж ж	=	Ž	О о	=	O	Ц ц	=	C	Ю ю	=	Ju
З з	=	Z	П п	=	P	Ч ч	=	Č	Я я	=	Ja

[1] Der Buchstabe Ë ë wird, sofern im russischen Text vorhanden, auch mit Ë ë wiedergegeben.

ABKÜRZUNGEN

für Standardwerke und Quellen, welche im Textteil des öfteren zitiert werden.

Allgemeine Nachschlagewerke, wie etwa die Große Sowjetenzyklopädie oder „Enciklopedičeskij slovar'" (Enzyklopädisches Wörterbuch), werden nicht besonders zitiert.

Die Bibliographie, und hier vor allem die Übersetzungen, wurde auf Grund der erreichbaren Literatur erstellt und mit Ergänzungen aus folgenden Werken versehen:

„Proizvedenija sovetskich pisatelej v perevodach no inostrannye jazyki 1945—1953" (Werke sowjetischer Schriftsteller in fremdsprachigen Übersetzungen 1945—1953, Moskau 1954).

„Russkie sovetskie pisateli — prozaiki" (Russische sowjetische Schriftsteller — Prosaiker, Bd. 1, Leningrad 1959).

A. N.	Akademija nauk SSSR, Istorija russkoj sovetskoj literatury, Bd. I, 1917—1929, Moskva 1958, und Bd. II, 1929—1941, Moskau 1960.
ANT	Antologija russkoj sovetskoj poezii 1917—1957. I, II. Gosud. izd. chudožestvennoj literatury, Moskva 1957.
KSB	Kleine Slavische Biographie, Wiesbaden 1958.
L.	Arthur Luther, Geschichte der Russischen Literatur, Bibliographisches Institut, Leipzig 1924.
L. E.	Literaturnaja enciklopedija, Moskva 1929.
S. L.	Sowjet-Literatur, Monatsschrift des Schriftstellerverbandes der UdSSR, Moskau.
Struve	Gleb Struve, Geschichte der Sowjetliteratur, Isar Verlag, München 1958.
T. V.	L. Timofeev i N. Vengerov, Kratkij slovar' literaturovedčeskich terminov, Moskva 1955.

AUTOREN

Achmátova Ánna Andréevna (Pseudonym für A. A. Gorénko)

Geb. 1888 in Südrußland, aus einer Adelsfamilie stammend. Mit N. *Gumilëv,* mit dem sie von 1910—1918 verheiratet war, zählt A. zu den hervorragendsten Vertretern der *Akmeisten.* Als eine der bedeutendsten Lyrikerin der russischen Literatur wird A. der Form nach stark von Puškin beeinflußt. Nachdem sie außer einigen in den dreißiger Jahren erschienenen Puškinstudien und einer Übersetzung des armenischen Dichters D. Varužan (Pervyj grech, Die erste Sünde, 1936) seit 1922 nichts mehr veröffentlicht hatte, meldete sich A. erst 1940 wieder mit einigen Gedichten in der Leningrader Zeitschrift „Zvezda" und mit einer Neuausgabe ihrer Gedichte im Sammelband „Iz šesti knig" (Aus sechs Büchern) zu Worte. In seiner programmatischen Rede „Über Wissenschaft und Kunst" setzte sich *Ždanov* im August 1946 eingehendst mit *Zoščenko,* mit den *Akmeisten,* und hier insbesondere mit A. als der Begründerin dieser „reaktionären literarischen Strömung", auseinander. Das Ergebnis dieser Verurteilung war ein Druckverbot für A., das erst 1950 wieder aufgehoben wurde. Obwohl A.s Dichtung nicht den Erfordernissen des *sozialistischen Realismus* entspricht und daher von der offiziellen sowjetischen Kritik kühl aufgenommen wird, wird A. immer wieder gedruckt und gern gelesen. Es soll jedoch auch nicht unerwähnt bleiben, daß der dichterische Wert der nach der Aufhebung des Schreibverbotes erschienenen Gedichte A.s gegenüber den früheren bedeutend geringer ist.

Večer (Abend, 1912)
Čëtki (Rosenkranz, 1914)
Belaja staja (Der weiße Schwarm, 1917)
Anno Domini (1922)
Iva (Die Weide, 1940)
Iz cikla ‚Slava miru' (Aus dem Zyklus ‚Ruhm dem Frieden', 1950)
Stichotvorenija (Gedichte, 1958)

Adamján Nóra (Eleonóra Geórgievna)

Geb. 1910 in Odessa als Tochter eines Arztes, schriftstellerisch tätig seit 1928. Neben Übersetzungen armenischer Schriftsteller ins Russische beschäftigte sich A. in ihrem Schaffen — vor allem Erzählungen — mit dem Thema „Die Frau".

Zolotaja mast' (Die goldene Farbe, 1955)
Vozvraščenie (Die Rückkehr, 1956)
Sestrënka (Schwesterchen, 1956)
Obed u sestry Erik (Das Mittagmahl bei der Schwester Erik, 1958)
U sinich gor (In den blauen Bergen, 1957)

Deutsche Übersetzungen

In den blauen Bergen, übers. v. E. Margolis, Moskau, S. L. 1957.

Afinogénov Aleksándr Nikoláevič

1904—1941. A. gehörte in den zwanziger Jahren zu der Künstlergruppe des sog. *Proletkultes.* Seine späteren Werke können als typisch für die Sowjetliteratur der dreißiger Jahre angesehen werden. Der Wert früherer Theaterstücke A.s liegt weniger im Künstlerischen als vielmehr im Dokumentarischen, wobei als beste Werke „Strach" (Die Angst) und „Dalëkoe" (Die Ferne) genannt werden können. Die Stücke des Autors zeichnen sich mehr durch psychologische Tiefe als durch Beherrschung des Theatertechnischen aus. A. kam 1941 bei einem Luftangriff auf Moskau ums Leben.

Malinovoe varen'e (Himbeerkonfitüre, 1926)
Čudak (Der Sonderling, 1928)
Strach (Die Angst, 1931)
Dalëkoe (Die Ferne, 1936)
Vtorye puti (Das zweite Gleis, 1939)
Mašen'ka (1940)
Nakanune (Am Vorabend, 1941)

Deutsche Übersetzungen

Ein Punkt in der Welt (Dalëkoe), übertragen v. L. Schwarz. Für die deutsche Bühne bearbeitet v. F. Treuberg, Berlin-Charlottenburg, Henschel. 1946.

Großvater und Enkelin (Mašen'ka), übers. v. M. Seldowitsch u. J. Berend-Groa, Berlin, Henschel. 1946.

Aleksandróvskij Vasílij Dmítrievič

1897—1934, als Sohn eines Bauern in Baskakov, Gouvernement Smolensk, geboren. A. arbeitete nach dem Besuch der Dorfschule in einer Lederfabrik in Moskau. Nach seiner Militärzeit von 1916—1917 kehrte A. 1918 nach Moskau zurück und schloß sich 1920 der eben gegründeten Dichtervereinigung *Kuznica* an. Seine erste Gedichtsammlung „Vosstanie" (Aufruhr) erschien 1919 in Moskau.

Vosstanie (Aufruhr, 1919)
Zvon solnca (Das Läuten der Sonne, 1923)
Stichi i poemy (Gedichte und Poeme, 1957)

Aligér (Aligér-Makárova) Margaríta Jósifovna

Geb. 1915, schriftstellerisch tätig seit 1933, absolvierte das Literarische Institut des Verbandes der Sowjetschriftsteller im Jahre 1937. A. ist Mitglied der KPdSU. Ihre Gefühlslyrik ist stark von den *Akmeisten*, vor allem von *Achmatova*, beeinflußt. Durch ihre scharfe Kritik an den Schattenseiten des sowjetischen Lebens lenkte A. die Aufmerksamkeit der Leitung der KPdSU auf sich. Aber es bedurfte erst einer von Chruščëv selbst ausgesprochenen Rüge, daß A. ihre Abweichungen von der Parteilinie als Fehler einbekannte.

God roždenija (Das Geburtsjahr)
Železnaja doroga (Die Eisenbahn, 1939)
Kamni s travoj (Steine mit Gras, 1940)
Pamjati chrabrych (Den Mutigen gewidmet, 1942)
Zoja (1942, *Stalinpreis* 1943)
Skazka o pravde (Das Märchen von der Wahrheit, 1945)
Pervye primety (Die ersten Merkmale, 1948)
Samoe glavnoe (Die Hauptsache, 1956)
Iz zapisnych knižek (Aus Notizbüchern, 1956)

Antokól'skij Pável Grigór'evič

Geb. 1896 in St. Petersburg, studierte Rechtswissenschaft. Seit 1943 ist A. Mitglied der KPdSU. Sein erster Gedichtband, in welchem ein ebenso starker Einfluß der französischen Literatur wie der *Akmeisten* (*Mandel'štam*) festzustellen ist, erschien 1922. In seinen vielfach pessimistischen Gedichten überwiegt das Intellektuelle über das intuitive Gefühl. A. ist als Schauspieler und Regisseur am Vachtangov-Theater in Moskau tätig.

Robesp'er i Gorgona (Robespierre und Gorgona, 1928)
Kommuna 1871 (Kommune 1871, 1931)
Bol'šie rasstojanija (Große Entfernungen, 1936)
Puškinskij god (Das Puškinjahr, 1938)
Polgoda (Ein halbes Jahr, 1942)
Železo i ogon' (Eisen und Feuer, 1942)
Fransua Villon (François Villon, 1943)
Koščej (Der Zauberer, 1943)
Syn (Der Sohn, 1943, *Stalinpreis* 1946)
Tret'ja kniga vojny (Das dritte Kriegsbuch, 1946)

Antónov Sergéj Petróvič

Geb. 1915 in Petrograd, von Beruf Ingenieur, seit 1944 schriftstellerisch tätig. A. tritt zuerst mit Gedichten hervor, geht aber dann zu Prosawerken über. In seinen letzten Erzählungen sind größere Reife und Sicherheit im Stil zu vermerken, z. B. in „Rasskaz bez geroja" (Erzählung ohne Held).

Vesna (Frühling, 1947)
Lena (1948)
Tamara Škurko (1948)
Po dorogam idut mašiny (Straßen in den neuen Tag, 1950)
Mirnye ljudi (Friedliche Menschen, 1951, *Stalinpreis*)
Pervaja dolžnost' (Die erste Anstellung, 1952)
Vasilëk (1957)
Rasskaz bez geroja (Erzählung ohne Held, 1957)

Deutsche Übersetzungen

In der einsamen Staniza, übers. v. Ilse Stieg, Berlin, Aufbau-Verlag. 1955.

Straßen in den neuen Tag (Po dorogam idut mašiny), übers. v. Margarete Spady, Berlin, Verlag Neues Leben. 1952.

Silberne Hochzeit, übers. v. Ingeborg Peschler-Gampert, Moskau, S. L. 1959.

Arbúzov Alekséj Nikoláevič

Geb. 1908 in Moskau. Er absolvierte die Theaterschule in Leningrad und trat als Schriftsteller 1930 mit der Aufführung seines Theaterstückes „Klass“ (Die Klasse) erstmals an die Öffentlichkeit. A. versteht es, aktuelle Themen des Sowjetlebens bühnenwirksam zu gestalten. Seine Stücke erfreuen sich in der Sowjetunion großer Popularität, so war z. B. das Stück „Tanja“ ein großer Publikumserfolg und erlebte seit 1939 bereits mehr als 1000 Aufführungen. Im Jahre 1941 organisierte A. in Moskau ein Jugendtheater.

Klass (Die Klasse, 1930)
Dal'njaja doroga (Der weite Weg, 1935)
Šestero ljubimych (Die sechs Lieblinge, 1935)
Tanja (1938)
Bessmertnyj (Der Unsterbliche, 1942)
Domik v Čerkizove (Das Häuschen in Čerkizova, 1943)
Vstreča s junost'ju (Begegnung mit der Jugend, 1947)
Goroda na zarje (Städte in der Morgenröte, 1957)
Dvenadcatyj čas (Die zwölfte Stunde, 1960)
Irkutskaja istorija (Eine Geschichte aus Irkutsk, 1960)

Deutsche Übersetzungen

Tanja. Dramatische Szenen in 4 Akten, übers. v. Dr. Zdravka Ebenstein, „Die Brücke“, Wien.

Der weite Weg. Lyrische Komödie in 3 Akten, übers. v. Erwin Arlt, Berlin, Henschelverlag. 1959.

Eine Geschichte aus Irkutsk, Schauspiel in 2 Aufzügen, übers. v. Regina Czoka, Moskau, S. L. 1960.

Árskij Pável Aleksándrovič

Geb. 1886 in Korolëvo, Gouvernement Smolensk, als Sohn einer Arbeiterfamilie. A. war seit seinem 15. Lebensjahr in den verschiedensten Berufen tätig und wurde 1905 wegen revolutionärer Tätigkeit in Sevastopol' verurteilt. Nach der Revolution schloß sich A. der Dichtervereinigung *Proletkul't* in Petrograd an, wo auch 1919 sein erster Gedichtband „Pesni bor'by“ (Kampflieder) erschien.

Pesni bor'by (Kampflieder, 1919)
Serp i molot (Sichel und Hammer, 1925)
Pesni i ballady (Lieder und Balladen, 1934)

Aséev Nikoláj Nikoláevič

Geb. 1889 als Sohn eines Angestellten, absolvierte die Realschule in Kursk und die Handelsschule in Moskau. Seine 1914 und 1916 erschienenen Gedichte kennzeichnen ihn als *Symbolisten* und Anhänger der *Kubofuturisten*. In den 1925 während seiner Tätigkeit bei der Zeitschrift *„Lef"* veröffentlichten „Liričeskie otstuplenija" (Lyrische Abweichungen) tritt A. scharf gegen das in der *NEP-Zeit* hochgekommene Spießertum auf. Die besondere Stärke des zum *Anarchismus* tendierenden, aber sehr begabten Dichters liegt in einem ungewöhnlichen Reichtum an Vergleichen. Wenn er auch unter dem Einfluß *Chlebnikovs* stand, wird A. allgemein als Nachfolger *Majakovskijs* angesehen. Manche halten ihn für „lyrischer und melodischer als Majakovskij" (R. Lelevič, L. E., Bd. 1, S. 269). 1941 wurde A. mit dem *Stalinpreis* ausgezeichnet.

Nočnaja flejta (Die Nachtflöte, 1914)
Okeanija (Okeanien, 1916)
Stal'noj solovej (Die stählerne Nachtigall, 1922)
Poema o Budënnom (Budennyj-Poem, 1923)
Poema o 26 bakinskich kommunistach (Poem von den 26 Kommunisten aus Baku, 1923)
Liričeskie otstuplenija (Lyrische Abweichungen, 1925)
Semën Prostakov (1928)
Dnevnik poeta (Tagebuch eines Dichters, 1929)
Rabota nad stichom (Die Arbeit am Vers, 1929)
Pamjati let. Sbornik stichotvorenij 1912—1955 (Erinnerung an vergangene Jahre, Gedichtsammlung 1912—1955, 1956)
Brigady kommunističeskogo truda (Brigaden kommunistischer Arbeit, 1958)

Deutsche Übersetzungen

Gedichte. Brigaden kommunistischer Arbeit, Schritte bergan, übers. v. Sepp Österreicher, Moskau, S. L. 1959.

Atárov Nikoláj Sergéevič

Geb. 1907 in Vladikavkaz, studierte Pädagogik in Vladikavkaz und Kunstgeschichte in Leningrad. 1945 war A. als Soldat in Wien. Seine ersten Werke erschienen 1930 in „Naši dostiženija" (Unsere Errungenschaften). A. wurde 1948 Mitarbeiter der „Literaturnaja gazeta" und später Chefredakteur der Zeitschrift „Moskva". Am 8. 8. 1957 wurde er von der „Literaturnaja gazeta" wegen Außerachtlassung der Parteilinie bei der Aufnahme von Beiträgen in die Zeitschrift „Moskva" streng gerügt.

Dvorec Sovetov (Sowjetpalast, 1939)
Istorija pervoj ljubvi (Die Geschichte einer ersten Liebe, 1955)

Deutsche Übersetzungen

Geschichte einer ersten Liebe, übers. v. Regina Czora, Moskau, S. L. 1957.

Ažáev Vasílij Nikoláevič

Geb. 1915, begann seine literarische Tätigkeit 1937 und absolvierte 1944 das Literarische Institut des Verbandes sowjetischer Schriftsteller. A.s bedeutendster Roman, „Fern von Moskau", gehört zu den Werken, die den Richtlinien *Ždanovs (Ždanovščina)* entsprachen, die sowjetische Wirklichkeit und den Eifer der Sowjetmenschen beim Wiederaufbau zu schildern. Das Werk wurde in 20 Sprachen übersetzt und erreichte eine Auflage von 1 635 000.

Daleko ot Moskvy (Fern von Moskau, 1948, *Stalinpreis* 1949)
Zoloto (Gold, 1946—47)

Deutsche Übersetzungen

Fern von Moskau, übers. v. A. Böltz, Berlin, Kultur und Fortschritt. 1951, 1953. Wien, Globus Verlag. 1951.

Babaévskij Semën Petróvič

Geb. 1909 im Gouvernement Char'kov, aus einer Bauernfamilie stammend. Während des Krieges war B. Frontberichterstatter. Gegenwärtig lebt er in Pjatigorsk. 1936 erschien sein erstes Buch, „Gordost'" (Der Stolz). Sein zweiteiliger Roman „Svet nad zemlëj" (Licht auf Erden), der 1949—1950 erschien und den *Stalinpreis* 1950 und 1951 erhielt, wurde in 26 Sprachen übersetzt und erlebte eine Auflage von 4 118 000. B.s Romane, die als typische Beispiele für die sog. *„lakirovka"* dienen, wurden nach Stalins Tod von der Kritik angeprangert (A. *Surkov* in der „Pravda" vom 19. 2. 1956). Die Erzählung „Sosedka" (Die Nachbarin), die in der Zeitschrift „Moskva" erschien, wurde dagegen wegen einer falschen Einstellung zur sowjetischen Wirklichkeit von der „Literaturnaja gazeta" am 8. 8. 1957 einer heftigen Kritik unterzogen.

Gordost' (Der Stolz, 1936)
Kubanskie rasskazy (Geschichten aus dem Kuban, 1940)
Kazaki na vojne (Die Kosaken im Krieg, 1946)
Staršij syn (Der älteste Sohn, 1956)
Na chutore Verbovom (Am Vorwerk Verbovoj, 1957)
Čužaja radost' (Das fremde Glück, 1957)
Sosedka (Die Nachbarin, 1957)
Kavaler zolotoj zvezdy (Der Ritter vom goldenen Stern, 1947, *Stalinpreis* 1949)
Svet nad zemlëj Bd. I. (Licht auf Erden, Bd. I 1949, *Stalinpreis* 1950)
Svet nad zemlëj Bd. II. (Licht auf Erden, Bd. II 1950, *Stalinpreis* 1951)

Deutsche Übersetzungen

Der Ritter des goldenen Sterns, übers. v. Alexander Böltz, Berlin, Verlag Kultur und Fortschritt. 1951, 1952, 1954.
Licht auf Erden, übers. v. Hilde Angarowa (Bd. I) u. Hildegard Olbrich (Bd. II), Berlin, Verlag Kultur u. Fortschritt. 1952.
Unterwegs (Erzählungen), übers. v. Inge Gamperl, Moskau, S. L. 1959.

Bábel' Isáak Emmanuílovič

Geb. 1894 in Odessa, aus einer jüdisch-orthodoxen Familie stammend. B., der von *Gor'kij* sehr gefördert wurde, veröffentlichte seine ersten Geschichten noch vor der Revolution. In den zwanziger Jahren zählte er zu den populärsten Schriftstellern der Sowjetunion. Elemente eines zynisch-sensiblen *Realismus* und einer scharfen Beobachtungsgabe geben seinen Werken ein besonderes Gepräge. B. war später politischer Kommissar bei der Roten Armee, wurde in den dreißiger Jahren als *Trockist* verfolgt und ist seit 1938 verschollen. Nachdem er lange Zeit von der sowjetischen Kritik totgeschwiegen worden war, wurde B. von der „Literaturnaja gazeta" am 9. 12. 1957 rehabilitiert.

Odesskie rasskazy (Geschichten aus Odessa, 1924)
Konarmija (Die Reiterarmee, 1926)
Benja Krik (1928)
Evrejskie rasskazy (Jüdische Erzählungen, 1928)
Načalo (Der Beginn, 1937)
Zakat (Sonnenuntergang, 1928)
Marija
Izbrannoe (Gesammelte Werke, 1957)

Deutsche Übersetzungen

Budjonnys Reiterarmee, übers. v. Dmitrij Umanskij, Berlin, Malik-Verlag. 1926.

Geschichten aus Odessa, übers. v. Dmitrij Umanskij, Berlin, Malik-Verlag. 1926.

Drei Welten, Erzählungen, übers. v. Dmitrij Umanskij, Berlin, Malik-Verlag. 1931.

Bagríckij Eduárd Geórgievič (Pseudonym für Džjúbin)

1895—1934, aus Odessa gebürtig. Sein erstes Werk erschien 1914 in Odessa. B. gehörte zu den *Konstruktivisten* und war einer der begabtesten Lyriker der Sowjetliteratur. In seinem Schaffen wurde er stark von *Chlebnikov* beeinflußt. Neben Übersetzungen von Robert Burns und Walter Scott behandelte er auch das Till-Eulenspiegel-Thema. B. war gegen jeglichen Wohlstand und die Zeit des Wiederaufbaus eingestellt, so z. B. im „Närrischen Fressen" (Ogoltelaja žratva) und im Poem „Die letzte Nacht" (Poslednjaja noč').

Jugo-zapad (Südwesten, 1928)
Duma pro Opanasa (Das Lied von Opanas, 1926)

Pobediteli (Die Sieger, 1932)
Poslednjaja noč' (Die letzte Nacht, 1932)
Fevral' (Februar, 1934)
Sobranie sočinenij v dvuch tomach (Gesammelte Werke in 2 Bänden, 1938)

Bartó Ágnija L'vóvna

Geb. 1902 in Moskau als Tochter eines Tierarztes. B. schreibt vor allem Kinderbücher und beschäftigt sich mit Problemen der Kindererziehung, wie z. B. in „Vas sejčas budet kasat'sja" (Bald wird es Sie angehen, 1956). Außerdem verfaßt sie auch Filmdrehbücher. Ihr Buch „Bratiška" (Brüderchen) ist der Völkerfreundschaft gewidmet und wurde in 29 Sprachen übersetzt. In ihren Büchern, die zu den besten Werken der russischen Jugendliteratur gehören, versteht es B., verschiedene Charaktere in ihrer klaren Sprache mit viel Humor treffend zu schildern. Für das Sammelwerk „Stichi detjam" (Gedichte für die Kinder) wurde sie 1950 mit dem *Stalinpreis* ausgezeichnet.

Bratiška (Brüderchen, 1928)
Devočka-revuša (Die Heul-Liese, 1930)
Snegir' (Der Gimpel, 1930)
Boltun'ja (Die Schwätzerin, 1939)
Rodnaja ulica (Die Straße meiner Kindheit, 1942)
Idët učenik (Es geht ein Schüler, 1944)
Nikita (1945)
Tvoj prazdnik (Dein Feiertag, 1947)
Ja živu v Moskve (Ich wohne in Moskau, 1947)
Zvenigorod (1948)
Emu četyrnadcat' let (Er ist 14 Jahre alt, 1949)
Stichi detjam (Gedichte für die Kinder, 1949, *Stalinpreis* 1950)
Dom pereechal (Ein Haus zieht um)
Mašen'ka (Maschenka)
Fonarik (Die kleine Laterne, 1958)

Deutsche Übersetzungen

Ein Haus zieht um, Berlin, Kultur und Fortschritt. 1949, übers. v. A. Thoss, Berlin, Kultur und Fortschritt. 1951.
Maschenka, Bukarest, Jugendverlag. 1952.

Gedichte. Der schreckliche Vogel u. Die ersten Schuhe, übers. v. Sepp Österreicher, Moskau, S. L. 1959.

Bážov Pável Petróvič

Geb. 1879. Er absolvierte 1899 das Priesterseminar in Perm', wurde aber Volksschullehrer. Als vorzüglicher Kenner des Urals wurde B. auch zu dessen Dichter. Er pflegte eine besondere Art der Märchenerzählung, die sogenannten „skazy", in welchen er das Leben und Wirken der Handwerker im Ural in außergewöhnlich zarten Tönen beschreibt, so z. B. in „Malachitovaja škatulka" (Die Schatulle aus Malachit). B.s Werke, deren erstes 1924 erschien, wurden bisher in 15 Sprachen übersetzt und erreichten eine Auflage von 7 195 000. Einige seiner Erzählungen wurden auch verfilmt („Die steinerne Blume" u. a.).

Ural'skie byli (Legenden aus dem Ural, 1924)
Malachitovaja škatulka (Die Schatulle aus Malachit, 1939, *Stalinpreis* 1943)
Dal'nee — blizkoe (Fern und doch nahe, 1946)
Kamennyj cvetok (Die steinerne Blume, 1938)
Ermakovy lebedi (Die Schwäne Ermaks, 1940)

Deutsche Übersetzungen
Das lebendige Feuer (Malachitovaja škatulka), Sagen aus dem Ural, übers. v. M. Spady, Berlin, Kultur und Fortschritt. 1952.
Legenden aus dem Ural, übertr. v. E. Gruber, Berlin, Zech. 1948.
Die Schwäne Jermaks, eine Sage aus dem Ural, übers. v. S. Kuschik, Nachw. v. X. Schaffgotsch, Wien, Die Brücke. 1949.
Fern und doch nah. Kindheitserinnerungen (Dal'nee — blizkoe), übers. v. Elisabeth u. Wladimir Wonsiatsky, Leipzig, Reclam. 1953.

Bédnyj Dem'ján (Pseudonym für Efím Alekséevič Pridvórov) 1883—1945, aus dem Dorfe Gubovka, Gouvernement Cherson, gebürtig. Er studierte zuerst an der militärmedizinischen Schule in Kiev, maturierte, und absolvierte 1908 die philologische Fakultät der Moskauer Universität. Seine ersten

Werke erschienen 1901 im Sammelwerk „Sbornik poetov i poetess“ (Sammelwerk der Dichter und Dichterinnen). 1912 trat B. der Kommunistischen Partei bei und wurde Mitarbeiter der „Pravda“ ab ihrem ersten Erscheinen am 5. Mai 1912. Die Bedeutung seiner literarischen Tätigkeit liegt hauptsächlich in der propagandistischen Wirkung seiner Fabeln und Feuilletons und Gedichte, die in seinem Schaffen bestimmend waren. Daneben versuchte er sich auch im Schauspiel: „Bogatyri“ (Die Recken). Von der Sowjetkritik wird B. zu den Satirikern gezählt.

Sobranie sočinenij I—XIX (1925—33)
Ausgewählte Werke (1948)
Znakomye lica, satiričeskie stichi, basni, fel'etony, epigrammy (Bekannte Gesichter, satirische Gedichte, Fabeln, Feuilletons, Epigramme, 1950)

Deutsche Übersetzungen
Ausgewählte Gedichte, Moskau, Zentralverlag der Völker der Sowjetunion. 1925.

Bek Aleksándr Al'frédovič

Geb. 1903 in Saratov. B. arbeitete 1920 in einer Lederfabrik in Moskau und begann seine schriftstellerische Tätigkeit mit Reportagen für die „Pravda“ und „Rabočaja Moskva“. Später wurde B. Berufsjournalist und Kritiker. In der Erzählung „Kurako“ wird das Leben von Michail K. Kurako, dem Altmeister der russischen Hochöfen, geschildert. Bekannt ist von B. vor allem der Roman „Volokolamskoe šosse“ (Die Wolokolamsker Chaussee), der das Jahr 1941 an der Ostfront behandelt.

Kurako (1934)
Volokolamskoe šosse (Die Wolokolamsker Chaussee, 1945)
Timofej — Otkrytoe serdce (Timofej — das offene Herz, 1948)
Pis'mo Lenina (Lenins Brief, 1956)
Žizn' Berežkova (Das Leben Berežkovs, 1956)

Deutsche Übersetzungen

Die Wolokolamsker Chaussee, übers. v. Hilde Angarowa, Wien, Globus-Verlag. 1947.

Timofej mit dem offenen Herzen, Berlin, Dietz. 1950.

Bélyj Andréj (Pseudonym für Borís Nikoláevič Bugáev)

1880—1934, studierte Naturwissenschaften an der Moskauer Universität und wurde 1904 Mitarbeiter der Zeitschrift „Vesy". B. ist einer der bedeutendsten Vertreter des *Symbolismus* und steht Kant, Schopenhauer und den Neukantianern nahe. Als Schüler des Anthroposophen Steiner sah B. in der russischen Revolution eine religiös-nationale Umwälzung, in der sich das russische Volk seiner messianistischen Sendung besinnen sollte. In seinen Werken liebt B. düstere, religiös-mystische Stimmungen. Die Verfallsstimmung der vorrevolutionären Zeit begleitete ihn zeitlebens. Nach ungefähr einjährigem Exil in Berlin kehrte B. 1923 nach Rußland zurück und bemühte sich krampfhaft, seine Dichtung in den Dienst der Revolution zu stellen, was aber bei seiner religiösen Weltanschauung ein wenig überzeugendes Unterfangen war. Durch seine kühnen sprachlichen und stilistischen Experimente in Poesie und Prosa übte B. einen großen Einfluß auf die jungen Schriftsteller der nachrevolutionären Periode aus. Als Vertreter einer *dekadenten* Weltanschauung wurde er jedoch von der Sowjetkritik (*Gor'kij*, *Ždanov*) abgelehnt.

Zoloto v lazuri (Gold in Himmelblau, 1904)
Pepel (Asche, 1909)
Urna (Die Urne, 1909)
Pervoe svidanie (Das erste Stelldichein, 1921)
Posle razluki (Nach der Trennung, 1922)
Serebrjanyj golub' (Die silberne Taube, 1910)
Peterburg (Petersburg, 1916)
Kotik Letaev (1918)
Prestuplenie Nikolaja Letaeva (Das Verbrechen des Nikolaj Lataev, 1921)
Na rubeže dvuch stoletij (An der Grenze zweier Jahrhunderte, 1930)

Moskovskij čudak (Ein Moskauer Sonderling, 1933)
Moskva pod udarom (Moskau in Gefahr, 1933)
Maski (Masken, 1933)

Deutsche Übersetzungen
Petersburg, übers. v. Gisela Droble, Wiesbaden, Insel-Verlag. 1959.

Berggól'c Ól'ga Fëdorovna

Geb. 1910 in St. Petersburg, aus einer Arztensfamilie stammend. B. absolvierte 1926 die Mittelschule und 1930 die philologische Fakultät der Leningrader Universität. Seit 1940 ist sie Mitglied der KPdSU. Während der Kriegszeit, in der sie zu einer bedeutenden Dichterin heranreifte, war B. beim Leningrader Rundfunk tätig. Sie begann ihre literarische Tätigkeit 1926 und veröffentlichte 1934 den ersten Band Erzählungen. B. ist eine kluge und begabte Schülerin der *Akmeisten,* insbesondere von Anna *Achmatova.* Sie gehört zu den ersten Schriftstellern der Sowjetunion, welche die Zeit des *Tauwetters* aufrichtig begrüßten.

Leningradskaja tetrad' (Das Leningrader Heft, 1942)
Leningradskij dnevnik (Das Leningrader Tagebuch)
Tvoj put' (Dein Weg, 1945)
Stichi i poemy (Gedichte und Poeme, 1946)
Govorit Leningrad (Hier spricht Leningrad, 1946)
Pervorossijsk (1950, *Stalinpreis* 1951)
Stichotvorenija i poemy (Gedichte und Poeme, 1951)
Izbrannoe (Ausgewähltes, 1954)
Lirika (Lyrik, 1955)
Otvet (Die Antwort, 1956)
Dnevnye Zvëzdy (Tagessterne, 1959)

Bezyménskij Aleksándr Il'íč

Geb. 1898 in Žitomir, absolvierte das Gymnasium in Vladimir und die Handelsschule in Kiev. Seit 1916 ist B. Mitglied der Kommunistischen Partei und seit 1919 Mitglied des Komsomol. Um 1920 gehörte B. zu den offiziellen Sprechern der Kommunistischen Partei. Sein Schaffen ist damit parteipolitisch stark beeinflußt.

Junyj proletarij (Žizn' Miti) (Der junge Proletarier, Mitjas Leben, 1920)
K solncu (Der Sonne entgegen, 1921)
Partbilet 224 332 (Parteiausweis 224 332, 1924)
Izbrannye stichi (Ausgewählte Gedichte, 1925)
Feliks
Den' našej žizni (Ein Tag unseres Lebens, 1930)
Vystrel (Der Schuß, 1930)
Tragedijnaja noč' (Tragische Nacht, 1932—49)
K zapadu ot El'by (Von der Elbe nach Westen, 1956)

Deutsche Übersetzungen

Gedichte des Zornes, übertr. v. Gerty Rath, Bukarest, Cartea Rusă. 1950.

Blok Aleksándr Aleksándrovič

1880—1921, geb. in St. Petersburg, aus einer Professorenfamilie stammend. Nach Absolvierung des Gymnasiums studierte B. zuerst an der juridischen, dann an der philologischen Fakultät in Petersburg. Schon im Alter von 5 Jahren begann er Gedichte zu schreiben. Im Jahre 1898 lernte er die Tochter des berühmten Chemikers Mendeleev kennen, die später seine Frau wurde. Nach einigen harmonischen Jahren begannen die Krisen in B.s Leben. Er empfand das Mißlingen der Revolution von 1905 als schweren Schlag und ging ins Ausland. Enttäuscht kehrte er dann nach Rußland zurück und begann wieder sein ausschweifendes Leben. Nach der Oktoberrevolution wurde er verhaftet, jedoch bald wieder freigelassen. *Gor'kij*, der B. nach Möglichkeit unterstützte, wollte ihm die Genehmigung erwirken, ins Ausland fahren zu dürfen. Diese Bestrebungen blieben jedoch ohne Erfolg. B. starb am 20. August 1921. Er ist einer der größten russischen Lyriker, einer der hervorragendsten Vertreter des russischen *Symbolismus*. Sein ganzes Schaffen war dem Thema „Rußland" gewidmet. Das Poem „Die Zwölf" (Dvenadcat') gehört zu den genialsten Werken über die russische Revolution.

Iz posvjaščenij (Aus Widmungen, 1903)
Stichi o prekrasnoj dame (Verse über eine schöne Dame, 1904)
Neznakomka (Die Unbekannte, 1906, 1911)
Nečajannaja radost' (Unerwartete Freude, 1907)
Snežnaja maska (Die Schneemaske, 1907)
Zemlja v snegu (Erde im Schnee, 1908)
Roza i krest (Rose und Kreuz, 1916)
Dvenadcat' (Die Zwölf, 1918)
Skify (Die Skythen, 1918)

Deutsche Übersetzungen

Die Zwölf, übertr. v. Wolfgang E. Groeger, Berlin, Newa-Verlagsgesellschaft. 1921.

Die Stille blüht, Ausw. u. übertr. v. Johannes v. Guenther, München, Weismann. 1947.

Gesammelte Dichtungen, übertr. v. Johannes v. Guenther, München, Weismann. 1947.

Die Unbekannte, übers. v. A. Rohde-Liebenau, Berlin, Aufbau-Bühnen-Vertrieb. 1946.

Skythen, übers. v. R. v. Walter, Berlin 1920. Rose und Kreuz, übers. v. W. E. Groeger, Berlin. 1922.

Brjúsov Valérij Jákovlevič

1873—1924, geb. in Moskau als Sohn eines vermögenden Kaufmanns. B. genoß eine ausgezeichnete linguistische Ausbildung: er beherrschte 8 Sprachen. Er hatte auch einen ausgeprägten Sinn für Kritik und war Führer und Mittelpunkt der *Dekadenten* und *Symbolisten*. *Gor'kij* nannte ihn „den kultiviertesten russischen Schriftsteller“ (1917). B., ein Feind des zaristischen Regimes, war 1905 Sozialist und wurde 1920 Mitglied der Kommunistischen Partei. Während des ersten Weltkrieges schrieb er patriotische Gedichte und nach der Revolution Hymnen auf die proletarische Revolution. B. übersetzte Vergil, Goethe, Emile Verhaeren, Romain Rolland, armenische Dichter und viele andere. Nach ihm wurde auch das Moskauer Institut für Kunst und Literatur benannt.

Russkie simvolisty (Russische Symbolisten, 1894—95)
Chefs d'œuvre (1895)

Tertia vigilia (1901)
Urbi et Orbi (1903)
V takie dni (In solchen Tagen, 1919—21)
Serp i molot (Sichel und Hammer, 1921)
SSSR (1923)
Izbrannye proizvedenija 3 Bde. (Ausgewählte Werke, 1926)

Deutsche Übersetzungen

Einzelne Gedichte, übers. v. Alexander Eliasberg, Russische Lyrik der Gegenwart, München. 1907. Johannes von Guenther, Neuer russischer Parnass, Berlin. 1911. Karl Roellinghoff, Rußlands Lyrik in Übertragung und Nachdichtung, Wien. 1920.

Bubennóv Michaíl Semënovič

Geb. 1909 als Sohn eines Bauern in Sibirien. Kindheit und Jugend verbrachte er im Altaigebiet. Er ist seit 1951 Mitglied der KPdSU. Seit den ersten Nachkriegsjahren zählt B. zur Prominenz der russischen Schriftsteller. Sein erstes Werk, die Novelle „Gremjaščij god" (Das dröhnende Jahr), handelt in Sibirien und ist den Reformen des anlaufenden 1. Fünfjahrplans gewidmet. Für den Roman „Belaja berëza" (Weiße Birke) wurde B. 1948 mit dem *Stalinpreis* ausgezeichnet. Das Buch gehört zu jener Serie von Werken, die ihren Stoff aus den Ereignissen des zweiten Weltkriegs schöpften.

Gremjaščij god (Das dröhnende Jahr, 1932)
Bessmertie (Unsterblichkeit, 1940)
Belaja berëza (Weiße Birke, 1947, *Stalinpreis* 1948, 1952 2. Teil)
Ogon' v tajge (Feuer in der Tajga, 1953)

Deutsche Übersetzungen

Die weiße Birke, übers. v. Veronica Ensslen, Berlin, Verlag Volk und Welt. 1955, 1956.

Unsterblichkeit, übers. v. Ilse Berger, Berlin, Verlag des Ministeriums für nationale Verteidigung. 1956. Übers. v. Alfred Kittner und Ilse Goldmann, Bukarest, Verlag Cartea rusă. 1956.

Budáncev Sergéj Fëdorovič

Geb. 1896 im Gouvernement Rjazan'. B. wurde als Schriftsteller erst nach der Revolution bekannt. Wegen seiner un-historischen Schilderung und individualistischen Einstellung in seinen Romanen wurde er von der sowjetischen Kritik heftig angegriffen.

Mjatež (Meuterei, 1923)
Provest' o stradanijach uma (Erzählung über die Leiden des Geistes, 1929)
Sobranie sočinenij (Gesammelte Werke, 1929)
Izbrannoe (Ausgewähltes, 1936)

Bulgákov Michaíl Afanás'evič

1891—1940. B.s Vater war Professor der Theologie an der Geistlichen Akademie in Kiev, B. selbst wandte sich dem Ärzteberuf zu und absolvierte 1916 seine Studien an der Universität in Kiev. Bis zu seiner Übersiedlung nach Moskau im Jahre 1921 lebte B. in Kiev und Vladikavkaz. Seine literarische Tätigkeit begann er 1919. B. schrieb Dramen und Belletristik. Er war ein begabter Dichter, war aber nicht in der Lage, den ideologischen Wünschen der Partei zu entsprechen, zum Beispiel wurden die Erzählungen in dem Sammelband „Diavoliada" von der Sowjetkritik wegen angeblich einseitiger Darstellung des sowjetischen Lebens abgelehnt. Die Aufführung des Theaterstückes „Beg" (Der Lauf) wurde am 24. 10. 1928 wegen seiner zu nachgiebigen Haltung gegenüber dem politischen Gegner verboten. Die bekanntesten Werke B.s sind das Schauspiel „Dni Turbinych" (Die Tage der Geschwister Turbin), das die Umarbeitung des Romans „Belaja gvardija" (Weiße Garde) ist. Der Stil B.s ist oft phantasievoll und sarkastisch, etwa wie in seiner Komödie „Zojkina kvartira" (Zojkas Wohnung). Im allgemeinen setzte sich B. in der Sowjetliteratur nicht durch, er war einer von jenen, die die *innere Emigration* vorzogen.

Diavoliada (Teufelsspuck, 1924)
Belaja gvardija (Die weiße Garde, 1924)
Dni Turbinych (Die Tage der Geschwister Turbin, 1924)
Zojkina kvartira (Zojkas Wohnung)

Mol'er (Molière, 1936)
Poslednie dni (Die letzten Tage, 1943 in Moskau aufgeführt; behandelt Puškins Schicksal)

Deutsche Übersetzungen
Die Tage der Geschwister Turbin, Die Weiße Garde, übers. v. Käthe Rosenberg, Berlin-Charlottenburg, S. Kagansky. 1928.
Sojkas Wohnung. Komödie in 4 Aufz. übers. v. Erich Boehme, Berlin, I. Ladyschnikow. 1929.
Alexander Puschkin (Poslednie dni). Schauspiel, übers. v. P. Hamm, Berlin, Henschel. 1948, 1950.

Čakóvskij Aleksándr Borísovič

Geb. 1913 in St. Petersburg als Sohn eines Arztes. Č., Chefredakteur der Zeitschrift „Inostrannaja literatura", ist seit 1938 auf literarischem Gebiet tätig. Sein Schaffensgebiet erstreckt sich in erster Linie auf Erzählungen und Skizzen. Bekannt wurde er 1948 durch seinen Roman „U nas uže utro" (Bei uns ist schon Morgen), der das Leben der Fischer auf Südsachalin und den Kurilen schildert.

Mirnye dni (Friedliche Tage)
Eto bylo v Leningrade (Es war in Leningrad, 1945)
U nas uže utro (Bei uns ist schon Morgen, 1948, *Stalinpreis* 1949)
Dorogi uchodjaščie v dal' (Wege, die in die Ferne führen, 1959)
Chvan Čer stoit na postu (Huan Tscher hält Wacht)
Tridcat' dnej v Pariže (30 Tage in Paris, 1956)
God žizni (Ein Jahr Leben, 1956)

Deutsche Übersetzungen
Es war in Leningrad, übers. v. Ina Tinzmann, Berlin-Leipzig, SWA-Verlag. 1947. Berlin, Verlag Kultur und Fortschritt. 1950.
Bei uns ist schon Morgen, übers. v. Veronica Ensslen, Berlin, Verlag Kultur und Fortschritt. 1950.
Friedliche Tage, übers. v. Alfred Edgar Thoss, Berlin, Verlag Kultur und Fortschritt. 1950. Berlin, Verlag der Nation. 1952.
Huan Tscher hält Wacht. Nach der Übers. v. Marga Bork, Berlin, Verlag Kultur und Fortschritt. 1953.
Ein Jahr Leben, übers. v. Erich Einhorn, Moskau, S. L. 1957.

Čapýgin Alekséj Pávlovič

1870—1937, bäuerlicher Abstammung. Er schrieb Bücher mit übertrieben „echter“ Sprache des siebzehnten Jahrhunderts, so daß seine historischen Romane eine schwerverständliche Lektüre wurden. Ein gewisser folkloristischer Wert ist ihnen aber nicht abzusprechen.

Belyj skit (Die weiße Einsiedelei, 1915)
Razin Stepan (1927)
Guljaščie ljudi (Fahrendes Volk, 1935)

Deutsche Übersetzungen

Erst lernen, dann heiraten. Schauspiel in 1 Aufz. bearb. v. L. S., Moskau, Zentralverlag der Völker der Sowjetunion. 1927.
Stepan Razin. Nach d. Übers. v. Dr. Paul Reissert, Berlin, Verlag Kultur und Fortschritt. 1953, 1954.

Chlébnikov Velemír (Víktor) Vladímirovič

1885—1922, absolvierte das Gymnasium in Kazan', wo er auch später an der naturwissenschaftlichen Fakultät der Universität studierte. Die ersten Gedichte Ch.s erschienen schon 1906. Zuerst ein Anhänger der *Symbolisten,* wandte sich Ch. bald den *Futuristen* zu. Von ihm stammen die *„zaumnye“* Gedichte, die mit Wortneubildungen (z. B. „bobeobi“, „amechagi“) überladen sind. In seinen Werken idealisierte Ch. die slawische Vergangenheit. Am 28. Juni 1922 starb er in geistiger Umnachtung. In seinem Nachruf schreibt V. *Majakovskij* in „Krasnaja nov'“, 1922, N. 4/8, S. 305: „Ich empfinde es als meine Pflicht, in meinem eigenen Namen, sowie auch in dem meiner Freunde, der Dichter *Aseev,* Burljuk, *Kručënych,* Kamenskij und *Pasternak,* schwarz auf weiß zu erklären, daß wir ihn zu unserem Lehrer der Poesie und zu den prachtvollen, ehrlichen Rittern unseres Kampfes um die Dichtung zählen.“

Šaman i Venera (Schamane und Venus, 1912)
Vila i Lešij (Vila und der Nachtgeist, 1913)
Vojna v mušelovke (Der Krieg in der Mausefalle)
Ladomir (1920)

Noč' pered sovetami (Die Nacht vor den Sowjets, 1921)
Novejšaja russkaja poezija (Die moderne russische Poesie, 1921)
Ustrug Razina (1922)
Nastojaščee (Das Echte, 1922)
Zangezi (1922)
Pračka (Die Wäscherin, 1922)
Sinie okovy (Die blauen Fesseln, 1922)
Neizdannye proizvedenija (Unveröffentlichte Werke, 1940)

Čukóvskij Kornéj Ivánovič (Pseudonym für N. I. Korničúk)
Geb. 1882 in St. Petersburg, absolvierte das Gymnasium in Odessa. Seit 1901 Mitarbeiter der Zeitung „Odesskie novosti", ging Č. als deren Korrespondent 1903 nach London. Nach seiner Rückkehr gab er 1905 die satirische Zeitschrift „Signal" heraus. 1916 redigierte Č. auf Aufforderung *Gor'kijs* die Kinderseite der Zeitschrift „Parus". Als Mitarbeiter der „Pravda" und „Krasnaja nov'" befaßte sich Č. mit Übersetzungen und literarhistorischen Arbeiten. Seit dem Erscheinen seines ersten Kinderbuches, „Priključenija Krokodila Krokodiloviča" (Die Abenteuer des Krokodil Krokodilovič), im Jahre 1919 ist Č. hauptsächlich auf dem Gebiete der Kinderliteratur tätig.

Literarhistorische Arbeiten
Ot Čechova do našich dnej (Von Čechov bis in unsere Tage, 1908)
Poezija grjaduščej demokratii (Die Poesie der künftigen Demokratie, 1914)
Kniga o sovremennych pisateljach (Ein Buch über moderne Schriftsteller, 1914)
Lica i maski (Gesichter und Masken, 1914)
Kniga ob Aleksandre Bloke (Das Alexander Blok-Buch, 1922)
Masterstvo Nekrasova (Die Kunst Nekrasovs, 1952)

Kinderbücher
Krokodil (1919)
Mojdodyr (1923)
Ot dvuch do piati (Von zwei bis fünf, 1925)
Telefon (1926)
Mucha Cekotucha (Die Fliege Cekotucha, 1927)
Tarakanišče (Die Riesenschabe, 1942)

Deutsche Übersetzungen

Was der Lore passierte (Mojdodyr). Lustige Geschichte, übers. v. W. Fischer, Wien, Globus. 1946.

Märchen. Verdrehte Welt, übers. v. W. Fischer, Wien, Globus. 1946.

Čulkóv Geórgij Ivánovič

Geb. 1879 in Moskau, einer Adelsfamilie entstammend. Č. war Mitarbeiter von Zeitschriften wie „Novyj put'", „Voprosy žizni" u. a. Er machte sich als Schriftsteller und Kritiker einen Namen und ließ in seinen Werken *symbolistische* Strömungen erkennen. Nach der Oktoberrevolution wandte er sich dem historischen Roman zu. Von der Sowjetkritik wird Č. heute nicht mehr erwähnt. (nach KSB)

Mjatežniki (Rebellen, 1926)
O P'ere Volchovskom (Über Pierre Volchovskoj, 1930)

Čumandrín Michaíl Fëdorovič

Geb. 1905 in Tula. Er war zuerst Fabriksarbeiter und ergriff später die Laufbahn eines Korrespondenten und Schriftstellers und wurde als solcher auch Leiter des *RAPP.* 1925 wurde Č. Mitglied der KPdSU. Er fiel 1939/40 im Finnlandkrieg. Obwohl er in seinen Erzählungen und Romanen die Fabrik und den Arbeiter in den Mittelpunkt der Darstellung rückt, wurde Č. dennoch des öfteren von der sowjetischen Kritik als Schwärmer für kleinbürgerliche Ideale genannt. (nach KSB)

Skloka (Intrige)
Rodnja (Verwandtschaft)
Fabrika Rable (Rables Fabrik)
Belyj kamen' (Weißer Stein)
Germanija (Deutschland)

Cvetáeva Marína Ivánovna

1894—1941, geb. in Moskau als Tochter eines Kunsthistorikers. C. studierte längere Zeit an der Sorbonne in Paris. Sie ging 1922 in die Emigration, aus der sie erst 1938 nach Rußland zurückkehrte. 1941 beging sie in Kazan' Selbstmord durch Erhängen. Die Hauptthemen in C.s literarischem Schaffen sind die Liebe und die Vergangenheit. Sie macht mit Geschmack viele stilistische Experimente, ohne die Grenzen des Verständlichen zu verlassen. Eine wohlwollende Beurteilung durch *Erenburg* in der „Literaturnaja Moskva" (zweiter Band) führte 1957 zu einer ausführlichen Polemik.

Večernij al'bom (Ein Album für den Abend, 1910)
Vërsty (Die Wersten, 1922)
Car'-Devica (Die Zarentochter, 1922)
Proza (Prosa, 1953)
Den' poezii (Der Tag der Poesie, 1956)

Deméntiev Nikoláj Stepánovič
wurde 1927 in Leningrad geboren. Nach Absolvierung der Leningrader Hochschule für das Wassertransportwesen war D. in Novosibirsk als Ingenieur tätig. Nach Verteidigung seiner wissenschaftlichen Dissertation wurde ihm der Titel eines Kandidaten der technischen Wissenschaften zuerkannt. In Novosibirsk begann er, sich auch schriftstellerisch zu betätigen. Seine ersten Erzählungen, „Katja", „Der erste Brief", „Unsere Liebe" und „Großvaters Enkel", die 1952/53 in der Zeitschrift „Sibirskie ogni" erschienen, wurden zu einem Sammelband vereinigt. 1958 veröffentlichte D. drei Kurzromane: „Der Mann vom Kuban'", „Meine Wege" und „Hinaus ins Leben". (nach S.L.)

Moi dorogi (Meine Wege, 1958)

Dikóvskij Sergéj Vladímirovič
1907—1940, geb. in Moskau, aus einer Lehrerfamilie stammend. In der Zeit nach dem Bürgerkrieg erwarb sich D. als Zeitungskorrespondent durch seine Reisen eine gründliche Kenntnis der Sowjetunion. 1940 fiel er im Krieg gegen Finnland. In seinen Werken behandelt er Themen über den Fernen Osten, vor allem das Leben der Waldarbeiter, Jäger, Fischer und der Grenzbewohner.

Zastava N (Grenzposten N, 1933)
Komendant Ptič'ego ostrova (Der Komandant der Vogelinsel)
Konec ‚Sago-Maru' (Das Ende der ‚Sago-Maru')
Patrioty (Patrioten, 1937)
Prikljućenija katera Smelogo (Die Abenteuer des Kutters Smelyj, 1940)
Egor Cygankov (1950)

Deutsche Übersetzungen

Die Abenteuer des Kutters Smely, übers. v. Rolf Brömel, Berlin, Verlag Neues Leben. 1952.
Der Kommandant der Vogelinsel, übers. v. M. Spady, Berlin, Kultur und Fortschritt. 1952.
Das Ende der ‚Sago-Maru', übers. v. M. Spady, Berlin, Kultur und Fortschritt. 1952.
Im Leuchtturm, Aus dem Novellenzyklus „Die Abenteuer des Kutters Smely", übers. v. Juri Elperin, Moskau, S. L. 1957.

Dolmatóvskij Evgénij Arónovič

Geb. 1915 in Moskau. D.s erste Gedichte wurden zuerst in den Zeitungen der Komsomolorganisation veröffentlicht. Nachdem er eine Zeitlang beim Bau der Moskauer Untergrundbahn gearbeitet hatte, besuchte D. dann das Gor'kij-Institut für Literatur und ging nach Beendigung seiner Studien nach dem Fernen Osten. Den zweiten Weltkrieg machte D. als Kriegsberichterstatter mit. In den ersten Nachkriegsjahren tat er sich als Verfasser von verschiedenen Gedichten mit antiwestlicher bzw. antiamerikanischer Tendenz hervor.

Izbrannoe (Ausgewähltes, 1948)
Slovo o zavtrašnem dne (Das Lied vom morgigen Tag, 1949)

Deutsche Übersetzungen

Das Lied vom morgigen Tag, übers. v. A. Thoss, Berlin, Kultur und Fortschritt. 1951.

Dúdin Michaíl Aleksándrovič

Geb. 1916 im Dorfe Klenëvo, Gouvernement Kostroma, als Sohn einer Bauernfamilie. Studierte an der Lehrerbildungsanstalt Ivanovo.

Stichi i poemy (Gedichte und Poeme, 1944)
Kostry na perekrëstkach (Freudenfeuer an Straßenkreuzungen, 1945)
V stepjach Salavata (In den Steppen von Salavata, 1949)
Posle meteli (Nach dem Schneesturm, 1956)

Dudíncev Vladímir Dmítrievič

Geb. 1918 in der Ukraine, studierte in Moskau Rechtswissenschaften. Nach der Genesung von einer Verwundung, die er in der Schlacht um Leningrad erlitten hatte, wirkte D. bei einem Militärgericht in Sibirien. Jetzt wohnt D. in Moskau. Die ersten Publikationen D.s, Gedichte und Erzählungen, erschienen um 1938 in verschiedenen Zeitungen und Zeitschriften. Sein erstes Buch ist eine Sammlung von Kurzgeschichten. 1956 erschien sein Roman „Der Mensch lebt nicht vom Brot allein". Das Buch wurde u. a. auch ins Deutsche übersetzt und löste im Westen eine rege Diskussion zum Thema *Tauwetter* aus.

U semi bogatyrej (Bei den sieben Recken, 1952)
Na svoëm meste (Am rechten Platz, 1953)
Ne chlebom edinym (Der Mensch lebt nicht vom Brot allein, 1956)
Novogodnjaja skazka (Ein Neujahrsmärchen, 1960)

Deutsche Übersetzungen

Der Mensch lebt nicht vom Brot allein, übers. v. Ingo-Manfred Schille, Hamburg, Verlag der Stern-Bücher. 1957. Hamburg, S. M. Bücher. 1960.

Erenbúrg Il'já Grigór'evič

Geb. 1891 in Kiev, aus einer bürgerlichen, jüdischen Familie stammend. E. genoß eine gute Schulbildung und ging im Alter von 18 Jahren nach Paris, wo er schon 1910 seine ersten Gedichte veröffentlichte. Nach achtjährigem Aufenthalt in Paris kehrte er 1917 nach Rußland zurück und erlebte die Revolution in der Ukraine. Wegen seiner ursprünglichen Ablehnung des bolschewistischen Regimes ging er wieder ins Ausland, kehrte aber 1923 nach Rußland zurück und wurde einer der erfolgreichsten sowjetischen Schriftsteller, der Rußland des öfteren auch im Ausland vertrat. In jüngster Vergangenheit wurde E. wegen seines Romans „Ottepel'" (*Tauwetter*) und einiger kritischer Aufsätze (vgl. *Cvetaeva*) wegen zu liberaler Auslegung der nachstalinistischen Politik von der Sowjetkritik gerügt. Trotzdem blieb seine Stellung als einer der bedeutendsten zeitgenössischen Sowjetschriftsteller unerschüttert.

Chulio Churenito (1922)
Žizn' i gibel' Nikolaja Kurbova (Leben und Ende des Nikolaj Kurbov, 1923)
Trest D. E. (Trust D. E., 1923)
Ljubov' Žanny Nej (Die Liebe der Jeanne Ney, 1923)
Rvač (1925)
Trinadcat' trubok (Dreizehn Pfeifen, 1923)
Leto 1925 goda (Der Sommer des Jahres 1925, 1926)
Zagovor ravnych (Die Verschwörung der Gleichen, 1928)
Den' vtoroj (Der zweite Tag, 1934)
Ne perevodja dychanija (Ohne Atempause, 1935)
Padenie Pariža (Der Fall von Paris, 1942 *Stalinpreis*)
Burja (Der Sturm, 1947, *Stalinpreis* 1948)
Devjatyj val (Die neunte Woge, 1951)
Ottepel' (Tauwetter, 1954)

Deutsche Übersetzungen

Die ungewöhnlichen Abenteuer des Julio Jurenito, übers. v. Alexander Eliasberg, Berlin, Welt-Verlag. 1923. Berlin, Malik-Verlag. 1929.

Trust D. E. Die Geschichte der Zerstörung Europas, übers. v. Lia Calman, Berlin, Welt-Verlag. 1925.

13 Pfeifen, übers. v. Bert Schiratzki, Basel, Rhein-Verlag. 1926. Berlin, Malik-Verlag. 1930.

Michail Lykow (Rvač), übers. v. Hans Ruoff, Berlin, Malik-Verlag. 1927.

Die Liebe der Jeanne Ney, übers. v. Waldemar Jollos, Basel, Rhein-Verlag. 1926, 1928. Berlin, Malik-Verlag. 1931.

Die Verschwörung der Gleichen, übers. v. Hans Ruoff, Berlin, Malik-Verlag. 1928.

Der zweite Tag, Moskau-Leningrad, Verlagsgenossenschaft ausländischer Arbeiter in der UdSSR. 1935.

Ohne Atempause, London, Malik-Verlag. 1936. Übers. v. Lotte Schwarz u. Otto Wyss, Leipzig, Volk und Buch Verlag. 1948.

Der Fall von Paris, Zürich, Steinberg-Verlag. 1945. Übers. v. E. Sabel, Berlin-Leipzig, SWA-Verlag. 1947. Übers. v. Hans Ruoff, Berlin, Aufbau-Verlag. 1947, 1951, 1952, 1953, 1954.

Der Sturm, übers. v. Maria Riwkin, Moskau, Verlag für fremdsprachige Literatur. 1948. Berlin, Verlag Volk und Welt. 1949, 1952, 1953, 1955.

Die neunte Woge, nach d. Übers. v. Alfred Kurella, Bd. 1, 2, Berlin, Verlag Volk und Welt. 1953, 1954. Moskau, Verlag für fremdsprachige Literatur. 1953, 1954.

Tauwetter, übers. v. Wera Rathfelder, Berlin, Verlag Kultur und Fortschritt. 1957.

Esénin Sergéj Aleksándrovič

1895—1925, geb. im Dorfe Konstantinovo, Gouvernement Rjazan', als Sohn eines Bauern. Auf Grund seiner Abstammung und seiner Erziehung war E. mit dem bäuerlichen Leben und der religiösen Tradition des russischen Dorfes wohlvertraut. Er begann bereits im Alter von 14 Jahren Gedichte zu schreiben. Nach dem Besuch der Dorfschule und einer Kirchenschule ging E. nach Moskau, um Verkäufer zu werden. Er besuchte dort die Volkshochschule und veröffentlichte 1916 seine erste Gedichtsammlung „Radunica". Nach seiner Übersiedlung nach St. Petersburg lernte er auch *Blok* kennen. Er wurde bald der berühmteste russische Lyriker und einer der bekanntesten Vertreter der Gruppe der *Imaginisten*. In seinen Werken, in denen er sich als großartiger Landschaftsschilderer zeigt, läßt er immer wieder seine Sehnsucht nach seinem Heimatdorf zum Durchbruch kommen. Berauscht von seinem Erfolg, gibt er sich jedoch in der Stadt einem ausschweifenden Leben hin. Nach der Scheidung seiner Ehe mit der Tänzerin Isadora Duncan, der er auch nach Frankreich und Amerika gefolgt war, heiratete E. im Jahre 1923 eine Enkelin Tolstojs. Am 28. Dezember 1925 verübte E. in seiner Wohnung in Leningrad Selbstmord durch Erhängen und Öffnen der Pulsadern.

Radunica (1916, Name der ersten Woche nach Ostern)
Nebesnyj barabanščik (Der himmlische Trommler, 1916)
Sorokoust (1920, Name für ein Gebet)
Tovarišč Inonija (Genosse Inonija, 1920)
Ispoved' chuligana (Das Bekenntnis eines Taugenichts, 1920)
Pugačëv (1921)
Ballada o dvadcati šesti (Die Ballade von den Sechsundzwanzig, 1924)
Rus' sovetskaja (Rußland der Sowjets, 1924)
Moskva kabackaja (Moskau der Kneipen, 1924)
Kapitan zemli (Kapitän der Erde, 1925)
Anna Snegina (1925)
Sočinenija (Werke, 2 Bde., 1956)

Deutsche Übersetzungen

Verklärung, übers. v. Tartakower, Der neue Merkur, 5. Jg. Heft 7. 1921.

Evtušénko Evgénij Aleksándrovič

Geb. 1933 als Sohn eines Staatsangestellten in der Station Zima an der Transsibirischen Eisenbahn im Rayon Irkutsk. Nach Absolvierung der Zehnjahresschule studierte E. ab 1951 am Gor'kij-Institut in Leningrad. E., dessen Werke seit 1949 gedruckt werden, wurde wegen seiner Gedichte und insbesondere wegen seiner Verserzählung „Zima" von der sowjetischen Kritik gerügt. Man warf ihm westliche Tendenzen vor. Daraufhin wurde E. aus dem Komsomolverband ausgeschlossen. Der Dichter bekannte seine Fehler ein und versprach, „sich zu bessern". E. ist ein Schriftsteller, der einen auffallenden Drang nach Freiheit und Originalität bekundet.

Zemlja. Noč' pered vystupleniem (Erde. Die Nacht vor dem Aufbruch, 1951)
Razvedčiki grjaduščego (Die Kundschafter der Zukunft, 1952)
Tretij sneg (Der dritte Schnee, 1955)
Šosse Entuziastov (Die Straße der Enthusiasten, 1956)

Zima (1956)
Otkuda vy (Woher kommt ihr, 1958)

Fadéev Aleksándr Aleksándrovič

1901—1956, geb. in Kimry, Gouvernement Tver' (jetzt Kalinin), als Sohn eines Volksschullehrers. Seine Kindheit und frühe Jugend verbrachte F. im Fernen Osten. Im Jahre 1918 trat er der Kommunistischen Partei bei und nahm 1919—1920 an den Kämpfen in Sibirien teil. Seit 1939 war F. Mitglied des ZK der KPdSU und Deputierter des Obersten Rates der UdSSR. Ursprünglich war F. in der *RAPP*-Gruppe, stellte sich aber nach 1932 um und wurde ein führendes Mitglied des *Schriftstellerverbandes* der SU. Bis zu Stalins Tod im Jahre 1953 hatte F. auch maßgeblichen Einfluß auf die Formulierung der Anforderungen, die von der Partei an die sowjetischen Schriftsteller gestellt wurden. Einige Wochen nach der Entstalinisierung beging F. am 13. Mai 1956 Selbstmord durch Erschießen. Er verfaßte Romane, Novellen und neben Erzählungen für die Sowjetliteratur richtungweisende, kritische Abhandlungen in den führenden sowjetischen Tageszeitungen. Seine Bücher wurden in 58 Sprachen übersetzt und erreichten eine Auflage von 11 119 000.

Protiv tečenija (Gegen den Strom, 1923)
Razliv (Hochwasser, 1923)
Razgrom (Die Neunzehn, 1927)
Poslednij iz Udege (Der letzte Udehe, 1929—36, geplant waren 6 Bde., nicht vollendet, 5. Teil 1941)
Molodaja gvardija (Die junge Garde, 1946, *Stalinpreis*)
Čërnaja metallurgija (Die schwarze Metallurgie, 1954, nur einzelne Kapitel)

Deutsche Übersetzungen

Kommissare, übers. v. K. Stürmer, Moskau, Zentralverlag der Völker der Sowjetunion. 1927.
Die Neunzehn (Razgrom) Berlin, Verlag für Literatur und Politik. 1928. Wien-Berlin, Verlag für Literatur und Politik. 1932. Neubearbeitet v. Nell Held, Moskau, Verlag für fremdsprachige

Literatur. 1927, 1948. München, Weismann. 1949. Übers. v. Dr. Arnold Boettcher, Berlin, Dietz. 1955. Übers. v. Hilde Angarowa, Leipzig, Reclam. 1926.

Der letzte Udehe, übers. v. Eduard Schiemann, Bd. 1, Wien-Berlin, Verlag für Literatur und Politik. 1932. Bd. 2, übers. v. Thea Schnittke, Moskau-Leningrad, Verlagsgenossenschaft ausländischer Arbeiter in der UdSSR. 1934.

Die junge Garde, Wien, Verlag Die Brücke. 1948. Berlin, Verlag Volk und Welt. 1949, 1953, 1954.

Fajkó Alekséj Micháјlovič

Geb. 1893, gehört zu den sowjetischen Dramatikern, welche ihre Laufbahn im realistischen Stil der zwanziger Jahre begannen und die Schilderung der sowjetischen Wirklichkeit zum Thema ihrer dramatischen Werke nahmen. (Vgl. *Afinogenov, Kiršon, Pogodin* u. a.)

Ozero Ljul' (Der Ljul'-See, 1923)
Učitel' Bubus (Der Lehrer Bubus, aufgeführt 1925)
Čelovek s portfelem (Der Mann mit der Aktentasche, 1928)
Kapitan Kostrov (Kapitän Kostrov, 1946)
Ne sotvori sebe kumira (Du sollst keinem Götzen dienen, 1956)

Fédin Konstantín Aleksándrovič

Geb. 1892 in Saratov. F.s Vater stammte aus dem Bauernstand, seine Mutter war eine Adelige. F. absolvierte 1903 die Handelsschule und studierte von 1911 bis 1914 Volkswirtschaft. Um seine Studien zu vollenden, ging er nach Deutschland, wurde während des Krieges interniert und 1918 ausgetauscht. Nach seiner Rückkehr nach Rußland war F. im Kommissariat für Volksbildung und als Journalist tätig. Er war auch mit *Gor'kij* befreundet. Seine ersten literarischen Versuche sollen bereits 1913 veröffentlicht worden sein. 1920 schloß sich F. den *Serapionsbrüdern* an und veröffentlichte in deren Almanach seine ersten Erzählungen. Hauptthema seiner Werke ist das Verhalten der Intelligenz zur Revolution.

Seit 1934 gehört F. zu den Leitern des *Schriftstellerverbandes* der SU. Seine Werke wurden in 14 Sprachen übersetzt und erreichten eine Auflage von 4 547 000.

Goroda i gody (Städte und Jahre, 1924)
Brat'ja (Die Brüder, 1928)
Podhiščenie Evropy (Der Raub Europas, 1934—35)
Pervye radosti (Frühe Freuden, 1945—46)
Neobyknovennoe leto (Ein ungewöhnlicher Sommer, 1947—48)
Sanatorij Arktur (Sanatorium Arktur)
Sobranie sočinenij (Gesammelte Werke, 1954)

Deutsche Übersetzungen

Städte und Jahre, übers. v. Dimitrij Umanskij, Berlin, Malik-Verlag. 1927. Berlin, Verlag Volk und Welt. 1948. Zürich, Universum Verlag. 1949. Berlin, Verlag der Nation. 1952. Übers. v. Georg Schwarz, Berlin, Aufbau-Verlag. 1960.

Die Brüder, übers. v. Erwin Honig, Berlin, Neuer Deutscher Verlag. 1928. Stuttgart, Behrendt-Verlag. 1947. Übers. v. Ena v. Baer, Leipzig, Insel-Verlag. 1954.

Frühe Freuden, übers. v. Hilde Angarowa, Moskau, Verlag für fremdsprachige Literatur. 1948, 1950. Leipzig, P. List. 1951. Berlin, Aufbau-Verlag. 1955.

Ein ungewöhnlicher Sommer, übers. v. Hilde Angarowa, Bd. 1 u. 2, Berlin, Verlag Kultur und Fortschritt. 1950, 1951. Moskau, Verlag für fremdsprachige Literatur. 1950.

Sanatorium Arktur, übers. v. Maria Riwkin, Berlin, Verlag Kultur und Fortschritt. 1956.

Foménko Vladímir Dmítrievič

Geb. 1911 in Černigov als Sohn eines Angestellten. F. verbrachte seine Kindheit in Rostov am Don und begann seine literarische Tätigkeit 1946 mit Erzählungen über den Wiederaufbau von Rostov.

Odna stročka (Eine Zeile, 1951)
Čelovek v stepi (Der Mensch in der Steppe, 1958)

Forš Ól'ga Dmítrievna (Pseudonym für A. Térek)

Geb. 1873 als Tochter einer Offiziersfamilie. F. begann ihre literarische Tätigkeit 1908 mit der Veröffentlichung von Erzählungen, später wandte sie sich mit Erfolg dem historischen Roman zu. In „Sovremenniki" (Zeitgenossen) schildert sie das Leben Gogol's in Rom, in einer Trilogie behandelt sie die Zeit Radiščevs (um 1800). Im Roman „Symbolisten" schildert F. das Leben der russischen Schriftsteller knapp vor der Revolution von 1917.

Moskovskie rasskazy (Moskauer Erzählungen, 1925)
Odety kamnem (In Stein gehüllt, 1925)
Sovremenniki (Zeitgenossen, 1926)
Gorjačij cech (Heiße Werkabteilung, 1932)
Simvolisty (Symbolisten, 1932)
Pod kupolom (Unter der Kuppel, 1933)
Radiščev (1934—39, Trilogie)
Michajlovskij zamok (Das Schloß Michajlovskij, 1946, I. Teil einer Trilogie über Leningrad)
Pervency svobody (Die Erstgeborenen der Freiheit, 1953)

Deutsche Übersetzungen

In Stein gehüllt, übers. v. Wolfgang E. Groeger, Leipzig, Dr. F. Fikentscher. 1926.
Die Kaiserin und der Rebell (Radiščev), übers. v. Alexander Böltz, Berlin, Verlag der Nation. 1957.

Fúrmanov Dmítrij Andréevič

1891—1926, geb. im Dorfe Sereda, Gouvernement Kostroma, als Sohn eines Kellners. F. verbrachte seine Kindheit in Ivanovo-Voznesensk, wo er auch die Realschule absolvierte. 1912 inskribierte er an der Moskauer Universität, im gleichen Jahre erschienen auch seine ersten Gedichte. Zu Beginn des ersten Weltkrieges ging F. als Sanitäter freiwillig an die Front. Erst Sozialrevolutionär, dann *Anarchist*, trat F. 1918 der Kommunistischen Partei bei. Im Jahre 1922 beendete er seine Studien an der Fakultät für Sozialwissenschaften. Er war politischer Kommissar in der Armee Čapaevs, später Vorsitzender des Stadtsowjets in Ivanovo, wo er mit Frunze bekannt wurde. 1923 war F. Sekretär im *RAPP*. Das Hauptthema in F.s Werken ist der Bürgerkrieg. Sein bekanntestes Werk ist der Roman „Čapaev", dessen Handlung übrigens einem russischen Film (1934) zugrunde liegt.

Krasnyj desant (Die rote Landung, 1922)
Čapaev (1923)
V semnadcatom godu (Im Jahre 1917, 1923)
Mjatež (Meuterei, 1923—25)
Invalid (Der Invalide, 1925)
Kak ubili otca (Wie sie den Vater erschlugen, 1925)
Tovarišč M. V. Frunze pod Užoj (Genosse M. V. Frunze an der Uža, 1925)
Morskie berega (Die Meeresufer, 1926)

Deutsche Übersetzungen

Die roten Helden (Krasnyj desant), übers. v. Aleksander Videns, Berlin, Verlag der Jugendinternationale. 1928.

Tschapajew, Moskau, Zentralverlag der Völker der Sowjetunion. 1928. Übers. v. Eduard Schiemann, Zürich, Ring-Verlag. 1934. Übers. v. Ellen Walden, Berlin, Verlag Kultur und Fortschritt. 1951, 1953. Bearb. v. Hilde Angarowa, Moskau, Verlag für fremdsprachige Literatur. 1955.

Meuterei, übers. v. Dora Hofmeister, Berlin, Verlag Kultur und Fortschritt. 1955.

Gajdár Arkádij (Pseudonym für Arkádij Petróvič Gólikov) 1904—1941, bekannt hauptsächlich als Verfasser von Kinderbüchern. Seine Jugend verbrachte er in Arzamas. Ab 1919 nahm G. aktiv an der Revolution als Rotarmist teil. Von seinen Werken ist die Novelle „Timur i ego komanda" (Timur und sein Trupp) am bekanntesten.

RVS (1925)
Škola (Die Schule, 1930)
Voennaja tajna (Kriegsgeheimnis, 1935)
Čuk i Gek (Čuk und Gek, 1939)
Timur i ego komanda (Timur und sein Trupp, 1940)

Deutsche Übersetzungen

Timur und seine Freunde. Jugendroman, übers. v. F. Grün, Wien, Globus. 1947. Timur und sein Trupp, übers. v. L. Klementinowskaja, Berlin, SWA. 1947.

Tschuk und Gek, Bukarest, Jugendverlag. 1951.
Schule des Lebens (Škola), übers. v. J. Tinzmann, Berlin, Kinderbuchverlag. 1951.

Gerásimov Sergéj Apollinárievič

Geb. 1906, ist Mitglied der KPdSU und des Obersten Sowjets. G., Volkskünstler der Sowjetunion, ist bekannt als Schauspieler und als Regisseur seiner eigenen Dramen. Für seine Filme „Učitel'" (Der Lehrer, 1939), „Molodaja gvardija" (Junge Garde, 1948) und „Osvoboždënnyj Kitaj" (Das befreite China, 1950) erhielt G. drei *Stalinpreise*. Außerdem wurde unter seiner Regie der Film „Tichij Don" (Der stille Don) gedreht.

Učitel' (Der Lehrer, 1939)
Naši dni (Unsere Tage, 1940)
Geroj našej epochi (Der Held unserer Zeit, 1956)

Gérman Júrij Pávlovič

Geb. 1910 in Riga. G. begann seine schriftstellerische Tätigkeit um 1929 und wurde in den dreißiger Jahren durch seinen Roman „Naši znakomye" (Unsere Bekannten) bekannt. Die Veröffentlichung des Romans „Podpolkovnik medicinskoj služby" (Oberstleutnant des medizinischen Dienstes), die 1949 in der Zeitschrift „Zvezda" begonnen wurde, mußte eingestellt werden, weil der Charakter des Helden nicht positiv im Sinne der von der Partei an die Literatur gestellten Anforderungen war.

Bi cheppi (Viel Glück)
Bednyj Genrich (Der arme Heinrich, 1934)
Naši znakomye (Unsere Bekannten, 1936)
Aleksej Žmakin (1938)
Syn naroda (Der Sohn des Volkes, 1939)
Podpolkovnik medicinskoj služby (Oberstleutnant des medizinischen Dienstes, 1949, nicht vollendet)
Rossija molodaja (Das junge Rußland, 1952, Roman aus der Zeit Peter d. Gr.)

Za tjuremnoj stenoj (Hinter der Gefängnismauer, 1956)
Rasskazy o Felikse Dzeržinskom (Erzählungen über Felix Dzeržinskij)
Delo, kotoromu ty služiš' (Der Sache, der du dienst, 1958, Ärzteroman)

Deutsche Übersetzungen

Viel Glück (Bi cheppi), London, Free Austrian Books. 1945.
Schwert und Flamme. Erz. über Feliks Dzeržinskij. übers. v. Tamara Krause, Berlin, Verlag Blick nach Polen. 1952, 1953.

Gladków Fëdor Vasíl'evič

1883—1958, geb. im Gouvernement Saratov als Sohn eines verarmten Bauern. Seine ersten, gedruckten Werke erschienen schon 1899. Als politischer Verbannter wurde G. nach der Revolution des Jahres 1905 Lehrer in Sibirien und später im Kuban'-Gebiet. 1920 trat G. der Kommunistischen Partei bei und schloß sich der in diesem Jahre entstandenen Dichtergruppe *Kuznica* an. Die ersten Romane G.s, „Die Ausgestoßenen" (1912) und später „Das feurige Roß", erschienen 1922, sind in der Komposition noch sehr schwach. Bekannt und berühmt wurde G. erst durch seinen Roman „Zement" (1925), der als erster Industrie- und Wiederaufbauroman angesehen wird. G.s Bücher wurden in 27 Sprachen übersetzt und erreichten eine Gesamtauflage von 5 938 000.

Ognennyj kon' (Das feurige Roß, 1922)
Cement (Zement, 1925)
Staraja sekretnaja (Früher im Zuchthaus, 1927)
P'janoe solnce (Trunkene Sonne, 1927)
Krov'ju serdca (Mit dem Blut des Herzens, 1928)
Novaja zemlja (Neue Erde, 1930)
Energija (Energie, 1938)
Kljatva (Der Schwur, 1945)
Povest' o detstve (Erzählung von meiner Kindheit, 1949, *Stalinpreis* 1950)
Vol'nica (Die Freischärler, 1950, *Stalinpreis* 1951)
Mjatežnaja junost' (Rebellische Jugend, 1956)

Deutsche Übersetzungen

Marussja stiftet Verwirrung (Pjanoe solnce), übers. v. Josef Kalmer u. Boris Krotkow, Wien, E. P. Tal & Co. 1930.

Ugrjumov erzählt vom Zuchthaus (Staraja sekretnaja), übers. v. Josef Kalmer u. Boris Krotkow, Leipzig-Wien, E. Prager. 1931.

Neue Erde, übers. v. Olga Halpern, Moskau, Verlagsgenossenschaft ausländischer Arbeiter in der UdSSR. 1932. Wien-Berlin, Verlag für Literatur und Politik. 1932.

Zement, übers. v. Olga Halpern, Berlin-Wien, Verlag für Literatur und Politik. 1927. Moskau, Verlagsgenossenschaft ausländischer Arbeiter in der UdSSR. 1932. Übers. v. Alfred Edgar Thoss, Berlin, Verlag Kultur und Fortschritt. 1949, 1950, 1951. Cement u. 4 Erz., übers. v. Wera Rathfelder u. Liselotte Remané, 5. erw. Aufl., Berlin, Verlag Kultur und Fortschritt. 1956.

Energie, Moskau-Leningrad, Verlagsgenossenschaft ausländischer Arbeiter in der UdSSR. 1935.

Der Schnee schmilzt (Povest' o detstve), übers. v. S. Cornelius Bengmann, Eisenach-Kassel, Röth. 1956.

Glínka Gleb Aleksándrovič

Geb. 1903 in Moskau. Wie G. von sich selber schreibt, ist er „nie Parteimitglied gewesen". Er absolvierte im Jahre 1925 das Valerij-Brjusov-Institut. Bis um das Jahr 1928 war G. nur als Lyriker tätig, wandte sich aber ab dieser Zeit der Prosa zu. Befruchtend wirkten auf ihn seine vielen Reisen, besonders in die Nordgebiete Rußlands. Er trug an der Moskauer Universität Theorie der Literaturgeschichte vor und war auch in der Redaktion der Zeitschrift „Sovetskij pisatel'" tätig. In seinem Schaffen stand G. der Dichtergruppe *Pereval* nahe. Derzeit lebt G. in den USA.

Vremena goda (Die Jahreszeiten, 1926)
Izrazcovaja pečka (Der Kachelofen, 1929)
Ešelon opazdyvaet (Der Echelon verspätet sich, 1932)
Istoki mužestva (Die Quellen der Tapferkeit, 1935)
Pavlov na Oke (Pavlov an der Oka, 1936)
Na perevale (Auf dem Pass, 1954, New York)

Golódnyj Michaíl (Pseudonym für Michaíl Semënovič Epštéin)
1903—1946, geb. in Bachmut, Gouvernement Ekaterinoslav, als Sohn einer Arbeiterfamilie. G. arbeitete schon im Alter von 12 Jahren in einer Fabrik und kam 1924 nach Moskau, wo er die Arbeiterhochschule (Rabfak) und das Valerij-Brjusov-Institut besuchte. Seine erste Gedichtsammlung, „Svai" (Die Pfähle), erschien 1922 in Char'kov.

Svai (Die Pfähle, 1922)
Izbrannoe (Auswahl, 1956)

Gorbátov Borís Leónt'evič
1908—1954, geb. im Donbass. G. begann seine schriftstellerische Tätigkeit 1922. Seine erste Novelle, „Jačejka" (Die Zelle), erschien 1928. Das Hauptthema in G.s Werken ist die Arbeiterschaft und die Komsomolbewegung. Seine Bücher wurden in 49 Sprachen übersetzt und erreichten bis 1958 eine Gesamtauflage von 9 993 000.

Naš gorod (Unsere Stadt, 1930)
Jačejka (Die Zelle, 1928)
Gornyj pochod (Der Feldzug in den Bergen, 1932)
Mastera (Meister, 1933)
Moë pokolenie (Meine Generation, 1933)
Obyknovennaja Arktika (Die gewöhnliche Arktis, 1938)
Bocman s ‚Gromoboja' (Der Bootsmann von ‚Gromoboj', 1938)
Bol'šaja voda (Das große Wasser, 1939)
Aleksej Kulikov – boec (Der Landser Alexej Kulikov, 1942)
Pis'ma tovarišču (Briefe an einen Genossen, 1942)
Rasskazy o soldatskoj duše (Geschichten über die Soldatenseele, 1943)
Nepokorënnye (Die Unbeugsamen, 1943, *Stalinpreis* 1946)
Donbass (1951)

Deutsche Übersetzungen

Die Unbeugsamen, Stockholm, Neuer Verlag. 1944. Auch unter dem Titel ‚Die sich nicht beugen ließen', übers. v. Nikolaus Hovorka, Wien, ‚Die Brücke'. 1946. Rudolstadt, Greifenverlag. 1950.

Die gewöhnliche Arktis, übers. v. Veronica Ensslen u. Miron Broser, Berlin, Verlag Tägliche Rundschau. 1947. Auch unter dem Titel

‚Die Geburt auf dem Gurkenland', bearb. v. Hanns A. Windorf. Rudolstadt, Greifenverlag. 1952.
Donbass, übers. v. Ernst Hube, Berlin, Tribüne. 195. Übers. v. Otto Braun, Bukarest, Verlag Cartea rusă. 1954.
Meine Generation, übers. v. Marie Jacob, Rudolstadt, Greifenverlag. 1954.
Das große Wasser. Der alte Bootsmann, Erzählungen, bearb. v. Hanns A. Windorf, Leipzig, Reclam. 1955.
Nach Jahresfrist (Brief an einen Genossen), übers. v. Hugo Huppert, Wien, Stern-Verlag. 1946.

Gorélov Iván Pávlovič

Geb. 1910 im Gebiet von Krasnodar. G. absolvierte die literarische Fakultät der Pädagogischen Hochschule und ist seit 1933 schriftstellerisch tätig. Im selben Jahr erschienen auch seine kleinen Skizzen über die Bergleute im Donezbecken in Buchform. Während des „Vaterländischen Krieges" war er im Einsatz an der Front. Von G.s literarischen Werken sind am bedeutendsten seine „Humoristischen Erzählungen", „Kornblumen" und „Das Familiengeheimnis".

Žrec Femidy (Der Priester der Gerechtigkeit, 1955)
Razljubil (Er hörte auf zu lieben, 1955)
Zolotye bukaški (Goldene Käfer, 1957)
San'ka (Sanja, 1957)
Deutsche Übersetzungen
Sanja, übers. v. Juri Elperin, Moskau, S. L. 1957.

Gorodéckij Sergéj Mitrofánovič

Geb. 1884 in St. Petersburg. Nach dem Besuch des Gymnasiums studierte G. an der historisch-philosophischen Fakultät der Universität St. Petersburg. Während des Krieges war er Korrespondent und leitete 1921 die Zeitung „Izvestija", später war G. in der Redaktion der Zeitschrift „Iskusstvo trudjaščimsja" tätig. 1907 erschien seine erste Gedichtsammlung. Vor der Revolution gehörte G. zu den *Akmeisten.*

Gór'kij

Izbrannye liričeskie i liriko-epičeskie stichotvorenija 1905—1935 (Ausgewählte lyrische und lyrisch-epische Gedichte 1905—1935, 1936)

Gór'kij Maksím (Pseudonym für Alekséj Maksímovič Péškov) 1868—1936, geb. in Nižnij Novgorod, dem heutigen Gor'kij, als Sohn armer Leute. Im Hause seiner Großeltern machte er schwere Kindheitsjahre durch. Da er von klein auf gezwungen war, mitzuverdienen, genoß er keine geregelte Schulbildung. Trotzdem war er sehr belesen und von Natur aus außergewöhnlich begabt. Seine turbulente und abenteuerliche Jugend beschrieb G. in „Meine Kindheit", „Unter fremden Menschen" und „Meine Universitäten". 1892 veröffentlichte er seine erste Erzählung, „Makar Čudra", welche ihn bald populär machte. 1905 war G. der inoffizielle, aber allseits anerkannte Vertreter der Linksradikalen. Er war mit Lenin, Stalin und vielen anderen prominenten Revolutionären befreundet. Wegen seiner Lungenkrankheit verbrachte G. viele Jahre im Ausland, vor allem in Italien auf Capri (1907 bis 1913, 1920 bis 1928). Nach der Oktoberrevolution brachte er wohl seine Ablehnung des roten Terrors zum Ausdruck, bejahte aber die bolschewistische Ideologie. Sein großes Verdienst bestand vor allem in der Fürsorge, die er in der Zeit der Not den russischen Künstlern angedeihen ließ. Sein feines Sprachgefühl machte ihn zum „obersten Richter", zu einem entscheidenden Kritiker seiner Zeit und Förderer junger Talente. G. gehört zu den Gründern und Klassikern des *sozialistischen Realismus.* Seine Erinnerungen an L. N. Tolstoj, A. Čechov, Lenin und andere Zeitgenossen nehmen in der Memoirenliteratur einen beachtlichen Platz ein.

G. starb am 18. Juni 1936, angeblich von Jagoda vergiftet. Seine Bücher sind bisher in 72 Sprachen übersetzt worden und haben eine Gesamtauflage von 78 382 000 erreicht.

Makar Čudra (1892)
Čelkaš (1895)
V stepi (In der Steppe, 1897)

Gór'kij

Mal'va (1897)
Foma Gordeev (1899)
Troe (Die Drei, 1900)
Na dne (Nachtasyl, 1902)
Vragi (Die Feinde, 1906)
Mat' (Die Mutter, 1908)
Detstvo (Meine Kindheit, 1913)
V ljudjach (Unter fremden Menschen, 1915)
Vospominanija o L've Nikolaeviče Tolstom (Erinnerungen an Lev Nikolaevič Tolstoj, 1919)
Moi universitety (Meine Universitäten, 1923)
Delo Artomonovych (Das Werk der Artomonovs, 1926)
Žizn' Klima Samgina (Das Leben des Klim Samgin, 1936)
O literature (Über die Literatur, 1937)

Deutsche Übersetzungen

Erinnerungen an Lew Nikolajewitsch Tolstoj, München, Verlag Der neue Merkur. 1920, erg. Aufl. 1921. Übers. v. Erich Boehme, Leipzig, Insel-Verlag. 1928.

Erlebnisse und Begegnungen, (Vospominanija), übers. v. Erich Boehme, Berlin, I. Ladyschnikow. 1924.

Das Werk der Artomonows, übers. v. Klara Brauner, Berlin, Malik-Verlag. 1927. Düsseldorf, Progress-Verlag. 1957. Berlin, Aufbau-Verlag. 1946, 1952. Moskau-Leningrad, Verlagsgenossenschaft ausländischer Arbeiter in der UdSSR. 1934. Berlin-Leipzig, SWA-Verlag. 1947. Berlin, Verlag Tägliche Rundschau. 1949.

Erinnerungen an Zeitgenossen (Vospominanija), übers. v. Erich Boehme, Berlin, Malik-Verlag. 1928. Berlin, Aufbau-Verlag. 1951, 1953.

Das Leben des Klim Samgin, übers. v. Rudolf Selke, Berlin, Sieben-Stäbe-Verlag. 1929, 1930. Buch 1, übers. v. Hans Ruoff, Berlin, Aufbau-Verlag. 1952, 1953. Essen, Verlag Dein Buch. 1953. Buch 2, übers. v. Hans Ruoff, Berlin, Aufbau-Verlag. 1953. Buch 3, übers. v. Hans Ruoff, Berlin, Aufbau-Verlag. 1955. Buch 4, übers. v. Hans Ruoff, Berlin, Aufbau-Verlag. 1957.

Ausgewählte Werke, Bd. 1—5, Moskau-Leningrad, Verlagsgenossenschaft ausländischer Arbeiter in der UdSSR. 1934. Wien, Globus-Verlag. 1947.

Erzählungen, Bd. 1—6, Berlin, Aufbau-Verlag. 1953 ff.

Mit wem seid Ihr, Meister der Kunst? Aufsätze, Reden, Briefe. Aus. u. Nachw. v. Hans Marquardt, bearb. v. Hilde Angarowa, Leipzig, Reclam. 1957.
Werke, Bd. 1—3, Berlin, Aufbau-Verlag. 1946.
Mutter, übers. v. A. Hess, Berlin, Aufbau-Verlag. 1946, 1951, 1952, 1953.
Meine Universitäten, übers. v. Erich Boehme, Berlin, Aufbau-Verlag. 1953.
Nachtasyl. Szenen aus der Tiefe in 4 Akten, übers. v. A. Scholz, Leipzig, Reclam. 1950, 1952.
In der Steppe. Novellen, Berlin-Leipzig, Volk und Wissen. 1947.
Die Feinde. Dramatische Szenen, übers. v. O. Potthof, Berlin, Henschelverlag Kunst und Gesellschaft. 1946.
Meine Kindheit, übers. v. A. Scholz, Berlin. 1917.
Tschelkasch (Čelkaš), übers. v. Ilse Mirus, Geschichten aus dem alten und neuen Rußland, München, Nymphenburger Verlagsh. 1958.

Gránin Daniil Aleksándrovič

Geb. 1919 in Petrograd, wo er auch seine frühe Kindheit und Jugend verbrachte und die Zehnjahresschule und die Technische Hochschule absolvierte. Er begann seine Laufbahn als Ingenieur am Kirovwerk. 1941 meldete er sich freiwillig an die Front. 1949 erschien seine erste Erzählung, „Variant vtoroj" (Die zweite Variante), in der Zeitschrift „Zvezda". G. gehört heute zu den angesehensten und meistgelesenen Schriftstellern der Sowjetunion.

Jaroslav Domrovskij (Jaroslav Dombrowski, 1951)
Novye druz'ja (Neue Freunde, 1952)
Iskateli (Bahnbrecher, 1954)
Sobstvennoe mnenie (Eigene Meinung, 1956)
Posle svad'by (Nach der Hochzeit, 1958)

Deutsche Übersetzungen

Bahnbrecher, übers. v. E. Margolis, Berlin, Dietz. 1956, 1957. Bukarest, Verlag Cartea rusă. 1956.
Eigene Meinung, übers. v. Heddy Weerth, Stuttgart, Osteuropa. 1957.

Gribačëv Nikoláj Matvéevič

Geb. 1910 im Gouvernement Brjansk als Sohn einer Bauernfamilie. G. absolvierte 1932 das Technologische Institut als Hydrotechniker. 1933 schlug er die journalistische Laufbahn ein und veröffentlichte bereits 1935 in Petrozavodsk seine erste Gedichtsammlung. 1939—1940 war G. an der finnischen Front. 1943 wurde er Mitglied der KPdSU. In seiner Eigenschaft als Kriegsberichterstatter lernte G. in den folgenden Jahren auch Prag und Berlin kennen. 1945—1947 schlug er in seinen Arbeiten einen aggressiven Ton gegenüber den USA an. Das Hauptthema in seinen Werken während dieser Periode sind das Leben und die Verhältnisse auf den Kolchosen.

Severo-zapad (Nordwesten, 1935)
Stichi i poemy (Gedichte und Poeme, 1939)
Po frontovym dorogam (Auf den Straßen der Front, 1946)
Naša zemlja — stichotvorenija (Unser Land, Gedichte, 1946—52)
U kostra (Am Lagerfeuer, 1947)
Vesna v ‚Pobede' (Frühling auf (der Kolchose) ‚Pobeda', 1947, *Stalinpreis*)
Kolchoz ‚Bol'ševik' (Die Kolchose „Bolschewik", 1948, *Stalinpreis*)
V pochode (Auf dem Marsch, 1948)
O stichach dlja detej (Über Kindergedichte, 1952)
Bronzovaja bezdeluška (Eine kleine Bronzefigur, 1956)
Les i step' (Wald und Steppe, 1956)
Sčast'e (Glück, 1958)

Deutsche Übersetzungen

Wald und Steppe, übers. v. Juri Elperin, Moskau, S. L. 1958.
Glück, übers. v. Sepp Österreicher, Moskau, S. L. 1959.

Grin Aleksándr (Pseudonym für Aleksándr Stepánovič Grinévskij)

1880—1932, geb. in Vjatka (jetzt Kirov). Sein Schaffen stand unter dem Einfluß der romantischen Erzählungen *Gor'kijs*. Die Handlung in G.s Erzählungen spielt sehr oft im Ausland, auch ihre Helden sind öfters Nichtrussen. G., der sich wie *Gor'kij* in den verschiedensten Berufen versuchte, aber in Gegensatz zu ihm von seinem armseligen, entbehrungsreichen Leben nicht loskam, bringt in seinen märchenähnlichen Erzählungen mit ihren Phantasiehelden immer wieder seine unerschütterliche Lebensfreude und seinen Glauben an das Gute und Schöne zum Ausdruck. Von der offiziellen Sowjetkritik wird G. als wirklichkeitsfremder Phantast und *Kosmopolit* abgetan.

V Italii (In Italien, 1906)
Alye parusa (Das Purpursegel, 1921)
Beguščaja po volnam (Wogengleiter, 1928)
Sobranie sočinenij (Gesammelte Werke, 1928, abgebrochen beim 8. Bd.)
Fantastičeskie povesti i novelly (Phantastische Erzählungen und Novellen, 1934)
Rasskazy (Erzählungen, 1935)
Nedotroga (Ein Rührmichnichtan, 1936)

Deutsche Übersetzungen

Das Purpursegel, übers. v. L. Kementinowskaja, Berlin-Leipzig, SWA-Verlag. 1946, 1948. Leipzig, Insel-Verlag. 1952, 1954, 1956.
Wogengleiter (Beguščaja po volnam), bearb. v. Hannes A. Windorf, Rudolstadt, Greifenverlag. 1949.

Grόssman Leonίd Petrόvič

Geb. 1888 in Odessa als Sohn eines Arztes. G. selbst schlug aber die juristische Laufbahn ein und wurde als Literarhistoriker durch Arbeiten wie z. B. „Oneginskaja strofa" (Onegins Versform), „Bakunin v ‚Besach'" (Bakunin in den ‚Dämonen') und „Kompozicija romanov Dostoevskogo" (Aufbau der Romane bei Dostoevskij) bekannt. In seinen Werken vertritt G. die Schule der *Formalisten*. Gegenwärtig ist er im *Gosizdat* tätig.

Ruletenburg (Roulettenburg, 1932, Dostoevskij in Deutschland)
Barchatnyj diktator (Der samtene Diktator, 1938, aus dem Leben Alexander II. und Loris-Melikovs)
Zapiski d'Aršiaka (Die Aufzeichnungen d'Archiacs, 1937, aus Puškins letzten Lebenstagen)
Gesammelte Werke, 5 Bde. (1928)

Gróssman Vasílij Semënovič

Geb. 1905 in Berdičev als Sohn eines Ingenieurs und einer Lehrerin. G. absolvierte die Realschule in Kiev und studierte an der Universität in Kiev und Moskau. Sehr umstritten ist sein 1952 in „Novyj mir“ erschienener Roman „Za pravoe delo“ (Für eine gerechte Sache). In diesem wird die Schlacht von Stalingrad geeschildert. Nach der Sowjetkritik sei diese Schilderung viel zu viel mit Philosophie überladen und vor allem werde die Rolle der Partei im Kampf gegen den Faschismus zu wenig gewürdigt.

V gorode Berdičeve (In der Stadt Berdičev, 1934)
Stepan Kol'čugin (1937—1940), 3 Teile.
Narod bessmerten (Dies Volk ist unsterblich, 1942)
Stalingrad (1943)
Gody vojny (Die Kriegsjahre, 1941—1945)
Za pravoe delo (Für eine gerechte Sache, 1954)

Deutsche Übersetzungen

Dies Volk ist unsterblich, übers. v. Hilde Angarowa, Moskau, Verlag für fremdsprachige Literatur. 1946.
Stalingrad, Moskau, Verlag für fremdsprachige Literatur. 1947.
Stepan Koltschugin, übers. v. Leon Nebenzahl, Bd. 1, 2, Berlin, Dietz. 1953.
Stalingrad verteidigt sich, Stalingrad greift an, übers. v. Hilde Angarowa, Wien, Stern-Verlag. 1946.

Gudzénko Semën Petróvič

1922—1953, geb. in Kiev in der Familie eines Angestellten. Nach der Absolvierung der Mittelschule im Jahre 1939 studierte G. am Institut für Geschichte, Philosophie und Literatur in Moskau. Im zweiten Weltkrieg ging G. als Freiwilliger an die Front und nahm an den Kämpfen vor Moskau teil. Er wurde auch mit dem Orden „Roter Stern“ ausgezeichnet. Später war er bei verschiedenen Soldatenzeitungen tätig. In der Nachkriegszeit unternahm er ausgedehnte Reisen durch die Sowjetunion, die ihn in die Karpaten, nach Tuva und Mittelasien führten. Seine ersten Gedichte wurden 1941 in einer Armeezeitung veröffentlicht. Die erste Gedichtsammlung erschien 1944 in Moskau unter dem Titel „Odnopolčane" (Regimentskameraden). (nach ANT)

Zakarpatskie stichi (Gedichte aus den Karpaten, 1948)
Bitva (Die Schlacht, 1948)
Novye kraja (Neue Länder, 1953)
Stichi i poemy (Gedichte und Poeme, 1942—52)

Gumilëv Nikoláj Stepánovič

1886—1921, geb. in Kronstadt, wo sein Vater Marinearzt war. G. verlebte seine Jugend in Carskoe Selo, absolvierte das Gymnasium in Petersburg und ging nach Abschluß seiner Studien im Jahre 1906 nach Paris. Dort hörte er an der Sorbonne Vorlesungen über Kunst und Literatur. 1910 heiratete er Anna Gorenko, welche unter dem Namen Anna *Achmatova* berühmt wurde. Die Ehe wurde 1918 geschieden. G. bereiste Europa, Afrika und den Nahen Osten. 1914 rückte er freiwillig ein und wurde an der Front ausgezeichnet. G. wurde zwei Wochen nach *Bloks* Tod, trotz *Gor'kijs* Bemühungen ihm zu helfen, wegen konterrevolutionärer Tätigkeit erschossen. G. war, zusammen mit *Gorodeckij*, der Begründer der *Akmeisten*. Von 1909 bis 1917 redigierte G. die Zeitschrift „Apollon". Er gilt als einer der talentiertesten russischen Lyriker des 20. Jahrhunderts.

Put' Konkvistadorov (Der Weg der Konquistadoren, 1905)
Žemčuga (Die Perlen, 1910)
Čužoe nebo (Der fremde Himmel, 1911)
Kolčan (Der Köcher, 1916)
Otravlennaja tunika (Die vergiftete Tunika, 1918)
Šatër (Das Zelt, 1921)
Ognennyj stolb (Der Feuerpfahl, 1921)

Gúsev Víktor Michájlovič

1909—1944, geb. in Moskau, aus einer bürgerlichen Familie stammend. G. begann seine literarische Tätigkeit 1927 und wurde vor allem durch seine vielen volkstümlichen Lieder, wie z. B. „Pesnja o Moskve" (Das Lied von Moskau), „Ja russkij čelovek" (Ich bin ein russischer Mensch), „Naša Moskva" (Unser Moskau) u. a., bekannt. Für seine Filme „Svinarka i pastuch" (Die Schweinemagd und der Hirt), und „V šest' časov večera posle vojny" (Um sechs Uhr abends nach dem Krieg) wurde G. 1942 und 1946 mit dem *Stalinpreis* ausgezeichnet.

Pochod veščej (Der Marsch der Dinge, 1929)
Geroi edut v kolchoz (Die Helden fahren auf die Kolchose, 1931)
Molodoj čelovek (Der junge Mann, 1933)
Slava (Der Ruhm, 1935)
Sočinenija v 2-ch tomach (Werke in 2 Bd., 1955)

Il'énkov Vasílij Pávlovič

Geb. 1897. I.s literarisches Schaffen erstreckt sich hauptsächlich auf Romane und Erzählungen. Die während der dreißiger Jahre erschienenen Romane I.s schildern die Zeit des ersten Fünfjahresplans und des „sozialistischen Wiederaufbaus". Der bekannteste dieser Romane, „Veduščaja os'" (Die Treibachse), wurde von *Gor'kij* wegen seiner künstlerischen Mängel kritisiert. In seinem 1950 mit dem *Stalinpreis* ausgezeichneten Roman „Bol'šaja doroga" (Der große Weg) setzte sich I. mit den Verhältnissen auf dem Kolchosdorf nach dem Kriege auseinander.

Veduščaja os' (Die Triebachse, 1931)
Solnečnyj gorod (Die Sonnenstadt, 1935)
Rodnoj dom (Das Vaterhaus, 1942)
Na tot bereg (Ans jenseitige Ufer, 1945)
Bol'šaja doroga (Der große Weg, 1949, *Stalinpreis* 1950)

Deutsche Übersetzungen

Die Triebachse, übers. v. E. Korniez, Zürich, Ring-Verlag. 1933. Moskau-Leningrad, Verlagsgenossenschaft ausländischer Arbeiter in der UdSSR. 1935.

Der große Weg, übers. v. Roland Schacht, Berlin, Verlag Kultur und Fortschritt. 1952.

Il'f Il'já (Pseudonym für Il'já Arnól'dovič Fáinsil'berg) 1897—1937, geb. in Odessa, aus einer kleinbürgerlichen, jüdischen Familie stammend. I. begann 1918 seine literarische Tätigkeit, in deren Verlauf er durch seine — mit seinem Freund E. *Petróv* („Il'f i Petróv") verfaßten — Satiren und dem satirischen Roman „Zwölf Stühle" hervortrat. „Die Hauptcharaktere dieser Bücher sind den Sowjets sozial fremde und feindlich gesinnte Elemente, getarnt als naive und zugleich geistreiche Menschen. Das Auffallende ist, daß diese Leute meistens klüger sind als ihre Umgebung" (El'sberg, Nasledie Gogolja i Ščedrina v sovetskoj satire, Moskau 1954, S. 111).

Dvenadcat' stul'ev (Zwölf Stühle, 1928)
Zolotoj telënok (Das goldene Kalb, 1931)
Odnoetažnaja Amerika (Das einstöckige Amerika, 1936)
Zapisnye knižki (Notizbücher, 1939, posthum)
Graf Sredizemskij (1957, posthum)

Deutsche Übersetzungen

Ein Millionär in Sowjetrußland (Zolotoj telënok), übers. v. Elsa Brod, Mary v. Pruss-Glowatzky u. Rich. Hoffmann, Nachwort v. A. Lunačarskij, Berlin-Wien-Leipzig, Zsolnay. 1932. Auch unter dem Titel Das goldene Kalb, übers. v. Enrico Italiener, Stockholm, Neuer Verlag. 1946.

Zwölf Stühle, übers. v. Elsa Brod u. Mary v. Pruss-Glowatzky, Hamburg, Rowohlt. 1954.

Vgl. *Petrov.*

Il'ín M. (Pseudonym für Il'já Jákovlevič Maršák) 1895—1953, geb. in der Stadt Ostrogorsk im Gouvernement Voronež. I wurde Ingenieur und begann im Jahre 1925 populärwissenschaftliche Bücher in einer für Kinder verständlichen Sprache über die verschiedensten technischen Errungenschaften und physikalischen Probleme zu schreiben.

Solnce na stole (Die Sonne auf dem Tisch, 1925)
Čërnym po belomu (Schwarz auf weiß, 1928)
Sto tysjač počemu (Hunderttausendmal warum, 1929)
Kak avtomobil' učilsja chodit' (Wie das Auto gehen lernte, 1930)

Rasskaz o velikom plane (Erzählung über den großen Plan, 1930)
Gory i ljudi (Berge und Menschen, 1935)
Rasskazy o veščach (Erzählungen über die Dinge, 1936)
Čelovek i stichija (Der Mensch und die Naturgewalt, 1947)
Putešestvie v atom (Die Reise ins Atom, 1948)
Pokorenie prirody (Die Eroberung der Natur, 1950)
Preobrazovanie planety (Die Umgestaltung des Planeten, 1951)

Deutsche Übersetzungen

Berge und Menschen, Wien, Globus-Verlag. 1946.

Der Mensch bezwingt die Natur (Pokorenie prirody), Wien, 1951. Auch unter dem Titel Besiegte Natur, übers. v. P. Weibel, Berlin, Volk und Welt. 1951.

Die Umgestaltung unseres Planeten, Berlin, Volk und Welt. 1952.

Was uns die Dinge erzählen, übertr. v. E. Sabel, Berlin, SWA-Verlag. 1947, 1948.

Die Sonne auf dem Tisch, Berlin, Volk und Welt. 1948.

100 000 × warum, Berlin, Volk und Welt. 1947, 1948, 1951.

Wolkenschieber und Wettermacher (Čelovek i stichija), übers. v. A. Thoss, Berlin, Volk und Welt. 1950. Auch unter dem Titel Der Mensch und die Naturkräfte, übers. v. W. Lorenz, 3 Teile, Bukarest, Staatsverlag. 1950.

Schwarz auf Weiß. Die Entstehung der Schrift, Zürich, Steinberg. 1945.

Înber Véra Michájlovna

Geb. 1890 in Odessa, aus einer kleinbürgerlichen Familie stammend. In der ersten Zeit ihrer literarischen Tätigkeit, die sie 1911 begann, schloß sich I. den *Dekadenten* an, trennte sich aber wieder von ihnen und wandte sich um 1920 der Gruppe der *Konstruktivisten* zu. Stil und Inhalt ihrer 1925 erschienenen „Erzählungen" verraten bereits zunehmende Reife. Die Jahre der Blockade Leningrads (1941 bis 1944) inspirieren sie zu tiefen, gedankenvollen Werken. In „Vdochnovenie i masterstvo" (Inspirationen und Kunst) versteht es I., in kurzen, treffenden Sätzen über die geheimnisvollen Vorgänge in der Seele des Künstlers bei seiner schöpferischen Arbeit zu erzählen.

Pečal'noe vino (Trauriger Wein, 1914)
Gor'kaja uslada (Bittere Süße, 1917)
Brennye slova (Vergängliche Worte, 1922)
Mal'čik s vesnuškami (Der Knabe mit den Sommersprossen, 1926)
Synu, kotorogo net (Dem Sohn, der nicht da ist, 1927)
Sojuz materej (Der Bund der Mütter, 1933)
Putevoj dnevnik (Das Reisetagebuch, 1939)
Pulkovskij meridian (Der Meridian von Pulkovo, 1942)
Rasskazy (Erzählungen, 1925)
Počti tri goda (Leningradskij dnevnik) (Fast drei Jahre. Aus einem Leningrader Tagebuch, 1945, *Stalinpreis*)
Mesto pod solncem (Der Platz an der Sonne)
Put' vody (Der Weg des Wassers, 1948)
Izbrannye proizvedenija (Ausgewählte Werke, 1954)
Lenin v Ženeve (Lenin in Genf, 1956)
Vdochnovenie i masterstvo (Inspirationen und Kunst, 1957)

Deutsche Übersetzungen

Der Platz an der Sonne, übers. v. Elena Frank, Berlin, Malik-Verlag. 1929. Leipzig, P. List. 1949, 1952. Leipzig, Reclam. 1954.
Fast drei Jahre. Aus einem Leningrader Tagebuch, Berlin, SWA-Verlag. 1946, 1947.
Ein Bergspaziergang (Kapitel aus „Lenin in Genf"), übers. v. Sepp Österreicher, Moskau, S. L. 1957.

Isakóvskij Michaíl Vasíl'evič

Geb. 1900 im Dorfe Glotovka im Gouvernement Smolensk als Sohn einer Bauernfamilie. Wegen finanzieller Schwierigkeiten mußte er bald das Studium aufgeben und arbeitete von 1921 bis 1931 als Mitarbeiter der Smolensker Zeitung „Rabočij put'". 1931 übersiedelte I. nach Moskau und widmete sich ganz seiner schriftstellerischen Tätigkeit. Sein erster Gedichtband, „Elektrisches Licht unterm Strohdach", fand auch die Wertschätzung *Gor'kijs.* In den folgenden Jahren veröffentlichte I. noch mehrere Sammlungen von volksliedhaften Gedichten, auf welchem Gebiet er ein wahrer Meister war. Viele seiner Gedichte wurden vertont und wurden so als Lieder in ganz Rußland bekannt, wie z. B. „Katjuša". Bis jetzt sind I.s Gedichte bei einer Gesamtauflage von 1 682 000 in 8 Sprachen übersetzt worden.

Rodnoe (Heimat, 1924)
Provoda v solome (Elektrisches Licht unterm Strohdach, 1927, *Stalinpreis* 1943, 1949)
Izbrannoe (Ausgewähltes, 1950)
Sočinenija v dvuch tomach (Werke in zwei Bänden, 1956)
Pjatnadcat' pesen (Fünfzehn Lieder)

Deutsche Übersetzungen
Fünfzehn Lieder, übers. v. Maximilian Schick, Moskau, Verlag für fremdsprachige Literatur. 1954.
Heimat, übers. v. Sepp Österreicher, Moskau. S. L. 1958.

Ivánov Vsévolod Vjačeslávovič

1895—1955, geb. im Oorte Lebjažij, im Gebiet Semipalatinsk, als Sohn einer Lehrerfamilie. I. betätigte sich in den verschiedensten Berufen, so z. B. als Schauspieler, Zirkusartist und Druckereiarbeiter. Die besten Werke I.s handeln vom Bürgerkrieg, den er übrigens in Sibirien selbst mitmachte. Diese Werke zeichnen sich durch ihre schwungvolle und kontrastreiche Schilderung des Lebens und außergewöhnlicher Begebenheiten und Ereignisse in den Bürgerkriegsjahren aus. Am bekanntesten davon sind „Partisanen" und „Panzerzug 14-69". I., der als Klassiker der Sowjetprosa bezeichnet wird, gehörte der Gruppe der *Serapionsbrüder* an.

Partizany (Partisanen, 1919)
Bronepoezd N 14-69 (Panzerzug 14-69, 1921)
Cvetnye vetra (Farbige Winde, 1922)
Golubye peski (Blauer Sand, 1923)
Vozvraščenie Buddy (Buddhas Rückkehr, 1923)
Severostal' (Nordstahl, 1925)
Tajnoe tajnych (Das Geheimnis der Geheimnisse, 1927)
Pochoždenija fakira (Abenteuer eines Fakirs, 3 Teile, 1935)
Djadja Kostja (Onkel Kostja, 1944)

Dvenadcat' molodcov iz tabakerki (Die zwölf Burschen aus einer Tabakdose, 1936)
Moë otečestvo (Mein Vaterland, 1941)
Na Borodinskom pole (Am Feld von Borodino, 1943)
Parchomenko (1939)
Vstreči s Maksimom Gor'kim (Begegnungen mit Maxim Gor'kij, 1947)

Deutsche Übersetzungen

Panzerzug 14-69, übers. v. Eduard Schiemann, Hamburg, C. Hoym Nachf. 1923. Übers. v. Arnold Boettcher, Leipzig, Reclam. 1955.
Abenteuer eines Fakirs, übers. v. T. Tschernaja, Moskau, Verlagsgenossenschaft ausländischer Arbeiter in der UdSSR. 1936. Zürich, Oprecht. 1937.
Aleksander Parchomenko (Parchomenko), übers. v. Robert Krickmann, Berlin, Dietz. 1955.
Ausgewählte Erz., übers. v. Erwin Honog, Berlin, Malik-Verlag. 1929.

Jákovlev Aleksándr Stepánovič

1886—1953, geb. in der Stadt Vol'sk, im Gouvernement Saratov, als Sohn eines Anstreichers. J., der seine schriftstellerische Tätigkeit erst während der Revolution begann, stellte mit unbestechlicher Wahrhaftigkeit in der Schilderung der sowjetischen Wirklichkeit und der Vergangenheit, hier vor allem des Lebens der Arbeiter und Bauern in der vorrevolutionären Zeit, die Entwicklung und Entstehung des sogenannten Sowjetmenschen in den Mittelpunkt seines Schaffens.

Mužik (Der Bauer, 1922)
Oktjabr' (Oktober, 1923)
Ošibki (Fehler, 1923)
Čelovek i pustynja (Der Mensch und die Wüste, 1926)
Sëmka (1927)
Pobeditel' (Der Sieger, 1927)
Žizn' i priključenija R. Amundsena (Leben und Abenteuer R. Amundsens, 1932)
Pioner Pavel Morozov (Pionier Pavel Morozov, 1938)
Tajna Saratovskoj zemli (Das Geheimnis des Saratover Landes, 1946)

Stupeni (Die Stufen, 1947)
Izbrannye proizvedenija (Ausgewählte Werke, 1957)

Jášin Aleksándr Jákovlevič (Pseudonym für A. Popóv)

Geb. 1913 im Dorfe Bludnovo, im Gouvernement Vologda, als Sohn einer Bauernfamilie. Er wurde Volksschullehrer und absolvierte knapp vor Ausbruch des zweiten Weltkrieges das Gor'kij-Institut für Literatur in Moskau. Hauptthema in J.s Werken, deren erstes 1928 erschien, ist der Mensch im E-Werk und beim Neulandeinsatz. In „Alëna Fomina" schildert J. die starke, innere Haltung der sowjetischen Frau. J. ist seit 1941 Mitglied der KPdSU.

Pesni severu (Lieder für den Norden, 1934)
Mat' (Die Mutter, 1940)
Alëna Fomina (1949, *Stalinpreis* 1950)
Sovetski čelovek (Der Sowjetmensch, 1951—56)
Ryčagi (Die Hebel, 1956)
S Leninym (Mit Lenin, 1956)
Svežij chleb (Frisches Brot, 1957)
Deutsche Übersetzungen
Mit Lenin, übers. v. Franz Leschnitzer, Moskau, S. L. 1959.

Júgov Alekséj

wurde erst in jüngster Zeit der breiten Öffentlichkeit bekannt, und zwar durch einen historischen Roman aus dem Mittelalter um Aleksandr Nevskij und einige hervorragend geschriebene Erzählungen und Romane, deren Themen er aus dem gegenwärtigen Leben nahm.

Ratoborcy (Die Streiter, 1949)
Otvažnoe serdce (Das mutige Herz, 1955)
Na bol'šoj reke (Am großen Strom, 1956)

Karaváeva Ánna Aleksándrovna

geb. 1893 in Perm', aus einer bürgerlichen Familie stammend. Nach Absolvierung des Gymnasiums war K. in verschiedenen

Berufen, u. a. auch als Dorfschullehrerin, tätig. Als Schriftstellerin schloß sich K., die seit 1926 Mitglied der KPdSU ist, vorerst der *Pereval*-Gruppe und später dem *VAPP*-Verband an. In ihren Werken ist die Dorfthematik vorherrschend, doch zeigt sie auch für die russische Vergangenheit Interesse, wie z. B. in „Zolotoj kljuv“ (Der goldene Schnabel), in welchem der Schauplatz der Handlung Sibirien zur Zeit Katharinas II. ist.

Fligel' (Flügel, 1922)
Zolotoj kljuv (Der goldene Schnabel, 1925)
Dvor (Der Hof, 1926)
Ryžaja mast' (Die Fuchsfarbe, 1927)
Lesozavod (Sägewerk, 1928)
Bajan i jabloko (Der Sänger und der Apfel, 1933)
Ogni (Die Lichter, 1943)
Vesennij šum (Frühlingsrauschen, 1946)
Razbeg (Anlauf, 1946—48)
Rodnoj dom (Das Vaterhaus, 1950, *Stalinpreis*)

Deutsche Übersetzungen

Fabrik im Walde (Lesozavod), übers. v. Alexandra Ramm, Berlin, Verlag der Jugendinternationale. 1930. Moskau, Verlagsgenossenschaft ausländischer Arbeiter in der UdSSR. 1932.

Das Vaterhaus, übers. v. Ernst Ehlers, Berlin, Verlag Neues Leben. 1952.

Kasátkin Iván Michájlovič

1880—1938 (?), geb. im Dorfe Baranovicy, im Gouvernement Kostroma. K. war bäuerlicher Abstammung und durchlebte eine schwere Jugend. Er war genötigt, sich sein Brot früh zu verdienen und sich in den verschiedensten Berufen zu verdingen. So war er z. B. als Schlosser, Maschinist, Heizer, Elektriker und Sägewerksarbeiter tätig. Lesen und Schreiben begann er erst mit 13 Jahren zu erlernen. Im Jahre 1902 zog er nach St. Petersburg, nahm eine Arbeit in einer Buchdruckerei an und begann im gleichen Jahre auch seine literarische Tätigkeit. Zwischen 1902—1905 wurde K. dreimal wegen revolutionärer Betätigung verhaftet. Er wurde auch mit *Gor'kij* bekannt. Diese Bekanntschaft blieb nicht ohne Einfluß auf sein literarisches Schaffen, so daß seine Werke in der Folge auch in größeren Zeitschriften abgedruckt wurden. Der Band „Lesnaja byl'" war das erste Buch, das 1919 im Verlag des CIK (Central'nyj ispolnitel'nyj komitet, Zentrales Exekutivkomitee) erschien. Von 1925 bis 1935 war K. Redakteur der „Krasnaja niva" und des „Kolchoznik". Im Jahre 1938 wurde er verhaftet und wahrscheinlich im gleichen Jahr erschossen.

Lesnaja byl' (Eine Waldsage, 1919)
Izbrannye rasskazy (Ausgewählte Erzählungen, 1957)

Kassíl' Lev Abrámovič

Geb. 1905 in Sloboda Pokrovskaja (dem heutigen Engel's) als Sohn eines Arztes; seine Mutter war Musiklehrerin. Nach Abschluß seiner Gymnasialstudien studierte K. an der Moskauer Universität und befreundete sich mit *Majakovskij*. Auf literarischem Gebiet ist K., dessen Werke seit 1925 gedruckt werden, vor allem als Verfasser von Kinderbüchern bekannt geworden.

Konduit i Švambranija (1931)
Čeremyš brat geroja (Sein großer Bruder)
Vratar' respubliki (Der Torhüter der Republik)
Majakovskij sam (Majakovskij selbst)
Dorogie moi mal'čiški (Meine lieben Knaben, 1949)
Ulica mladšego syna (Die Straße des jüngsten Sohnes, 1949, gemeinsam geschrieben mit M. L. Poljanskij, *Stalinpreis* 1951)
Delo vkusa (Geschmacksache, 1958)
Velikoe protivostojanie (Die große Opposition, 1957)

Deutsche Übersetzungen

Das Mädchen Sima (Velikoe protivostojanije), übers. v. Ernst Hube, Berlin, Verlag Neues Leben. 1949. Auch unter dem Titel ‚Das Mädchen Ustja', übers. v. Ernst Hube, bearb. v. Günter Gehrmann, Berlin, Verlag Neues Leben. 1949.

Sein großer Bruder (Čeremyš brat geroja), übertr. v. M. Brichmann, Berlin. Altberliner Verlag. 1950, 1953.

Katáev Iván Ivánovič

1902—1942, gehörte zu den begabtesten Mitgliedern der *Pereval*-Gruppe. Sein Roman „Moloko“ (Milch, 1930) wurde als typisches Werk dieser Gruppe wegen sentimentaler Einstellung verurteilt. Um 1937, in der Zeit der großen Säuberungen, wurde K. in die Verbannung geschickt; 1957 wurde er rehabilitiert.

Katáev Valentin Petróvič

Geb. 1897 in Odessa als Sohn einer Lehrerfamilie. Als junger Mann schrieb er Gedichte, welche im „Odesskij listok“ und in St. Petersburger Illustrierten erschienen. 1915 wurde K. Soldat und Kriegskorrespondent, 1918—1920 diente er in der Roten Armee. Seit 1922 lebt K., der Inhaber des Leninordens ist, in Moskau und betätigt sich als Schriftsteller. Von K.s Werken wurden besonders bekannt „Ja syn trudovogo naroda“ (Ich bin ein Sohn des arbeitenden Volkes), eine historisch-objektive Darstellung des Themas Revolution und Bürgerkrieg mit gleichzeitiger Hervorkehrung des russischen Nationalstolzes, sowie das Buch „Beleet parus odinokij“ (Es blinkt ein einsam Segel), eine meisterhafte Schilderung der Erlebnisse zweier junger Burschen aus Odessa während der Revolution von 1905. „Vremja vperëd“ (Im Sturmschritt vorwärts) ist einer jener vielen, anfangs der dreißiger Jahre erschienenen Romane, die die Errichtung von ausgedehnten Industrieanlagen schildern. K.s Bücher sind bisher in 52 Sprachen übersetzt worden und erreichten eine Gesamtauflage von 11 344 000.

Otec (Der Vater, 1925)
Rastratčiki (Die Defraudanten, 1927)
Beleet parus odinokij (Es blinkt ein einsam Segel, 1936)
Ja syn trudovogo naroda (Ich bin ein Sohn des arbeitenden Volkes, 1937)
Šël soldat s fronta (Es kam ein Soldat von der Front, 1938)
Žena (Seine Frau, 1943)

Syn polka (Der Sohn des Regiments, 1945, *Stalinpreis* 1946)
Avangard (Die Avantgarde, 1926)
Kvadratura kruga (Die Quadratur des Kreises, 1928)
Vremja vperëd (Im Sturmschritt vorwärts! 1932)
Flag (Die Flagge, 1942)
Za vlast' sovetov (In den Katakomben von Odessa, 1949, nach Parteikritik umgeschrieben 1951)
Chutorok v stepi (Steppenweiler, 1956)

Deutsche Übersetzungen

Die Defraudanten, übers. v. Richard Hoffmann, Wien, Paul Zsolnay Verlag. 1928.

Das Wunder in der Wüste (Šël soldat s fronta), Bühnenscherz in 1 Aufzg., Engels, Staatsverlag der ASSRdWD. 1938.

Ninotschka (Žena), übers. v. Maurice Hirschmann, Wien, 1946. Andermann Verlag. Auch unter dem Titel ‚Seine Frau', übers. v. Miron Broser, Berlin, Verlag Tägliche Rundschau. 1947.

Es blinkt ein einsam Segel, übers. v. L. Klementinovskaja, Berlin-Leipzig, SWA-Verlag. 1947. Nach der Übers. v. Ina Tinzmann, Berlin, Verlag Kultur und Fortschritt. 1951, 1956.

Ein weißes Segel einsam gleitet, übers. v. Otto V. Wyss, Wien, Volksbuchverlag. 1951.

Im Sturmschritt vorwärts! (Vremja vperëd), übers. v. Willy Koellner, Berlin-Leipzig, SWA-Verlag. 1947. Nach der Übers. v. Tittelbach, Berlin, Aufbau-Verlag. 1954.

Der Sohn des Regiments, übers. v. Georg Koch, 2. Aufl., Berlin, Verlag Neues Leben. 1954.

In den Katakomben von Odessa (Za vlast' sovetov), übers. v. Veronica Ensslen, Berlin, Verlag Kultur und Fortschritt. 1955.

Die Flagge, übers. v. K. Alexander, Auswahl russischer Reportagen, Wien, Stern-Verlag. 1946.

Kavérin Venjamín Aleksándrovič (Pseudonym für Zil'bérg)

Geb. 1902 in Pskov, aus einer Künstlerfamilie stammend. Er absolvierte 1924 die Universität in Leningrad. Sein erstes literarisches Werk, die Erzählung „Odinnadcataja aksioma" (Der elfte Grundsatz), erschien bereits 1921. In seinen Romanen erweist sich K. als meisterhafter Darsteller überaus spannender Begebenheiten und als genauer Kenner der sowjetischen Jugend. K., der auch Literarhistoriker ist und der Gruppe der *Serapionsbrüder* angehörte, wurde nach Erscheinen seines Romans „Otkrytaja kniga“ (Das offene Buch), dem ersten Band einer Trilogie, von der Sowjetpresse wegen einseitiger Darstellung der sowjetischen Wirklichkeit heftig kritisiert und beschuldigt, ein *Formalist* zu sein.

Devjat' desjatych sud'by (Neun Zehntel des Schicksales, 1926)
Skandalist, ili večera na Vasil'evskom ostrove (Der Unruhestifter oder die Abende auf der Vasilevskij-Insel, 1928)
Ispolnenie želanij (Die Erfüllung der Wünsche, 1936)
Dva kapitana (Zwei Kapitäne, 1940—1945, *Stalinpreis* 1946)
Otkrytaja kniga (Das offene Buch, 1949, 1. Teil)
Doktor Vlasenkova (Doktor Vlasenkova, 1952)
Poiski i nadeždy (Bestrebungen und Hoffnungen, 1956)

Deutsche Übersetzungen

Zwei Kapitäne, übers. v. Hilde Angarowa u. Miron Broser, Berlin-Leipzig, SWA-Verlag. 1946—1947. Berlin, Aufbau-Verlag. 1955.
Doktor Tatjana Wlassenkowa, übers. v. Marga Bork, Berlin, Verlag Kultur und Fortschritt. 1953.
Glückliche Jahre (Otkrytaja kniga), übers. v. Veronica Ensslen, Berlin, Verlag Kultur und Fortschritt. 1954.

Kazakévič Emmanuil Génrichovič

Geb. 1913 in Kremenčug, Gouvernement Poltava, als Sohn einer jüdischen Volksschullehrerfamilie. K. arbeitete einige Zeit im Fernen Osten (u. a. war er Kolchosvorsitzender und Mitarbeiter von Komsomolzeitungen) und war 1941—1945 Soldat. Als solcher machte er auch die Einnahme Berlins mit. Seit 1944 ist K. Mitglied der KPdSU. Seine ersten, in den dreißiger Jahren erschienenen Bücher, wie z. B. „Doroga v Birobidžan“ (Der Weg nach Birobidžan), „Bol'šoj mir“ (Die große Welt) u. a., schrieb K. in Jiddisch. Von seinem Werk „Serdce druga“ (Das Herz des Freundes) schreibt die Große Sowjetenzyklopädie, daß es „bedeutende ideologische Fehler“ enthalte.

Zvezda (Der Stern, 1947, *Stalinpreis* 1948)
Dvoe v stepi (Zwei in der Steppe, 1948)

Vesna na Odere (Frühling an der Oder, 1949, *Stalinpreis* 1950)
Serdce druga (Das Herz des Freundes, 1953)
Dom na ploščadi (Das Haus am Platz, 1956)

Deutsche Übersetzungen

Frühling an der Oder, übers. v. Benita v. Rimscha, Berlin, Verlag Volk und Welt. 1953, 1954, 1956.

Kazáncev Aleksándr Petróvič

wurde 1906 in der Stadt Akmolinsk (Kazachstan) als Sohn einer Angestelltenfamilie geboren. 1930 absolvierte er die Technologische Hochschule in Tomsk und war dann als Ingenieur tätig. Ende der dreißiger Jahre begann K. wissenschaftlich-utopische Werke zu verfassen. Der erste große Roman dieser Art, „Die flammende Insel" (1941), wurde von den jugendlichen Lesern sehr gut aufgenommen. Später veröffentlichte er die Bücher „Die Arktisbrüder" und „Der Polartraum". Außer wissenschaftlich-utopischen Romanen schrieb K. einige Novellen sowie Skizzen, die die Errungenschaften der sowjetischen Wissenschaft und Technik popularisieren. (nach S.L.)

Kázin Vasílij Vasíl'evič

Geb. 1898 in Moskau. Der Vater war Handwerker und ermöglichte seinem Sohn den Besuch der Realschule. 1918 organisierte K. die Moskauer Arbeiterjugend. 1920 wurde er Mitglied der Moskauer Literatengruppe *Kuznica,* schloß sich dann aber der Gruppe *Kosmist* in Petrograd an, wo auch 1922 seine erste Gedichtsammlung erschien. Die Mitglieder dieser Gruppe hielten sich für rechtgläubige Kommunisten und vertraten die Auffassung, daß Kollektivismus und die Arbeit in der Fabrik die einzigen, eines modernen Dichters würdigen Themen seien.

Rabočij maj (Arbeitermai, 1922)
Ljubov' i lis'ja šuba (Die Liebe und der Fuchspelz, 1925)
Stichotvorenija (Gedichte, 1956)

Ketlínskaja Véra Kazimírovna

Geb. 1906. Ihr erstes Buch „Natka Mičurina“ (1922) widmete sie der Arbeiterjugend. K., die seit 1927 Mitglied der KPdSU ist, behandelt vor allem politische und technische Themen. Dabei verzettelt sie sich aber in der technischen Terminologie derart, daß der Laie z. B. bei der Lektüre von „Dni našej žizni“ (Die Tage unseres Lebens) nur mühsam dem Gang der Handlung folgen kann. Ihre „geringe Gestaltungskraft“ wird aber, nach den Worten *Fadeevs*, durch die „ideologisch richtige Tendenz“ kompensiert. Im Roman „Mužestvo“ (Der Mut) schildert K. die Entstehung einer neuen Stadt in der Taiga.

Mužestvo (Der Mut, 1938)
V osade (Die Belagerung, 1947, *Stalinpreis* 1948)
Dni našej žizni (Die Tage unseres Lebens, 1952)

Deutsche Übersetzungen

Der Mut, übers. v. Dr. Ernst Busse, Berlin, Verlag Neues Leben. 1950, 1954.

Kirsánov Semën Isaákovič

Geb. 1906 in Odessa als Sohn eines Schneiders, gehört zu den Anhängern *Majakovskijs*. Sein Werk „Die sieben Tage der Woche“, erschienen im „Novyj mir“ 1956, gehört zur *Tauwetterliteratur*. Ansonsten ist K. ein echter Sohn der Revolution, ein begeisterter Sowjetmensch und talentierter Dichter, welcher sogar in der schweren Zeit der dreißiger Jahre eine allegorische Form in seiner Verserzählung „Zoluška“ (Aschenbrödel) fand, um seiner Phantasie Ausdruck verschaffen zu können. Übrigens gilt „Zoluška“ als sein bestes Werk. Derzeit ist K. Redakteur der Zeitschrift „Sowjetliteratur“.

Pricel (Das Visier, 1926)
Stichi v stroju (Verse im Dienst, 1930)
Pjatiletka (Fünfjahresplan, 1930)
Udarnyj kvartal (Das Viertel der Stoßarbeiter)
Tovarišč Marks (Genosse Marx, 1932)
Zoluška (Aschenbrödel, 1934)

Poema o rabote (Das Poem über die Arbeit, 1934)
Geran', mindal', fialka (Geranium, Mandel und Veilchen, 1937)
Nebo nad Rodinoj (Der Himmel über der Heimat, 1947)
Aleksandr Matrosov (1949)
Makar Mazaj (1950)
Veršina (Der Gipfel, 1954)
Sem' dnej nedeli (Die sieben Tage der Woche, 1956)
Deutsche Übersetzungen
Das Blümchen, übers. v. Franz Leschnitzer, Moskau, S. L. 1958.

Kiršón Vladímir Michájlovič

1902—1938 (?), absolvierte 6 Klassen Gymnasium, trat 1918 als Komsomolec in die Rote Armee ein und wurde 1920 Mitglied der Kommunistischen Partei. Ab 1925 lebte K. in Moskau und war Sekretär der *VAPP* und dann der *RAPP*, welcher Gruppe er zusammen mit Averbach, *Fadeev*, *Libedinskij* u. a. angehörte. K. wurde 1938 (?) hingerichtet und 1957 rehabilitiert. In seinem literarischen Schaffen war K. hauptsächlich Dramatiker, der mit Vorliebe zeitnahe, aktuelle Themen behandelte.

Konstantin Terechin (1926)
Rel'sy gudjat (Die Schienen summen, 1927)
Gorod vetrov (Die Stadt der Winde, 1928)
Chleb (Brot, 1930)
Sud (Das Gericht, 1933)
Čudesnyj splav (Die wunderbare Legierung, 1934)
Deutsche Übersetzungen
Die wunderbare Legierung, Komödie in 3 Akten, Moskau, Verlagsgenossenschaft ausländischer Arbeiter in der UdSSR. 1936.

Kljúev Nikoláj Alekséevič

1886—1937, geb. im Gouvernement Vologodsk als Sohn eines Bauern. Seine Mutter unterrichtete ihn im Lesen und Schreiben. Er kannte Rußland „von Solovki bis China". In seinem dichterischen Schaffen gehört K. zu den *Symbolisten* und wurde von *Esenin* als sein älterer Bruder bezeichnet. Valerij *Brjusov* half ihm bei der Herausgabe seines ersten Gedichtbandes (1908). 1933 wurde K. nach Narymsk verschickt, wo er im August 1937 starb.

Bratskie pesni (Brüderliche Lieder, 1909)
Lesnye byli (Waldsagen, 1913)
Mirskie dumy (Die weltlichen Gedanken, 1914)
Pesni solncenosca (Die Lieder des Sonnenträgers, 1920)
Pogorel'ščina (Das Abgebrannte), um 1925 geschrieben, aber nie gedruckt, jedoch viel im Manuskript gelesen. Auch die Verserzählung „Pesn' o Velikoj Materi" ist noch nicht im Druck erschienen. K. schrieb vor seiner Deportation noch Gedichte, die angeblich „unerreicht schön" waren, aber nie gedruckt wurden. (Ivanov-Razumnik, Novoe Slovo, Berlin, 20. 12. 1942)
Polnoe sobranie sočinenij (Gesammelte Werke Bd. I, II, 1954)

Klyčków Sergéj (Pseudonym für Sergéj Antónovič Lesenków) 1889—1941 (?), geb. im Dorfe Dubrovki, Gouvernement Tver'. Ein *Bauerndichter*, der in seinen Werken an *Esenin* und *Kljuev* erinnert. Um 1924 wandte er sich der Prosa zu und schrieb mit Folklore überladene Romane aus dem Leben des Dorfes in der Zeit der Revolution. K. wurde in den dreißiger Jahren verhaftet und es ist anzunehmen, daß er in einem Konzentrationslager umkam.

Domašnie pesni (Häusliche Lieder)
Sacharnyj nemec (Der Zuckerdeutsche)
Čertuchinskij balakir (Der Schwätzer aus Čertuchino)
alle zwischen 1924—1930
V gostjach u žuravlej (Bei den Kranichen zu Gast, 1930)
Stichi (Gedichte, 1936)

Knórre Fëdor Fëdorovič

Geb. 1903 in St. Petersburg als Sohn eines Ingenieurs. 1919 war K. als Freiwilliger in der Roten Armee und arbeitete dann am Leningrader Theater. Schriftstellerisch ist K. seit 1925 tätig und hat u. a. über 20 Filmdrehbücher geschrieben.

Neizvestnyj tovarišč (Der unbekannte Genosse, 1938)
Tvoja bol'šaja sud'ba (Dein großes Schicksal, 1948)
Mat' (Die Mutter, 1951)
Bez obložki (Ohne Umschlag, 1953)
Utro (Der Morgen, 1954)
Rasskazy (Erzählungen, 1955)

Kóčetov Vsévolod Anísimovič

Geb. 1912 in Novgorod. Nach dem Besuch der Siebenjahresschule in Leningrad arbeitete K. als Hafenarbeiter und in einer Schiffswerft. Er studierte dann am Landwirtschaftlichen Technikum und war ab 1931 auf Kolchosen und Sowchosen im Gebiete von Moskau und Leningrad tätig. 1935 wurde K. wissenschaftlicher Mitarbeiter einer landwirtschaftlichen Versuchsstation bei Leningrad und wandte sich 1938 dem Journalistenberuf zu. Von 1955 bis 1959 bekleidete er den Posten des Chefredakteurs der „Literaturnaja gazeta".

Na Nevskich ravninach (An den flachen Ufern der Neva, 1946)
Predmest'e (Die Vorstadt, 1947)
Komu svetit solnce (Wem die Sonne scheint, 1948)
Pod nebom rodiny (Unter dem Himmel der Heimat, 1950)
Žurbiny (Die Žurbins, 1952)
Molodost' s nami (Die Jugend ist mit uns, 1954)
Brat'ja Eršovy (Die Brüder Eršov, 1958)

Deutsche Übersetzungen

Familie Shurbin, nach der Übers. v. Hildegard Olbrich, Berlin, Verlag Kultur und Fortschritt. 1953. Übers. v. O. Braun, Bukarest, Verlag Cartea Rusă. 1953. Moskau, Verlag für fremdsprachige Literatur. 1954.

Die Brüder Jerschow (gekürzt), übers. v. Regina Czora, Moskau, S. L. 1959.

Korolénko Vladímir Galaktiónovič

1853—1921, ein sehr bekannter und gerne gelesener Prosaiker, der zum Lager der russischen Intelligenz zählte. In allen seinen Werken kehrt er immer wieder seinen Glauben an das

Gute im Menschen hervor. K., der von der zaristischen Regierung sechs Jahre in die Verbannung nach Sibirien geschickt wurde, war einer der ersten, die von den Sowjets sofort als einer der ihrigen anerkannt wurde, und dies vor allem deshalb, weil ihn Lenin schon 1907 als einen „progressiven Schriftsteller" bezeichnet hatte.

Son Makara (Der Traum des Makar, 1885)
V durnom obščestve (In schlechter Gesellschaft, 1885)
Slepoj muzykant (Der blinde Musiker, 1886)
Les šumit (Der Wald rauscht, 1886)
Reka igraet (Der Fluß spielt, 1892)
Bez jazyka (Ohne Sprache, 1895)
Istorija moego sovremennika (Die Geschichte meines Zeitgenossen, 4 Bde., 1906—1922)

Deutsche Übersetzungen

Als die Bandura sang (Sibirische Erzählungen), Cornelius Bergmann, Eisenach, Erich-Röth-Verlag. 1949.

Der Wald rauscht, übers. v. Felix Loesch, Dr. Cornelius Bergmann, Katharina Gilde, Berlin, Aufbau-Verlag. 1953. übers. v. Ilse Mirus, Geschichten aus dem alten und neuen Rußland, München, Nymphenburger Verlagsh. 1958.

Die Geschichte meines Zeitgenossen, übers. v. Rosa Luxemburg und Hermann Asemissen, Berlin, Rütten & Loening-Verlag. 1953.

Kinder im grauen Stein, übers. v. Dr. Cornelius Bergmann, Eisenach, Erich-Röth-Verlag. 1952.

Der blinde Musiker, übers. v. A. Markow, Halle. 1892.

In schlechter Gesellschaft, übers. v. J. Grünberg, Leipzig, Reclam. 1893.

Koževnikov Alekséj Venedíktovič

Geb. 1891 im Gouvernement Vjatka, aus einer Bauernfamilie stammend. K. wurde Volksschullehrer und studierte nach dem Bürgerkrieg am Literarischen Institut in Moskau. Schriftstellerisch ist K. seit 1924 tätig. Bemerkenswert ist sein Roman „Veniki" (Die Besen), eine packende Schilderung des

Lebens der Matrosen an der Wolga mit stimmungsvollen Landschaftsbeschreibungen.

Pervyj priz (Der erste Preis, 1927)
Zolotaja golot'ba (Die goldenen Bande, 1927)
Veniki (Die Besen, 1928)
Brat okeana (Bruder des Ozeans, 1946)
Živaja voda (Belebendes Wasser, 1950)

Deutsche Übersetzungen

Bruder des Ozeans, übers. v. Ena v. Baer, Berlin, Altberliner Verlag. 1949, 1951.

Belebendes Wasser, übers. v. Erwin Skalka, Berlin, Verlag Kultur und Fortschritt. 1951. Wien, Globus-Verlag. 1952.

Kožévnikov Vadím

Geb. 1909 in Narymsk, Westsibirien, wohin seine Eltern wegen revolutionärer Tätigkeit verbannt worden waren. Seine Kindheit verbrachte er in Sibirien. 1925 begann K. seine Studien an der Literarisch-Ethnologischen Fakultät der Moskauer Universität und war nach deren Beendigung bei verschiedenen Zeitungen und Zeitschriften tätig. In seinen Werken befaßt sich K. mit Fragen der Industrialisierung des Landes.

Ognennaja reka (Der Feuerstrom, 1949)
Vstreči v Kitae (Begegnungen in China, 1954)
Na dal'nem severe (Im fernen Norden, 1956)
Zare navstreču (Dem Morgenrot entgegen, 1957)

Deutsche Übersetzungen

Tima, der kleine Sibirier (Zare navstreču), übers. v. Jutta Janke, Berlin, Verlag Neues Leben. 1959.

Kručënych Alekséj Eliséevič

Geb. 1886. Er gehörte mit *Chlebnikov* und *Majakovskij* zu den führenden *Futuristen,* lehnte radikal die Vergangenheit der russischen Literatur ab und war neben *Aseev, Majakovskij* und *Pasternak* ein eifriger Mitarbeiter der Zeitschrift „*Lef*". K. versuchte sich auch in der „*zaumnaja*"-Dichtung (B. Arvatov, „Rečetvorčestvo" in Lef Jahrg. 1923, Nr. 2, S. 83).

Zaumniki (1922)
Pervoe maja (Der erste Mai, 1923)

Kuprín Aleksándr Ivánovič
1970—1938, geb. in der Stadt Nervočat, im Gouvernement Penza, aus einer Beamtenfamilie stammend. K. besuchte vorerst die Kadettenschule, dann die Militärschule in Moskau und diente 1890—1894 als Offizier. Er lebte in Kiev, Žitomir, Rostov am Don und Odessa. Nach der Revolution emigrierte K., kehrte aber 1937 wieder nach Rußland zurück. Er schrieb spannende, naturalistische Erzählungen und Romane aus dem zeitgenössischen Leben. Aber „sobald er seinen Blick vom Einzelnen zum Allgemeinen zu erheben sucht, weiß er sich keinen Rat. Aber wo er beim Einzelnen bleibt, da zeigt er sich immer als Meister des Alltagsrealismus". (L.)

Poslednij debjut (Das letzte Debut, 1889)
Doznanije (Die Untersuchung, 1894)
Millioner (Der Millionär, 1895)
Čudesnyj doktor (Der Wunderdoktor, 1897)
Moloch (Der Moloch, 1896)
Poedinok (Das Duell, 1904)
Granatovyj braslet (Das Granatarmband, 1911)
Jama (Die Gruft, 1909)
Junkera (Offiziersschüler, 1933)
Jeanette (1933)

Deutsche Übersetzungen

Erzählungen, übers. v. H. Harff, Stuttgart. 1904.
Das Duell (Poedinok), übers. v. A. Heß, Stuttgart. 1905.
Der Moloch, übers. v. J. Herzmark, Wien. 1907. Berlin, Reiter & Loeming. 1954.
Die Gruft (Jama), übers. v. C. Philips, München. 1910.
Das Granatarmband, übers. v. A. Villard, München. 1911. Übers. v. Ilse Mirus, Geschichten aus dem alten und neuen Rußland, München, Nymphenburger Verlagsh. 1958.
Olesja und andere Novellen, übers. v. F. Krantz, Berlin. 1911.
Der weiße Pudel, übers. v. Margarete Spady, Berlin, Verlag Kultur und Fortschritt. 1955.

Kuznecóv Anatólij

geb. 1930, lebte während der deutschen Besetzung in Kiev. K. hatte eine abenteuerreiche Jugend: er war Zigarettenverkäufer, Schüler in einer Ballettschule, versuchte sich in der Malerei und Bildhauerei und arbeitete noch 1952 als Bauarbeiter. Mit der Veröffentlichung seiner ersten Werke im Jahre 1957 machte K., nun Student am Literarischen Gor'kij-Institut, die Kritik auf sich aufmerksam.

Zachar Zacharyč i Ton'ka (Zachar Zacharyč und Ton'ka, 1957)

Zapiski molodogo čeloveka, prodolženie legendy (Die Aufzeichnungen eines jungen Menschen, die Fortsetzung einer Legende, 1957)

Deutsche Übersetzungen

Die Legende geht weiter (aus den Aufzeichnungen eines jungen Menschen), übers. v. Regina Czora, Moskau, S. L. 1957.

Lavrenëv Borís Andréevič

Geb. 1891. L., von Beruf Kavallerieoffizier, begann 1913 zunächst Gedichte zu schreiben, um sich später ganz der Literatur zu widmen. Anfangs lehnte er sich an die *Futuristen*, dann aber an *Gumilëv* an. L. ist ein sehr dynamischer und phantasiereicher Schriftsteller. Seine Werke sind bereits in 14 Sprachen übersetzt worden und in mehr als 1 470 000 Exemplaren erschienen.

Gala-Peter (1916)

Veter (Der Wind, 1924)

Zvëzdnyj cvet (Die Sternblume, 1924)

Sorok pervyj (Der Einundvierzigste, 1924)

Mir v stëklyške (Die Welt in einer Glasscheibe, 1926)

Krušenie respubliki Itl' (Der Untergang der Republik Itl', 1926)

Sed'moj sputnik (Der siebente Gefährte, 1927)

Razlom (Die Bresche, 1928)

Za tech, kto v more (Für die auf See, 1945, *Stalinpreis* 1946)

Golos Ameriki (Die Stimme Amerikas, 1949, *Stalinpreis* 1950)

Deutsche Übersetzungen

Der Einundvierzigste, nach der Übers. v. Eugen W. Mewes, Berlin, Verlag der Jugendinternationale. 1928.

Die Stimme Amerikas, Drama in 4 Akten, übers. v. K. Roose, Berlin, Henschel. 1950. Übers. v. I. Goldmann, Bukarest, Verlag Cartea rusă. 1950.

Für die auf See, Schauspiel in 3 Akten, übers. v. E. Baer, Berlin, Henschel. 1952.

Die Bresche, Schauspiel in 4 Aufz., übers. v. H. Rodenberg, Berlin, Henschel. 1950.

Lébedev-Kumáč Vasílij Ivánovič

1898—1949, geb. in Moskau als Sohn eines Schusters. Nach dem Besuch des Gymnasiums absolvierte er die historisch-philologische Fakultät der Moskauer Universität. 1940 wurde L.-K. Mitglied der KPdSU und später Deputierter des Obersten Sowjets der RSFSR. L.-K. war Mitarbeiter vieler Zeitschriften („Bednota", „Gudok", „Rabočaja gazeta", „Krokodil", „Krasnoarmeec" u. a.), Verfasser von vielen Filmdrehbüchern und von vielen Texten zu Liedern, die in der Vertonung von A. V. Aleksandrov, I. O. Dunaevskij, J. S. Miljutin, M. I. Blatner u. a. sehr populär geworden sind. L.-K. war mit *Majakovskij* und D. *Bednyj* befreundet. Er galt viele Jahre hindurch als der offizielle Poet der Sowjetunion. 1941 wurde ihm der *Stalinpreis* verliehen.

Kniga pesen (Das Buch der Lieder, 1938)
Stichotvorenija i pesni (Gedichte und Lieder, 1950)
Pesni (Lieder, 1953)

Populäre Liedertexte

Marš vesëlych rebjat (Der Marsch der fröhlichen Jugend, 1934)
Široka strana moja rodnaja (Groß ist mein Heimatland, 1935)
Moskva majskaja (Moskau im Mai, 1937)

Lenč Leoníd

Geb. 1905 im Gouvernement Smolensk. Er absolvierte die Fakultät für Wirtschaftswissenschaften an der Universität in

Rostov. Seit 1925 schreibt er Skizzen und Feuilletons für die Presse. Seine erste Erzählung wurde im Jahre 1929 veröffentlicht. Seit 1934 ist L. ständiger Mitarbeiter der satirischen Zeitschrift „Krokodil". Während des Krieges war er Frontberichterstatter der Zeitung „Zerschlagen wir den Feind". L. ist Verfasser vieler humoristischer Erzählungen, von denen mehr als ein Dutzend in Sammelbänden erschienen sind. Auch als Dramatiker machte sich L. einen Namen. Von ihm stammen die Bühnenwerke „Pavel Grekov", „Talente", sowie mehrere kleinere satirische Stücke.

Sinus (1934)
Talant (Talente, 1949)
Refleksy (Reflexe, 1955)
Ekzempljar (Exemplar, 1956)
Okroška (Eine kalte Kvassuppe, 1927)
Trudnaja služba (Schwerer Dienst, 1957)
Nervnyj tik (Das nervöse Zucken, 1957)
Pomidor i treska (Die Tomate und der Kabeljau, 1958)
Prochor i Lord (Prochor und der Lord, 1958)
Udačnaja ženit'ba (Gelungene Heirat, 1958)

Deutsche Übersetzungen

Talente, Scherz in 1 Aufz., übers. v. Günter Richter, Halle, Mitteldeutscher Verlag. 1951.

Humoresken, übers. v. Erwin Johann Bach, Berlin, Eulenspiegel-Verlag. 1955.

Erzählungen. Die Beichte, Romantik, Die unsterbliche Handschrift, übers. v. Heddy Hofmaier, Moskau, S. L. 1958.

Leónov Leoníd Maksímovič

Geb. 1899 in Moskau. Sein Vater, ein Journalist, stammte aus einer Bauernfamilie aus dem Gouvernement Kaluga. Nach Beendigung seiner Studien trat L. in die Rote Armee ein. 1922 ließ er sich in Moskau nieder und veröffentlichte im selben Jahr auch seine ersten Erzählungen. *Gor'kij* bezeichnete L. als einen jungen Dostoevskij. Sein bestes Werk ist der Roman „Der Dieb" (1927). L., dem zweimal der *Stalinpreis* verliehen wurde, gehört zu den begabtesten zeitgenössischen Schriftstellern. Seine Werke wurden bisher bei einer Gesamtauflage von 2 790 000 Exemplaren in 9 Sprachen übersetzt.

Zapiski Andreja Petroviča Kovjakina (Die Memoiren des Andrej Petrovič Kovjakin, 1924)
Konec melkogo čeloveka (Das Ende eines kleinen Mannes, 1924)
Barsuki (Die Dachse, 1924)
Vor (Der Dieb, 1927)
Sot' (Aufbau, 1930)
Professor Skutarevskij (1932)
Doroga na okean (Der Weg zum Ozean, 1936)
Našestvie (Invasion, 1942, *Stalinpreis* 1943)
Lënuška (1943, *Stalinpreis* 1944)
Russkij les (Russischer Wald, 1953)
Sobranie sočinenij (Gesammelte Werke, 1953)

Deutsche Übersetzungen
Die Bauern von Wory (Barsuki), übers. v. Bruno Prochaska und Dmitrij Umanskij, Wien, P. Zsolnay. 1926.
Der Dieb, übers. v. Dmitrij Umanskij und Bruno Prochaska, Bd. 1, 2, Berlin, P. Zsolnay. 1928.
Aufbau, übers. v. Richard Hoffmann, Wien, P. Zsolnay. 1930. Auch unter dem Titel ‚Das Werk im Urwald', übers. v. Alexander Böltz, Berlin, Verlag Kultur und Fortschritt. 1949.
Professor Skutarewskij, übers. v. Dora Hofmeister, Berlin, Verlag Kultur und Fortschritt. 1956.

Libedinskij Júrij Nikoláevič

Geb. 1898 in Odessa als Sohn eines Arztes. Seine Kindheit verbrachte L. zum Teil im Ural, wo sein Vater in einem großen Werk tätig war. 1921 trat er der Kommunistischen Partei bei und hatte einige Jahre hindurch politische Posten in der Roten Armee inne. Hauptfigur in allen seinen Werken ist der Kommunist bei seiner Arbeit in der Partei, beim Aufbau einer neuen Gesellschaftsordnung. L.s Romane und Novellen sind in erster Linie als Zeitdokumente von Wert. Sein Roman „Roždenie geroja" (Die Geburt eines Helden), eine Schilderung des Kampfes eines kommunistischen Kommissars gegen seine menschlichen Schwächen und Neigungen, löste innerhalb der *RAPP* heftige Kontroversen aus, in deren Verlauf die Gegner L.s siegreich blieben und das Werk als nicht dem Aufbau des Sozialismus entsprechend verurteilten.

Nedelja (Eine Woche, 1922)
Sergo (1957)
Zavtra (Morgen, 1923)
Komissary (Die Kommissare, 1926)
Roždenie geroja (Die Geburt eines Helden, 1930)
Gory i ljudi (Berge und Menschen, 1948)
Zarevo (Feuerschein, 1952)
Utro sovetov (Der Morgen der Sowjets, 1957)

Deutsche Übersetzungen

Ein Woche, übers. v. Eduard Schiemann, Hamburg, C. Hoym Nachf. 1923.

Berge und Menschen, übers. v. Josi v. Koskull, Bd. 1, 2, Berlin, Verlag Volk und Welt. 1954.

Feuerschein, übers. v. Hermann Alemissen, Bd. 1, 2, Berlin, Verlag Kultur und Fortschritt. 1956.

Lídin Vladímir Gérmanovič

Geb. 1894 in Moskau, studierte am Institut für Ostsprachen in Moskau und wurde dann Rotarmist. Seine literarische Tätigkeit, die er 1915 begann, erstreckt sich auf Romane, Skizzen und Erzählungen. Aber erst die letzten Arbeiten L.s erreichten dichterisches Niveau.

Nord (1925)
Idut korabli (Es fahren die Schiffe, 1926)
Puti vërsty (Die Straßen und die Wersten, 1927)
Otstupnik (Der Abtrünnige, 1928)
Iskateli (Die Sucher, 1930)
Mužestvo (Die Tapferkeit, 1930)
Mogila neizvestnogo soldata (Das Grab des unbekannten Soldaten, 1931)
Velikij ili tichij (Der Große oder der Stille, 1932)

Syn (Der Sohn, 1935)
Bol'šaja reka (Der große Strom, 1938)
Doroga na zapad (Der Weg nach Westen, 1940)
Izgnanie (Die Verbannung, 1947)
Dve žizni (Zwei Leben)
Korobka iz beresty (Die Schachtel aus Birkenrinde, 1955)
Drevnjaja povest' (Eine alte Sage, 1956)
Dalëkij drug (Der ferne Freund, 1956)
Mocart (Mozart, 1957)
Djuny (Die Dünen, 1957)

Deutsche Übersetzungen

Der Abtrünnige, übers. v. Olga Halpern u. Eugen W. Mewef, Berlin, Drei-Kegel-Verlag. 1928.
Vier Erzählungen, übers. v. Maximilian Schick, Moskau, Meshdunarodnaja kniga. 1939.
Zwei Leben, Nach der Übers. v. B. Tutenberg, Berlin, Verlag Kultur und Fortschritt. 1951.

Lugovskój Vladimir Aleksándrovič

1901—1957, geb. in Moskau als Sohn eines Lehrers. Seine literarischen Arbeiten, die ersten davon vornehmlich Gedichte über den Bürgerkrieg, werden seit 1924 gedruckt. L. übersetzte viel aus den Werken von Dichtern der Volksdemokratien und aus der uzbekischen und aserbeidschanischen Literatur. Der Grundton seines Schaffens ist optimistisch, er war „von den frühesten Versen an bestrebt, zu sagen, daß das Leben auf Erden zum Glücke und nicht zu sinnlosem Untergang geschaffen ist“ (Autobiographie).

Evropa (Europa, 1932)
Žizn' (Das Leben, 1933)
Dangara (1935)
Kaspijskoe more (Das Kaspische Meer, 1936)
Kraj ljubimyj (Das geliebte Land, 1952)
Tebe, Ukraina! (Dir, Ukraine! 1954)
Avtobiografija (Autobiographie, 1957)

Deutsche Übersetzungen

Über mich selber (Avtobiografija), übers. v. Franz Leschnitzer, Moskau, S. L. 1958.

Gedichte. Der Stern, übers. v. Sepp Österreicher, Damals wars, übers. v. Franz Leschnitzer, Moskau, S. L. 1958.

Lunačárskij Anatólij Vasíl'evič

1875—1933, geb. in Poltava als Sohn eines Angestellten. Schon im Alter von 17 Jahren schloß sich L. der revolutionären Bewegung an und war auch mit Lenin und *Gor'kij* befreundet. Mit den Revolutionären in der Emigration stand L. unter dem Decknamen Vojnov in Verbindung (1904). Nachdem er 1905 für einige Zeit eingesperrt wurde, ging L. nach seiner Freilassung ins Ausland und kehrte 1917 nach Rußland zurück. L. war der erste Volkskommissar für Bildungswesen und war in dieser Eigenschaft ein eifriger Förderer vieler Experimente im Schulwesen, in der Kunst, sowie — im ersten Stadium der Revolution — von Versuchen, die zur Schaffung des sogenannten *Proletkultes* abzielten. Nach 1929 oblag ihm nur mehr die Aufsicht über die wissenschaftlichen Institutionen. L. starb 1933 in Mentone, knapp bevor er seinen Posten als sowjetischer Botschafter in Madrid antreten sollte. Seine zahlreichen literarischen Arbeiten sind in der Sowjetunion bis heute noch nicht in gesammelter Form erschienen.

Oliver Kromvel (Oliver Cromwell, 1920)
Osvoboždënnyj Don Kichot (Der befreite Don Quichotte, 1922)
Teatr i revolucija (Theater und Revolution, 1924)

Deutsche Übersetzungen

Der befreite Don Quichotte, Schauspiel in 9 Bildern, übers. v. J. Gotz, Volksbühnen-Verlags- u. Vertriebs-Ges. 1925.

Lunc Lev Nátanovič

1901—1924, geb. in St. Petersburg als Sohn einer Intellektuellenfamilie. Er absolvierte 1918 das Gymnasium und beendete 1922 seine Universitätsstudien. Als Anhänger der bürgerlichen Weltanschauung vertrat er die Forderung, daß die Kunst unabhängig von der Politik, und der Schriftsteller frei von allen Vorschriften und Beschränkungen sein müsse. Als

Theoretiker der *Serapionsbrüder* verfaßte er 1922 auch deren Manifest „Warum wir Serapionsbrüder sind". L., dessen literarisches Schaffen vornehmlich Dramen und Erzählungen umfaßt, starb 1924 in einem Sanatorium bei Hamburg.

Vne zakona (Vogelfrei, 1921)
V pustyne (In der Wüste, 1922)
Počemu my ‚Serapionovy brat'ja' (Warum wir Serapionsbrüder sind, 1922)
Ob ideologii i publicistike (Über Ideologie und Publizistik, 1922)
Na zapad! (Nach Westen! 1923)
Obez'jany idut (Die Affen kommen, 1923)
Bertrand de Born (1922)
Gorod pravdy (Die Stadt der Wahrheit, 1924)

Majakóvskij Vladímir Vladímirovič

1893—1930, geb. im Dorfe Bagdadi in Georgien, wo sein Vater, ein verarmter Adeliger, Forstaufseher war. Nach dem Tode des Vaters übersiedelte die Familie 1906 nach Moskau und M. besuchte für kurze Zeit das humanistische Gymnasium. 1908 wurde er wegen revolutionärer Betätigung verhaftet. M. war auch darauf bedacht, seine revolutionäre Gesinnung durch ungewöhnliche Kleidung und auffallendes Benehmen öffentlich zu bekunden. Durch seine revolutionäre Einstellung und seine Verachtung für die Kunst der Vergangenheit fühlte er sich von der Bewegung der *Futuristen* angezogen, deren hervorragendster Vertreter er schließlich wurde. Der Beginn seiner literarischen Tätigkeit fällt in das Jahr 1912. Er zählte auch zu den Mitunterzeichnern des Manifests der *Futuristen*, „Poščëčina obščestvennomu vkusu" (Eine Ohrfeige dem öffentlichen Geschmack), das im selben Jahre veröffentlicht wurde. In seinem revolutionären Eifer nach einer „Entpoetisierung" der dichterischen Sprache kam er den radikalen Forderungen der *Futuristen* sehr entgegen. Seit 1915 war M. auch mit *Gor'kij* befreundet. Durch die Macht seines Vortrags bei den Lesungen seiner Gedichte auf seinen Reisen durch Rußland erwarb sich M. große Popularität. Die Verwendung von umgangssprachlichen und derben Ausdrücken in seinen vom Wortakzent beherrschten, neuartigen, rhythmischen Versen ließ ihn zum Dichter des revolutionären Plakats und politischer Kampfparolen werden. M. ist heute der meistübersetzte Dichter Sowjetrußlands. Allein in der Zeit von 1917 bis 1947 wurden seine Werke in 54 Sprachen übersetzt und erreichten eine Auflage von 4 668 000 Exemplaren. Am 14. April 1930 beging M. Selbstmord durch Erschießen. Seine Theaterstücke, in der Hauptsache Satiren, die in der Sowjetunion wegen ihrer Verhöhnung sowjetischer, bürokratischer Einrichtungen lange nicht gespielt wurden, gehören heute wieder zum täglichen Repertoire.

Vladimir Majakovskij (1915)
Oblako v štanach (Wolke in Hosen, 1915)
Vojna i mir (Krieg und Frieden, 1916)
Misterija Buff (Mysterium Buffo, 1918)
Levyj marš (Linker Marsch, 1919)
150 000 000 (1921)
Vladimir Il'ič Lenin (1924)
Chorošo (Gut und Schön, 1927)
Klop (Die Wanze, 1928)
Banja (Das Bad, 1929)
Vo ves' golos (Aus vollem Halse, 1930)
Polnoe sobranie sočinenij (Gesammelte Werke, 1955—1956)

Deutsche Übersetzungen

150 000 000, übers. v. Johannes R. Becher, Berlin, Malik-Verlag. 1925. Übers. v. Alfred Edgar Thoss. Berlin, Verlag Volk und Welt. 1950.

Zwei Dichtungen: Wladimir Iljitsch Lenin, Gut und schön, übers. v. Hudo Huppert, Moskau, Meshdunarodnaja Kniga. 1940.

Ausgewählte Gedichte, übertr. v. Hugo Huppert, Berlin, SWA-Verlag. 1946. Berlin, Verlag Volk und Welt. 1953.

Wolke in Hosen, übers. v. Alfred Edgar Thoss, Berlin, Verlag Volk und Welt. 1949.

Aus vollem Halse, übers. v. Johannes v. Guenther, Berlin, SWA-Verlag. 1950.

Sowjetjugend, Gedichte, übers. v. Paul Wiens, Berlin, Verlag Neues Leben. 1951.

Ausgewählte Gedichte, ausgew. u. m. einem Nachwort vers. v. Werner Creutziger, übers. v. Hugo Huppert u. Alfred Edgar Thoss, Leipzig, Reclam. 1953.

Makárenko Antón Semënovič

1888—1939, geb. in der Stadt Belopol'e im Gouvernement Cherson. Er begann seine Tätigkeit 1905 als Arbeiterlehrer in einer Eisenbahnerschule in der Stadt Krjukov bei Kremenčug. Von 1920 bis 1928 leitete er eine Kolonie für verwahrloste Kinder. Seine Erfahrungen auf dem Gebiete der Pädagogik wertete M. in vielen Büchern und Vorlesungen aus und verfaßte auch eine Reihe theoretischer, pädagogischer Abhandlungen.

Marš tridcatogo goda (Der Marsch des Jahres 1930, 1932)
Pedagogičeskaja poema (Der Weg ins Leben, 1935)
Čest' (Die Ehre, 1938)
Flagi na bašnjach (Flaggen auf den Türmen, 1938)
Kniga dlja roditelej (Ein Buch für Eltern)
Pedagogičeskie sočinenija (Pädagogische Werke)

Deutsche Übersetzungen

Der Weg ins Leben, nach der Übers. v. Ingo-Manfred Schille, Berlin, Aufbau-Verlag. 1950, 1951, 1953, 1954.

Flaggen auf den Türmen, übers. v. Erich Salewski, Berlin, Aufbau-Verlag. 1952, 1953, 1954. Berlin, Verlag Kultur und Fortschritt. 1957.

Ein Buch für Eltern, übers. v. Larissa Bortnowsky u. Maria Steim, Berlin, Aufbau-Verlag. 1954.

Vorträge über Kindererziehung, herausgegeben v. G. S. Makarenko u. W. N. Kolbanowskiu, übers. v. A. Böltz. Berlin-Leipzig, Volk u. Wissen. 1949, 1950.

Einige Schlußfolgerungen aus meiner pädagogischen Erfahrung, Berlin, Verlag Volk und Wissen. 1954.

Malýškin Aleksándr Geórgievič

1892—1938, geb. im Dorfe Bogorodeckoe, im Gouvernement Penza, als Sohn einer Bauernfamilie; die Kindheit verbrachte

M. in der Stadt Mokšan. Nach Beendigung seiner Studien an der philologischen Fakultät in St. Petersburg trat M. in die Rote Schwarzmeerflotte ein. Als Schriftsteller war M. ab 1912 tätig. Seine Werke gelten als Musterbeispiel für den *sozialistischen Realismus*. Wenn auch M. dessen Spielregeln getreulich befolgte, d. h. aktuelle Themen im Einklang mit der sozialistischen Interpretation unter Hervorhebung der heldenhaften Natur des Sowjetmenschen zu behandeln, so brachte er es doch zuwege, in seinen Werken dem Leser auch die rein menschliche Seite seiner Helden vor Augen zu führen (z. B. Šelechov in „Sevastopol'").

Uezdnaja ljubov' (Die Liebe in der Provinz, 1914)
Polevoj prazdnik (Das Fest auf dem Felde, 1914)
Padenie Daira (Der Fall von Dair, 1923)
Fevral'skij s-ezd (Die Februar-Tagung, 1927)
Sevastopol' (1930)
Ljudi iz zacholust'ja (Menschen aus Krähwinkel, 1938)

Deutsche Übersetzungen

Der dreizehnte Winter (Menschen aus Krähwinkel), übers. v. Elisabeth u. Wladimir Wonsiatsky, Leipzig, Staackmann. 1951. Glück, Kapitel aus dem Roman „Menschen aus Krähwinkel", Moskau, S. L. 1958.

Mandel'štám Ósip Emíl'evič

1891—193?, stammte aus einer bürgerlich-jüdischen Familie. Er war ein hervorragender Vertreter der vorrevolutionären *Akmeisten*. Als entschiedener Anhänger der westeuropäischen Kultur stand M. der Revolution geistig fern und trat auch in der nachrevolutionären Literatur nicht hervor. Trotzdem gelang es ihm, sich noch jahrelang in der sowjetischen Literatur, wenn auch in bescheidenem Ausmaß, zu behaupten. Neben verschiedenen Gedichtbänden veröffentlichte M. auch Prosaerzählungen und literarkritische Abhandlungen. 1932 wurde er verhaftet und deportiert; über sein Ende ist nichts Genaues bekannt.

Kamen' (Der Stein, 1913)
Tristia (1922)
Stichotvorenija (Gedichte, 1928)
Šum vremeni (Der Lärm der Zeit, 1925)
O poezii (Über die Dichtkunst, 1928)
Sobranie sočinenij (Gesammelte Werke, 1955, New York)

Maršák Samuíl Jákovlevič

Geb. 1887 in Voronež. Er studierte in Ostrogorsk, St. Petersburg und London. M., der auch mit *Gor'kij* befreundet war, ist der Begründer der sowjetischen Kinderliteratur. 1942 wurde er mit dem *Stalinpreis* für politische Satiren ausgezeichnet. Er übersetzte auch Shakespeare, Byron, Heine und Petöfi. Für die Shakespeareübersetzung wurde ihm 1949 der *Stalinpreis* verliehen. Außerdem wurde er mit dem Leninorden und mehreren anderen Auszeichnungen dekoriert. Das erste Kinderbuch M.s, „Detki v kletke" (Kinderchen im Käfig), erschien bereits 1923, als er Mitarbeiter der Kinderzeitschrift „Novyj Robinson" und der *„Molodaja gvardija"* war.

Detki v kletke (Kinderchen im Käfig, 1923)
Skazka pro kozla (Ein Märchen von einem Ziegenbock, 1941)
Dvenadcat' mesjacev (Zwölf Monate, 1943, *Stalinpreis* 1946)
Počta voennaja (Die Feldpost, 1944)
Kruglyj god (Das ganze Jahr, 1945)
Koškin dom (Das Katzenhaus, 1945)
Ledjanoj ostrov (Die Eisinsel, 1947)
Kak pečatali knigu etu (Wie dieses Buch gedruckt wurde, 1951)
Mister Tvister (Mister Twister)
Mel'nik, mal'čik i osël (Der Müller, der Knabe und der Esel)
Na straže mira (Auf Friedenswacht)
Otkuda stol prišël? (Wo kommt der Tisch wohl her?)
Raznocvetnaja kniga (Das bunte Buch)
Stichi dlja detej (Gedichte für Kinder, 1950, *Stalinpreis* 1951)
Pritča o gluposti (Das Gleichnis von der Torheit, 1955)
Slučaj po doroge (Eine Begebenheit unterwegs, 1955)
Pro gippopotama (Über das Flußpferd, 1956)

Skazka pro carja i pro sapožnika (Das Märchen vom Zaren und dem Schuster, 1956)

V načale žizni — Stranicy vospominanij (Am Anfang des Lebens — Seiten aus den Erinnerungen, 1960)

Deutsche Übersetzungen

Die 12 Monate, Märchen, übers. v. G. Ausländer, Wien, Globus-Verlag. 1947. Ein Wintermärchen, übers. u. bearb. v. H. Wolf, Leipzig, Buch-Verlag. 1948.

Kinderchen im Käfig, Nachdicht. v. E. Weinert, Berlin, Holz-Verlag. 1947, 1952.

Wie euer Buch gedruckt wurde, übers. v. P. Wiens, Berlin, Kinderbuchverlag. 1952.

Der Ritt auf dem Esel (Mel'nik, mal'čik i osël), eine Geschichte für groß und klein, übertr. o. E. Wildberger, Berlin-Leipzig, Volk und Wissen Verlag. 1946.

Mister Twister, übers. v. E. Haacken, Berlin-Dresden, Kinderbuchverlag. 1950.

Auf Friedenswacht, übers. v. P. Wiens, Berlin, Kinderbuchverlag. 1952.

Wo kommt der Tisch wohl her? übers. v. P. Wiens, Berlin, Kinderbuchverlag. 1952.

Das bunte Buch, übers. v. A. Thoss u. N. Ludwig, Berlin, Kultur und Fortschritt. 1949.

Der Narr, übers. v. Sepp Österreicher, Moskau, S. L. 1957.

Märchen. ‚Das Märchen von den zwei Katzen' und ‚Die Satzzeichen', übers. v. Sepp Österreicher, Moskau, S. L. 1959.

Martýnov Leoníd Nikoláevič

Geb. 1905 in Omsk als Sohn eines Beamten. M. absolvierte 4 Klassen Mittelschule und arbeitete ab 1920 bei verschiedenen Zeitungen. Als Korrespondent machte er ausgedehnte Reisen durch die Sowjetunion. Auf literarischem Gebiet beschäftigte sich M. viel mit Übersetzungen von Werken verschiedener Sowjetvölker und der Volksdemokratien ins Russische. Sein Erstlingswerk, „Stichi i proza" (Gedichte und Prosa), erschien 1939 in Omsk. Seit 1957 werden die Gedichte M.s wegen ideologischer Abweichungen von der Sowjetkritik abgelehnt.

Interessant ist seine Charakterisierung der Beziehungen zwischen der kommunistischen und nichtkommunistischen Welt in dem Gedicht „Pervorodstvo" (Oktjabr' 1956/12); u. a. vertritt er die Ansicht, daß die Sowjetunion weder ein Land der Armen noch der Reichen, sondern einfach ein neues Land sei.

Poemy (Poeme, 1940)
Lukomor'e (Meeresbucht, 1945)
Krasnye vorota (Das rote Tor, 1952)
Gedichte (1955)
Gedichte (1957)

Meléšin Stanisláv

Geb. 1928 im Dorfe Belogorka, im Gebiet von Penza, als Sohn eines Bauern. M. lebte eine Zeitlang im Nordural, wo er auch seine Militärdienstzeit verbrachte. Dort lernte er den kleinen Volksstamm der Mansi kennen, von dem seine erste Sammlung von Erzählungen und Reportagen, „Die Tasmanov", handelt. M. absolvierte 1955 die Gor'kij-Literaturhochschule und trat 1956 dem Sowjetischen *Schriftstellerverband* bei. Während und nach seiner Hochschulzeit erschienen von M. weitere Bücher, z. B. „Drei in der Taiga", „Patsche Rumal", „Wesensverwandte", „Ljubava".

V doroge (Unterwegs, 1954)

Deutsche Übersetzungen

Ein Schuß in der Taiga, übers. v. Erich Eichhorn, Moskau, S. L. 1958.

Michalków Sergéj Vladímirovič

Geb. 1913 in Moskau; sein Vater war Professor an einer landwirtschaftlichen Schule. 1927 übersiedelte die Familie nach Pjatigorsk. Nach Beendigung der Zehnjahresschule im Jahre 1930 kehrte M. jedoch wieder nach Moskau zurück und nahm an verschiedenen geologischen Expeditionen teil. Sein erstes literarisches Werk, ein Gedichtband, erschien im Jahre 1936. M. schreibt Gedichte für Kinder und die heranwachsende Jugend und verfaßt politische Fabeln im Stile Krylovs. In den ersten

Tagen des zweiten Weltkrieges ging M. als Korrespondent an die Front. 1943 verfaßte er den Text für die neue Sowjethymne. Seit 1950 ist M. Mitglied der KPdSU. Von seinen Bühnenwerken sind die 1949 erschienenen Stücke „Ja choču domoj" (Ich will nach Hause) wegen seiner — in der Nachkriegszeit von der Partei eifrig geförderten — antiwestlichen Tendenz, sowie „Il'ja Golovin" wegen der Darstellung des Lebens Šostakovič' am bemerkenswertesten.

Tom Kenti (1938)
Vesëlye snovidenija (Heitere Träume, 1945)
Vesëlye putešestvenniki (Fröhliche Reisegefährten)
Osoboe zadanie (Eine ungewöhnliche Aufgabe, 1946)
Krasnyj galstuk (Das rote Halstuch, 1947)
Prikljućenija zajki (Die Abenteuer eines Hasen)
Razgovor s synom (Gespräch mit dem Sohn)
Ja choču domoj (Ich will nach Hause, 1949)
Il'ja Golovin (1949, *Stalinpreis* 1950)
Smech i slëzy (Lachen und Weinen)
Pesni prostych ljudej (Lieder einfacher Leute, 1951)
Raki (Krebse, 1952)
Sočinenija 2 Bde. (Werke, 2 Bde., 1954)
Basni (Fabeln, 1957)

Deutsche Übersetzungen

Fröhliche Reisegefährten, Bukarest, Jugendverlag. 1951.

Ausgewählte Fabeln. Nachdichtung v. Bruno Tutenberg, Berlin, Verlag Kultur und Fortschritt. 1955.

Ilja Golovin und seine Wandlung. Schauspiel in 3 Akten, übers. v. Wangenheim, Berlin, Henschel. 1950.

Das rote Halstuch, Schauspiel in 3 Akten, übers. v. P. Hamm, Halle (S), Mitteldeutscher Verlag. 1952.

Der fleißige Hase (Priključenija zajki), nachgedichtet v. W. Forberg, Berlin, Kultur und Fortschritt. 1951. Gespräch mit dem Sohn, Nachdichtung v. P. Wiens, Berlin, Kinderbuchverlag. 1952.

Lachen und weinen. Ein lustiges Traumspiel in 3 Akten, 7 Bildern, 5 Zwischenspielen und mit einem Prolog, übers. v. E. Walden, Berlin, Aufbau-Bühnen-Betrieb. 1946.

Ich will nach Hause, Bukarest, Cartea rusă. 1950.

Musátov Alekséj Ivánovič

Geb. 1911 im Dorfe Lizunovo, im Gouvernement Vladimir. Von seinen Werken, die seit 1930 im Druck erscheinen, sind die Novellen aus der Nachkriegszeit bemerkenswert.

Stožary (1948, *Stalinpreis* 1950)
Dragocennoe zerno (Das kostbare Korn, 1949)
Dom na gore (Das Haus auf dem Berg, 1951)
Čerëmucha (Der Faulbaum, 1952)
Krutye tropy (Steile Pfade, 1955)
Bol'šaja vesna (Der große Frühling, 1957)

Nagíbin Júrij Márkovič

Geb. 1920 in Moskau. N. wollte Filmregisseur werden, wandte sich aber schließlich der schriftstellerischen Tätigkeit zu. Seine Werke erscheinen seit 1940. N. gehört zu den produktivsten sowjetischen Novellisten. Er wurde bekannt durch seine Erzählung „Chazarskij ornament" (Das chasarische Ornament), die in den 1956 erschienenen Sammelband sowjetischer Dichter, „Literaturnaja Moskva", aufgenommen, aber von der Kritik abgelehnt wurde, da sie angeblich nicht der sowjetischen Wirklichkeit entspricht.

Čelovek s fronta (Der Mann von der Front, 1943)
Bol'šoe serdce (Das große Herz, 1944)
Dve sily (Zwei Kräfte, 1944)
Gvardejcy na Dnepre (Die Garde am Dnepr, 1945)
Zerno žizni (Der Kern des Lebens, 1948)
Pokupka kop'ja (Der Kauf einer Lanze, 1950)
Trubka (Die Tabakspfeife, 1952)
Zimnij dub (Die winterliche Eiche, 1953)
Kombajnery (Mähdrescherführer, 1954)
Syn (Der Sohn, 1955)
Trudnoe sčastie (Schweres Glück, 1956)
Meščerskie storoža (Die Wächter von Meščera, 1956)
Svet v okne (Das Licht im Fenster, 1957)
Poslednjaja ochota (Die letzte Jagd, 1957)

Deutsche Übersetzungen

Die Tabakspfeife, übers. v. Juri Elperin, Moskau, Verlag für fremdsprachige Literatur. 1955.

Schwer erkämpftes Glück, übers. v. Regina Czora, Moskau, S. L. 1957.

Narin'jáni Semën Davídovič

Geb. 1908 in Taškent. N. ist seit 1924 Journalist und war als solcher bei „Komsomol'skaja pravda", „Ogonëk" und „Pravda" tätig. In seinen Werken spiegeln sich seine Erfahrungen wider, die er beim Bau der Stalingrader Traktorenfabrik und der Moskauer Metro sammelte.

Ljudi bol'ševistskich tempov (Menschen mit sowjetischem Tempo)

Anonim (Anonym, 1953)

Sbornik fel'etonov (Feuilletons. Sammelwerk)

Nedogónov Alekséj Ivánovič

1914—1948, stammte aus einer Arbeiterfamilie. Der Beginn seiner dichterischen Tätigkeit fällt in das Jahr 1934. Von 1939 bis 1946 war N. Soldat. Die Dichtungen N.s, vornehmlich sein Kolchospoem „Flag nad sel'sovetom" (Die Flagge über dem Dorfsowjet), für das ihm 1948 der *Stalinpreis* verliehen wurde, sind stark parteipolitisch gefärbt. Er hielt sich nämlich streng an die Forderungen der Partei, aktuelle Probleme des sowjetischen Lebens im Lichte eines überschäumenden Optimismus darzustellen, wodurch der dichterische Wert seiner Werke stark beeinträchtigt wurde.

Flag nad sel'sovetom (Die Flagge über dem Dorfsowjet, 1947, *Stalinpreis* 1948)

Ausgewählte Werke (1949)

Nekrásov Víktor Platónovič

Geb. 1911. N., der seit 1944 Mitglied der KPdSU ist, studierte in Kiev Architektur. Seine Romane wirken durch ihre echte, aufrichtige, aus dem unmittelbaren Erleben heraus geschriebene Darstellung, die frei von jeder politischen Tendenz ist.

In der Novelle „In der Heimatstadt", die auch im Ausland bald bekannt wurde, behandelt N. das Problem des Verhältnisses zu denen, die während der deutschen Besetzung in ihrer Heimatstadt verblieben waren.

V okopach Stalingrada (In den Schützengräben von Stalingrad, 1946, *Stalinpreis* 1947)
Sem' cvetov radugi (Die sieben Farben des Regenbogens, 1950)
V rodnom gorode (In der Heimatstadt, 1954)

Deutsche Übersetzungen

In den Schützengräben von Stalingrad, übers. v. Nadeshda Ludwig, Berlin, SWA-Verlag. 1948. Berlin-Hamburg-Stuttgart-Baden-Baden, Rowohlt. 1949. Berlin, Aufbau-Verlag. 1954.
Ein Mann kehrt zurück, Berlin, Verlag Kultur und Fortschritt. 1957.

Nevérov Aleksándr Sergéevič (Pseudonym für Skóbelev) 1886—1923, geb. im Dorfe Novikovo, im Gouvernement Samara. Sein Vater, ein Bauer, diente einige Zeit als Unteroffizier in einem St. Petersburger Garderegiment. Seine Mutter war Analphabetin. N. wuchs in der Familie seines Großvaters auf, die nach Sibirien übersiedelte. Er war zuerst Lehrling in einer Druckerei, arbeitete aber später bei einem Kaufmann. Im Jahre 1903 trat N. ins Lehrerseminar ein und erhielt nach 3 Jahren sein Diplom als Volksschullehrer. Er schrieb hauptsächlich Erzählungen aus dem Leben der Lehrer, der Landgeistlichkeit und der Bauern. Im Jahre 1922 übersiedelte N. nach Moskau. Er war mit *Gor'kij* und *Korolenko* befreundet, die ihn beide förderten.

Serye dni (Graue Tage, 1910)
Učitel' Strojkin (Der Lehrer Strojkin, 1911)
Mar'ja bol'ševička (Maria die Bolschewistin, 1921)
Taškent — gorod chlebnyj (Taschkent, die brotreiche Stadt, 1923)
Gusi — lebedi (Gänse — Schwäne, 1923)

Deutsche Übersetzungen

Taschkent, die brotreiche Stadt, übers. v. Maria Einstein, Berlin, Neuer Deutscher Verlag. 1925. Engels, Deutscher Staatsverlag. 1938.

Nikándrov Nikíta Nikándrovič (Pseudonym für Ševcóv)

Geb. 1878 als Sohn eines Postbeamten. N., der die Laufbahn eines Ingenieurs für Verkehrswesen einschlug, stand in regem Briefwechsel mit L. Tolstoj. 1905 wurde er wegen revolutionärer Umtriebe verbannt. Von 1910 bis 1914 lebte er in der Emigration. Seine erste, 1905 geschriebene Erzählung wurde 1906 in der Zeitschrift „Mir Božij" veröffentlicht. 1928—1929 erschien erstmals eine Sammlung seiner Erzählungen.

Povesti i rasskazy (Novellen und Erzählungen, 1958)

Nikítin Nikoláj Nikoláevič

Geb. 1895 in St. Petersburg, aus einer Beamtenfamilie stammend. Ab 1915 studierte er an der Universität, 1918 diente er als Freiwilliger in der Roten Armee. N. schreibt vornehmlich Erzählungen — die erste erschien 1922 —, in denen er das Leben des russischen Menschen während der Revolution und der Bürgerkriegsjahre schildert. „Wer die ‚ornamentale', ‚dynamische' Prosa mit ihren Licht- und Schattenseiten studieren will, findet kein besseres Material als die Erzählungen N.s der Jahre 1921—1923" (Struve). Allerdings wendet sich N. von dieser Thematik dann ab. Die Dostoevskijnovelle (Hier lebte Dostoevskij) hat das Interesse der Öffentlichkeit erneut auf N. gelenkt.

Prestuplenie Kirika Rudenko (Das Verbrechen des Kirik Rudenko, 1928)

Pogovorki o zvëzdach (Sprichwörter über die Sterne, 1934)

Baku (Apšeronskaja noč') (Baku, eine Nacht in Apšeron, 1937)

Eto bylo v Kokande (Es begann in Kokanda, 1939)

Severnaja avrora (Nordlicht, 1950, *Stalinpreis* 1951)

Zdes' žil Dostoevskij (Hier lebte Dostoevskij, 1956)

Deutsche Übersetzungen

Nordlicht (Severnaja avrora), übers. v. Alfred Kurella, 2. Aufl., Moskau, Verlag für fremdsprachige Literatur. 1955.

Nikoláev Aleksándr

Geb. 1925 in Moskau als Sohn eines Metallgraveurs. Vor dem Kriege arbeitete N. als Mähdrescherführer. Nach dem Kriege, den er als Artillerist mitmachte, absolvierte N. zunächst die juridische Fakultät der Moskauer Universität, später das Gor'kij-Literaturinstitut in Moskau. Sein Schaffensweg als Dichter begann im Jahre 1944, als er an der Front war. Sein erster Gedichtband, „Unterwegs", erschien 1956. In den letzten Jahren wurden Gedichte von N. vielfach in Zeitschriften veröffentlicht. (nach S. L.)

Nikoláeva Galína Evgén'evna (Pseudonym für Voljánskaja)

Geb. 1914 im Dorfe Usmanka, im Gebiet von Tomsk, als Tochter eines Beamten. N. studierte Medizin und schlug nach Beendigung ihrer Studien die wissenschaftliche Laufbahn ein. Nach einer medizinischen Lehrtätigkeit in Gor'kij in den Jahren 1938 bis 1942 stand N. von 1942 bis 1945 als Ärztin im Fronteinsatz. Der Beginn ihrer literarischen Tätigkeit fällt in das Jahr 1945. Von 1948 bis 1950 war N. Korrespondentin der „Literaturnaja gazeta". Von ihren Werken, die bisher bei einer Gesamtauflage von 1 976 000 in 23 Sprachen übersetzt wurden, ist am bekanntesten der Roman „Žatva" (Die Ernte), eine im Sinne der Forderungen der Partei geschriebene Glorifizierung der Helden der Arbeit. Dieser Roman wurde zu einem Film, „Vozvraščenie Vasilija Bortnikova" (Die Rückkehr Vasil Bortnikovs), und in ein Theaterstück, „Vysokaja volna" (Die hohe Welle), gemeinsam mit S. Radzinskij umgearbeitet.

Gibel' komandarma (Der Tod des Armeeführers, 1945)
Skvoz' ogon' (Durchs Feuer, 1946)
Žatva (Die Ernte, 1950, *Stalinpreis*)
Čerez desjatiletie (Nach einem Jahrzehnt, 1955)
Povest' o direktore MTS i glavnom agronome (Die Geschichte von dem Direktor der MTS und dem Chefagronomen, 1955)
Bitva v puti (Schlacht unterwegs, 1957)

Deutsche Übersetzungen

Ernte, übers. v. Otto Braun, Moskau, Verlag für fremdsprachige Literatur. 1952. Berlin, Verlag Kultur und Fortschritt. 1952, 1953, 1954. Bukarest, Verlag Arlus-Cartea rusă. 1953. Berlin, Aufbau-Verlag. 1955, 1956.

Die Geschichte Nastja Kowschowas (Povest' o direktore MTS i glavnom agronome), übers. v. Pauline Schneider, Bukarest, Verlag Cartea rusă. 1955.

Schlacht unterwegs, einige Kapitel aus dem Roman, übers. v. Juri Elperin, Moskau, S. L. 1958.

Nikúlin Lev Veniamínovič

Geb. 1891 in Žitomir, stammt aus dem Theatermilieu. Seit 1940 ist N. Mitglied der KPdSU. Im Roman „Rossii vernye syny" (Rußlands treue Söhne, übers. ‚Im geheimen Auftrag') schildert er den Feldzug 1813—1814.

Nikakich slučajnostej (Es gibt keine Zufälle, 1924)
Vremja, prostranstvo, dviženie, 2 Bde. (Zeit, Raum, Bewegung, 1932)
Ljudi russkogo iskusstva (Menschen der russischen Kunst, 1947)
Rossii vernye syny (Rußlands treue Söhne, 1950, *Stalinpreis* 1951)

Deutsche Übersetzungen

Im geheimen Auftrag (Rossii vernye syny), übers. v. R. Fischer, Berlin, Rütten u. Loening. 1953.

Nílin Pável Filíppovič

Geb. 1908 in Irkutsk. Sein erstes Werk, der Roman „Ein Mann geht bergauf", erschien 1935. Während des Krieges war N. Berichterstatter. Aus dieser Zeit stammt u. a. die Erzählung „Die Lebenslinie". Nach dem Kriege verfaßte N. das Bühnenstück „Auf der weiten Welt", den Roman „Die Reise nach Moskau", die Erzählung „Probezeit", sowie einige Novellen. Von N. stammt auch des Drehbuch des vieldiskutierten Films „Ein großes Leben". N. ist ein sehr begabter Künstler, der es versteht, mit wenigen Worten eine große Wirkung in der Aussage zu erzielen. Er wagt es auch, unangenehme Fragen offen zu diskutieren (z. B. „Žestokost'", deutsch „Hart auf hart").

Na belom svete (Auf der weiten Welt, 1947)
Poezdka v Moskvu (Die Reise nach Moskau, 1955)
Žučka (1955)
Ispytatel'nyj srok (Probezeit, 1956)
Žestokost' (Hart auf hart, 1956)

Deutsche Übersetzungen

Genosse Wenka (Žestokost'), übers. v. Wera Rathfelder, Berlin, Verlag Deutsche Volksbücher. 1960.
Probezeit, übers. v. Juri Elperin, Moskau, S. L. 1957.
Hart auf hart (Žestokost'), übers. v. Hilde Angarowa, Moskau, S. L. 1958.

Njurnbérg-Šárov Aleksándr Izraílevič

Geb. 1909 in Kiev. Als Korrespondent war N.-Š. während des Krieges in Deutschland, Ungarn, ČSR und Österreich. Von seinen Werken sind am bekanntesten:

Bol'šaja ljubov' (Große Liebe)
Vozvraščenie (Die Rückkehr)
Žizn' (Das Leben)
Batal'on Borisa Ivanoviča (Bataillon Boris Ivanovič)
Žizn' pobeždaet (Das Leben siegt)

Nóvikov-Pribój Alekséj Sílyč

1877—1944, geb. im Dorfe Matveevka, im Gouvernement Tambov. N.-P. nahm als Matrose an der Schlacht von Tsushima teil, die er auch in seinem gleichnamigen Roman schildert. Die Werke N.-P.s wurden erstmalig im Jahre 1907 gedruckt, von der Zensur jedoch verboten. N.-P. schrieb damals unter dem Pseudonym A. Zatërtyj. Als politischer Emigrant lebte N.-P. auch in Frankreich, England, Spanien, Italien und Afrika. Eine Zeitlang war er auch bei *Gor'kij* auf Capri. Nach dem Kriege schrieb N.-P. vornehmlich Seemannsgeschichten.

Morskie rasskazy (Seegeschichten, 1917)
More zovët (Das Meer ruft, 1919)
Podvodniki (U-Bootmatrosen, 1923)

Solënaja kupel' (Das salzige Taufbecken, 1929)
Begstvo (Die Flucht, 1931)
Madagaskar (1932)
Cusima (Tsushima, 1932—1940, *Stalinpreis* 1941)
V drejfe (In der Drift, 1935)
V buchte ‚Otrada' (In der ‚Otrada'-Bucht)

Deutsche Übersetzungen
In der ‚Ostrada'-Bucht, Bukarest, Verlag Cartea rusă. 1953.
Zwei Seegeschichten, übertr. v. H. Wolf, Leipzig, Insel-Verlag. 1952.

Obradóvič Sergéj Aleksándrovič

1892—1956, geb. in Moskau, aus einer Handwerkerfamilie stammend. Nach dem ersten Weltkrieg, den er als Soldat mitmachte, betrieb O. in Moskau literarische Studien und wurde Mitglied der Künstlervereinigung *Kuznica*. Er leitete auch den Kulturteil der „Pravda". Im Jahre 1921 veröffentlichte O. seine erste Gedichtsammlung, „Vzmach" (Aufschwung).

Vzmach (Aufschwung, 1921)
Izbrannye stichi (Ausgewählte Gedichte, 1935)
Dorogi (Straßen, 1947)

Ógnev Nikoláj (Pseudonym für Michaíl Grigór'evič Rózanov)

1888—1938, war von Beruf Lehrer und befaßte sich schon aus diesem Grunde viel mit Erziehungsproblemen. Bei der Zeitschrift „Oktjabr'" leitete er auch eine Zeitlang das Jugendreferat. Wegen seines Interesses an der Jugend und den jungen Schriftstellern wurde O. auch von *Gor'kij* sehr geschätzt (s. Literaturnaja gazeta vom 30. 6. 1938). Auf literarischem Gebiet wurde O. vor allem durch seinen aufsehenerregenden Roman „Dnevnik Kosti Rjabceva" (Das Tagebuch des Schülers Kostja Rjabzev) bekannt. Neben der geschickt gewählten Form ist das Buch deswegen besonders bemerkenswert, weil es eine Vorstellung von den Experimenten vermittelt, die während der Revolution und der zwanziger Jahre in den höheren Schulen durchgeführt wurden, und weil es eine wirklichkeitsnahe Schilderung des Lebens der Jugend der ersten Sowjetgeneration in den Schulen ist. Der zweite Teil des Romans, „Ischod Nikpetoža“ (Der Abgang des Nikpetož) ist jedoch von weit geringerem literarischen und zeitdokumentarischen Wert. Von der offiziellen Sowjetkritik wird O. heutzutage vollkommen ignoriert.

Šči respubliki (Die Kohlsuppe der Republik)
Evrazija (Eurasien)
Dnevnik Kosti Rjabceva (Das Tagebuch des Kostja Rjabcev, 1926 bis 1927)
Ischod Nikpetoža (Der Abgang des Nikpetož)
Tri izmerenija (Drei Dimensionen)

Deutsche Übersetzungen

Das Tagebuch des Schülers Kostja Rjabzew, übers. v. Maria Einstein, Berlin, Verlag der Jugendinternationale. 1927.
Kostja Rjabzew auf der Universität (Ischod Nikpetoža), übers. v. Maria Einstein, Berlin, Verlag der Jugendinternationale. 1927.

Oléša Júrij Kárlovič

Geb. 1899 in Elizavetgrad, dem heutigen Kirovograd, aus einer Intellektuellenfamilie stammend. Seine Jugendjahre verbrachte O. in Odessa. Er wurde dann Journalist und veröffentlichte seine Feuilletons und Verse unter dem Pseudonym „Zubilo“ (Meißel) in der Zeitung „Gudok“. Allgemein bekannt wurde O. aber erst mit der Veröffentlichung seines Romans „Zavist’“ (Neid) im Jahre 1927 (als Theaterstück „Zagovor čuvstv“ — Die Verschwörung der Gefühle). Das immer wiederkehrende Grundthema in O.s Schaffen ist die Darstellung der Auseinandersetzung zwischen der „alten“ und der „neuen“ Welt. Da sich der Dichter in diese „neue“ Welt nicht einfügen konnte, wurde er von der sowjetischen Kritik heftig angegriffen, worauf O. Ende der dreißiger Jahre verschwand. Die im Jahre 1956 erfolgte Wiederveröffentlichung des Romans „Die drei Dicken“ und die in Vorbereitung befindliche Neuauflage des Romans „Neid“ lassen auf seine Rehabilitierung schließen. (nach KSB)

Zavist’ (Neid, 1927)
Tri tolstjaka (Die drei Dicken, 1928)
Ljubov’ (Liebe, 1929)
Višnëvaja kostočka (Der Kirschkern, 1930)
Spisok blagodejanij (Die Liste der Wohltaten, 1931)
Strogij junoša (Ein strenger junger Mann, 1943), als Filmdrehbuch verfaßt.

Ósin Dmítrij Dmítrievič

Geb. 1906 in Smolensk als Sohn eines Angestellten. Vor Beginn seiner literarischen Tätigkeit war O. als Redakteur bei verschiedenen Provinzzeitungen tätig, z. B. bei „Brjanskij rabočij“, „Rabočaja Samara“ u. a. Seine ersten Werke wurden 1925 veröffentlicht. O.s Lyrik erreicht besonders dann bedeutende Kraft, wenn er über seine Heimat schreibt: „V boru za Orlan’ju“ (In den Wäldern von Orlan’).

Sorevnovanie (Der Wettbewerb, 1933)
My nastupaem (Wir rücken vor, 1934)
Prazdnik vozvraščenija (Das Fest der Rückkehr, 1947)
Rannej vesnoj (Vorfrühling, 1954)
V boru za Orlan’ju (In den Wäldern von Orlan’, 1956)
Na novom zavode (In einem neuen Betrieb, 1956)
Sila žizni (Die Kraft des Lebens, 1957)
Van’ka Loban (1958)
Dal’nie poezda (Fernzüge, 1958)

Ósipov Valérij

Geb. 1930 in Moskau als Sohn eines Ingenieurs. O. absolvierte 1954 das Institut für Journalistik an der Moskauer Universität. Auf literarischem Gebiet ist O. bereits seit seinem 19. Lebensjahr tätig; er schreibt Gedichte, Skizzen und Erzählungen. Im Herbst 1956 reiste er als Korrespondent der „Komsomol’skaja pravda" nach Jakutien. Dort sammelte O. viele interessante Berichte über das Leben der jungen Geologen und Entdecker von Diamantenfeldern. Auf einem solchen Bericht beruht die Erzählung „Ein Brief, der nicht aufgegeben wurde". (nach S. L.)

Neotpravlennoe pis'mo (Ein Brief, der nicht aufgegeben wurde, 1957)

Solnce podnimaetsja na Vostoke (Die Sonne geht im Osten auf, 1958. V. Kitaev und V. Osipov)

Deutsche Übersetzungen

Ein Brief, der nicht abgeschickt wurde, übers. v. Juri Elperin, Moskau, S. L. 1958.

Ostróvskij Nikoláj Alekséevič

1904—1936, geb. im Dorfe Vilija, im Gouvernement Volyn', als Sohn eines Schlossers. Während der Kriegsjahre übersiedelte die Familie aus Wolhynien ins Landesinnere. Nachdem O. wegen unbotmäßigen Benehmens während des Religionsunterrichts aus der Schule ausgeschlossen worden war, war er gezwungen, frühzeitig ins Berufsleben einzutreten. In der Folge war O. dann in den verschiedensten Berufen, so als Hirte, Schankbursche, Abwäscher, beschäftigt. Von 1914 bis 1918 war er als Lagerarbeiter in Šepetovka, einem Eisenbahnknotenpunkt in der Provinz, tätig. Dort schloß er sich den Revolutionären an und wurde 1919 Soldat in der Roten Armee. In den Kämpfen bei Lemberg wurde er schwer verwundet. 1924 wurde O. Mitglied der Kommunistischen Partei. Im Alter von 23 Jahren erkrankte er schwer; zu einer völligen Lähmung trat eine fortschreitende Erblindung. In diesem Zustand völliger Hilflosigkeit wurde O. Schriftsteller und diktierte vom Krankenbett aus seinen Roman „Wie der Stahl gehärtet wurde", der wegen seiner Verherrlichung der kommunistischen Idee zu einem Musterbeispiel für den *sozialistischen Realismus* wurde. Nach seinem Tode erschien der erste Teil des unvollendeten

Romans „Die Sturmgeborenen", der das Leben der heranwachsenden Jugend während der Bürgerkriegsjahre schildert.

Kak zakaljalas' stal' (Wie der Stahl gehärtet wurde, 1934, als Buch 1935)

Roždënnye burej (Die Sturmgeborenen, 1936)

Deutsche Übersetzungen

Wie der Stahl gehärtet wurde, Kiev, Staatsverlag der nationalen Minderheiten. 1937. Berlin, Verlag Neues Leben. 1947, 1948. Bearb. v. Maja Bregmann u. Nell Held, Moskau, Verlag für fremdsprachige Literatur. 1953. Nach der Übers. v. Nelly Drechsler, Berlin, Verlag Neues Leben. 1954, 1956.

Die Sturmgeborenen, übers. v. Rose Wittfogel, Moskau, Verlag für fremdsprachige Literatur 1947. ‚Die im Sturm Geborenen', Kiev; Staatsverlag der nationalen Minderheiten der UdSSR. 1936.

Ovéčkin Valentín Vladímirovič

Geb. 1904 in Taganrog, aus einer Beamtenfamilie stammend. Von 1941 bis 1945 war O. Kriegsberichterstatter. Seit 1943 ist er Mitglied der KPdSU. Die erste Erzählung O.s, „Savel'ev", erschien 1927 in der Zeitung „Bednota". Das Hauptthema in seinen Werken ist das Leben auf dem Kolchoz („Rajonnye budni", deutsch „Alltag im Rayon"). O.s Erzählungen tragen einen belehrenden und damit publizistischen Charakter.

Kolchoznye rasskazy (Kolchozerzählungen, 1935)

S frontovym privetom (Grüße von der Front, 1945)

Bab'e leto (Altweibersommer, 1947)

Nastja Kolosova (1949)

Rajonnye budni (Alltag im Rayon, 1952)

V tom že rajone (Im gleichen Rayon, 1954)

Svoimi rukami (Mit eigenen Händen, 1956)

Trudnaja vesna (Schwerer Frühling, 1956)

Deutsche Übersetzungen

Erzählungen. In einer Kollektivwirtschaft, übers. v. Harry Schnittke, Moskau, Verlag für fremdsprachige Literatur. 1955.

Frühlingsstürme (Trudnaja vesna), Berlin, Verlag Kultur und Fortschritt. o. J.

Panfërov Fëdor Ivánovič

1896—1960, aus einer Bauernfamilie stammend. P., Mitglied der KPdSU seit 1926, war Deputierter des Obersten Sewjets. Nachdem er zu Beginn seiner schriftstellerischen Tätigkeit einige Theaterstücke verfaßt hatte, errang P. um 1930 mit der Veröffentlichung der beiden ersten Bände seines vierteiligen Romans „Bruski“ (Die Genossenschaft der Habenichtse) seinen ersten großen Erfolg. So wie viele andere Bücher, die in den Jahren des 1. Fünfjahrplans erschienen, hatte er die Kollektivierung der Landwirtschaft zum Thema. Ein paar Jahre später jedoch richtete *Gor'kij* in seinem Sprachreinigungsbestreben gegen das Werk heftige Angriffe, da seine Sprache zu vulgär und mit zu vielen Dialektausdrücken durchsetzt wäre.

Pachom (1920—22)
Naši zemli (Unser Land, 1922)
Mužiki (Die Bauern, 1924)
Ot derevenskich polej (Von den Dorffeldern, 1926)
V predutrennjuju ran' (Vor Morgendämmerung, 1927)
Bruski (Schleifsteine, 1928—1937)
Bor'ba za mir (Der Kampf um den Frieden, 1947, *Stalinpreis* 1948)
V strane poveržennych (Im Lande der Besiegten, 1948, *Stalinpreis* 1949)
Bol'šoe isskustvo (Die große Kunst, 1949)
Kogda my krasivy (Wenn wir schön sind, 1952)
Nedavnee prošloe (Die unmittelbare Vergangenheit, 1952)
Volga matuška reka (Mütterchen Wolga, 1958. Bd. 1: „Udar“ (Der Schlag), Bd. 2: „Razdumie (Die Meditation)

Deutsche Übersetzungen

Die Genossenschaft der Habenichtse (Bruski), übers. v. Edith Hajós, Berlin, Verlag für Literatur und Politik. 1928. Bd. 2, Wien-Berlin, Verlag für Literatur und Politik. 1931. Auch unter d. Titeln ‚Mit festem Schritt‘, Moskau-Leningrad, Verlagsgenossenschaft ausländischer Arbeiter in der UdSSR. 1934; ‚Wolgabauern‘, übers. v. Arthur Nestmann, bearb. u. Nachwort v. Lothar Kampe. Bd. 1, 2, Dresden, Sachsenverlag. 1953.

Panóva Véra Fëdorovna

Geb. 1905 in Rostov am Don. P. war von 1922 bis 1935 als Korrespondentin tätig. Ihr erstes literarisches Werk, „Il'ja Kosogor", erschien im Jahre 1939. Der breiteren Öffentlichkeit wurde P. jedoch erst durch ihre Kriegsnovelle „Sputniki" (Weggenossen) und die Nachkriegsromane „Kružilicha" (Menschen aus Kružilicha) und „Jasnyj bereg" (Helles Ufer) bekannt; diese Werke zeichnen sich vor allem durch eindrucksvolle Charakterschilderungen aus. Obwohl mit *Stalinpreisen* ausgezeichnet, wurden sie zusammen mit dem während der sogenannten Tauwetterperiode erschienenen Roman „Vremena goda" (Die Jahreszeiten), einer Darstellung des Lebens der obersten Schichten der sowjetischen Gesellschaft, auf dem 2. Sowjetischen Schriftstellerkongreß im Dezember 1954 wegen der indifferenten Einstellung der Verfasserin zum *sozialistischen Realismus* einer heftigen Kritik unterzogen. Die Werke P.s sind bisher in 21 Sprachen übersetzt worden und haben eine Auflage von 3 122 000 Exemplaren erreicht.

Devočki (Mädchen, 1945)
Sputniki (Weggenossen, 1946, *Stalinpreis* 1947)
Kružilicha (1947, *Stalinpreis* 1948)
Jasnyj bereg (Helles Ufer, 1948, *Stalinpreis* 1949)
Vremena goda (Die Jahreszeiten, 1953)
Serëža (1955)
Staraja Moskva (Das alte Moskau, 1956)
Sentimental'nyj roman (Ein sentimentaler Roman, 1958)

Deutsche Übersetzungen

Menschen aus Krushilicha (Kružilicha), übers. v. Nadeshda Ludwig, bearb. v. Walter Bergstraßer, Berlin, Verlag Kultur und Fortschritt. 1949, 1951. Übers. v. Eva Priester, Wien, Globus-Verlag. 1950.

Helles Ufer, übers. v. Hans Bruschwitz, Leipzig, P. List. 1951, 1952.

Weggenossen, übers. v. Veronika Ensslen, Berlin, Aufbau-Verlag. 1952, 1954. Auch unter dem Titel ‚Weggefährten', Berlin, Paul Zsolnay. 1948.

Serjoscha, übers. v. E. Müller-Kamp, Bonn, Schimmelbusch & Co. 1957.

Pasternák Borís Leonídovič

1890—1960, geb. in Moskau als Sohn eines jüdischen Künstlerehepaares. Er studierte zunächst an der Universität in Moskau bei Skrjabin Musik, wandte sich aber später dem Kunstgeschichte- und Philosophiestudium zu. Zu Studienzwecken reiste P. auch nach Deutschland und Italien und kehrte knapp vor dem Ausbruch der Revolution nach Rußland zurück. P. hatte schon im Jahre 1912 begonnen, sich auf literarischem Gebiet zu betätigen, und sich dabei eng an die radikalsten Vertreter der *futuristischen* Bewegung anzuschließen; in Buchform erschienen seine Erstlingswerke jedoch erst einige Jahre später. Da P. nicht geneigt war, in seinen Dichtungen aktuelle Themen im Sinne des *sozialistischen Realismus* zu behandeln, war er wiederholten Angriffen von seiten der offiziellen sowjetischen Kritik ausgesetzt. Dies mag wohl auch ein Grund dafür sein, daß er sich als vorzüglicher Sprachkönner und Übersetzer vornehmlich mit der Übertragung Shakespearescher Dramen und Goethes Faust ins Russische befaßte. Den ihm 1958 für seinen Roman „Doktor Živago" zugesprochenen Nobelpreis für Literatur nahm P. aus politischen Gründen nicht an.

Bliznec v tučach (Der Zwilling in den Wolken, 1914)
Poverch bar'erov (Über den Barrieren, 1917)
Sestra moja žizn' (Meine Schwester — das Leben, 1922)
Temy i var'jacii (Themen und Variationen, 1923)
Spektorskij (1926)
Devjat'sot pjatyj god (Das Jahr 1905, 1927)
Lejtenant Šmidt (Leutnant Schmidt, 1927)
Ochrannaja gramota (Der Geleitbrief, 1931)
Vtoroe roždenie (Die zweite Geburt, 1932)
Na rannich poezdach (In Frühzügen, 1943)
Zemnoj prostor (Irdische Weite, 1945)
Doktor Živago (1958)

Deutsche Übersetzungen

Doktor Schiwago, übers. v. Reinhold von Walter, Frankfurt a. M., S. Fischer Verlag. 1958.

Geleitbrief (Ochrannaja gramota), übers. v. Gisela Druhla, Frankfurt/M., Ullstein-Buch. 1958.

Wenn es aufklärt (Eine Auswahl), übers. v. Rolf Dietrich Keil, Frankfurt/M., Fischer Verlag. 1960.

Paustóvskij Konstantín Geórgievič

Geb. 1892 in Moskau. P. entstammte einer Eisenbahnerfamilie, absolvierte das Gymnasium in Kiev und studierte einige Zeit an der Universität in Moskau. Nachdem er am Bürgerkrieg teilgenommen und später in den verschiedensten Berufen gearbeitet hatte, wurde P. 1925 Schriftsteller. Seine erste literarische Arbeit, eine Erzählung, war bereits 1911 erschienen. Die ersten Werke P.s sind voll von der Romantik des sowjetischen Wiederaufbaus und zeugen von seiner Vorliebe für das Großartige in der Natur. Später schöpft P. seine Thematik vornehmlich aus dem Leben russischer Künstler (Levitan, Kiprenskij, Lermontov, Puškin).

Morskie nabroski (Skizzen über das Meer, 1925)
Vstrečnye korabli (Schiffe, die sich begegnen, 1928)
Blistatel'nye oblaka (Prachtvolle Wolken, 1929)
Kara Bugaz (1932)
Kolchida (Kolchis, 1934)
Romantiki (Schwärmer, 1935)
Čërnoe more (Das Schwarze Meer, 1936)
Isaak Levitan (1937)
Orest Kiprenskij (1937)
Taras Ševčenko (1939)
Severnaja povest' (Nordische Erzählung, 1939)
Poručik Lermontov (Oberleutnant Lermontov, 1941)
Dalëkie gody (Ferne Jahre, 1946)
Povest' o lesach (Sagen aus den Wäldern, 1948)
Zimnjaja istorija (Eine Wintergeschichte, 1948)
Stal'noe kolečko (Das eiserne Ringlein, 1949)

Naš sovremennik (Unser Zeitgenosse, 1949)
Roždenie morja (Die Geburt eines Meeres, 1952)
Bespokojnaja junost' (Unruhige Jugend, 1955)

Deutsche Übersetzungen

Die Kolchis, übers. v. J. Kagan, Moskau, Verlagsgenossenschaft ausländischer Arbeiter in der UdSSR. 1936. Berlin, Aufbau-Verlag. 1946.
Erzählungen, übers. v. Ina Tinzmann, Berlin-Leipzig, SWA-Verlag. 1947, 1948.
Aus ferner Jugend (Dalëkie gody), übers. v. Richard Hoffmann, Wien, Erasmus-Verlag. 1947.
Eine Wintergeschichte (Zimnjaja istorija), übers. v. Horst Wolf, Berlin-Leipzig, SWA-Verlag. 1948.
Nordische Novelle (Severnaja povest'), übers. v. Maximilian Schick, Berlin, Dietz. 1949.
Das eiserne Ringlein (Stal'noe kolečko), u. a. Erz., übers. v. Liselotte Remané, Berlin, Verlag Lied der Zeit. 1949.
Der alte Nachen u. a. Erz., übers. v. Horst Wolf, Leipzig, Reclam. 1952, 1955.
Segen der Wälder (Povest' o lesach), übers. v. Robert Carl Siehr, Berlin, Altberliner Verlag. 1952. Auch unter dem Titel ‚Eine Geschichte vom Walde' bekannt, übers. v. Alfred Kittner u. Ilse Goldmann, Bukarest, Verlag Cartea rusă. 1955.
Ferne Jahre, übers. v. Josi v. Koskull, Berlin, Aufbau-Verlag. 1955.
Kara-Bugaz, Der Mensch erobert die Wüste, übers. v. Ruthenberg, Wien, Globus-Verlag. 1948.
Das Mädchen aus dem Norden (Severjanka), Schauspiel in 1 Aufz., Berlin, Gesellschaft für deutsch-sowjetische Freundschaft. 1952.

Pavlénko Pëtr Andréevič

1899—1951, geb. in St. Petersburg, aus einer Beamtenfamilie stammend. P. war seit 1920 Mitglied der Kommunistischen Partei, nahm am Bürgerkrieg teil und wurde später Abgeordneter des Obersten Rates der Sowjetunion. Als Beauftragter für Außenhandelsbeziehungen unternahm P. Mitte der zwanziger Jahre Reisen in die Türkei, in den Vorderen Orient, nach Griechenland, Italien und Frankreich. Diese Reisen fanden in seinem ersten literarischen Werk, „Asiatskie rasskazy" (Asiatische Erzählungen, 1929) und den in den folgenden Jahren erschienenen Reiseschilderungen ihren Niederschlag. Einen grundlegenden Erfolg in der sowjetischen Literatur errang P. mit seinem 1937 erschienenen Roman „Na vostoke" (Im Osten), einer Schilderung des Lebens in den sowjetischen Grenzgebieten im Fernen Osten, die dem Zweck diente, der sowjetischen Öffentlichkeit die Gefahren einer Bedrohung der Aufbauarbeit in den dortigen Gebieten durch einen japanischen Angriffskrieg vor Augen zu führen. P., der auch mit *Stalinpreis* und Leninorden ausgezeichnet wurde, verfaßte auch Filmdrehbücher und war Mitarbeiter beim Film „Aleksandr Nevskij". In den Jahren 1949—1951 veröffentlichte er Reiseskizzen über USA, Italien und Deutschland. Seine Werke wurden bis jetzt in 38 Sprachen übersetzt und erreichten eine Auflage von 7 157 000.

Asiatskie rasskazy (Asiatische Erzählungen, 1929)
Stambul i Turcija (Stambul und die Türkei, 1930)
Pustynja (Die Wüste, 1932)
Putešestvie v Turkmenistan (Reise nach Turkmenistan, 1932)
Barrikady (Barrikaden, 1932)
Na vostoke (Im Osten, 1937)
Sčastie (Das Glück, 1947, *Stalinpreis* 1948)
Stepnoe solnce (Steppensonne, 1949)
Golos v puti (Stimme unterwegs, 1948)
Truženiki morja (Die Werktätigen des Meeres, 1952 posthum)

Deutsche Übersetzungen

Barrikaden, Moskau-Leningrad, Verlagsgenossenschaft ausländischer Arbeiter in der UdSSR. 1934. Übers. v. Tschornaja. Leipzig, Volk und Buch Verlag. 1948.

Das Glück, übers. v. Veronica Ensslen, Berlin, Verlag Tägliche Rundschau. 1949. Leipzig-München, P. List. 1949, 1950, 1951, 1952.

Steppensonne, übers. v. Hilde Angarowa, Berlin, Verlag Kultur und Fortschritt. 1952, 1954. Leipzig, Reclam. 1954.

Ruf auf dem Weg (Golos v puti), Bukarest, Verlag Cartea rusă. 1954. Auch unter dem Titel ‚Stimme unterwegs', Berlin, Verlag Kultur und Fortschritt. 1954.

Petróv Evgénij Petróvič (Pseudonym für Katáev)

1903—1942, geb. in Odessa als Sohn einer Lehrerfamilie. P., ein Bruder von Valentin *Kataev*, war Freund und Mitarbeiter von Il'ja *Il'f*, mit dem er gemeinsam zwischen 1927 und 1937 eine Reihe humoristischer und satirischer Werke verfaßte. P. fiel im Jahre 1942 als Berichterstatter bei Sevastopol'.

Ostrov mira (Die Insel des Friedens, 1940)
Frontovoj dnevnik (Fronttagebuch, 1942)
Gemeinsam mit Il'f:
Dvenadcat' stul'ev (Zwölf Stühle, 1928)
Zolotoj telënok (Das goldene Kalb, 1931)
Odnoetažnaja Amerika (Das einstöckige Amerika, 1930)

Deutsche Übersetzungen

Die Insel des Friedens. Ein Lustspiel in 4 Akten, übers. v. G. Tanewa, Berlin, Henschel und Sohn. 1947.

Vgl. *Il'f*.

Pil'nják Borís Andréevič (Pseudonym für Vogáu)

1894—1937 (?), geb. in Možajsk als Sohn eines Tierarztes, der seinerseits einer wolgadeutschen Familie entstammte. P. absolvierte die Realschule in Nižnij Novgorod (dem jetzigen Gor'kij) und besuchte dann ein Handelsinstitut in Moskau. Seine ersten Erzählungen erschienen bereits im Jahre 1909, der Beginn seines eigentlichen literarischen Schaffens wird jedoch durch die Veröffentlichung seiner Novelle „Celaja žizn' " (Ein ganzes Leben) im Jahre 1915 gekennzeichnet. Von den jungen Dichtern der nachrevolutionären Zeit gehörte P. zu den ersten, die sich die Revolution zum Hauptthema ihres literarischen Schaffens erkoren. Durch seinen im Jahre 1922 veröffentlichten Roman „Golyj god" (Das nackte Jahr) errang P. für Jahre eine führende Position in der Sowjetliteratur. Dieser

Roman stellt eigentlich nur eine ungezwungene Zusammenstellung von Erzählungen dar, die zum Teil auch als selbständige Erzählungen veröffentlicht oder in andere derartige Romane eingebaut wurden. Zu einer ausgewachsenen politischen Sensation wurde die im Jahre 1927 veröffentlichte Erzählung „Povest' o nepogašennoj lune" (Die Geschichte vom nichtverlöschten Mond), welche in verschlüsselter Form die auf Befehl Stalins erfolgte Ermordung des Revolutionsgenerals Frunze zum Thema hatte. P. unternahm auch Reisen, die ihn nach Japan und Amerika führten und die dann in verschiedenen Werken verarbeitet wurden. Gewisse, an konterrevolutionäre Ideen anklingende Äußerungen in seinem Werk „Krasnoe derevo" (Mahagoni) bewirkten P.s Ausschluß aus dem *RAPP*. P. soll im Jahre 1937 erschossen worden sein, sein Tod wurde jedoch offiziell nicht bestätigt.

Golyj god (Das nackte Jahr, 1922)
Mašiny i volki (Maschinen und Wölfe, 1924)
Povest' o nepogašennoj lune (Die Geschichte vom nichtverlöschten Mond, 1927)
Korni japonskogo solnca (Die Wurzeln der japanischen Sonne, 1927)
Kitajskij dnevnik (Chinesisches Tagebuch, 1927)
Krasnoe derevo (Mahagoni, 1929)
Volga vpadaet v Kaspijskoe more (Die Wolga mündet ins Kaspische Meer, 1930)
O'kej (OK, 1931)
Kamni i korni (Steine und Wurzeln, 1934)

Deutsche Übersetzungen

Die Wolga fällt ins Kaspische Meer, übers. v. Erwin Honig m. e. Beitrag v. Karl Radek, Berlin, Neuer deutscher Verlag. 1930.

Platónov Andréj Platónovič (Pseudonym für Kliméntov)

1896—1951, geb. in Voronež, einer Arbeiterfamilie entstammend. Nach Beendigung des Bürgerkrieges, an dem er teilgenommen hatte, studierte P. Elektrotechnik. P., dessen erstes literarisches Werk im Jahre 1921 veröffentlicht wurde, gehörte zu den begabtesten Mitgliedern der *Pereval*-Gruppe und erfreute sich der Förderung durch *Gor'kij*. Wegen seiner allzu realistischen und schonungslosen Darstellung der Nachkriegsverhältnisse und der Kollektivierung wurde P. in der Folge heftig kritisiert.

Gvardejcy čelovečestva (Gardisten der Menschheit, 1928—1946)
Izbrannye rasskazy (Ausgewählte Erzählungen, 1958)

Pogódin Nikoláj Fëdorovič (Pseudonym für Stukálov)

Geb. 1900 in der Stanica Gundrovskaja am Don als Sohn einer Bauernfamilie. P., der seine Laufbahn als Journalist begann, ist einer der bekanntesten sowjetischen Dramatiker. Seine Stücke behandeln vornehmlich Themen der sowjetischen Aufbauarbeit und der neueren sowjetischen Geschichte (Lenin). Der allgemeinen Kampagne gegen den Westen in den ersten Nachkriegsjahren schloß sich P. mit dem antiamerikanischen Stück „Missurijskij val's" an. Einen besonders großen Theatererfolg verzeichnet das Stück „Sonet Petrarki", da es die ansonsten in der Sowjetliteratur gemiedene „Nur-Liebe" zum Thema hat. Seit 1949 ist P. verdienter Künstler der RSFSR.

Temp (Tempo, 1929, umgearbeitet 1930)
Poema o topore (Das Poem von der Axt, 1930, umgearbeitet 1931)
Posle bala (Nach dem Ball, 1932, umgebarbeitet 1934)
Moj drug (Mein Freund, 1932)
Aristokraty (Aristokraten, 1934, umgearbeitet 1935)
Čelovek s ruž'ëm (Der Mann mit der Flinte, 1937, *Stalinpreis* 1941)
Kremlëvskie kuranty (Das Glockenspiel des Kreml, 1941)
Missurijskij val's (Missouri-Walzer, 1949)
Sonet Petrarki (Das Sonett Petrarcas, 1956)
Tret'ja patetičeskaja (Die dritte Pathetique, 1958)

Deutsche Übersetzungen

Der Mann mit der Flinte. Schauspiel in 3 Akten und 12 Bildern, Engels, Deutscher Staatsverlag. 1939.

Aristokraten. Ein sowjetisches Drama, Berlin, Henschel. 1946.

Der Missouri-Walzer. Die neue Variante. Schauspiel in 4 Akten, übers. v. A. Thoss. Berlin, Henschel. 1951.

Appassionata. Trilogie, dritter Teil, übers. v. Juri Elperin, Moskau, S. L. 1959.

Polevój Borís Nikoláevič (Pseudonym für Kámpov)

Geb. 1908, ist seit 1940 Mitglied der KPdSU. Von 1941 bis 1945 Korrespondent der „Pravda", machte sich auf literarischem Gebiet während der ersten Nachkriegsjahre durch die Veröffentlichung von Dokumentarberichten aus der Kriegszeit einen Namen. Später verfaßte er noch verschiedene Erzählungen und Reiseberichte. Die Werke P.s, der Delegierter des Obersten Sowjets der RSFSR ist, wurden bei einer Gesamtauflage von 8 361 000 in 36 Sprachen übersetzt.

Gorjačij cech (Die unruhige Zeche, 1940)
Ot Belgoroda do Karpat (Von Belgorod bis in die Karpaten, 1945)
Povest' o nastojaščem čeloveke (Die Erzählung vom wahren Menschen, 1946, *Stalinpreis* 1947)
Neugasimoe plamja (Die unauslöschliche Flamme, 1947)
My — sovetskie ljudi (Wir sind Sowjetmenschen, 1948, *Stalinpreis* 1949)
Vernulsja (Heimkehr, 1949)
Zoloto (Gold, 1950)
Sovremenniki (Zeitgenossen, 1952)
Moskvička (Die Moskauerin, 1955)
Nikolaič i Nina (Nikolaič und Nina, 1956)
Amerikanskij dnevnik (Amerikanisches Tagebuch, 1956)
Glubokij tyl (Hinterland, 1958)

Deutsche Übersetzungen

Der wahre Mensch, übers. v. Oswald Tornberg, Dresden, Sachsenverlag. 1950, 1951, 1952, 1953. Berlin, Verlag Kultur und Fortschritt. 1956.

Gold. Der deutschen Fassung liegt eine Übersetzung v. M. Bork zugrunde, Berlin, Kultur und Fortschritt. 1953, 1954, 1955.

Neue Erzählungen, übers. v. Hilde Angarowa u. M. Paul, Bukarest, Verlag Arlus-Cartea rusă. 1953.

Frontlinie Eisenstraße (My — sovetskie ljudi), nach der Übers. v. Wolfgang Müller, Berlin, Verlag Kultur und Fortschritt. 1954.

Druckfehlerverzeichnis

Seite 9, Zeile 10: v perevodach na inostrannye statt: v perevodach no inostrannye

Seite 16, Zeile 12: 1934 statt: 1943

Seite 23, Zeile 4: 1879-1950 statt: Geb. 1879

Seite 62, Zeile 15: Geb. 1895 im Orte statt: 1895-1955, geb. im Orte

Seite 77, Zeile 4: 1870-1938 statt: 1970-1938

Seite 78, Zeile 17: 1891-1559 statt: Geb. 1891

Seite 125, Zeile 7: 1875-1958, geb. statt: Geb. 1875

Seite 157, Zeile 24: estetstvo statt: estestvo

Heimkehr, übers. v. Arnold Boettcher, Leipzig, Reclam. 1954.
Zeitgenossen, übers. v. Hilde Angarowa u. Gertrud Daberkow-Schmid, Berlin, Verlag Kultur und Fortschritt. 1955.
Der Querkopf (Gorjačij cech), übers. v. Dora Hofmeister, Berlin, Verlag Kultur und Fortschritt. 1956.
Skizzen in der Zeitung, Berlin, Dietz. 1953.
Hinter der Front, übers. v. Peter Murkel, Moskau, S. L. 1959.

Popóvkin Evgénij Efímovič

Geb. 1907. Er absolvierte die literarische Fakultät der Moskauer Universität. Seit 1927 ist P. Mitglied der KPdSU. Als linientreuer Sowjetschriftsteller richtete P. während des 3. Plenums des Sowjetischen Schriftstellerverbandes im Mai 1957 heftige Angriffe gegen die im Sammelband „Literaturnaja Moskva" vertretenen Autoren und beschuldigte sie, die kommunistische Ideologie „aufzuweichen".

Družba (Freundschaft, 1934)
Bol'šoj razliv (Die große Überschwemmung, 1947)
Sem'ja Rubanjuk (Die Familie Rubanjuk, 1951, *Stalinpreis* 1952)

Príšvin Michaíl Michájlovič

1873—1954, geb. im Dorfe Chruščëvo bei El'zy im Gouvernement Orël, einer Kaufmannsfamilie entstammend. Wegen marxistischer Umtriebe von 1897 bis 1899 in Haft, studierte P. dann in Leipzig Bodenkultur. P.s vorzügliche Kenntnis der russischen Natur und Tierwelt, die er sich auf vielen Fußwanderungen durch die Weiten Nordrußlands erwarb, kommt in seinen stimmungsvollen Gedichten und Erzählungen immer wieder zum Ausdruck. Er wurde darin von Turgenevs „Aufzeichnungen eines Jägers" beeinflußt.

V kraju nepuganych ptic (Im Land der zahmen Vögel, 1905)
Čërnyj arab (Der schwarze Araber, 1911)
V kraju deduški (Im Lande des Großvaters, 1923—1945)
Kalendar' prirody (Der Naturkalender, 1925)
Rodniki Berendeja (Berendejs Quellen, 1926)

Kaščeeva cep' (Kaščevs Kette, 1923—1936)
Žen'-šen' (Dschen-Schen, 1932)
Kladovaja solnca (Der Sonnenspeicher, 1945)
Molodoj kolchoznik (Der junge Kolchozbauer, 1955)
Neopublikovannye zapiski (Unveröffentlichte Aufzeichnungen, 1956)

Deutsche Übersetzungen

Dschen-Schen, übers. v. Dr. Irene Barth, Vorw. v. Maxim Gorki, Wien, Scholle-Verlag. 1947. Übers. v. Manfred von Busch, red. v. Joachim Barckhausen, Leipzig, Reclam. 1951, 1952. Leipzig, Insel-Verlag. 1955. Auch unter dem Titel ,Ginseng', München, Nymphenburger Verlagsbuchh. 1960.

Der Sonnenspeicher, übers. v. Nadesha Ludwig, Berlin-Leipzig, SWA-Verlag. 1949.

Die Flöte Pans (Erzählungen und Skizzen), übers. v. Manfred von Busch, Berlin, Verlag Volk und Welt. 1948.

Meine Landsleute (Tiernovellen), übers. v. Juri Elperin, Moskau, S. L. 1957.

Geheimnisse des Waldes (V kraju deduški), übers. v. J. Dembovski, Berlin, Holz. 1952, 1953.

Der schwarze Araber, übers. v. A. Eliasberg, München. 1917.

Prokóf'ev Aleksándr Andréevič

Geb. 1900 im Gebiet des Ladogasees als Sohn eines Fischers. 1919 trat P. der Kommunistischen Partei bei und nahm auch an den Bürgerkriegskämpfen aktiv teil. Während des 2. Weltkrieges war P. an der finnischen Front im Einsatz. In seinen Gedichten lehnt er sich stark an den Wortschatz der russischen Volkspoesie an.

Polden' (Mittag, 1931)
Ulica krasnych zor' (Die Straße des Morgenrots, 1931)
Rossija (Rußland, 1944, *Stalinpreis* 1946)
Stichotvorenija (Gedichte, 1950)
V puti (Unterwegs, 1953)
Junost' (Jugend, 1955)

Deutsche Übersetzungen

Mond, übers. v. Veronika Chorwat, Moskau, S. L. 1958.

Rádov Geórgij Geórgievič

Der Dichter wird von der sowjetischen Kritik der gleichen „neuen Richtung“ zugeordnet wie V. *Ovečkin*, V. *Tendrjakov*, D. *Granin*, G. *Troepol'skij*. Im Gegensatz zu den *lakirovščiki* sehen diese Dichter die Konflikte des heutigen russischen Lebens in ihrer wahren Sicht.

Šef (Der Chef, 1954)
Zvëdy (Sterne, 1955)
Na ulice kazačej (Auf der Kosakenstraße, 1955)
Četyre stročki (Vier Zeilen, 1956)
Čekmarëv (1957)
Voskresnyj rasskaz (Sonntagserzählung, 1958)
Tëšča (Die Schwiegermutter, 1958)

Réjsner Larísa Micháјlovna

1895—1926, geb. in Odessa, aus einer Intellektuellenfamilie stammend. Sie begann ihre schriftstellerische Tätigkeit im Jahre 1907, wobei sie stark unter dem Einfluß der *Akmeisten*, vor allem *Gumilëvs*, stand. In ihren Gedichten verwendet sie häufig Metaphern. 1914, erst 19 Jahre alt, gab R. zusammen mit ihrem Vater die Zeitschrift „Rudin“ heraus. Bei Ausbruch der Revolution schließt sie sich sofort dieser an und wird 1918 Kommissar des Moskauer Generalstabs. 1918—1919 verfaßte R. lyrisch-dramatische Skizzen über den Bürgerkrieg, welche 1924 in einem Band „Die Front“ erschienen.

Afganistan (Afghanistan, 1923)
Hamburg na barrikadach (Hamburg auf den Barrikaden, 1923)
Front (Die Front, 1924)
Ugol', železo i živye ljudi (Kohle, Eisen und lebende Menschen, 1924)
Dekabristy (Die Dekabristen, 1925)

Románov Pantelejmón Sergéevič

1884—1938, geb. im Dorfe Petrovskoe im Gouvernement Tula. R. absolvierte das Gymnasium in Tula und studierte Rechtswissenschaft an der Moskauer Universität. Er begann seine literarische Tätigkeit im Jahre 1917. R. wurde zum Chronisten der nachrevolutionären Wirklichkeit. Mit Vorliebe befaßte er sich in seinen Werken mit Fragen der modernen Ehe und den Beziehungen des Mannes mit der „befreiten" Frau. In der Behandlung der Themen, zum Beispiel in den Erzählungen „Komnata" (Das Zimmer), „Svjataja ženščina" (Die heilige Frau) und anderen, nimmt das Anekdotenhafte einen breiten Raum ein. Von der sowjetischen Kritik wird R. als destruktiv bezeichnet.

Bez čerëmuchi (Ohne Myrten, 1926)
Tovarišč Kisljakov (Genosse Kisljakov, 1930)
Rus' (Rußland, 1936) 5 Bde.

Deutsche Übersetzungen

Drei Paar Seidenstrümpfe (Tovarišč Kisljakov), übers. v. Markus Joffe, Berlin, Universitas. 1932.

Roždéstvenskij Robért Ivánovič

Geb. 1932 im Dorfe Kosicha im Rayon Kosichinskij (Altajgebiet), entstammt einer Offiziersfamilie. 1950 inskribierte er an der Karelo-Finnischen staatlichen Universität, trat aber bald ins Gor'kij-Institut für Literatur über, das er im Jahre 1956 absolvierte. Sein literarisches Debut feierte R. bereits im Jahre 1949. Sein erster Gedichtband, „Flagi vesny" (Flaggen des Frühlings), erschien 1955 in Petrozavodsk. (nach ANT)

Moja ljubov' (Meine Liebe, 1956)
Stichi i poemy (Gedichte und Poeme, 1956)

Rybakóv Anatólij Naúmovič (Pseudonym für Arónov)

Geb. 1911. R. studierte Volkswirtschaft und diente 1941—1945 als Soldat. Seine Werke werden seit 1948 veröffentlicht. Bekannt ist R. durch seinen Roman „Voditeli" (Menschen am Steuer) geworden.

Kortik (Der Marinedolch, 1950)
Voditeli (Menschen am Steuer, 1950, *Stalinpreis* 1951)
Ekaterina Voronina (1955)

Deutsche Übersetzungen

Menschen am Steuer, übers. v. Alexander Böltz, Berlin, Verlag Kultur und Fortschritt. 1951, 1953.
Der Marinedolch (Kortik), übers. v. B. Pasch, Berlin, Verlag Neues Leben. 1953.

Safónov Vadím Andréevič

Geb. 1904 in Kerč auf der Krim als Sohn eines Eisenbahningenieurs. Mit 16 Jahren trat S. ins Berufsleben ein und arbeitete als Gehilfe in einer Mühle und später bei einem Fischer. Seine literarische Tätigkeit begann er im Januar 1923 mit Gedichten, Erzählungen und Skizzen. Das erste größere Werk S.s, „Lamarck und Darwin", das dem Genre nach als wissenschaftliche Belletristik bezeichnet werden kann, erschien 1930. Seit dieser Zeit veröffentlichte S. mehr als 20 Bücher, darunter „Erde in Blüte", „Der Weg in die Weite", „Auf den Bergen ist Freiheit" und das unlängst vollendete Reiseskizzenbuch „Reise in ein fremdes Land". (nach S.L.)

Doroga na prostor (Der Weg in die Weite, 1945)
Zemlja v cvetu (Die Erde in Blüte, 1949)
Besstrašie (Furchtlosigkeit, 1951)
V Zakarpatskoj Ukraine (Transkarpaten-Ukraine)

Deutsche Übersetzungen

Furchtlosigkeit, Bukarest, Verlag Cartea rusă. 1953.
Transkarpaten-Ukraine, Berlin, SWA. 1948.

Šaginján Mariétta Sergéevna

Geb. 1888 in Moskau als Tochter eines Arztes. Š ist armenischer Herkunft. Seit 1942 ist sie Mitglied der KPdSU. 1945 promovierte sie zum Doktor der Philosophie. In ihrem dichterischen Schaffen gehörte sie in ihrer Jugend der Richtung der *Symbolisten* an, stellte sich aber in den dreißiger Jahren auf den offiziellen *sozialistischen Realismus* um. Ihre Werke wurden bei einer Gesamtauflage von 1 386 000 Exemplaren in 6 Sprachen übersetzt.

Pervye vstreči (Erste Begegnungen, 1909)
Svoja sud'ba (Das eigene Schicksal, 1923)
Priključenija damy iz obščestva (Die Abenteuer einer Dame aus der Gesellschaft, 1923)
Mess-Mend (1935) 3 Teile
KiK (K und K, 1928)
Gidrocentral' (Das Wasserkraftwerk, 1930)
Taras Ševčenko (1945)
Gëte (Goethe, 1950)
Sem'ja Ul'janovych (Die Familie Uljanov, 1957)
Dela i ljudi Armenii (Leben und Leute in Armenien, 1942—1943)
Ural v oborone (Ural im Abwehrkampf, 1944)
Po dorogam pjatiletki (Auf den Wegen des Fünfjahresplanes, 1947)
Putešestvie po sovetskoj Armenii (Reise durch Sowjetarmenien, 1950, *Stalinpreis* 1951)

Deutsche Übersetzungen

Abenteuer einer Dame, übers. v. Maria Einstein, Berlin, Malik-Verlag. 1924.
Das Wasserkraftwerk (Gidrocentral'), übers. v. Helene Korinetz, Moskau-Leningrad, Verlagsgenossenschaft ausländischer Arbeiter in der UdSSR. 1934. Zürich, Ring-Verlag. 1934. Übers. v. Alexander Böltz, Berlin, Dietz. 1952.
Leben und Leute in Armenien, übers. v. E. Rosenberg, Berlin, SWA. 1947.
Eine Reise durch Sowjetarmenien, übers. v. F. Loesch, Berlin, Kultur und Fortschritt. 1953.
Goethe, übers. v. Traute Stein, Berlin, Verlag Kultur und Fortschritt. 1954.
Die Familie Uljanov, Berlin, Verlag Kultur und Forschritt. 1959.

Ščipačëv Stepán Petróvič

Geb. 1899 im Dorfe Ščipači, im Gouvernement Perm', als Sohn einer Bauernfamilie. Im Jahre 1919 trat er in die Rote Armee ein und wurde Mitglied der Kommunistischen Partei. Von 1922 bis 1929 war Š. Lehrer an Militärschulen in Sevastopol' und Moskau. In den folgenden Jahren war Š. als Redakteur tätig und widmete sich in der Folge wissenschaftlicher Arbeit. Seine ersten Gedichte erschienen 1923 im Druck. „Die ersten zehn Jahre seines dichterischen Schaffens waren für ihn eine Zeit des beharrlichen Suchens nach dem eigenen Weg. 1936 verfaßte Š. mehrere lyrische Gedichte, die von seiner Berufung als Lyriker zeugen" (S. L. 1959/4). 1956 veröffentlichte Š. die autobiographische Prosaerzählung „Berëzovyj sok" (Der Birkensaft).

Gedichte (1948, *Stalinpreis* 1949)
Domik v Šušenskom (Das Häuschen in Šušenskoe, 1944)
Pavlik Morozov (1950, *Stalinpreis* 1951)
Berëzovyj sok (Der Birkensaft, 1956)

Deutsche Übersetzungen

Liebesgedichte, Berlin, Verlag Kultur und Fortschritt. 1950.
Lyrische Gedichte, übers. v. Alfred Kurella, Moskau, Verlag für fremdsprachige Literatur. 1952.
Gedicht. Der Tag, da Lenin zur Welt kam, übers. v. Franz Leschnitzer, Moskau, S. L. 1959.

Sejfúllina Lídija Nikoláevna

1889—1954, geb. in der Stanica Varlamova im Gouvernement Orenburg. Der Vater war Pfarrer, die Mutter stammte aus einer bäuerlichen Familie. In ihren Adern floß auch Tatarenblut. S. wurde 1906 Lehrerin, ab 1917 war sie vorerst im Ural, später in Sibirien in der Volksbildung tätig. Ihre in den zwanziger Jahren erschienenen Werke behandeln vornehmlich das Leben auf dem Dorf in den ersten Jahren der Revolution und des Bürgerkrieges.

Pravonarušiteli (Die Rechtsbrecher, 1922)
Aleksander Makedonskij (Alexander von Mazedonien, 1922)
Peregnoj (Humus, 1922)
Mužickij skaz o Lenine (Bäuerliche Erzählungen über Lenin, 1924)
Virineja (1925)
Sobstvennost' (Eigentum, 1933)

Tanja (1934)
Molodost' (Die Jugend, 1934)
Na svoej zemle (Auf eigener Scholle, 1941—1945)

Deutsche Übersetzungen

Der Ausreißer (Pravonarušiteli), übers. v. Maria Einstein, Berlin, Malik-Verlag. 1925. Göttingen, Verlag Öffentliches Leben. 1948.
Wirineja, übers. v. Maria Einstein, Berlin, Malik-Verlag. 1925. Übers. v. Hans Ruoff, Berlin, Malik-Verlag. 1930, 1931.

Sel'vínskij Il'já L'vóvič

Geb. 1899, aus einer bürgerlichen Familie aus Simferopol' stammend. Er studierte zunächst an einem katholischen Gymnasium in Konstantinopel, wurde dann Matrose, nahm am Bürgerkrieg teil und immatrikulierte dann an der Moskauer Universität. S. gilt als hervorragender Vertreter der *Konstruktivisten.* Seine ersten Gedichte erschienen 1926. Einige seiner Gedichte wurden von der Sowjetkritik zur Zeit *Ždanovs* als ideologisch labil gestempelt.

Uljalaevščina (1927)
Zapiski poeta (Die Aufzeichnungen eines Dichters, 1928)
Puštorg (1929)
Pao-Pao (1932)
Ryzar' Joann (Der Bauernarzt, 1956)
General Brusilov (1943)
Livonskaja vojna (Der livländische Krieg, 1944)

Deutsche Übersetzungen

Der Bauernarzt (Ryzar' Joann), Tragödie in 5 Akten, übertr. v. A. Rohde-Liebenau, Berlin, Aufbau-Bühnen-Vertrieb. 1946.

Semënov Sergéj Terént'evič

1868—1922, geb. im Dorfe Andreevskaja, im Gouvernement Moskau, als Sohn eines Bauern. S. begann seine literarische Tätigkeit im Jahre 1887 und stand in der Frühzeit seines Schaffens unter dem Einfluß von Leo Tolstoj. In den Werken, die nach 1917 erschienen, behandelt S. das Leben im sowjetischen Dorf.

Novoe krest'janskoe chozjajstvo (Die neue bäuerliche Wirtschaft, 1922)
Novyj chozjain (Der neue Herr, 1924)

Sëmuškin Tíchon Zachárovič

Geb. 1900 in Staraja Kutlja, im Gouvernement Penza. Er studierte an der Universität Moskau und war in der Folge als Mitglied verschiedener Expeditionen, vor allem auf Čukotka, tätig. Er stellte das erste čukotische Wörterbuch zusammen und schreibt auch in seinen Werken hauptsächlich über das Leben dieses Volkes. S. ist seit 1952 Mitglied der KPdSU. Seine Werke wurden bei einer Auflage von 2 196 000 Exemplaren in 26 Sprachen übersetzt.

Na Čukotke (Im Land der Tschukatschen, 1939)
Škola na Čukotke (Die Schule auf Čukotka, 1931)
Russkaja Amerika (Russisches Amerika, 1947)
Alitet uchodit v gory (Alitet geht in die Berge, 1948, *Stalinpreis* 1949)

Deutsche Übersetzungen

Brand in der Polarnacht (Alitet uchodit v gory), übers. v. Veronica Ensslen (1. Buch) u. Otto Braun (2. Buch), Berlin, Verlag Kultur und Fortschritt. 1949, 1951, 1953, 1955. Auch unter dem Titel ‚Alitet geht in die Berge', übers v. Otto Braun, Moskau, Verlag für fremdsprachige Literatur. 1950, 1952.

Im Land der Tschukatschen (Na Čukotke), übers. v. F. Loesch, Berlin, Verlag Kultur und Fortschritt. 1953.

Serafimóvič Aleksándr Serafímovič (Pseudonym für Popóv)

1863—1949, geb. in Nižne-Kurmojarskaja Stanica (Kosakendorf) als Sohn eines Kosakenoffiziers. Seine Jugend verbrachte S. in ärmlichen Verhältnissen. Politisch stand er den Sozialdemokraten nahe und wurde ein prominenter Mitarbeiter in *Gor'kijs* literarischer Gruppe *Znanie*. Während seiner Studien in St. Petersburg lernte er dort Lenins älteren Bruder (A. J. Uljanov) kennen und arbeitete mit ihm an der revolutionären Bewegung, was schließlich zu seiner Verhaftung und Verbannung führte, in der er bis 1890 lebte. Während dieser Zeit begann er seine literarische Tätigkeit, als deren erstes Werk 1889 eine Erzählung veröffentlicht wurde. Bei Ausbruch der Revolution war S. einer der ersten namhaften Schriftsteller der älteren Generation, die für die neuen Machthaber Partei ergriffen. 1942 wurde im der *Stalinpreis*, später auch der Leninorden verliehen. Seine Werke wurden in 42 Sprachen übersetzt und erreichten eine Auflage von 10 993 000 Bücher.

Na l'du (Auf der Eisscholle, 1887)

Na Presne (Im Stadtviertel Presnja, 1905—1907)

Mërtvye na ulicach (Tote auf den Straßen, 1907)

Gorod v stepi (Stadt in der Steppe, 1907—1910)

Myšinoe carstvo (Das Reich der Mäuse, 1913)

Vstreča (Begegnung, 1915)

Galina (1917)

Mar'jana (Marianne, 1918)

Železnyj potok (Der eiserne Strom, 1924)

Deutsche Übersetzungen

Der eiserne Strom, übers. v. Eduard Schiemann, Berlin, Neuer Deutscher Verlag. 1925. London, Malik-Verlag. 1935. Moskau-Leningrad, Verlagsgenossenschaft ausländischer Arbeiter in der UdSSR. 1935. Berlin-Leipzig, SWA-Verlag. 1947. Moskau, Verlag für fremdsprachige Literatur. 1948. Berlin, Verlag Kultur und Fortschritt. 1952. Nachw. v. Ralf Schröder, Leipzig, Reclam. 1955.

Marianne. Bühnenstück in 4 Aufz., bearb. v. G. Luft, Moskau, Zentralverlag der Völker der Sowjetunion. 1928.

Stadt in der Steppe, übers. v. I. Dölling, bearb. u. Nachw. v. Günter Pössiger, Weimar, Thüringer Volksverlag. 1953.

Im Stadtviertel Presnja, übers. v. Alfred Kittner u. Ilse Goldmann, Bukarest, Verlag Cartea rusă. 1955.

Ausgewählte Werke, übers. v. Friedrich Schwarz, Bd. 1 und 2, Berlin, Aufbau-Verlag. 1956.

Galina, übers. v. Horst Wolf, Leipzig, Reclam. 1953.

Auf der Eisscholle, übers. v. E. Kolodny, Char'kov, Zentralverlag. 1930.

Sergéev-Cénskij Sergéj Nikoláevič

Geb. 1875 im Dorfe Preobraženskoe, im Gouvernement Tambov, als Sohn eines Offiziers. S.-C. ergriff den Beruf eines Lehrers und betätigte sich ab 1901 auf literarischem Gebiet. Seine frühen Arbeiten behandeln das Leben der russischen Intelligenz nach der Revolution von 1905 und sind von der *dekadenten* Stimmung der damaligen Zeit überschattet. Später widmet sich S.-C. hauptsächlich historischen Romanen, in denen er den Krimkrieg und Ereignisse des ersten Weltkrieges behandelt, z. B. „Puški vydvigajut" (Geschütze gehen in Stellung). Seit 1943 ist S.-C. Mitglied der Akademie der Wissenschaften und wurde auch mit dem Leninorden ausgezeichnet.

Dumy i grëzy (Gedanken und Träume, 1901)

Tundra (1903)

Valja (1914)

Preobraženie Rossii (Rußlands Umgestaltung, eine Romanfolge, wird seit 1917 geschrieben)

Sevastopol'skaja strada (Die heißen Tage von Sevastopol', 3 Bde. 1938, *Stalinpreis* 1941)

Nastojaščie ljudi (Echte Menschen, 1943)

Deutsche Übersetzungen

Die heißen Tage von Sevastopol (Sevastopol'skaja strada), übers. v. Josefine Kieseritzky, Bd. 1 und 2. Berlin, Rütten & Loening. 1953.

Der Obstgarten, übers. v. Elisabeth u. Wladimir Wonsiatsky, Leipzig, Reclam. 1955.

Símonov Konstantín (Kiríll) Michájlovič

Geb. 1915 in Petrograd als Sohn eines Offiziers. 1942 wurde S. Mitglied der KPdSU und später Abgeordneter des Obersten Sowjets der RSFSR. Im Jahre 1938 absolvierte er das Gor'kij-Institut für Literatur. Seine Werke, die seit 1934 erscheinen, wurden bisher in 38 Sprachen übersetzt und haben eine Auflage von 15 987 000 erreicht. Viele Gedichte S.s sind Allgemeingut geworden, wie z. B. „Ubej ego!" (Töte ihn!), „Ždi menja" (Warte auf mich), „Ty pomniš', Alëša, dorogi Smolenščiny..." (Die Straßen von Smolensk bleiben unvergeßlich, Alëša...).

Pavel Cërnyj (1938)

Nastojaščie ljudi (Echte Menschen, 1938)

Dorožnye stichi (Reisegedichte, 1939)

Suvorov (1939)

Istorija odnoj ljubvi (Die Geschichte einer Liebe, 1940, als Umarbeitung „Obyknovennaja istorija" Eine gewöhnliche Geschichte, 1940)

Pobeditel' (Der Sieger, 1941)

Daleko na vostoke (Fern im Osten, 1941)

Paren' iz našego goroda (Ein Bursche aus unserer Stadt, 1941, *Stalinpreis* 1942)

Russkie ljudi (Russische Menschen, 1942, *Stalinpreis* 1943)

Dni i noči (Tage und Nächte, 1944, *Stalinpreis* 1946)

Tak i budet (So wird es sein, 1944)

S toboj i bez tebja (Mit dir und ohne dich, 1944)

Pod kaštanami Pragi (Unter den Kastanien von Prag, 1945)

Russkij vopros (Die russische Frage, 1946, *Stalinpreis* 1947)

Druz'ja i vragi (Freunde und Feinde, 1948, *Stalinpreis* 1949)

Čužaja ten' (Der fremde Schatten, 1949, *Stalinpreis* 1950)

Torvarišči po oružiju (Waffenbrüder, 1950—1952)

Dobroe imja (Der gute Ruf, 1953)

Stichi 1954 goda (Gedichte des Jahres 1954, 1954)

Živye i mërtvye (Die Lebenden und die Toten, 1959)

Deutsche Übersetzungen

Die russische Frage. Schauspiel in 3 Aufz. u 7 Bildern, Berlin, Verlag Tägliche Rundschau. 1947. Übers. v. Ilja Bakkal, bearb. v. Theodor Popp, Berlin, Henschel & Sohn. 1947.

Tage und Nächte, übers. v. E. Margolis und R. Czora, Berlin-Leipzig, SWA-Verlag. 1947. Neubearb. v. Siegfried u. Lydia Behrsing, Berlin, Verlag Volk und Welt. 1948, 1953.

Freunde und Feinde, übers. v. Hugo Huppert, Moskau, Verlag für fremdsprachige Literatur. 1950.

Lyrik eines Jahrzehnts (Ausgewählte Gedichte), übertr. v. Edgar Thoss, Berlin, Verlag Kultur und Fortschritt. 1952.

Der fremde Schatten. Drama in 4 Akten, 6 Bildern, übers. v. Veronica Ensslen, Berlin, Aufbau-Bühnen-Vertrieb. 1950.

So wird es sein. Ein Stück in 3 Akten u. 6 Bildern, übertr. v. M. Einstein, Berlin-Charlottenburg, Henschel. 1947.

Wart auf mich! übers. v. Klara Blum, Auswahl russischer Reportagen, Wien, Stern-Verlag. 1946.

Der Sohn, Kazachisches Sprichwort (aus der Sammlung ‚Mit dir und ohne dich'), übers. v. Sepp Österreicher, Moskau, S. L. 1957.

Die Lebenden und die Toten, übers. v. Alexander Kaempfe und Maria Lampus, Berlin, Verlag bei Kindler. 1960.

Šklóvskij Víktor Borísovič

Geb. 1893. Š. studierte an der St. Petersburger Universität Literatur und stand zu Beginn seiner literarischen Laufbahn („Voskresenie slova", Die Auferstehung des Wortes, 1914 und „Svincovyj žrebij", Das bleierne Los, 1914) den *Futuristen* nahe. Später wandte er sich jedoch dem *Formalismus* zu und gehörte im Jahre 1914 zu den Mitbegründern der Vereinigung *Opojaz.* Seit dem Jahre 1929, als der *Formalismus* von der Partei als eine im Widerspruch zur kommunistischen Ideologie stehende literarische Richtung verurteilt wurde, wandte sich S. dem historischen Roman zu.

Iskusstvo kak priëm (Die Kunst als Methode, 1917)
O teorii prozy (Über die Theorie der Prosa, 1925)

Tret'ja fabrika (Die dritte Fabrik, 1926)
Marko Polo (1932)
Minin i Požarskij (1940)
Zametki o proze russkich klassikov (Bemerkungen über die Prosa russischer Klassiker, 2. Auflage 1955)
Čtoby lučše znat' drug druga ... (Um einander besser zu kennen ..., 1956)

Slúckij Borís Abrámovič

Geb. 1919 in Slavjansk, im Gebiet Stalinsk, als Sohn eines Angestellten. S. absolvierte die Mittelschule in Char'kov und studierte 1937—1941 Rechtswissenschaft und am Gor'kij-Institut für Literatur. Im Jahre 1941 ging er als Freiwilliger an die Front. Im selben Jahr begann er, sich auch literarisch zu betätigen. Nach Kriegsende, von 1948 bis 1952, war S. beim Rundfunk tätig. Seine Gedichte erfreuten sich in der Literaturnaja gazeta vom 28. 7. 1956 einer wohlwollenden Kritik *Erenburgs*.

Gedichtsammlung Pamjat' (Erinnerung, 1957)

Smirnóv Sergéj Sergéevič

Geb. 1915 in Petrograd. Im Jahre 1931 arbeitete S. in einem elektromechanischen Werk in Char'kov und studierte von 1932 bis 1937 am Energetischen Institut in Moskau. Von 1937 bis 1941 war er Student am Gor'kij-Literaturinstitut. Während des 2. Weltkrieges war S. vorerst Soldat, später Kriegsberichterstatter. Im Jahre 1946 trat er der KPdSU bei und war in der Folge bei der Moskauer Organisation des sowjetischen *Schriftstellerverbandes* tätig. Als Schriftsteller ist S. erst nach dem Krieg bekannt geworden, vor allem durch seine Kriegsschilderungen.

V bojach za Budapešt (In den Kämpfen um Budapest, 1947)
Dinastija Kazancevych (Die Dynastie Kazancev, 1949)

Stalingrad na Dnepre (Stalingrad am Dnepr, 1954)
Na poljach Vengrii (Auf den Feldern Ungarns, 1954)
Krepost' nad Bugom (Die Festung am Bug, 1955)
Krepost' na granice (Die Festung an der Grenze, 1956)

Deutsche Übersetzungen

Die Dynastie der Kasanzews, übertr. v. A. Nestmann, Berlin, Dietz. 1952.

Smirnóv Sergéj Vasil'evič

Geb. 1913 in Jalta. S. absolvierte das Gor'kij-Institut für Literatur in Moskau und veröffentlichte sein Erstlingswerk im Jahre 1934. Sein erster Gedichtband erschien 1948 („Freunde"). Zusammen mit den Schriftstellern *Gribačëv* und Krivickij verfaßte S. im Jahre 1956 das Reiseskizzenbuch „Wunderschöne Desna". S. ist der Sekretär des *Schriftstellerverbandes* der UdSSR.

S novym godom (Prosit zum neuen Jahre, 1950)
V gostjach i doma (Zu Gast und daheim, 1958)

Sóbolev Leoníd Sergéevič

Geb. 1898 in Irkutsk als Sohn eines Offiziers. Er besuchte die Kadettenschule in St. Petersburg und diente von 1918 bis 1931 in der Kriegsmarine. Auf literarischem Gebiet ist S. seit 1925 tätig. Er behandelte in seinen Werken zunächst Themen über die russische Flotte, später spezialisierte er sich auf die kazachische Literatur. S. ist Vorsitzender des *Schriftstellerverbandes* der RSFSR.

Kapital'nyj remont (Die Generalreparatur, 1932)
Morskaja duša (Die Seele des Meeres, 1942, *Stalinpreis* 1943)
Zelënyj luč (Der grüne Strahl, 1954)

Deutsche Übersetzungen

Der grüne Strahl, übers. v. Juri Elperin, Berlin, Verlag des Ministeriums für Nationale Verteidigung. 1956.

Sofrónov Anatólij Vladímirovič

Geb. 1911 in Minsk, verbrachte seine Jugend am Don. Er absolvierte im Jahre 1937 die literarische Fakultät des Pädagogischen Instituts in Rostov. Seine ersten literarischen Arbeiten entstanden bereits im Jahre 1930. Der Schwerpunkt der Dichtung S.s liegt in zeitgenössischen Dramen, die in ihrem psychologischen Aufbau zwar etwas primitiv, aber wegen ihrer aktuellen Thematik sehr erfolgreich sind. Seit 1940 ist S. Mitglied der KPdSU.

Solnečnye dni (Sonnige Tage, 1934)
Storona Donskaja (Das Land am Don, 1940)
Stepnye soldaty (Soldaten der Steppe, 1944)
V odnom gorode (In einer Stadt, 1946, *Stalinpreis* 1948)
Moskovskij charakter (Der Moskauer Charakter, 1949, *Stalinpreis* 1949)
Kar'era Beketova (Die Karriere Beketovs, 1949)
Serdce ne proščaet (Das Herz vergibt nicht, 1954)
Den'gi (Geld, 1956)
Čelovek v otstavke (Ein Mann außer Dienst, 1957)

Deutsche Übersetzungen

In einer Stadt. Schauspiel in 3 Aufz. u. 6 Bildern, übers. v. E. Baer, Berlin, Henschel. 1952.
Gedicht. Morgen in Delhi, übers. v. Sepp Österreicher, Moskau, S. L. 1959.

Šólochov Michaíl Aleksándrovič

Geb. am 24. Mai 1905 in Kružilin im Dongebiet. Er besuchte das Gymnasium, verließ es aber 1918 wegen der Revolutionswirren. Seit 1922 lebt Š. meist in Moskau. 1932 trat er der KPdSU bei und wurde 1936 Deputierter zum Obersten Sowjet der UdSSR. Seine Laufbahn als Schriftsteller begann Š. im Jahre 1923 mit der Veröffentlichung seiner ersten Erzählung in der Zeitung „Junošeskaja pravda". Das Hauptthema in Š.s Schaffen ist das Leben der Kosaken. Mit seinem in epenhafter Breite angelegten Roman „Tichij Don" (Der stille Don) errang er sowohl in der Sowjetunion als auch im Ausland einen einzigartigen Erfolg. Š. gilt in der SU als klassischer Vertreter des *sozialistischen Realismus.* Er ist sicherlich einer der begabtesten und innerlich freiesten Dichter der russischen Literatur der Gegenwart. Seine Werke wurden bei einer Auflage von 20 559 000 Exemplaren bisher in 55 Sprachen übersetzt.

Donskie rasskazy (Erzählungen vom Don, 1925)
Tichij Don (Der stille Don, 1928—1940, *Stalinpreis* 1941)
Podnjataja celina (Neuland unterm Pflug, 1932)
Nauka nenavisti (Die Wissenschaft des Hasses, 1942)
Oni sražalis' za rodinu (Sie kämpften für die Heimat, 1943—1954)
Pervenec velkich stroek (Der erste Großbau, 1952)
Sud'ba čeloveka (Das Schicksal des Menschen, 1956—1957)

Deutsche Übersetzungen

Der stille Don, übers. v. Olga Halpern, Berlin, Verlag für Literatur und Politik. 1929. Bd. 2, Berlin, Verlag für Literatur und Politik. 1930. Übers. v. Olga Halpern, Bd. 1—3, London, Malik-Verlag. 1934—1936. Bd. 1, Moskau-Leningrad, Verlagsgenossenschaft ausländischer Arbeiter in der UdSSR. 1935. Bd. 1—3, Zürich, Büchergilde Gutenberg. 1943. München-Leipzig-Freiburg, P. List. 1947. Bd. 1—2, Berlin, Verlag Volk und Welt. 1947. 6. Aufl. Bd. 1—2, Berlin, Verlag Volk und Welt. 1953. Bd. 3—4, übers. v. E. Margolis und R. Czora, Berlin, Verlag Volk und Welt. 1948. 7. Aufl. Bd. 1—4, übers. v. Olga Halpern (Bd. 1, 2), E. Margolis und R. Czora (Bd. 3, 4), Berlin, Verlag Volk und Welt. 1953, 1954. Buch 4, übers. v. E. Margolis und R. Czora, neu bearb. v. Maximilian Schick, Moskau, Verlag für fremdsprachige Literatur. 1954. 8. Aufl. neubearb. u. übers. v. Maximilian Schick, Berlin, Verlag Volk und Welt. 1957.

Neuland unterm Pflug, übers. v. Boris Krotkow und Georg Stephan Stoessler, Wien, Büchergilde Gutenberg. 1945. Bd. 1, Berlin, SWA-Verlag. 1946, 1947. Neubearb. v. Nelly Held, Berlin, Verlag Volk und Welt. 1952, 1954, 1955, 1956.

Der erste Großbau, Bukarest, Cartea rusă Verlag. 1952.

Ein Menschenschicksal, übers. v. Juri Elperin, Moskau, S. L. 1957.

Sie kämpften für ihr Vaterland (Kapitel aus dem Roman ‚Oni szažalis' za rodinu'), übers. v. Hilde Angarowa, Moskau, S. L. 1959.

Schule des Hasses (Nauka nenavisti), übers. v. Hilde Angarowa, Wien, Stern-Verlag. 1946.

Sologúb Fëdor Kuz'míč (Pseudonym für Tetérnikov)

1863—1927, ist einer der prominentesten Vertreter des russischen *Symbolismus.* Charakteristisch für ihn ist die in seinen Werken vorherrschende Verfallsstimmung und Angst vor der Wirklichkeit. S. vertrat bis 1917 revolutionäre Ideen, ging aber nach der Revolution in die *innere Emigration.* Er blieb wohl weiterhin in Rußland, konnte aber wie viele andere Intellektuelle keinen Anschluß an das neue Leben finden. Von S. stammt auch eine Übersetzung von Voltaires „Candide".

Melkij bes (Der kleine Teufel, 1905)
Pobeda smerti (Der Sieg des Todes, 1907)
Založniki (Geiseln, 1909)
Ljubov' nad bezdnami (Liebe über Abgründen, 1914)
Zaklinatel'nica zmej (Die Schlangenbeschwörerin, 1921)

Sótnik Júrij Vjačeslávovič

Geb. 1914 in Vladikavkaz als Sohn eines Malers. Er absolviert die Mittelschule in Moskau und war dann bei den Zeitschriften „Bezbožnik", „Vožak", „Pioner", „Smena" usw. tätig. Sein literarisches Schaffen erstreckt sich auf Kinderliteratur und Erzählungen.

Archimed Vovki Grušina (1946)
Pro naši dela (Von unseren Taten, 1946)
Nevidannaja ptica (Der Wundervogel, 1950)
Čelovek bez nervov (Der Mensch ohne Nerven, 1950)
Chvostik (Das Schwänzchen, 1953)

Deutsche Übersetzungen

Der Wundervogel, übers. v. H. Linke, Berlin, Kinderbuchverlag. 1951.

Von unseren Taten, Bukarest, Jugendverlag. 1950.

Der Mensch ohne Nerven und eine andere Erzählung, übers. v. H. Linke, Berlin, Kinderbuchverl. 1951.

Stávskij Vladímir Petróvič

1900—1943, geb. in Penza. S. trat bereits als Achtzehnjähriger der Kommunistischen Partei bei und wurde später auch zum Deputierten in den Obersten Sowjet gewählt. Am 14. November 1943 fiel er in den Kämpfen bei Nevel'. S. begann bereits 1922, sich literarisch zu betätigen, blieb jedoch als Dichter in seiner Entwicklung stecken. Die Komposition seiner Werke war nicht immer genügend durchdacht, die Vergleiche darin zu gekünstelt, wie z. B. in „Razbeg" (Der Anlauf). Manche Details sind geradezu grotesk. Trotzdem wirkt seine Schilderung, besonders in den Kriegsberichten, ursprünglich und frisch.

Stanica (Das Kosakendorf, 1929)
Razbeg (Der Anlauf, 1931)
Sil'nee smerti (Stärker als der Tod, 1932)
Kolchoznye zapiski (Kolchozskizzen, 1932)
Vojna (Krieg, 1941)

Štéjn Aleksándr Petróvič

Geb. 1906 in Samarkand als Sohn eines Angestellten. Er studierte an der Universität Leningrad und begann bereits als Sechzehnjähriger seine schriftstellerische Tätigkeit. In der Sowjetliteratur machte sich Š. vor allem als Dramatiker einen Namen. Während der Ära *Ždanovs* trat er vornehmlich als Verfasser von anti*kosmopolitischen* und historischen Stücken hervor.

Zakon česti (Der Ehrenkodex, 1948)
Flag admirala (Die Admiralsflagge, 1950)
Prolog (1955)
Personal'noe delo (Eine persönliche Angelegenheit, 1954)
Gostinica ‚Astorija' (Hotel Astoria, 1957)

Deutsche Übersetzungen

Ehrengericht (Zakon česti), nach dem Szenarium des gleichnamigen Mosfilms, übers. v. A. Thoss, Berlin, Deutsch. Filmverleih. 1950.

Eine persönliche Angelegenheit (Personal'noe delo), Bühnenspiel in 4 Aufz., übers. v. Gerty Rath, Bukarest, Verlag Cartea rusă. 1956.

Surkóv Alekséj Aleksándrovič

Geb. 1899 im Kreis Rybinsk, Gouvernement Jaroslavl', als Sohn einer Bauernfamilie. S. ist ein vielpublizierter Dichter, der gerne in der Öffentlichkeit auftritt. Nach den frühen Jugendjahren, welche er als Arbeiter in den verschiedensten Berufen in St. Petersburg verbrachte, trat er in die Rote Armee ein und wurde 1925 Mitglied der Kommunistischen Partei, später wurde er Deputierter des Obersten Sowjets der UdSSR. Als eifriger Verfechter der von der Partei für die Sowjetliteratur erlassenen Richtlinien errang S. eine führende Stellung im Sowjetischen *Schriftstellerverband.* Auf dem 2. Sowjetischen Schriftstellerkongreß im Dezember 1954 hielt er als Erster Sekretär des Verbandes das Hauptreferat. Als Dichter stellte sich S. zum ersten Mal im Jahre 1930 mit einem Gedichtband vor. In vielen seinen Gedichten spielt der Kampf, gepaart mit einem unauslöschlichen Haß gegen den Feind, eine vorherrschende Rolle. Verschiedene solcher Gedichte wurden auch vertont, so z. B. „Pesnja smelych“ (Das Lied der Kühnen) von V. Belyj. S.s Werke wurden bisher bei einer Auflage von 1 348 000 Exemplaren in 4 Sprachen übersetzt.

Pesnja smelych (Das Lied der Kühnen, 1941)
Dekabr' pod Moskvoj (Dezember vor Moskau, 1942)
B'ëtsja v tesnoj pečurke ogon' (Im Öflein lodert das Feuer, 1942)
Pobeda (Der Sieg, 1943, *Stalinpreis* 1946)
Miru — mir! (Der Welt den Frieden, 1950, *Stalinpreis* 1951)
Vostok i zapad (Der Osten und der Westen, 1957)

Deutsche Übersetzungen

Der Welt den Frieden (Miru — mir!), übertr. v. Alfred Edgar Thoss, Berlin, Verlag Volk und Welt.

Einem Altersgenossen, übers. v. Franz Leschnitzer, Moskau, S. L. 1957.

Svetlóv Michail Arkád'evič

Geb. 1903 in Dnepropetrovsk, einer Handwerkerfamilie entstammend. Seine ersten literarischen Werke schrieb S. unter dem Einfluß einer abstrakten Kunstrichtung, wie sie von den der Künstlergilde *Kuznica* angehörenden Dichtern vertreten wurde. In späteren Jahren versuchte sich S. auch in lyrischen Theaterstücken, deren Themen er jedoch dem modernen Leben entnahm, so z. B. in „Brandenburgskie vorota" (Das Brandenburger Tor).

Rel'sy (Geleise, 1923)
Granada (1926)
Pesnja o Kachovke (Das Lied von Kachovka, 1935)
Skazka (Märchen, 1939)
Dvadcat' let spustja (Zwanzig Jahre später, 1940)
Dvadcat' vosem' (Achtundzwanzig, 1942)
Stichi o Lize Čajkinoj (Gedichte über Lisa Čajkina, 1942)
Rossija (Rußland, 1956)
S novym sčast'em (Mit neuem Glück, 1956)
Brandenburgskie vorota (Das Brandenburger Tor, 1946)
Zdravstvuj, universitet! (Sei gegrüßt, Universität!, 1952)

Deutsche Übersetzungen

Das goldene Tal (Skazka), übers. v. H. Zinner, Berlin, Henschel. 1950.
Granada, übers. v. Sepp Österreicher, Moskau, S. L. 1957.

Tarásov-Rodiónov Aleksándr Ignát'evič

1885—?, stand seit 1905 in der bolschewistischen Bewegung und kämpfte während der Revolution in der Roten Armee. Nach seiner Rückkehr ins Zivilleben war T.-R. als Untersuchungsrichter beim Obersten Gerichtshof tätig. In den dreißiger Jahren fiel er einer Säuberung zum Opfer. T.-R. hatte sich auch als Romancier versucht, doch war ihm wenig Erfolg beschieden.

Šokolad (Schokolade, 1922)
Fevral' (Februar, 1928; der erste Teil einer Trilogie ‚Tjažëlye šagi' — Schwere Schritte)
Ijul' (Juli, 1933; der zweite Teil der Trilogie ‚Tjažëlye šagi' — Schwere Schritte)

Deutsche Übersetzungen

Schokolade, übers. v. Alexandra Ramm, Berlin-Wilmersdorf, Verlag der Zeitschrift ‚Die Aktion'. 1924.
Februar, übers. v Olga Halpern, Potsdam, G. Kiepenheuer. 1928.
Juli, übers. v. Olga Halpern, Berlin, Neuer Deutscher Verlag. 1932.

Tendrjakóv Vladímir Fëdorovič

Geb. 1923 im Vologdagebiet als Sohn eines Angestellten. Nach dem Kriege studierte T. am Gor'kij-Institut für Literatur und bereiste nach dessen Absolvierung (1951) im Auftrage der Zeitschrift „Ogonëk" die Sowjetunion. T. gehört zu den talentiertesten Prosaikern der jüngeren Generation. Er ist ein guter Beobachter des Lebens im Kolchozdorf, durch ihn erfährt man auch, wie die junge Generation das Problem des modernen Dorflebens sieht.

Sredi lesov (Mitten in den Wäldern, 1954)
Ne ko dvoru (Der fremde Hof, 1954)
Saša otpravljaetsja v put (Sascha macht sich auf den Weg, 1956)
Tugoj uzel (Der feste Knoten; zweite Fassung zu ‚Sascha macht sich auf den Weg', 1957)
Čudotvornaja (Die Wundertätige, 1958)
Uchaby (Morast, 1958)
Trojka, semërka, tuz (Dreier, Siebener, As, 1960)

Deutsche Übersetzungen

Erzählungen (Der Fremde u. a.), übers. v. Juri Elperin und Dora Hofmeister, Berlin, Verlag Kultur und Fortschritt. 1956.
Der fremde Hof, übers. v. Juri Elperin, Bukarest, Verlag Cartea rusă. 1956.
Morast, übers. v. Juri Elperin, Moskau, S. L. 1957.

Tíchonov Nikoláj Semënovič

Geb. 1896 in St. Petersburg als Sohn eines Handwerkers. Nach dem Besuch der Handelsschule diente T. während des ersten Weltkrieges bei den Husaren, 1918 trat er in die Rote Armee ein. Gegenwärtig ist T. Deputierter des Obersten Sowjets der UdSSR, seit 1950 ist er auch Präsident des sowjetischen Komitees zum Schutze des Friedens. Der Beginn seiner literarischen Tätigkeit ist durch seinen Beitritt zu den *Serapionsbrüdern* im Jahre 1922 gekennzeichnet. Die Gedichte aus seinen ersten Schaffensjahren haben fast ausschließlich Krieg und Bürgerkrieg zum Thema. Gegen Ende der zwanziger Jahre begann T. in zunehmendem Maße Prosawerke mit romantischer Thematik zu schreiben. T. ist einer der reifsten und kultiviertesten Dichter der Sowjetunion.

Orda (Die Horde, 1922)
Braga (Dünnbier, 1922)
Krasnye na Arakse (Die Roten am Araks, 1924)
Riskovannyj čelovek (Der Wagehals, 1927)
Kočevniki (Nomaden, 1931)
Vojna (Krieg, 1931)
Klinki i tačanki (Klingen und Militärwagen, 1932)
Kljatva v tumane (Der Schwur im Nebel, 1933)
Večnyj tranzit (Der ewige Transit, 1934)
Ten' druga (Der Schatten des Freundes, 1936)
V lesach, na poljanach mšistych (In den Wäldern und auf moosigen Waldblößen, 1941)
Kirov s nami (Kirov ist mit uns, 1941)
Rastët, šumit vichr' narodnoj slavy (Es wächst und rauscht der Sturm des nationalen Ruhms, 1941, *Stalinpreis* 1942)
Ognennyj god (Das flammende Jahr, 1942)
Leningradskie rasskazy (Leningrader Erzählungen, 1942)
Stichi o Jugoslavii (Gedichte über Jugoslavien, 1947)
Gruzinskaja vesna (Gruzinischer Frühling, 1948, *Stalinpreis* 1949)
Dva potoka (Zwei Ströme, 1951)
Na vtorom vsemirnom kongresse storonnikov mira (Auf dem 2. Weltkongreß der Friedenskämpfer, 1951, *Stalinpreis* 1952)
Beloe čudo (Das weiße Wunder, 1956)

Deutsche Übersetzungen

Erzählungen aus Pakistan (aus „Dva potoka"), übers. v. Josefine Kieseritzky, Berlin, Rütten & Loening. 1952. Auch unter dem Titel ‚Reiseskizzen aus Pakistan', Bukarest, Verlag Cartea rusă. 1952.

Gedichte (Auswahl), übertr. v. Alfred Edgar Thoss, Potsdam, Rütten & Loening. 1950.

Tolstój Graf Alekséj Nikoláevič

1882—1945, geb. in Nikolaevsk, im Gouvernement Samara, war mütterlicherseits mit Turgenev verwandt. Nach der Absolvierung der Realschule trat er in das St. Petersburger Technologische Institut ein, beendete aber seine Studien nicht, sondern schlug die literarische Laufbahn ein. In Provinzzeitungen erschienen im Jahre 1905 seine ersten Gedichte, 1908 die ersten Erzählungen („Staraja bašnja", Der alte Turm). Während des ersten Welkrieges entfaltete T. eine reiche literarische Tätigkeit, er schrieb vor allem über den Untergang der vorrevolutionären russischen Gesellschaft („Čudaki", Sonderlinge). In manchen seiner Werke ist T. von Dostoevskij beeinflußt, so z. B. in „Chromoj barin" (Der hinkende Herr). Nach der Revolution schloß er sich zunächst der weißen Bewegung an, ging dann 1919 ins Ausland, kehrte aber 1923 nach Rußland zurück. Sein literarisches Schaffen ist gewaltig: Romane, Theaterstücke, viele Bände Novellen, Filmdrehbücher und hunderte von Artikeln. T. wurde Mitglied der Akademie der Wissenschaften, Deputierter des Obersten Sowjets, *Stalinpreis*träger und Inhaber vieler anderer Ehrungen und Auszeichnungen. T. reiste auch in vielen politischen und kulturellen Missionen als Vertreter der Sowjetregierung, zuweilen auch als Botschafter, ins Ausland. Nach *Gor'kijs* Tod war T. „Doyen der russischen Schriftsteller". Bisher erschienen seine Werke in mehr als 30 Millionen Exemplaren, übersetzt in 50 Sprachen. Am bekanntesten ist sein Roman „Pëtr I." (Peter I.).

Zavolž'e (Jenseits der Wolga, 1909—1910)
Čudaki (Sonderlinge, 1911)
Chromoj barin (Der hinkende Herr, 1912)
Detstvo Nikity (Nikitas Kindheit, 1920)
Ljubov' — kniga zolotaja (Die Liebe ist ein goldenes Buch, 1922)
Rukopis' najdennaja pod krovat'ju (Das unter dem Bett gefundene Manuskript, 1923)
Golubye goroda (Blaue Städte, 1925)
Pochoždenija Nevzorova, ili Ibikus (Die Abenteuer Nevzorovs, oder Ibykus, 1925)
Giperboloid inženera Garina (Das Hyperboloid des Ingenieurs Garina, 1925), später umgearbeitet und umbenannt in
Diktator Garina (Diktator Garina, 1927)
Sojuz pjati (Der Bruder der Fünf, 1926)
Čërnaja pjatnica (Schwarzer Freitag, 1926)
Gadjuka (Die Viper, 1928)
Čërnoe zoloto (Schwarzes Gold, 1931)
Chleb (Brot, 1937)
Choždenie po mukam (Der Leidensweg, 1919—1941, *Stalinpreis* 1943; Trilogie)
Den' Petra (Peters Werktag)
Pëtr I. (Peter I., Teil 1: 1929—30, Teil 2: 1933—34, Teil 3: 1944 bis 1945, *Stalinpreis* für Teil 1 u. 2: 1941)
Rasskazy Ivana Sudarëva (Ivan Sudarëvs Erzählungen, 1942)
Ivan Groznyj (Ivan der Schreckliche, 1943, *Stalinpreis* 1946)
Trudnye gody (Schwere Jahre, 1943)

Deutsche Übersetzungen

Höllenfahrt (Choždenie po mukam), übers. v. Alexander Eliasberg, München, C. H. Beck'sche Verlh. 1922. Auch unter dem Titel ‚Leidensweg', eine Trilogie (Die Schwestern — Das Jahr achtzehn — Trüber Morgen). Drei Bücher in einem Band, übertr. v. M. Schick, Berlin, SWA-Verlag. 1947. Berlin, Aufbau-Verlag. 1953, 1955.

Zar Peters Werktag (Den' Petra), übers. v. Alexander Eliasberg, München, Orchis-Verlag. 1923.

Das Geheimnis der infraroten Strahlen (Giperboloid inženera Garina), übers. v. A. Wasserbauer, Berlin, Neuer Deutscher Verlag.

1927. Auch unter dem Titel ‚Geheimnisvolle Strahlen', übers. v. Anneliese Bauch, Berlin, Verlag Kultur und Fortschritt. 1957.

Peter der Große, übers. v. M. Schick, Moskau, Verlag für fremdsprachige Literatur. 1949, 1950, 1953. Berlin, Aufbau-Verlag. 1950, 1951, 1952, 1953, 1955, 1956.

Brot (Die Verteidigung von Stalingrad), Engels, Deutscher Staatsverlag. 1939. Moskau, Meshdunarodnaja kniga. 1939. Übers. v. Paul Kutzner, Leipzig, Volk und Buch Verlag. 1948, 1951. Berlin, Aufbau-Verlag. 1953.

Nikitas Kindheit, Berlin, SWA-Verlag. 1949. Übers. v. Dr. Cornelius Bergmann, Eisenach, Röth. 1950. Übers. v. Maria Hoerll, Göttingen, Deuerlich. 1954.

Iwan Sudarjows Erzählungen, übers. v. Ilse Goldmann und Alfred Kittner, Bukarest, Verlag Cartea rusă. 1953.

Ibykus (Pochoždenija Nevzorova, ili Ibikus), übers. v. Christine Patzer, Berlin, Aufbau-Verlag. 1956.

Ivan der Vierte (Ivan Groznyj), Drama in 2 Teilen, übers. v. H. Rodenberg, Berlin, Aufbau-Bühnen-Vertrieb. 1946.

Die Liebe. Komödie in 3 Aufz., übers. v. Johannes v. Guenther, München, Orchis-Verlag. 1923.

Die Viper, übers. v. Pauline Schneider, Bukarest, Verlag Cartea rusă. 1956.

Der schwarze Freitag, übers. v. Felix Loesch, Berlin, Aufbau-Verlag. 1956.

Bund der Fünf (und andere Erzählungen. 1910—1944), übers. v. Erwin Tittelbach u. a., Berlin, Aufbau-Verlag. 1953, 1954.

Trenëv Konstantín Andréevič

1878—1945, geb. im Dorfe Bakšeevka, im Gouvernement Char'kov. T. war bäuerlicher Herkunft. Er studierte im geistlichen Seminar und beendete 1903 am St. Petersburger Archäologischen Institut und an der Priesterakademie seine Studien. Im Jahre 1921 bezog T. zur Erweiterung seiner Kenntnisse die Fakultät für Bodenkultur an der Tavričeskij Universität. Seine literarische Tätigkeit begann T. im Jahre 1898 mit der Veröffentlichung von Erzählungen, in späteren Jahren betätigte er sich als Dramatiker. T., der auch mit

Gor'kij befreundet war, war einer der ersten Dichter, der es wagte, die Gestalt Lenins auf die Bühne zu stellen. Seine Werke, von denen das Bürgerkriegsdrama „Ljubov' Jarovaja" am bekanntesten ist, wurden in 6 Sprachen übersetzt und erreichten eine Auflage von 883 000 Exemplaren.

Na jarmarke (Auf dem Jahrmarkt, 1913)
Erzählungen und Skizzen, 1941—1945
Pugačëvščina (1924)
Ljubov' Jarovaja (1926, *Stalinpreis* 1941)
Žena (Die Gattin, 1928)
Opyt (Der Versuch, 1933)
Gimnazisty (Gymnasiasten, 1936)
Na beregu Nevy (Am Ufer der Neva, 1937)
Anna Lučinina (1941)
Navstreču (Dem Ziel entgegen, 1942)
Polkovodec (Der Feldherr [Kutuzov], 1944)

Tret'jakóv Sergéj Michájlovič

1892—1939 (?), geb. in Riga als Sohn eines Lehrers. Nach dem Besuch des russischen Gymnasiums und der juridischen Fakultät der Moskauer Universität war T. von 1919 bis 1922 als Mitarbeiter der „Krasnoe znamja" und des „Dal'nevostočnyj telegraf" in Vladivostok tätig. Im Jahre 1919 veröffentlichte T. auch seine erste Gedichtsammlung. Nach Moskau zurückgekehrt, wurde T. Mitarbeiter der Zeitschrift *„LEF"* und einer der bedeutendsten Vertreter der *Futuristen.* In der 1927 entstandene Gruppe „Der neue *LEF"* wurde T. ein eifriger Fürsprecher einer von den konventionellen Kunstbegriffen freien, auf das Alltagsleben der Gesellschaft konzentrierten Reportage- und Tatsachenliteratur. In den Jahren der Kollektivisierung arbeitete T. auf einer Kolchose. In den dreißiger Jahren fiel er einer „Säuberung" zum Opfer.

Ryči, Kitaj! (Brülle, China! 1924)
Rečevik (1929)
Tysjača i odin trudoden' (Tausendundein Arbeitstag)

Deutsche Übersetzungen

Brülle, China, Spiel in 5 Bildern, übers. v. Leo Lania, Berlin, J. Ladyschnikow. 1929.

Den Schi-Chua. Bio-Interview, übers. v. Alfred Kurella, Berlin, Malik-Verlag. 1932.

Tausendundein Arbeitstag (Tysjača i odin trudoden'), Moskau-Leningrad, Verlagsgenossenschaft ausländischer Arbeiter in der UdSSR. 1935.

Tvardóvskij Aleksándr Tŕifonovič

Geb. 1910 in Zagor'e, im Gouvernement Smolensk, als Sohn eines Dorfschmiedes. Zur Zeit der Kollektivisierung war T. Korrespondent verschiedener Smolensker Zeitungen. Im Jahre 1930 veröffentlichte er seinen Gedichtband „Put' k socializmu" (Der Weg zum Sozialismus). 1938 wurde er Mitglied der KPdSU und studierte Geschichte und Philosophie in Moskau. Während des Krieges war T. Berichterstatter von Soldatenzeitungen. T. ist einer der einfallsreichsten und geistvollsten Schriftsteller der Sowjetunion. Sein bekanntestes Werk aus der Vorkriegszeit ist „Strana Muravija" (Wunderland Muravija), eine humorvolle Schilderung der Abenteuer eines Bauern auf der Suche nach einem Land, in dem es noch ein Privateigentum und keine Kollektivwirtschaften gibt. Das geistreiche Epos „Vasilij Tërkin", eine Charakterisierung des russischen Soldaten, kann mit Jaroslav Hašeks Werk „Der brave Soldat Švejk" verglichen werden. Bis zum Jahre 1954, als T. als leitender Redakteur des „Novyj mir" durch *Simonov* ersetzt wurde, hatten seine Werke eine Auflage von 3 681 000 Exemplaren erreicht und waren in 15 Sprachen übersetzt worden.

Dnevnik predsedatelja (Tagebuch eines Kolchosvorsitzenden, 1932)
Strana Muravija (Wunderland Muravia, 1936, *Stalinpreis* 1941)
Vasilij Tërkin (1941—1945, *Stalinpreis* 1946)
Dom u dorogi (Das Haus am Wege, 1946, *Stalinpreis* 1947)
Za dal'ju dal' (In fernster Ferne, 1953)
Pečniki (Ofensetzer, 1958)

Deutsche Übersetzungen

Wunderland Muravia, übers. v. Alfred Kurella, Berlin, Verlag Volk und Welt. 1954.

Die Jungvermählten (aus ‚Za dal'ju dal'‘), übers. v. Sepp Österreicher, Moskau, S. L. 1958.

Ofensetzer, übers. v. Regina Czora, Moskau, S. L. 1957.

Tynjánov Júrij Nikoláevič

1894—1943, geb. in der Stadt Režica, im Gouvernement Vitebsk, als Sohn eines Arztes. Er absolvierte 1918 die historisch-philologische Fakultät in Petrograd und war von 1921 bis 1930 am Institut für die Geschichte der russischen Poesie tätig. Im Jahre 1921 schloß sich T. als Literarhistoriker und hervorragender Puškinkenner den *Formalisten* an. Seine Werke fallen durch ihren außerordentlich reichen Wortschatz und die Kultiviertheit der Sprache auf. Sei es aus Abneigung gegen die neue Zeit oder aus einer gewissen Scheu, in seinen Werken aktuelle Themen zu behandeln, jedenfalls konzentrierte sich T. in seinem Schaffen auf den literarhistorischen Roman, dem sich in der Folge auch andere Schriftsteller zuwandten.

Dostoevskij i Gogol' (Dostoevskij und Gogol', 1921)

Problema stichotvornogo jazyka (Das Problem der Verssprache, 1924)

Kjuchlja (Wilhelm Küchelbecker, 1925)

Smert' Vazir-Muchtara (Griboedov) (Der Tod des Vazir-Muchtar, 1928)

Podporučik Kiže (Sekondeleutnant Saber, 1928)

Archaisty i novatory (Archaisten und Neuerer, 1929)

Maloletnij Vitušišnikov (Der minderjährige Vitušišnikov, 1933)

Voskovaja persona (Die Wachsfigur)

Puškin (1936—1943)

Deutsche Übersetzungen

Wilhelm Küchelbecker (Kjuchlja). Dichter und Rebell, übers. v. M. Einstein. Berlin, Volk und Welt. 1947.

Sekundeleutnant Saber (Podporučik Kiže), übers. v. M. Einstein, Berlin, Volk und Welt. 1948. Leipzig, Insel-Verlag. 1954.

Ûrin Víktor Arkád'evič

Geb. 1924 in Char'kov. Während des Krieges war U. Kriegsberichterstatter der Zeitung „Na šturm". Im Jahre 1947 absolvierte er das Gor'kij-Institut für Literatur. Seine Werke werden seit 1937 veröffentlicht. U. schreibt Gedichte und Erzählungen. In seiner Lyrik ahmt er A. *Blok* nach.

Vesna pobeditelej (Der Frühling der Sieger, 1946)
Sčast'ju navstreču (Dem Glück entgegen, 1953)
Gde sejčas Ljuda? (Wo ist jetzt Ljuda? 1954)
Jugo-vostok (Südosten, 1955)
Rekam snjatsja morja (Die Flüsse träumen vom Meer, 1956)

Vasilénko Iván Dmítrievič

Geb. 1895 in Makeevka. V. war von 1922 bis 1934 in der Volksbildung tätig. In seinem 1946 erschienenen Sammelband erweist er sich als begabter Erzähler.

Volšebnaja škatulka (Die Zauberschatulle, 1937)
Artëmka v cirke (Artëmka im Zirkus, 1939)
Artëmka u gimnazistov (Artëmka bei den Gymnasiasten, 1944)
Plan žizni (Der Lebensplan, 1946)
Zakoldovannyj spektakel' (Das verhexte Schauspiel, 1949)
Zvëzdočka (Das Sternchen, 1950, *Stalinpreis*)
V nogu (Im Gleichschritt, 1952)

Deutsche Übersetzungen

Peps und Peter (Artëmka v cirke), übers. v. J. Koskull, Berlin-Dresden, Kinderbuchverlag. 1950.
Peter bei den Gymnasiasten (Artëmka u gimnazistov), übers. v. J. Koskull, Berlin-Dresden, Kinderbuchverlag. 1950.
Peter und die verhexte Theateraufführung (Zakoldovannyj spektakel'), übers. v. F. Schüler, Berlin, Kinderbuchverlag. 1953.
Das Sternchen, übers. v. J. Koskull, Berlin, Kinderbuchverlag. 1951. Bukarst, Jugendverlag. 1951.

Vasilévskij Vitálij

Geb. 1908 im Südural. Er absolvierte die philologische Fakultät der Höheren Kunstforschungskurse in Leningrad und ist seit 1925 als Journalist tätig. V. schreibt hauptsächlich Erzählungen und Novellen, wie z. B. „Offiziersfreundschaft“, „Gestern und heute“, „Es sangen die Mädchen ein Lied...“ u. a. Seine Erzählungen vermitteln vor allem einen guten Einblick in das sowjetische Alltagsleben. Langweile und Pessimismus überschatten das Gesamtbild seines Schaffens.

Komendant rečnoj perepravy (Der Kommandant der Flußfähre, 1955)
Skučnoe leto (Ein langweiliger Sommer, 1956)
Perekati-pole (Die Kollerdistel, 1957)

Vasíl'ev Sergéj Aleksándrovič

Geb. 1911 in der Stadt Kurgan, in Sibirien, als Sohn eines Beamten. Im Jahre 1927 zog er nach Moskau, wo er in der Stoffdruckabteilung einer Textilfabrik arbeitete und 1938 das Gor'kij-Institut für Literatur absolvierte. Gleich zu Beginn des zweiten Weltkrieges trat V. als Freiwilliger in die Rote Armee ein und betätigte sich als Frontberichterstatter. Der Beginn seiner literarischen Tätigkeit fällt in das Jahr 1931, zwei Jahre später erschien sein erster Gedichtband „Lebensjahre“. Hauptthema in V.s Schaffen ist der sowjetische Arbeiter. So schildert er in dem Buche „Moskauer Kohlenrevier“ (1948) die Arbeit des Kumpels, in „Sowjet-Moskau“ (1947) die Errungenschaften bei der Umgestaltung der Hauptstadt. Im Poem „Das Erste der Welt“ (1950) zeichnet V. die Gestalt des russischen Erfinders A. F. Možajskij, der das erste russische Flugzeug baute. Einen bedeutenden Platz im Schaffen V.s nehmen seine literarischen Parodien und Epigramme ein, die im satirischen Sammelband „Mit Rücksicht auf die Person“ enthalten sind. (nach S.L.)

Veresáev V. (Pseudonym für Vikéntij Viként'evič Smidóvič)

1867—1945, ein sehr populärer Sowjetschriftsteller, der sich schon vor der Revolution durch scharfsinnige, realistische Schilderungen gesellschaftlicher Ereignisse einen Namen gemacht hatte. Einen besonderen Erfolg verzeichnete er mit dem 1901 erschienenen, nach dem Leben geschriebenen Werk „Zapiski vrača“ (Memoiren eines Arztes). Von Bedeutung sind auch seine literarhistorischen Arbeiten über Dostoevskij, Leo Tolstoj und Puškin. Bekannt ist ferner seine Übersetzung der Ilias ins Russische.

Bez dorogi (Weglos, 1895)
Zapiski vrača (Memoiren eines Arztes, 1901)
Na povorote (Am Scheideweg, 1902)
Živaja žizn' (Lebendiges Leben, 1911)
V tupike (In der Sackgasse, 1922)
Puškin v žizni (Puškin lebt, 1926—1927)
Sëstry (Die Schwestern, 1933)

Deutsche Übersetzungen

Puschkin (Puškin v žizni). Sein Leben und Schaffen. SWA-Verlag, Berlin. 1947.

Vesëlyj Artëm (Pseudonym für Nikoláj Ivánovič Kočkuróv)

Geb. 1899 als Sohn eines Wolgastauers. Vor Beginn seiner literarischen Tätigkeit arbeitete V. als Fabrikarbeiter und als Fuhrmann. Später trat er der Kommunistischen Partei bei und nahm am Bürgerkrieg teil. V. experimentiert in seinen Werken viel in Sprache und Form. In seinem historischen Roman „Guljaj Volga“ besteht z. B. das Kapitel X nur aus dem Wort „Plyli“ (Sie schwammen). Seine Prosa erinnert mit ihren kurzen, abgerissenen Sätzen an die Verse *Majakovskijs* (Struve). V.s Lieblingsthemen sind die *anarchistischen*, russischen „vol'nica“ (Freischärler, Räuberbanden), die Matrosen der Revolutionszeit, die Kosaken Ermaks, des Eroberers von Sibirien. In seinen Werken sind auch so manche Einflüsse von *Chlebnikov*, Remizov und A. *Belyj* festzustellen.

Reki ognennye (Feurige Flüsse, 1923)
Strana rodnaja (Heimatland, 1925)
Rossija krov'ju omytaja (Rußland, im Blut gewaschen, 1931)
Guljaj Volga (1933)

Deutsche Übersetzungen

Heimatland (Strana rodnaja). Auszüge. Pokrovsk, Deutscher Staatsverlag der ASSR der Wolgadeutschen. 1925.

Virtá Nikoláj Evgén'evič (Pseudonym für Sévercev)

Geb. 1906 im Gouvernement Tambov. Er stammt aus der Familie eines Dorfgeistlichen und wuchs in ärmlichen, dörflichen Verhältnissen auf. In seiner Jugend erlebte er im Jahre 1920 im Gouvernement Tambov den gegen das kommunistische Regime gerichteten Bauernaufstand unter Antonov, den er auch in seinem ersten Erfolgsroman, „Odinočestvo“ (Allein geblieben), behandelt. Von 1923 bis 1935 war V. Mitarbeiter verschiedener Provinzzeitungen, während des finnischen Krieges und im 2. Weltkrieg war er Kriegsberichterstatter.

Odinočestvo (Allein geblieben, 1935, *Stalinpreis* 1941), der 1. Teil einer geplanten Trilogie

Zakonomernost' (Gesetzmäßigkeit, 1936) der 2. Teil der Trilogie, der 3. Teil wurde nicht veröffentlicht

Večernij zvon (Abendläuten, 1951), als 1. Teil eines sechsbändigen Romanzyklus geplant

Zemlja (Land, 1937, eine Bearbeitung von ‚Odino čestvo‘)

Chleb naš nasuščnyj (Unser tägliches Brot, 1947)

Stalingradskaja bitva (Die Stalingrader Schlacht, Drehbuch, 1947)

Zagovor obrečënnych (Die Verschwörung der Verdammten, 1948)

Deutsche Übersetzungen

Die Stalingrader Schlacht. Ein Drehbuch in literar. Form, übers. v. Dr. Johannes Krieger, Berlin-Leipzig, SWA-Verlag. 1948.

Allein geblieben (Odinočestvo), übers. v. Harry Schnittke, Moskau, Verlag für fremdsprachige Literatur. 1954.

Višnévskij Vsévolod Vitál'evič

1900—1951, hatte am Bürgerkrieg an der Wolga teilgenommen. Seine ersten literarischen Werke erschienen im Jahre 1920. Im Jahre 1937 wurde er Mitglied der KPdSU und wurde später auch stellvertretender Generalsekretär des Sowjetischen

Schriftstellerverbandes. Während des zweiten Weltkrieges schrieb V. Frontberichte aus dem belagerten Leningrad und nachher Berichte über die Nürnberger Prozesse. Bei einer Gesamtauflage von 936 000 Exemplaren wurden V.s Werke bisher in 16 Sprachen übersetzt.

Sud nad kronštadtskimi mjatežnikami (Gericht über die Kronstädter Meuterer, 1921)
Pervaja konnaja (Die erste Reiterarmee, 1929)
Poslednij rešitel'nyj (Der letzte entscheidende . . ., 1931)
Optimističeskaja tragedija (Eine optimistische Tragödie, 1932)
U sten Leningrada (An den Mauern Leningrads, 1943)
Nezabyvaemyj 1919 (Das unvergeßliche Jahr 1919, 1949, *Stalinpreis* 1950)
My iz Kronstadta (Wir aus Kronstadt, 1933)
My russkie ljudi (Wir Russen, 1937)

Deutsche Übersetzungen

Optimistische Tragödie. Schauspiel in 3 Akten, vom Verfasser autorisierte Bearb. v. F. Wolf, Berlin, Henschel. 1948.

Vol'kenštéjn Vladímir Michájlovič

Geb. 1883. V. machte sich in den zwanziger Jahren als Dramatiker und Theaterkritiker einen Namen. Er verfaßte u. a. eine Abhandlung über die Entwicklung des Dramas in den ersten 10 Jahren nach der Revolution („Dramatičeskaja literatura 1917—1927") und eine Monographie über Stanislavskij, den Leiter des Moskauer Künstlertheaters.

Ivan Groznyj (Ivan der Schreckliche, 1907)
Spartakus (1923)
Opyt mistera Vedda (Das Experiment des Mr. Vedd, wurde nicht veröffentlicht)
Gusary i golubi (Husaren und Tauben, 1928)
Telegramma iz Carskogo (Das Telegramm aus Zarskoe, 1934)

Volóšin (Kiriénko-Volóšin) Maksimilián Aleksándrovič

1877—1932, stand als *Symbolist* den *Akmeisten* nahe. Vor der Revolution lebte er lange Zeit in Paris. Sein erstes literarisches Werk erschien im Jahre 1900. Seine nach 1917 gedruckten Gedichte behandelten meist revolutionäre Themen. Da er nach dem Bürgerkrieg als Konterrevolutionär gebrandmarkt wurde, wurde ab 1925 von V. nichts mehr veröffentlicht. Er lebte bis zu seinem Tode in Koktebel' bei Feodosija auf der Krim.

Stichotvorenija (Gedichte, 1910)
Anno mundi ardentis (1916)
Iverija (1918)
Verchari (1919)

Zalýgin Sergéj Pávlovič

Geb. 1913 im Dorfe Durasovka, im Gouvernement Ufa. Z., von Beruf Landwirt und Hydrologe, arbeitete als Wissenschaftler in Omsk, wo er auch sein erstes Buch, einen Band Erzählungen, veröffentlichte. Einige weitere Erzählungen von ihm erschienen in Omsk und Novosibirsk.

Vtoroe dejstvie (Zweiter Aufzug, 1952)
Kak ja ustraival svoju doč' (Wie ich für meine Tochter gesorgt habe, 1956)
Funkcija (Funktion, 1957)
Bez peremen (Nichts Neues, 1958)
Svideteli (Zeugen, 1956)

Zamjátin Evgénij Ivánovič

1884—1937, geb. in Lebedjan, im Gouvernement Char'kov. Er studierte am Polytechnischen Institut in St. Petersburg und wurde Schiffsingenieur. Schon während seiner Studentenzeit trat Z. der Sozialdemokratischen Partei bei. Wegen seiner politischen Tätigkeit wurde er mehrmals verhaftet und schließlich deportiert, 1913 wurde er begnadigt. Z.s erste Erzählung erschien im Jahre 1908 in der Zeitschrift „Obrazovanie". Z., der als tragende Säule der *Serapionsbrüder* großen Einfluß auf eine Reihe junger Schriftsteller ausübte, wurde in seinem

Schaffen einerseits von Leskov, aber auch von Remizov und *Prišvin* beeinflußt. Die Veröffentlichung seines interessantesten Werkes, des Romans „My" (Wir), im Jahre 1929 löste eine heftige Kampagne gegen ihn aus, die zu seinem Austritt aus dem *RAPP* führte. Das Werk, eine groteske Schilderung des totalitären Staates, wurde von der offiziellen Kritik als eine Schmähung der bestehenden und künftigen kommunistischen Errungenschaften empfunden und als solches verurteilt. Z. wurde 1931 gestattet, die Sowjetunion zu verlassen, um sich im Ausland niederzulassen. Er starb 1937 in Frankreich.

Uezdnoe (Provinzielles, 1911)
Na kuličkach (Am Ende der Welt, 1914)
Ostrovitjane (Insulaner, 1917)
Lovec čelovekov (Menschenfänger, 1917)
Skazki dlja vzroslych detej (Märchen für erwachsene Kinder, 1922)
Navodnenie (Überschwemmung, 1926)
Nečestivye rasskazy (Pietätlose Geschichten, 1927)
Ogni sv. Dominika (Die Feuer des hl. Dominik, 1923)
Obščestvo početnych zvonarej (Die Gesellschaft der ehrenamtlichen Glockner, 1926), die Bühnenbearbeitung von ‚Ostrovitjane'
Blocha (Der Floh, 1925), nach Leskovs Erzählung „Der Linkshänder"
My (Wir, 1929)

Žárov Aleksándr Alekséevič

Geb. 1904 in Semënovskoe bei Moskau, stammt aus einer Bauernfamilie. Nach dem Besuch der Realschule begann Ž. im Jahre 1921 das Studium der Soziologie in Moskau. Er war auch als Redakteur der Zeitschriften „Komsomolija" und „Smena" tätig und zählte zu den Organisatoren der Vereinigung proletarischer Schriftsteller „*Molodaja gvardija*". Zu Beginn seiner dichterischen Tätigkeit stand Ž. stark unter dem Einfluß *Majakovskijs*.

Slovo o Povolž'e (Die Mär vom Wolgagebiet, 1921)
Skazal zadumčivo soldat (Nachdenklich sprach der Soldat, 1956)
Izbrannye proizvedenija (Ausgewählte Werke, 1956)

Zavalíšin Aleksándr Ivánovič

Geb. 1891. Der Abstammung nach Kosake, war Z. als Hirte, Dorfschreiber, Angestellter des Statistischen Amtes und als Redakteur tätig. Besondere Aufmerksamkeit lenkte Z. erstmals im Jahre 1926 auf sich, als er das Drama „Vor" (Der Dieb) veröffentlichte. Zur Zeit lebt Z. in der Emigration.

Ne te vremena (Andere Zeiten, 1925)
Skuki radi (Aus Langeweile, 1925)
Vor (Der Dieb, 1926)
Pervyj blin (Aller Anfang, 1927)
Partbilet (Das Parteibuch, 1927)
Častnoe delo (Privatsache, 1927)
Pepel (Die Asche, 1928)
Sapožnik agitator (Der Schuster als Agitator, 1928)
Fal'šivaja bumažka (Ein falsches Papier, 1929)
Sovetskie cenzory za rabotoj (Sowjetische Zensoren bei der Arbeit, 1950)

Zlóbin Stepán Pávlovič

Geb. 1903. In seinen Werken, deren erstes 1924 erschien, verrät er ein vorzügliches Sprachgefühl und Kenntnis der russischen Folklore. In seinen Romanen behandelt Z. gerne Themen aus der russischen Geschichte, so z. B. aus der Zeit der russischen Bauern- und Kosakenhelden Stepan Razin und Pugačëv (Salavat Julaev).

Salavat Julaev (1929)
Stepan Razin (1951, *Stalinpreis*)

Deutsche Übersetzungen

Der Adler vom Don (Stepan Razin), übers. v. Dr. Alois Rottensteiner, Bd. 1 u. 2. Berlin, Rütten & Loening. 19545. Wien, Zsolnay. 1955.

Zóščenko Michaíl Michájlovič

1895—1958, geb. in Poltava als Sohn eines Malers. Er studierte an der juridischen Fakultät der St. Petersburger Universität und zog 1915 als Freiwilliger in den Krieg. 1918 trat er in die Rote Armee ein. Seine Verbindung mit den *Serapionsbrüdern* im Jahre 1921 bedeutete den Beginn seiner literarischen Tätigkeit. Stark unter dem Einfluß Gogol's stehend, wandte sich Z. den täglichen Sorgen des kleinen Mannes zu. Er bediente sich in seinen vielen Erzählungen der Sprache der Halbgebildeten. Die Themen für seine Geschichten lieferten ihm die vielen Widerwärtigkeiten des Alltagslebens und die Schikanen, denen der Durchschnittsbürger oft seitens einfältiger Spießer hilflos ausgesetzt war. Gegen diese richtete Z. seinen humorvollen Spott. Solange er damit einen aus der alten Zeit stammenden Menschentyp angriff, war er dem Regime genehm. Im Laufe der Zeit kam aber ein neuer Spießertyp auf, der bereits der neuen Zeit entstammte. Diese „humoristische Kulturgeschichte" (*Gor'kij*) war nun nicht mehr im Einklang mit der Parteilinie. Kurz nach dem Erscheinen der Erzählung „Priključenija obez'jany" (Die Abenteuer eines Affen), die als ein Angriff auf das Sowjetregime und den sowjetischen Menschen gewertet wurde, richtete *Ždanov* im Jahre 1946 vernichtende Angriffe gegen Z. Nicht einmal die Zeit des *Tauwetters* nach Stalins Tod konnte Z. zu neuem Schaffen anregen. Z. war nicht nur in der Sowjetunion einer der meistgelesenen zeitgenössischen Schriftsteller, auch im Ausland ist sein Name bestens bekannt. Seine Werke wurden in alle Weltsprachen übersetzt. Stark autobiographischen Charakter trägt das unvollendete Buch „Sonnenaufgang".

Rasskazy Nazara Il'iča gospodina Sinebrjuchova (Die Erzählungen des Herrn Nazar Il'ič Sinebrjuchov, 1922)
Vesëlaja žizn' (Fröhliches Leben)
O čëm pel solovej (Was die Nachtigall sang)
Uvažaemye graždane (Geehrte Mitbürger, Bd. 1, 1926, Bd. 2, 1940)
Pis'ma pisatelju (Briefe an den Schriftsteller, 1929)
Vozvraščënnaja molodost' (Die wiedererlangte Jugend, 1933)
Golubaja kniga (Blaubuch, 1934)
Istorija odnoj žizni (Die Geschichte eines Lebens, 1936)

Pered voschodom solnca (Vor Sonnenaufgang, 1943)
Priključenija obez'jany (Die Abenteuer eines Affen, 1946)
Parusinovyj portfelj (Die Leinenmappe, 1950)

Deutsche Übersetzungen

Lustiges Abenteuer (Vesëloe priključenie), übers. v. J. M. Schubert, Heidelberg, Merlin-Verlag. 1927.

So lacht Rußland! übers. v. Mary v. Pruss-Glowatzky u. Elsa Brod, Prag, A. Synek. 1927.

Teterkin bestellt einen Aeroplan, übers. v. Josef Kalmer, Leipzig-Wien, Prager. 1931.

Der redliche Zeitgenosse (Uvažaemye graždane), übers. v. Grete Willinsky, Kassel, Schleber. 1947.

Was die Nachtigall sang. Satiren, Stuttgart, Reclam-Verlag. 1957.

Die Leinenmappe. Sowjetruss. Komödie in 3 Akten, übers. v. M. Einstein, Berlin, Henschel. 1950.

Anm.: Die angeführten Übersetzungen stellen in der Mehrzahl ausgewählte Erzählungen aus versch. Werken dar.

VERZEICHNIS SOWJETISCHER LITERARISCHER BEGRIFFE

Verzeichnis sowjetischer literarischer Begriffe

AKMEISMUS, AKMEISTEN

(vom griechischen akmē — der Gipfel), eine literarische Richtung, welche um das Jahr 1912 in Rußland entstand und bis 1922 von Bedeutung war. Ihr Zentrum war in Petrograd. An der Spitze dieser Richtung standen *Gumilëv, Mandel'stam,* Anna *Achmatova* u. a. m. Nach Ansicht der Akmeisten darf der Dichter das Unerkennbare und Unerforschbare nie außer acht lassen und trotzdem nur die unmittelbare Wahrheit verkünden. Die Form muß einfach und klar, die Sprache geschliffen sein. Wenn auch die offizielle Sowjetkritik im A. eine reaktionäre Bewegung sieht, übt er jedoch bis heute einen starken Einfluß auf die russische Poesie aus.

„An das Nichterkennbare immer denken, aber seine Gedanken darüber nicht mit mehr oder weniger wahrscheinlichen Mutmaßungen zu kränken — das ist das Prinzip des Akmeismus", schrieb E. *Gumilëv,* „Literaturnye manifesty" (Literarische Manifeste), Moskau, 1929, S. 44.

ANARCHISMUS, ANARCHISTEN

Die Sowjets sehen im A. ihren erbitterten Feind; nach ihrer Auffassung sollen die Anarchisten den vollendeten Individualismus verkünden und damit, über Nietzsche, die Vorläufer des Faschismus sein.

ÄSTHETENTUM

(esteststvo), subjektive Einstellung zur Wirklichkeit, zum Schönen in der Natur und Kunst. Das Ä. wird von der sowjetischen Kritik als Loslösung der Kunst vom Leben und von der Gesellschaft verurteilt. Es wird als Synonym für Ideenlosigkeit gebraucht.

BAUERNDICHTER

Unter diesem Begriff versteht man weniger Dichter bäuerlicher Abstammung, als vielmehr Poeten der Revolutionszeit, welche die bäuerliche Thematik behandelten, etwa in der Art von *Esenin,* der wohl als typischer B. bezeichnet werden kann. Neben ihm gehören *Kljuev, P. V. Orešin, Klyčkov* u. a. in diese Gruppe. Die ideologische Besonderheit bestand darin, daß sie zwar die Revolution akzeptierten, aber in ihr vor allem die mystische Erfüllung des langgehegten Wunschtraumes des russischen Bauerntums sahen und damit in einem meist sehr unklar ausgesprochenen Gegensatz zur offiziellen Deutung und zum tatsächlichen Leben standen. Die jüngsten B. kennen diese ideologische Gegensätzlichkeit nicht mehr. Der Unterschied zwischen den „jüngeren“ und „älteren“ B. wirkt sich vielleicht am deutlichsten im verwendeten Wortschatz aus. Der Wortschatz *Esenins* ist z. B. sehr reich an kirchlichen Ausdrücken (man möchte fast sagen, an „kirchlich-ländlichen“), welche den modernen B. weniger liegen, z. B. *Jašin* u. a. m.

BOL'ŠEVÍK

der Name entstand als Gegensatz zu Men'ševík, „als Ergebnis des Kampfes gegen die Men'scheviki“ (vgl. XIX. Parteitag der KPdSU, Neue Welt (1952/22). B. ist formell gleichbedeutend mit Kommunist, hatte jedoch in der Zeit des Bürgerkrieges einen nationalen Beigeschmack (Gegensatz zum internationalen „Kommunist“), welcher allerdings in den späteren Jahren verloren ging. Heute wird dem Worte B. ein moralischer Akzent verliehen.

BUDETLJÁNE

russischer Ausdruck für *Futuristen.* Dieser Ausdruck wurde zwar von einigen *Futuristen* gebraucht, ging aber in den russischen Sprachschatz nicht ein.

CENTRIFÚGA

vgl. Kubofuturismus.

DEKADENZ, DEKADENT

wird die Zeit zwischen der Revolution von 1905 und dem ersten Weltkrieg verallgemeinernd bezeichnet. Die sowjetische Kritik zählt zur D. so ziemlich alles, was nicht *sozialistischer Realismus* ist, vom *Impressionismus* bis zum Existenzialismus. Dekadent wird heute auch die westliche Kultur genannt, welche nach sowjetischer Meinung dem unweigerlichen Verfall ausgesetzt ist.

Verzeichnis sowjetischer literarischer Begriffe

DETIZDÁT

Jugendverlag.

EGOFUTURISMUS

eine Variation des extremen *Futurismus*. „Fetischistische“ Verehrung der Wortform, eine Modeerscheinung der ersten zwanzig Jahre des XX. Jahrhunderts. Hauptvertreter sind J. Severjanin, ferner B. A. *Lavrenëv* u. a. Eine nennenswerte Spur hat diese Richtung in der russischen Literatur nicht hinterlassen.

EMIGRATION

oder „innere Emigration“. Zur i. E. gehören Menschen, welche zwar in der Sowjetunion leben und auch nicht auswandern wollen, die Sowjetmacht aber ihrem Wesen nach ablehnen und sich aus jeglichem aktiven Leben in eine Art passiver Resistenz zurückgezogen haben. Es sind hauptsächlich Menschen, die zu stark in der vorrevolutionären Zeit verwurzelt sind und den Weg zum neuen Leben nicht finden konnten. Bei den Dichtern äußert sich dieser Zustand entweder durch die Scheu vor der Öffentlichkeit (z. B. *Sologub*) oder dadurch, daß der Autor seine Anschauungen dem Leser in erster Linie „zwischen den Zeilen“ mitteilt. (M. *Bulgakov*, E. *Zamjatin* u. a. m.)

EXPRESSIONISMUS, EXPRESSIONISTEN

kam in der russischen Dichtung anfangs des XX. Jahrhunderts auf. Die einzige Realität ist das subjektive Leben des Künstlers. Die Grundlage des künstlerischen Schaffens war für die Expressionisten nicht das unmittelbare Erlebnis (wie bei den *Impressionisten*), sondern das B e w u ß t s e i n des Erlebten. Diese Neigung zum Irrationalen sieht man in der Malerei etwa bei Van Gogh und O. Kokoschka. In der russischen Literatur sind L. Andreev, beim Theater E. B. Vachtangov, V. E. Mejerchol'd, A. J. Tairov, K. A. Madžanov die markantesten Vertreter dieser Richtung.

FORMALISMUS, FORMALISTEN

Trennung der Form vom Inhalt und Überbewertung der Form. Der extreme F. kann als *Dekadenz* bezeichnet werden. Die künstlerische Form ist für die F. Selbstzweck. In Rußland fand diese Bewegung in der Gruppe der *Kubofuturisten* ihre Vertreter, wurde aber durch die Partei verurteilt (O *Proletkul'tach* 1920 und im Erlaß der Partei über die Fragen der Ideologie 1946—1948). Nach L. *Grossmann* (Metod i stil', Moskau 1922) strebt der F. die „Vertiefung der Sprachstudien, der Komposition, der poetischen Technik und der künstlerischen Eigenart des jeweiligen Autors" an.

FOSP

Federacija ob-edinenij sovetskich pisatelej. Eine Organisation, welche beauftragt wurde, *RAPP, LEF, Pereval* und andere Schriftstellerorganisationen zu vereinigen, jedoch zu keiner nennenswerten Tätigkeit sich entfalten konnte.

FUTURISMUS, FUTURISTEN

Diese Bewegung, die durch die Ablehnung der Vergangenheit auf dem Gebiet der Kultur, der Moral, aber auch durch die Ablehnung der Gegenwart auffällt, entstand vor dem ersten Weltkrieg. Der F. war im wesentlichen eine negative und destruktive Bewegung. Sie zog im Namen einer unklar formulierten Kunst der Zukunft gegen die bürgerliche Kultur, alle Konventionen, sowie die Kunst der Vergangenheit zu Felde" (Struve). Im vorrevolutionären Rußland gehörten zu dieser Richtung Dichter der Gruppe „Gileja", die *Kubofuturisten* (D. D. Burljuk, V. V. *Chlebnikov,* V. V. Kamenskij, V. V. *Majakovskij* u. a.), dann die Gruppe „*Centrifuga*" (S. Bobrov, B. L. *Pasternak,* N. N. *Aseev*), Vertreter des *Egofuturismus* (I. Severjanin). Nach der Revolution gaben sich die *Futuristen* in der Zeitung „Iskusstvo kommuny" (1918—1919) und dann in der Zeitschrift „*Lef*" (1923—1925) als Vertreter des linksradikalen Flügels aus. Von der Partei wurde der F. 1932 als unzeitgemäß gebrandmarkt.

GOSIZDAT

Gosudarstvennoe izdatel'stvo — Staatsverlag.

IDEALISMUS

Nichtmaterialistische Philosophien werden von der materialistischen (marxistischen) Philosophie als I. bezeichnet und gelten schlechthin als unwissenschaftlich und reaktionär. Deswegen muß I. in sowjetischer Diktion als ein wenig aussagender Allgemeinbegriff verstanden werden.

IMAGINISMUS, IMAGINISTEN

formalistische literarische Strömung, die kurze Zeit vor dem ersten Weltkrieg in England auftrat (T. E. Hulme, H. Doolittle, Ezra Pound). Der I. kam in Rußland erst durch das Erste Manifest am 1. Februar 1919 auf. Zu den I. gehörten in Rußland vor allem Šeršenevič, *Kljuev*, Mariengof und *Esenin* (in der ersten Periode seines Schaffens). Der Kreis der I. zerfiel 1924. Das Typische am I. war die Vernachlässigung des Inhaltes. Betont wurde die Hebung der Form, der Vorstellungskraft. Das Lossagen der I. vom „täglichen Leben“, ihre Vorliebe für die russische Dorftradition und ihre politische Desinteressiertheit wird ihnen von der Sowjetkritik verübelt.

IMAGISMUS

Vgl. Imaginismus

IMPRESSIONISMUS, IMPRESSIONISTEN

laut sowjetischer Auffassung, eine rein bürgerliche, aus Frankreich stammende (zweite Hälfte des XIX. Jhd.) Kunstrichtung. Der I. bemüht sich, das Kunsterlebnis unmittelbar wiederzugeben. Die Art der Wiedergabe ist betont persönlich. Die Künstler des I. haben wenig Verständnis für das Leben ihrer Umgebung. Vorgeworfen wird ihnen ein ausgeprägter Individualismus. Sie überschätzen die Form zum Nachteil des Inhaltes. (nach T.V.)

INNERE EMIGRATION

Vgl. Emigration

INTERNATIONALISMUS, INTERNATIONALISTEN

unter I. werden in der SU vor allem Anhänger Trockijs verstanden.

JUNGE GARDE

Molodaja gvardija, ein Verlag, 1922 auf Beschluß des 5. Allrussischen Komsomolkongresses gegründet. Vor allem als Komsomolverlag gedacht; 1933 wurde die Kinderliteratur dem *Detizdat*

übertragen. Die Zeitschrift „Molodaja gvardija" (1922—1941) veröffentlichte Werke namhafter Schriftsteller, wie z. B. N. N. *Aseev*, V. *Majakovskij*, M. *Gor'kij*, D. *Bednyj*, A. *Neverov* u. a. m. Seit 1948 erscheint ein Almanach „Molodaja gvardija".
Ferner werden unter „Molodaja gvardija" auch die Untergrundkämpfer der kommunistischen Jugend im zweiten Weltkrieg verstanden (vgl. *Fadeev* „Molodaja gvardija").

KOLLEKTIVE ARBEIT

Künstlerkollektive sind in der Sowjetunion nicht selten. Nach der Meinung der Sowjetkritik sollen sie eine „große Zukunft" haben (T. V.). Gruppenarbeiten werden vor allem von Bildhauern, Malern aber auch hie und da von Dichtern (z. B. *Il'f i Petrov*) vorgelegt.

KOMPARATIVISMUS

die vergleichende Methode in der Literaturwissenschaft, wird von der Sowjetkritik als verderbliche und abwegige Methode der westeuropäischen Literaturwissenschaft bezeichnet. (T. V.)

KONSTRUKTIVISMUS, KONSTRUKTIVISTEN

ist nach sowjetischer Auffassung eine Verfallserscheinung der bürgerlichen Kunst und Literatur des XX. Jahrhunderts; entstanden nach dem ersten Weltkrieg. Die K. sehen in jeder, besonders in den rein technischen Erscheinungen unserer Zeit (Fabrik, Auto usw.) auch eine Kunst, die Kunst unserer Zeit. Diese Richtung blühte in der Sowjetunion eine Zeitlang und wurde dann von der Sowjetkritik verworfen. Sammelbecken dieser Kunstrichtung in Rußland war die 1923 von Il'ja *Sel'vinskij* in Moskau gegründete Vereinigung „Das literarische Zentrum", die erst 1930 aufgelöst wurde. Zu den K. gehörte u. a. auch der Dichter E. G. *Bagrickij* (1895—1934).

KOSMIST

Unter der Führung Bogdanovs (1873—1928) übernahm der *Proletkul't* die Aufgabe, eine spezifisch proletarische Literatur zu schaffen. Diese Vereinigung war besonders von 1918—1920 aktiv und gab als eigene Zeitschrift die „Proletarskaja kul'tura" heraus. 1920 gründeten einige proletarische Dichter, die sich vom *Pro-*

letkul't getrennt hatten, in Moskau die Gruppe *Kuznica.* Ihr Gegenstück in Petrograd nannte sich K. Zu ihnen gehörte u. a. S. A. *Gerasimov.*

KOSMOPOLITISMUS, KOSMOPOLITEN

eine Ideenwelt, für die das Wort „Ichbinderweltbürger" kennzeichnend ist. Nach der Meinung der Sowjetkritik bemühen sich die USA, die kosmopolitische Weltanschauung in der Welt zu verbreiten, um dadurch eine Voraussetzung für ihre Weltherrschaft zu schaffen. Besonders abwegig findet die Sowjetkritik die durch den K. entstehende Ablehnung der eigenen nationalen Kultur. Als politischer Vertreter des K. wird L. B. Trockij bezeichnet.

KRITISCHER REALISMUS

stellt wahrheitsgetreu das Negative des Lebens in seinen Kunstwerken dar (z. B. Gogols „Tote Seelen").

KUBISMUS

eine Nebenströmung des extremen *Futurismus;* das ganze Leben wird in elementare geometrische Formen zerlegt. Mariengof, Šeršenevič und Kusikov gehören mit einigen ihrer Werke dieser literarischen Richtung an. Der K. wird von der Sowjetkritik als reaktionär abgelehnt.

KUBOFUTURISMUS, KUBOFUTURISTEN

sucht eine Verbindung der klassischen Lyrik mit dem Zeitalter der Technik zu finden. Zu den K. gehörte unter anderem auch der junge N. N. *Aseev.*

KÚZNICA

eine Gruppe von Dichtern des damaligen *Proletkul't,* die in Moskau gegründet wurde (vgl. *Kosmist).* Die Dichter der K. besangen hauptsächlich den Arbeiter und seine Arbeit in der Fabrik. Nur Poletaev, einer der begabtesten aus dieser Gruppe, machte hierin eine Ausnahme und schrieb über den Arbeiter in seinem Heim, bei seiner Familie. Er gehörte auch zu den wenigen, die in ihren Dichtungen optimistische Anschauungen vertraten.

Die Vereinigung ging dann in dem im August 1921 gegründeten *VAPP* auf.

LAKIRÓVKA, LAKIRÓVŠČIK

bedeutet in der Sprache der Sowjetkritik eine Verschönerung der Gegenwart, eine schönfärberische Schilderung des Lebens, frei von allen Konflikten, im Sinne der Parteirichtlinien. „Lakirovščiki" wurden vor allem die Erfolgsdichter der Stalinära genannt, welche ihre Erfolge nicht ihrer künstlerischen Begabung, sondern der Art der Stoffwahl und Behandlung verdanken. Ein typisches Beispiel hierfür ist S. *Babaevskij* mit seinen Romanen „Kavaler zolotoj zvezdy", „Svet nad zemlëj" usw.

LAPP

Vgl. *VAPP*

LEF

Levyj front iskusstva — die linke Front der Kunst, eine 1923 in Moskau gebildete literarische Gruppe, welche die Zeitschrift „Lef" (1923—1925) und „Novyj lef" (1927—1928) herausgab und den *Futuristen* nahe stand. Die L.-Gruppe trat für eine „proizvodstvennuju literaturu", eine Literatur der Tatsachen, ein. Einer der bedeutendsten Vertreter des L. und Redakteur der genannten Zeitschriften war V. *Majakovskij* (1928 aus dem L. ausgetreten). Ferner gehörten ihr auch N. N. *Aseev,* B. *Pasternak,* A. *Kručënych,* S. *Tret'jakov,* V. *Chlebnikov,* A. *Fadeev* u. a. m. an.

LITERARISCHES ZENTRUM

Vgl. Konstruktivismus

LITO

Litodel, Literarische Abteilung des Kommissariates für Volksbildung.

LITODÉL

Vgl. LITO

LZK

Literarisches Zentrum der *Konstruktivisten.*

MAPP
Vgl. VAPP

MITLÄUFER
oder *Poputčiki.* So wurden Schriftsteller Ende der zwanziger Jahre genannt, welche die sowjetische Wirklichkeit zwar akzeptierten und vor allem eine politisch vollkommen loyale Haltung einnahmen, aber ihrer Herkunft nach nicht zu den proletarischen Dichtern gehörten und keine Parteigenossen waren. Ihre gesellschaftliche Gleichberechtigung wurde erst im Jahre 1932 durch die Auflösung und Verurteilung der *RAPP* gesichert. Zu den M. zählen folgende namhafte Dichter: *Esenin, Pil'njak,* Vsevolod *Ivanov, Tichonov, Leonov, Romanov, Kataev, Zoščenko, Ognev* u. a. m. Die Zeitschrift „Krasnaja nov' ", herausgegeben von Aleksandr Voronskij (1884—193?) stand den M. nahe.

MODERNISMUS
abgesehen von der im Westen üblichen Bezeichnung für die religiösen, philosophischen Strömungen des XIX. und XX. Jahrhunderts wird M. von den Sowjets als allgemeine Bezeichnung für verschiedene, nach sowjetischer Diktion als Verfallserscheinungen zu bezeichnende Kunstrichtungen gebraucht, zu denen auch *Impressionismus, Expressionismus* und *Konstruktivismus* zählen. Alles Reaktionäre, Volksfeindliche (antinarodnoe) und *Kosmopolitische* wird als M. gestempelt.

MOLODÁJA GVÁRDIJA
Vgl. Junge Garde

MYSTIZISMUS
eine der üblichen sowjetischen Definitionen: „Die Vertretung des M. in der gegenwärtigen bürgerlichen Gesellschaft beweist den Marasmus und die Verfaultheit der bürgerlichen Kultur, ist der Ausdruck der Angst der imperialistischen Bourgeoisie vor den Massen, welche für den Frieden, Freiheit und Sozialismus kämpfen."

NAPÓSTOVCY
Vgl. Vorpostler

NATURALISMUS

bemüht sich, als Kunstrichtung der Wirklichkeit in der getreuen Nachbildung des Lebens, der Sprache (mit allen lokalen Sprachbesonderheiten) usw. ähnlich zu sein. Ihm mangelt es an der Verallgemeinerung. E. Zola gilt als der größte Vertreter des N.

NEOREALISMUS

eine reaktionäre Schule der modernen Philosophie (besonders in Amerika und England), steht dem Machinismus nahe. N. propagiert subjektive, idealistische Thesen über die Identität des Gegenstandes und der Idee. Nach ihm sind die Mathematik und die Logik der einzigen Formen der rellen Welt. (nach der Kleinen Sowjetenzyklopädie)

NEP

Neue ökonomische Politik (nóvaja ekonomíčeskaja polítika). N. bezeichnet die Periode der teilweisen Rückkehr zu gewissen kapitalistischen Wirtschaftsformen. Eingeführt auf Grund eines Beschlusses des X. Parteitages im Frühjahr 1921. Diese wirtschaftliche Auflockerung war notwendig, um die nach dem Bürgerkrieg vollkommen zerrüttete Wirtschaft wiederherzustellen. Die N.-Periode ist im geistigen und besonders im gesellschaftlichen Leben des Landes durch das Aufkommen des Spießertums gekennzeichnet. Unternehmungslustige Elemente nützten die schnell entstandene Konjunktur zu einem geschmacklosen Wohlstand aus. *Il'f* und *Petrov, Zoščenko*, Pantelejmon *Romanov* und andere Schriftsteller (vor allem *Majakovskij*) greifen das Lächerliche dieser Zeit von verschiedenen Gesichtswinkeln aus an. Die Fünfjahrespläne und die Kollektivisierung (ab 1927) machten der N.-Periode ein Ende. In der Erinnerung der älteren Generation erscheint die N.-Zeit oft als Eldorado im Vergleich zu den Jahren 1918—1921 und den dreißiger Jahren.

NEPMÁN

N. wurden Menschen genannt, welche in der Zeit des *NEP* besonders erfolgreich waren. Auch — Schieber, Neureiche.

NIČEVÓKI

eine literarische Gruppierung (der Name kommt von „ničegó"), welche um das Jahr 1921 hervortrat.

NIHILISMUS, NIHILISTEN

ist die Ablehnung des Bestehenden. In den sechziger Jahren des XIX. Jahrhunderts entstand in der russischen Literatur der Typ des N., vor allem in der Gestalt des E. Bazarov (Turgenevs „Väter und Söhne"); die sowjetische Kritik lehnt die Bezeichnung N. für die Revolutionäre der sechziger und siebziger Jahre (XIX. Jahrh.) ab, bezeichnet aber selbst hie und da ihre eigenen Gegner als N.

NOVÁTORSTVO

Bezeichnung für das richtige Gefühl für das Neue (nóvyj, novátor) und Wertvolle in der Literatur. N. der Form nach ist *Formalismus* und ist schädlich; N. in der Ideenwelt ist notwendig und zu begrüßen (nach *Ždanov*).

OBJEKTIVISMUS

ist eine Bezeichnung für eine politisch desinteressierte Haltung, die von sowjetischer Seite nach dem Grundsatz „Wer nicht mit uns ist, ist gegen uns" verurteilt wird.

OPOJÁZ

Óbščestvo po izučéniju poetíčeskogo jazyká, Gesellschaft zum Studium der dichterisch-poetischen Sprache (1914—1923). Diese Gesellschaft war eine Gründung der *Formalisten* (V. B. *Šklovskij* u. a. m.).

PAPP

Vgl. VAPP

PEREVÁL

Die P.-Gruppe wurde im Jahre 1924 gegründet. Eine Anzahl von jungen Schriftstellern, vor allem Poeten, welche von der *Jungen Garde* (Molodaja gvardija) und „Oktober" (Oktjabr') kamen, waren für eine Zusammenarbeit mit den *Poputčiki* (Mitläufer). Zu ihnen zählten: Ivan *Kataev,* Andrej *Platonov,* der Kritiker Lešnëv, Gleb *Glinka* u. a. Politisch standen die meisten der „Perevalovcy" den *Trockisten* nahe und wurden so in den dreißiger Jahren Verfolgungen ausgesetzt.

POPÚTČIKI

Vgl. Mitläufer

PROLETKÚL'T

eine radikale Kunstanschauung, welche vor allem mit der Vergangenheit brechen wollte. An ihrer Spitze stand Bogdanov. Im Jahre 1920 wurde der P. von der kommunistischen Partei verurteilt und aufgelöst. Im gleichen Jahr konstituierte sich ein Teil der Moskauer P.-Dichter in der Gruppe *Kuznica*, in Leningrad in der *Kosmist*-Bewegung.

RAPP

Rossíjskaja associácija proletárskich pisátelej (Russische Vereinigung proletarischer Schriftsteller). Eine literarische Organisation, welche von 1925 bis 1932 bestand. Die ursprüngliche Aufgabe dieser Organisation war, die Sowjetliteratur vor bürgerlichen und antisowjetisch eingestellten Elementen zu schützen. R. übte „diktatorische Vollmachten aus und bestimmte die Politik, nach welcher sich alle Schriftsteller zu richten hatten, wenn sie in der Literatur weiter leben wollten" (Struve). Führer der R. war der Kritiker Averbach. Durch das Dekret vom 23. April 1932 wurde die R.-Organisation aufgelöst. Einige ihrer Mitglieder (Averbach) wurden verfolgt, den anderen gelang es, sich der neuen Situation anzupassen (Jurij *Libedinskij*).

REALISMUS

„ist die Grundmethode in der Kunst" (T. V.). Sein Gebot lautet: Lebenswahrheit ist der Leitfaden des Künstlers, der sich Mühe geben muß, ein Maximum davon in seinem Werk zu vermitteln (vgl. *Kritischer Realismus* und *sozialistischer Realismus*).

RÓSTA

Rossíjskoe telegráfnoe agéntstvo (Russische Telegrafenagentur), gegründet 1918, mit *TASS* 1925 fusioniert.

SCHRIFTSTELLERVERBAND DER RSFSR

wurde 1957 gegründet. Vorsitzender wurde Leonid *Sobolev*. Seit 1958 verfügt der S. über einen eigenen Verlag („Sovremennik") und gibt seine eigene Zeitschrift, „Literatura i žizn' ", heraus.

Verzeichnis sowjetischer literarischer Begriffe

SCHRIFTSTELLERVERBAND DER SU

Sojúz pisátelej SSSR. Auf Grund eines Beschlusses des ZK der Partei vom 23. 4. 1932 wurden alle literarischen Gruppen und Organisationen (insbesondere *RAPP*) aufgelöst und ein Schriftstellerverband (Sojuz sovetskich pisatelej) ins Leben gerufen, der alle gefügigen Dichter der Sowjetunion vereinigen sollte. Seine Aufgabe war, auch die Kunstrichtung für das ganze Land zu bestimmen (*Sozialistischer Realismus*). Die konstituierende Versammlung fand im August 1934 statt. Die erste, bis 1955 gültige Bezeichnung lautete „Sojuz sovetskich pisatelej". Die Mitgliederzahl stieg von 1500 im August 1934 auf 3695 im Dezember 1954. Der erste Ehrenpräsident des Verbandes war M. *Gor'kij*. Der S. hat auch einen eigenen Verlag (Sovetskij pisatel') und gibt als sein offizielles Organ die „Literaturnaja gazeta" heraus.

SERAPIONSBRÜDER

Serapiónovy brát'ja, eine literarische Gruppe, welche um 1921 in Petrograd enstand und bis in die Mitte der zwanziger Jahre eine bedeutende Rolle spielte. Sie wurde so nach E. T. A. Hoffmanns Erzählungen benannt. Die S. stellen die Kunst außerhalb der Politik; ihre daraus folgende apolitische Haltung wird ihnen von der Partei übelgenommen. Theoretiker dieser Gruppe war der Schriftsteller L. *Lunc*. Zu den S. gehörten u. a. Vs. *Ivanov*, N. *Tichonov*, K. *Fedin*, V. *Kaverin*, N. *Nikitin*, *Zamjatin*, *Leonov*, A. *Tolstoj*, u. a. m.

SOZIALISTISCHER REALISMUS

spiegelt das Leben in der revolutionären Entwicklung wider, d. h. das Leben als Erscheinungsform der sozialistischen Gesellschaft. Es wird der Kampf um den morgigen Tag gezeigt. Im s. R. wird das Leben des Volkes, der Nation gezeichnet und damit die nationale Form bewahrt (*Tichonov* über den s. R. in der „Pravda", 12. Februar 1958).

STALINPREIS

Stalinpreise wurden für hervorragende Leistungen in Kunst und Wissenschaft seit 1939 verliehen. In jeder Gruppe gab es verschiedene Preisklassen. Der erste Preis bestand aus der ansehnlichen Summe von 100 000 Rubeln. Unter den ersten Preisträgern für Literatur waren Aleksej *Tolstoj* für den dritten Teil seines

„Leidensweges", *Šolochov* für den dritten Teil des „Stillen Don", *Erenburg* für den „Fall von Paris", sowie *Virta, Simonov* und *Tichonov* (nach Struve).

SURREALISMUS

extrem formale Richtung in der Kunst. Die Quelle der Kunst liegt im Unterbewußtsein, im Traum, im Ilogismus (P. Picasso).

SYMBOLISMUS, SYMBOLISTEN

S. verzichtet auf die Erkenntnis der Wirklichkeit. Der Verstand kann die reale Wirklichkeit nicht erkennen, nur die Intuition allein ist fähig, zu erkennen und auch so in die Welt des Unfaßbaren einzudringen. Zu den Vertretern des S. zählt man K. D. Bal'mont, D. S. Merežkovskij, Z. Gippius, F. *Sologub*, A. *Belyj*, Vjačeslav Ivanov. Die hervorragendsten S. waren jedoch A. *Blok* und V. *Brjusov*. Außer *Blok* und *Brjusov* lehnten die meisten der S. den Bolschewismus ab und gingen entweder in die Emigration oder zogen sich aus dem öffentlichen Leben zurück.

TASS

Telegráfnoe Agéntstvo Sovétskogo Sojúza (Telegrafenagentur der Sowjetunion). Gegründet 1925.

TAUWETTER

ein Begriff, welcher in den Wortschatz des Westens für die Zeit der nachstalinistischen Auflockerung Eingang fand. Dies gilt besonders für die Zeit von 1953 bis 1956. Das Wort T. aus dem gleichnamigen Roman von I. *Erenburg* übernommen. T.-Literatur werden jene Werke genannt, welche die sowjetische Wirklichkeit während der genannten Periode kritisch darstellen (z. B. *Dudincev* „Nicht von Brot allein").

TAUWETTERLITERATUR

TROCKISMUS, TROCKISTEN

Die XVI. Parteikonferenz (1925) erklärte die Politik Trockijs und seiner Anhänger zum Gegner des Bolschewismus, und seither werden die Trockisten als dessen Feinde bezeichnet. Stalin führte gegen die Trockisten einen schonungslosen Kampf. T. vertreten die Idee der permanenten Revolution.

VAPP

Vserossíjskaja associácija proletárskich pisátelej (Allunionsvereinigung proletarischer Schriftsteller), eine Vereinigung, welche 1920 entstand. In ihr vereinigten sich die Schriftsteller der russischen Sowjetrepublik und der transkaukasischen Republiken. Nach dem Jahre 1928 war sie unter dem Namen *VOAPP* (Allunionsverband der Vereinigung proletarischer Schriftsteller) bekannt. Die Sektion in Moskau nannte sich *MAPP*, jene in Leningrad *LAPP* (Petrograd - *PAPP*). Alle diese Organisationen wurden am 23. April 1932 aufgelöst.

VOAPP

Vgl. VAPP

VORONSKISMUS

kommt von dem Namen des bedeutenden Sowjetkritikers und Literarhistorikers Voronskij. Dieser schloß sich in den zwanziger Jahren der Gruppe *Pereval* an, war als Anhänger *Trockijs* bekannt, wurde als solcher aus der Partei ausgeschlossen, und um 1937 fiel er einer Säuberung zum Opfer. V. wird in der Sowjetkritik als ein „ständiges Schimpfwort in der Kampagne gegen die *Pereval*gruppe" gebraucht. (Struve). Voronskijs größter Gegner war Averbach.

VORPOSTLER

russisch — napóstovcy. Diese literarische Gruppe entstand aus dem Kreis um Lelevič, der die Zeitschrift „Na postu" leitete (gegründet im Juni 1923, erschien bis 1925, zusammen sechs Nummern). Diese Schriftsteller waren meist proletarischer Abkunft, doch in ihrer Mehrheit keine Kommunisten, ja sie standen oft in Opposition zu den Führern der Partei. Zu diesen Dichtern gehörten außer G. Lelevič (Pseudonym für Laborij G. Kal'manson, geb. 1901), B. Volin, O. Brik, Aleksandr *Bezymenskij*, Jurij *Libedinskij* u. a. Ihre These war, daß die neue Literatur eine selbständige, proletarische Literatur sein müsse und bei niemandem zu lernen habe, also weg von der Tradition und den Klassikern. Ihre Tätigkeit bestand hauptsächlich in der Bekämpfung der *Mitläufer*. Von der Regierung wurden die V. als Volksfeinde gebrandmarkt.

ZAÚM'

oder „zaúmnaja poézija", eine unübersetzbare Neubildung, welche die „neue", begriffslose Poesie mit ihren neugebildeten, nur für den Augenblick gültigen Wörtern bezeichnen sollte. Beispiele hierzu liefern vor allem die Werke von *Chlebnikov, Kručënych* und anderen *Futuristen.* Theoretische Abhandlungen zur Rechtfertigung dieser „Poesie" wurden vor allem von B. Arvatov verfaßt („Rečetvorčestvo" in *Lef,* Jahrg. 1923, Nr. 2, S. 79—91).

ŽDÁNOVŠČINA, (ŽDANOV)

die fast ausschließlich in westlichen Publikationen gebrauchte Bezeichnung für die Ära der straffen Ausrichtung der sowjetischen Literatur und Kunst nach den ideologischen Forderungen der Kommunistischen Partei unter Andrej Aleksandrovič Ždanov (1896 bis 1948). Von entscheidender Bedeutung für die Entwicklung der Literatur waren Ž.s Rede auf dem Unionskongreß des Schriftstellerverbandes im Jahre 1934, „Über Kunst und Wissenschaft", und sein Referat über die Zeitschriften „Zvezda" und „Leningrad" im Jahre 1946, in welchem er die Richtlinien der Partei für die Literatur festlegte. Hatte Ž. im Jahre 1934 die Richtlinien im Sinne des *sozialistischen Realismus* festgelegt, so wiederholte er sie 1946 mit der Modifizierung, daß er von den Schriftstellern verlange, den Sowjetmenschen (sovetskij čelovek) als für die übrige Welt beispielgebend zu schildern. Wichtig war in Ž.s Reden von 1946 auch die Forderung, die Problematik des modernen Dorfes zu behandeln.

ZNÁNIE

Der Verlag Z. wurde 1893 in St. Petersburg gegründet. Nachdem *Gor'kij* an ihm teilnahm, wurde der Verlag zu einem Sammelpunkt der progressiven Schriftsteller Rußlands. Z. gab unter anderem Werke von *Gor'kij, Serafimovič, Kuprin* u. a. heraus.

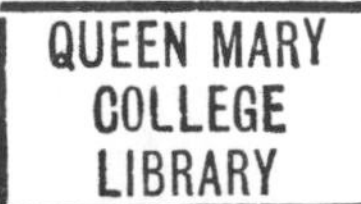

NAMENSINDEX

Kursiv gedruckte Seitenzahlen verweisen auf eine ausführliche Behandlung des Stichworts.

Namensindex

Namensindex

BEGRIFFSINDEX

BEIHEFTE ZUR
ZEITSCHRIFT FÜR ROMANISCHE PHILOLOGIE

BEGRÜNDET VON GUSTAV GRÖBER
FORTGEFÜHRT VON WALTHER VON WARTBURG
HERAUSGEGEBEN VON KURT BALDINGER

BAND 206

STEVEN N. DWORKIN

Etymology and Derivational Morphology: The Genesis of Old Spanish Denominal Adjectives in *-ido*

MAX NIEMEYER VERLAG TÜBINGEN
1985

Publication of this book has been made possible in part by a grant from the Horace H. Rackham School of Graduate Studies at the University of Michigan.

CIP-Kurztitelaufnahme der Deutschen Bibliothek

Dworkin, Steven N.:
Etymology and derivational morphology : the genesis of old Spanish denominal adjectives in -ido /
Steven N. Dworkin. – Tübingen : Niemeyer, 1985.
(Zeitschrift für romanische Philologie : Beihefte ; Bd. 206)
NE: Zeitschrift für romanische Philologie / Beihefte

ISBN 3-484-52206-2 ISSN 0084-5396

Satz: C. H. Beck'sche Buchdruckerei, Nördlingen
Druck: Sulzberg-Druck GmbH, Sulzberg im Allgäu

Table of Contents

Acknowledgement

It is a pleasure to acknowledge the help received from many quarters in the preparation of this monograph. I am deeply grateful to Professors Jerry R. Craddock, Clifford S. Leonard, Jr., Yakov Malkiel, and Ernst Pulgram for their insightful comments on an earlier draft of this study. I have incorporated many of their suggestions, but I alone remain responsible for remaining errors and stylistic infelicities. My warmest appreciation goes to the University of Michigan for the following generous assistance: I wish to thank the Horace H. Rackham School of Graduate Studies for a Faculty Fellowship which allowed me to complete the research for this monograph, the College of Literature, Science and the Arts for a grant which covered the costs of preparing the manuscript for submission, and the Department of Romance Languages for funding the computer time needed for text editing and processing. I owe a special debt of gratitude to David J. Billick who carefully and expertly prepared this monograph on the computers of the University of Michigan Terminal System.

CHAPTER ONE

Spanish Pseudo-Participial Adjectives in *-ido:* An Overview

Etymologists have long known that successful work in their specialty demands recourse to the knowledge furnished by all branches of historical grammar – phonology, morphology (inflectional, derivational, and compositional), syntax, and semantics. In a not too distant past, the masters of historical grammar fully understood the importance of etymology for their craft. The work of many first-rate scholars displays a happy balance between diachronically-slanted lexical pieces and essays in straight historical grammar. Within the fields of Latin and Romance studies, the names of Alfred Ernout, Friedrich Diez, Wilhelm Meyer-Lübke, and Max Leopold Wagner, each of whom authored both etymological dictionaries and historical grammars, spring immediately to mind. Although he never compiled a standard etymological dictionary, the research carried out by Ramón Menéndez Pidal shows an impressive interplay between historical grammar and etymology; his *Cid* Grammar (1908), his masterly *Orígenes del español* (1926; [3]1950), and the definitive version (1941) of his *Manual de gramática histórica española* were flanked by strings of impressive lexical vignettes[1] and the etymological vocabulary of the *Cantar de mío Cid.* Outside the Romance domain one may invoke in this context, by way of illustration, the names of Émile Benveniste[2], Pierre Chantraine, Antoine Meillet, and Edward Sapir.

Today's practitioners of Romance historical grammar, especially students of morphology and syntax, have tended to ignore the findings made available by the probings of etymologists into the histories of individual lexical items, word families, or semantic fields. This attitude has resulted in the well documented estrangement – to the disadvantage of all parties – of etymology and historical grammar. To a large extent etymologists have not exactly helped their own cause. With a few notable exceptions (such as Yakov Malkiel, Kurt Baldinger, and those few of their immediate disciples who have displayed some degree of commitment to etymological research), they have neglected to show concern with the implications of their findings for general linguistics and have been slow

[1] See especially his "Etimologías españolas", *Ro,* 29 (1900), 334-379, and "Notas para el léxico románico", *RFE,* 7 (1920), 1–36, an elaboration upon the Spanish material in the first edition of Wilhelm Meyer-Lübke, *REW.*

[2] For a retrospective of Benveniste's massive output viewed within the framework of this discussion, see Malkiel, "Lexis and Grammar – Necrological Essay on Émile Benveniste (1902–76)", *RPh,* 34:2 (1980), 160–94.

to take advantage of new insights provided by more experimentally minded linguists. Responsibility for rectifying this situation falls squarely on the shoulders of the etymologist, who can no longer afford the luxury of being a "pure" etymologist in the style of such luminaries as Paul Aebischer, Juan Corominas, and Johannes Hubschmid.

Among Romanists active today Yakov Malkiel has taken the lead in attempting to revitalize etymology and to restore a healthy balance with historical grammar[3]. Among his recent suggestions is the inclusion within the scope of etymology of the genesis and spread of affixal as well as of root morphemes. Certain intricate problems of derivational morphology may require the microscopic inspection of each lexical item in which the element in question makes an appearance.

Worthy of quotation in this context is the following observation made by Malkiel some thirty years ago:

> "it has become empirically known that word formation (that is, derivation and composition) which, with inflection proper, makes up morphology in the Indo-European languages, is best studied and practiced jointly with etymology; witness the output of researchers such as A. Ernout and M. L. Wagner who attack problem after problem of word origins and formative suffixes, simply because they have found the respective issues to be inextricably interwoven."[4]

Let me add here that Malkiel himself has consistently practiced what he has preached in these lines. His monographs on the growth of individual suffixes are accompanied by separate studies of pertinent lexical items (many etymologically opaque) which contain the formative under study. Such investigations may be especially necessary with non-native suffixes which at first enter a language as integral parts of loanwords (e.g., Sp. *-aje, -esco*)[5], and with affixes

---

[3] The vital connection between etymology and historical grammar has preoccupied Malkiel since the fifties. His most recent papers on the topic include: "The Interlocking of Etymology and Historical Grammar Exemplified with the Analysis of Spanish *desleír", Proceedings of the Second International Conference on Historical Linguistics,* ed. William M. Christie, Jr., (Amsterdam, 1976), pp. 285–310 (with Discussion at pp. 310–12); "Perspectives d'un renouvellement de l'étymologie romane", *Actes du XIIIe congrès international de linguistique et philologie romanes (Québec, 1971)* (Québec, 1976), pp. 967–86; "Etymology as a Challenge to Phonology: The Case of Romance Linguistics", *Lautgeschichte und Etymologie: Akten der VI. Fachtagung der Indogermanischen Gesellschaft, Wien 24–29 September 1978* (Wiesbaden, 1980), pp. 260–86; "Etymology: New Thoughts and Possibilities for its Rejuvenation", *Scritti linguistici in onore di G. B. Pellegrini,* I, (Pisa [1983]), pp. 589–634.

[4] "Etymology and the Structure of Word Families", *Word,* 10 (1954), 265–74, at 265.

[5] On *-aje* see Suzanne Fleischman's monograph, *Cultural and Linguistic Factors in Word Formation: An Integrated Approach to the Development of the Suffix -age,* UCPL 86 (Berkeley, London, and Los Angeles, 1977), esp. pp. 285–315. On *-esco* see Malkiel, "The Pan-European Suffix *-esco, -esque* in Stratigraphic Projection", *Papers in Linguistics and Phonetics to the Memory of Pierre Delattre,* ed. Albert Valdmann (The Hague, 1973), 357–87; and, Thomas J. Walsh, "Two Contrastable Approaches to Suffixal Derivation: The Case of Romance *-esco/-esque*", *RPh,* 33:4 (1980), 489–96.

which may have been generated from the language's internal derivational resources. The growth and spread in Hispano-Romance of one such problem suffix constitutes the central theme of this monograph.

Like its sister languages, Old Spanish had inherited from Latin a set of three suffix-stressed past participles, namely *-ado, -ido,* and *-udo,* attached to verbs in *-ar, -ir,* and *-er* respectively. These same morphemes (or their homonyms) came to perform other tasks in Hispano-Romance. A suffix *-ado* could be employed to form nouns indicative of secular or ecclesiastical jurisdictions (a function in which *-ado* often competed with OSp. *-adgo,* later *azgo,* the local reflex of -ĀTICU); witness *reinado* 'reign' ← *reino* 'kingdom', *principado* 'principate' ← *príncipe* 'prince', *condado,* 'county' ← *conde* 'count', *apostolado* 'papacy' ← *apóstol* 'apostle; Pope', *obispado* 'bishopric' ← *obispo* 'bishop' (alongside *principadgo, condadgo, apostoladgo, obispadgo*)[6]. Cognate formations are found in other Romance languages. In Old Spanish the suffix *-ido* was added to first conjugation verb bases to coin substantives denoting sounds, especially animal noises and cries, e.g., *balido* 'bleating' ← *balar* 'to bleat', *bramido* 'roaring' ← *bramar* 'to roar', *ladrido* 'barking' ← *ladrar* 'to bark'. This systematic use of *-ido* is peculiar to Hispano-Romance[7]. The Romance languages seem not to have used the descendants of -ŪTU in nominal derivation.

Latin has also bequeathed to the daughter languages the ability to coin denominal adjectives with the local reflexes of -ĀTU and -ŪTU. Using *-ado* Spanish created adjectives denoting 'resemblance, equipped with' (e.g., *alado* 'winged' ← *ala* 'wing', *anaranjado* 'orange-colored' ← *naranja* 'orange'), and using *-udo,* adjectives stressing the idea of 'exuberance, overabundance' (e.g., *barbudo* 'with a heavy beard' ← *barba* 'beard', *orejudo* 'long-eared' ← *oreja* 'ear'). However, medieval Hispano-Romance parted company with the other Romance languages by creating on its own a set of semantically negative denominal adjectives in *-ido,* for example *adolorido* 'sad, afflicted' ← *dolor* 'pain'; *descolorido* 'pale, colorless' ← *color* 'color'; *despavorido* 'scared' ← *pavor* 'fear'. It is the history of these denominal formations in *-ido* which I shall seek to explain in this monograph by integrating the findings of individual word studies with the analytic insights provided by the concept of multiple causation.

Medieval (and, to a lesser extent, modern) Hispano-Romance contains a series of what I shall label pseudo-participial adjectives displaying the terminal segment *-ido.* On the synchronic plane these adjectives do not function as the past participle of a corresponding *-er* or *-ir* verb. (In some cases writers and, I suspect, lexicographers have "artificially" coined the appropriate *-ir* verb.) Those *-ido* adjectives which genetically do continue such participles (a minority

---

[6] On the alternation *-adgo* ~ *-ado* (also learned *-ato*), see Suzanne Fleischman, "Factores operantes en la historia de un sufijo: El caso de *-azgo*", *Estudios ofrecidos a Emilio Alarcos Llorach,* III (Oviedo, 1978), pp. 75–85.

[7] Jerry R. Craddock and Emanuel S. Georges have examined at length this use of *-ido* in their article "The Hispanic Sound-Suffix *-ido*", *RPh,* 17:1 (1963), 87–107.

within the entire group) represent for the most part relics of verbs which had long ago fallen into disuse. A common semantic thread, namely the expression of a negatively-valued physical or mental state or, viewed from a different perspective, the absence or attenuation of the corresponding positive qualities, links the majority of the *-ido* adjectives which I shall discuss here.

A preliminary sifting of the material suggests a threefold division, depending on the nature of the base and the status of the *-ido* segment. In Group I, *-ido* is a segmentable suffix attached to a clearly identifiable nominal base, to which a prefix has been – in all likelihood, simultaneously, – added:

I. *adolorido* 'sad, afflicted' (*dolor* 'pain'), *amodorrido* 'sleepy, drowsy' (*modorra* 'drowsiness'), Ast. *asombríu* (with *íu* as the local equivalent of *-ido*) 'growing in the shade' (*sombra* 'shade'), *desabrido* 'insipid, unpleasant' (*sabor* 'taste'), *desanguido* 'anemic' (OSp. *sangue,* cf. mod. *sangre* 'blood'), *descolorido* 'pale, colorless' (*color* 'color'), OSp. *desertido* 'abandoned, uninhabited' (*desierto* 'desert'), OSp. *desfacido* 'angry' (*faz* 'face'), OSp. *desfamn-, desfambr-ido,* mod. *desh-* 'hungry, famished' (*famne* ~ *fambre,* mod. *hambre* 'hunger'), OSp. *(d)esmedrido* 'downhearted' (*miedo* 'fear'), *(d)espavorido* 'scared' (*pavor* 'fear'), Ast. *enganíu* 'hungry' (*gana* 'desire, want'), OSp. *enlexido* 'dirty' (*lixo* 'dirt, scum'), OSp. *entenebrido* 'darkened' (*tiniebras,* mod. *-blas* 'darkness'), OSp. *esbaforido* 'breathless, shocked' (*bafo* 'breath').

All these formations carry a negative connotation, reinforced in many instances by the prefix *(d)es-*.

In Group II, *-ido* seems to be affixed to adjectival bases, again as part of a parasynthetic derivational pattern:

II. *amortido* 'dead' (*muerto* 'dead'), *denegrido* 'blackened' (*negro* 'black'), *de-, re-sequido* 'very dry' (*seco* 'dry'), *des-, em-blanquido* 'whitened' (*blanco* 'white'), OSp. *empobrido* 'poor, impoverished' (*pobre* 'poor'), OSp. *endurido* 'hardened, obdurate' (*duro* 'hard'), OSp. *enflaquido* 'weakened' (*flaco* 'weak, thin'), *en-, re-gordido* 'swollen, excessively fat' (*gordo* 'fat'), OSp. *enloquido* 'mad' (*loco* 'mad, crazy'), OSp. *enralido* 'rendered sparse' ([vernacular] *ralo* 'sparse' vs [learned] *raro* 'rare, uncommon'), OSp. *ensangostido* 'narrowed down' (*angosto* 'narrow'), *renegrido* 'very black' *(negro),* OSp. *repretido* 'id.' (OSp. *prieto* 'black'), *revejido* 'prematurely aged' (*viejo* 'old'), *reverdido* 'green' (*verde* 'green').

Except for *des-, em-blanquido* and *reverdido,* all these items too have an decidedly negative flavor.

In the adjectives which comprise Group III, *-ido* can best be labeled a "suffixoid". An etymological analysis discloses at least three subclasses. Group III a *-ido* adjectives continue documented Latin bases in -ĪTU:

III a OSp. *bell-, vell-ido* 'handsome, beautiful', possibly traceable in the final analysis to MELLĪTU 'honey-like', OSp. *sencido* 'intact, virgin (of a field)' < SANCĪTU, ppc. of SANCĪRE 'to forbid entry', OSp. *transido* 'dead' < TRĀNSĪTU, ppc. of TRĀNSĪRE 'to cross over'.

Group III b adjectives originally functioned as participles of primary *-er* and *-ir* verbs:

III b *aterido* 'stiff with cold, shivering with cold' (OSp. **aterir;* cf. *aterecer*) alongside *entelerido* 'shivering with fear or fever', *desvaído* 'lank, gaunt' (**desvaír*), *esperido* 'exhausted, emaciated', (**esperir*), *florido* 'flowered' (**florir;* cf. *florecer,* Fr. *fleurir,* It. *fiorire*), OSp. *gracido* 'grateful' (*gracir* 'to thank'), *manido* 'spoiled', gamey (of meat)' (OSp. *man-er, -ir* 'to remain'), OSp. *tollido* (mod. *tull-*) 'paralyzed' (*toller* 'to take away').

A handful of borrowings, almost all Gallicisms adjusted to Spanish morphological conditions, constitutes Group III c:

OSp. *ardido'* ~ *fardido* (var. *faldrido*) 'astute, bold, daring' (OProv. *ardit,* OFr. *hardi* 'id.'), OSp. *(des)marrido* 'sad' (OFr. *marri* 'id.'), OSp. *(d)esmaído* 'feeble' (Cat. *esmait* 'worry, trouble'), *escaldrido* 'wise' (Cat. *escaltrit;* cf. It. *scaltrito*), *favorido* (It. *favorito*), *fornido* 'strong, robust' (OFr. *forni* 'id.' mod. *fourni*), *garrido* handsome, beautiful' (OFr. *garni* 'adorned, ornate'), OSp. *malbaylido* 'poorly cared for' (OFr. *mal-, maubailli* 'id.').

Once again a sizeable proportion of the Spanish adjectives are negatively tinged.

The assignment of adjectives to each group must remain flexible. The positive semantic value of *florido,* combined with the absence of a prefix, suggests that this adjective is more realistically viewed as a lexicalized past participle rather than as a denominal adjective extracted directly from *flor.* On the synchronic plane, many speakers of medieval Spanish at some point probably linked the formations gathered together in Group II directly to the underlying simple adjective; I shall argue below (Chapter three) that, genetically, most of these items are lexicalized past participles of de-adjectival *-ir* verbs which had given way to their *-ecer* doublets. If this claim is accurate, the adjectives gathered together in Group II are typologically related to the items found in Group III b, i.e., adjectives which originated as participles of *-er* or *-ir* verbs. The possible synchronic association of these items with the base adjective rather than with an obsolescent or moribund verb justifies setting these derived adjectives apart for analytical purposes. It is not inconceivable that certain Group II adjectives represent analogical formations derived directly from the relevant adjective. In like fashion the prefix observable in *enlexido* and *entenebrido,* tentatively placed in Group I, may indicate that these adjectives originally arose as past participles of the corresponding (obsolete) denominal *-ir* verbs. Rare and jocose *(a)quellotrido* can be classed with Group I if the base is assumed to be substantivized *aquellotro.*

From the diachronic perspective, Group I presents the greatest difficulties as a morphological class. True, Latin contained a handful of denominal adjectives in -ĪTUS, based for the most part on third-declension nouns:

AURĪTUS 'long-eared' (AURIS 'ear'), AVĪTUS 'ancestral' (AVUS 'grandfather'), CRINĪTUS 'with a mane' (CRĪNIS 'mane'), FOLLĪTUS 'equipped with a leather bag' (FOLLIS 'leather bag, bellows'), IGNĪTUS 'with fire' (IGNIS 'fire'), MELLĪTUS 'honey-like' (MEL 'honey'), ORBĪTUS 'circle-shaped' (ORBIS 'circle'), PATRĪTUS 'father-like' (PATER 'father'), PELLĪTUS 'dressed in skins' (PELLIS 'skin'), PENĪTUS 'equipped with a tail' (PENIS 'tail'), TURRĪTUS 'turreted' (TURRIS 'tower').

Late Latin records some -ĪTUS adjectives formed from first declension nouns: CAUDĪTUS 'with a tail' ← CAUDA 'tail' (cf. PENĪTUS), HERBĪTUS 'grassy' ← HERBA 'grass', LANĪTUS 'wooly' ← LĀNA 'wool' alongside CAUD-, HERB-, LĀN-ĀTUS[8]. Yet not one of these Latin adjectives underlies a Spanish denominal formation in Group I. The relevant Spanish items are semantically far removed from these Latin denominal adjectives in -ĪTUS. Whereas the latter denote 'equipped with, shaped like, related to' and are semantically positive or neutral, the Spanish denominal adjectives in *-ido* are negatively colored and in some cases (though, I hasten to emphasize, not in all) directly indicate the absence or lack of a given quality or feature.

Few Romance dialects display denominal adjectives which formally or semantically correspond to the Spanish *-ido* formations at issue. In some Medieval Portuguese texts Sp. *dolorido* and *descolorido* are matched by *doorido* and *escoorido*[9]. Ptg. *saborido,* not recorded before the sixteenth century (Gil Vicente) is probably a borrowing from Hispano-Romance (cf. Ast. *saboríu*)[10]. Edward L. Adams extracted from the dictionaries of Raynouard and Levy six such adjectives for Old Provençal: *acerit* 'steel-like' *(acier), aibit* 'perfect' (*aip* 'good quality'), *fraidit* 'rascally' (*fra[i]del* 'rascal'), *maestrit* 'artificial' (*maestre* 'master'), *poestadit* 'powerful' (*poestat* 'power'), *voltit* 'vaulted' (*volta* 'vault')[11]. I suspect, however, that Adams may have been misled by the way Raynouard listed these adjectives in his *Lexique romane.* Although in the heading for each entry the adjective ends in *-it,* the examples of these adjectives cited by Raynouard and by Levy-Appel in the *Provenzalisches Supplement-Wörterbuch* appear as *aib-, fraid-, po(d)estad-* and *volt-itz* (var. *-is*). As for *maestrit,* Levy-Appel also records *maistrir.* Therefore it seems that the adjectives presented by Adams do not bear a suffix cognate with the Spanish *-ido* under study here. The dictionaries of Godefroy and Tobler-Lommatszch both record the same example of OFr. *marmori* 'flecked with marble' and *savori* 'sweet tasting' (cf. Sp. *sabrido,* It. *saporito*). Wartburg labels both items as hapax legomena (*FEW,* 6, 366*b* and 11, 207*a*). The available evidence does not clearly indicate whether these adjectives are derivatives of *marmor* and *savor* or past participles of such OFr. verbs as **marmorir* and **savorir.*

---

[8] See C. V. Paucker, *ZVS,* 26 (1883), 417.

[9] Both adjectives appear in the *Cantigas de Santa Maria.* To the best of my knowledge the linguistic impact of Castilian on the Galician *Cantigas* has not been studied.

[10] In his *Portuguese Word Formation with Suffixes,* Language Dissertation No. 33 (Baltimore, 1941), § 122, Joseph H. D. Allen, Jr. notes that there is little evidence for the use of *-ido* to form derived adjectives in Portuguese. Allen recorded without comment OPtg. *dorido* (while correctly classifying *dolorido* as a Hispanism) and stated that *saborido,* if it were not a reflex of *SAPORĪTU, may be a rare example of a Portuguese denominal adjective in *-ido.*

[11] *Word-Formation in Provençal* (New York and London, 1913), University of Michigan Studies, Humanistic Series, vol. II, p. 304; Kristoffer Nyrop pointedly notes the absence of such adjectives in French; see his *Grammaire historique de la langue française,* III[2]: *Formation des mots* (Copenhagen, 1936), § 237, p. 122.

Max Leopold Wagner reports four pertinent formations in the Logudorese dialect of Sardinian: *famidu* 'starved' (cf. *famine* 'hunger') reminiscent of OSp. *desfamnido; ag-, in-ganidu* 'desirous' (*gana* 'desire', a Hispanism), a cognate of Ast. *enganíu; lanidu* and *limidu* 'mouldy, musty' (*lana* 'wool' and *limu* 'mould, must'). With regard to *lanidu,* Wagner declared that although he remains unaware of a verbal derivative of *lana* which may have mediated between the noun and *lanidu,* one might exist. Indeed, his etymological dictionary of Sardinian records Log. *(al)lanire*[12]. Late Latin LANĪTU may well be the source of *lanidu.* Like their Spanish counterparts, the Sardinian adjectives carry a negative connotation. Do these formations represent a native derivational pattern or are they an imitation of the Spanish scheme? It. *crinito* 'with a mane' is a reflex of CRĪNĪTU; cf. OFr. *crenu,* OProv. *crenut.* It. *saporito* 'tasty, flavorful' may have originated as the participle of *saporire,* although the *Dizionario etimologico italiano* of Battisti and Alessio documents the verb some two centuries later than the participle/adjective. Thus only in Spanish is there a significant corpus of denominal adjectives in *-ido.*

Almost all Spanish suffixes can be traced back to a formal prototype in the parent language. Obviously, not every derived formation in Spanish corresponds to an underlying Hispano-Latin lexical item containing the required suffix. More often than not, a few "leader words" organically transmitted from or through Hispano-Latin to Romance clearly constitute the model upon which speakers began to generate new derivatives. The number of such key formations need not be large. Malkiel has demonstrated that a single Latin adjective – CAPRŪNUS 'pertaining to a goat' ← CAPER 'he goat', CAPRA 'she-goat' – served as the starting point for the genesis and rapid expansion in Medieval Spanish of denominal adjectives in *-uno* derived from zoonyms[13]. Almost all Spanish nouns and adjectives with the suffix *-iego* (a formative which enjoyed considerable popularity in folk speech) were coined within Romance; the few such items traceable to Latin prototypes as *judiego* 'pertaining to the Jews' < JŪDAICU and *gallego* 'Galician' < GALLAECU may have provided at best the outlines of a formal model[14].

On the functional level, most suffixes have expanded their semantic scope beyond that of their underlying source. Usually the analyst can trace (or reconstruct with a high degree of plausibility) in a logical sequence the semantic evolution of a suffix as it passed from Latin to become an independent derivational morpheme in Romance. Viewed in strictly formal terms, *-ido* is indeed the heir to -ĪTU. Whereas Latin -ĪTU remained semantically neutral, Spanish

---

[12] *Historische Wortbildungslehre des Sardischen,* RH, 39 (Berne, 1952), § 91, p. 86; *Dizionario etimologico sardo,* II (Heidelberg, 1962) s.v. *lana.*

[13] "The Latin Background of the Spanish Suffix *-uno:* Studies in the Genesis of a Romance Formative", *RPh,* 4:1 (1950), 17–45; "Nuevas aportaciones para el estudio del sufijo *-uno*", *NRFH,* 13 (1959), 241–90.

[14] Malkiel, *The Hispanic Suffix -(i)ego: A Morphological and Lexical Study Based on Historical and Dialectal Sources,* UCPL, 4:3 (1951), 111–214.

-*ido* seems to carry a negative message in the bulk of the adjectives under study here. Only three of the non-participial -*ido* adjectives under discussion can be plausibly linked to identifiable Latin bases: OSp. *bell-, vell-ido,* whose etymological kernel may be MELLĪTU[15], OSp. *sencido,* which I still link to SANCĪTU[16] (while rejecting Eric P. Hamp's alternative proposal of *SINCĪTU[17]), and *transido,* traditionally linked to TRANSĪTU. The first two adjectives, semantically positive, may have played a certain role in furnishing a formal model for the minting of -*ido* adjectives bereft of a corresponding -*er* or -*ir* verb. It is unlikely that *transido* could have played the role of leader word; indeed, I shall suggest below the possibility of a foreign origin (OFr. *transi*) for *transido.*

The -*ido* adjectives which concern us clearly do not go back to a common source. Disparate linguistic events have come together to create this series within the framework of medieval Hispano-Romance. Diachronists have long realized that more than one force may lie behind a given linguistic mutation or creation, but before Malkiel's pioneering essay[18], no specialist had attempted to study systematically and at a high level of abstraction the mechanics of multiple causation. This concept invites a dual interpretation. On one hand, multiple causation can refer to a number of discrete factors whose combined action leads to the genesis and spread of a particular linguistic shift. In such a case, the analyst may attempt to identify and isolate primary from secondary factors and to rank the impact of the individual forces at work[19]. Approached from the other angle, however, multiple causation often appears to be synonymous (or to overlap) with the notion of polygenesis and subsequent formal convergence. Here a series of unconnected events may tend to yield an identical, or at least comparable, result. The latter view of multiple causation may prove invaluable in tracing the rise of a derivational suffix for which there seems to exist no clearcut single source. The close study of each lexical item displaying the pertinent formative element may disclose the various independent circumstances which came together to spawn a new derivational affix. Such will be the approach to the genetic study of the -*ido* adjectives under consideration in this monograph.

Although individual -*ido* adjectives (e.g., *aterido, bellido, garrido, sencido* all long-standing etymological cruxes) have received varying degrees of attention from scholars, no worker before 1946 bothered to examine these formatives as a derivational series. Many grammarians and linguists seemed unaware

---

15 Malkiel, "The Etymology of Hispanic *vel(l)ido* and *melindre*", *Lg,* 22 (1946), 284–316.

16 "The Genesis of OSp. *sencido:* A Study in Etymology and Multiple Causation", *RPh,* 33:1 (1979), 130–37.

17 "Old Spanish *sencido* Again," *RPh,* 36:1 (1982), 28–31 (with Editorial Post-Script by Y. M., 31–34).

18 "Multiple versus Simple Causation in Linguistic Change," *To Honor Roman Jakobson: Essays on the Occasion of his Seventieth Birthday* (1967), II, pp. 1228–1246.

19 "On Hierarchizing the Components of Multiple Causation," *Studies in Language,* 1 (1977), 81–107.

of this use of *-ido* as a derivational suffix. Nebrija's fairly comprehensive list of Spanish denominal suffixes contains no pertinent formations in *ido*[20]. The section on suffixes in Giovanni Miranda, *Osservationi della lingua castigliana* (1566) includes *dolorido, descolorido,* and *desabrido* which were accurately identified as derivatives of *dolor, color,* and *sabor.* The same three adjectives are also recorded in César Oudin, *Grammaire espagnolle expliquée en françoise* (^{3}1619) and Lorenzo Franciosini, *Grammatica spagnola e italiana* (1624). Friedrich Diez first set the tone for the standard treatment of these adjectives. In his survey of the progeny of Latin suffixes built around the consonantal pillar *-t-* Diez noted that -ĀTUS, -ĪTUS, -ŪTUS could form adjectives directly from nouns (for -ĪTUS he cited AURĪTUS, GALERĪTUS, and PELLĪTUS). He observed that the Romance languages, favored -ĀTU, but sparingly used -ĪTU in this way. On the Spanish side he chose as examples *bellido* (which he derived from *bello*), *garrido* (allegedly of Arabic origin), and *dolorido;* he erred by including *vellido,* which he glossed as 'hairy' (implying derivation form *vello* 'hair, fur'), seemingly unaware that this adjective represented only a variant spelling of *bellido*[21]. Paul Foerster[22] and Wilhelm Meyer-Lübke[23] echoed Diez to the point of repeating his examples (including the erroneous disjunction of *bell-* and *vell-ido*).

The turn of the century marked no major breakthrough. On the side of raw data Henry R. Lang[24], commenting on *desmaída* found in a Galician poem of the Archdeacon of Toro included in the *Cancionero de Baena* cited "similar formations", such as *endurido, desflaquido, enflaquido, desfamnido, enloquido,* and *denegrido.* He correctly equated *vellido* with *bellido* and OPtg. *velido* and noted *robido* (for expected *robado*) in the Leonese MS O of the *Alexandre.* He concluded: "The existence of such participial and adjectival forms in *-ido* alongside those in *-ado* is due to the fact that the Latin suffix ĪTUS served the same purposes as the more frequent ĀTUS" (170). Federico Hanssen[25] and Vicente García de Diego[26] were content to record the use of *-ido* in the minting of adjectives, and to select *dolorido* by way of illustration. José Alemany y

---

[20] See Book III, Chap. 4, "De los nombres denominativos," of his *Gramática de la lengua castellana* (1492), ed. Antonio Quilis (Madrid, 1980), pp. 170–72.

[21] The original edition of *Grammatik der romanischen Sprachen,* II (Bonn, 1838), p. 292f. offers no examples of pseudo-participial Sp. adjectives in *-ido.* The examples cited turn up in the third edition (1871), p. 357. In light of Optg. *velido,* his error with regard to *vellido* is all the more surprising coming from the pen of an authority on medieval Portuguese lyric poetry.

[22] *Spanische Sprachlehre* (Berlin, 1880), § 305.

[23] *Grammatik der romanischen Sprachen,* II: *Formenlehre* (Leipzig, 1892), § 447.

[24] *Cancioneiro gallego-castelhano: The Extant Galician Poems of the Gallego-Castilian Lyric School (1350–1450),* New York and London, 1902, 169f.

[25] *Gramática histórica de la lengua castellana* (Halle, 1913), § 299. Hanssen also included *vellido,* implying derivation from *vello.* The original German version (1910) did not mention these formations.

[26] *Elementos de gramática histórica castellana* (Burgos, 1914), p. 194.

Bolufer's treatment of Spanish word formation routinely linked all uses of *-ido* ultimately to inflectional ĪTU[27].

Ramón Menéndez Pidal's *Manual (elemental) de gramática histórica española* (¹1904; ⁶1941) does not contain a section devoted to derivational morphology. In his treatment of the "weak" past participles (§ 121) he states: "... en textos del siglo XIII o XIV se hallan algunos verbos en *-ar* con partic[ipio] *-ido: robido, amodorrido, desmaído,* y en ast[uriano] oriental subsiste *condeníu* por *condenado;* comp. lat. DOMĀRE, DOMITUS, [CREPĀRE], CREPITUM, y en Varrón DOLITUS por DOLĀTUS". Yet proparoxytonic DOMITU, CREPITU, and DOLITU in no way could have provided the model for the few participles in *-ido* of verbs in *-ar:* DOMITU survived only as the lexicalized adjective *duendo* 'tame(d)'; CREPITU may ultimately underlie *grieta* 'crack, fissure', while DOLITU has left no traces in Hispano-Romance. John Lihani repeats this statement and adds to the list *desertido* alongside *desertar*[28]. Menéndez Pidal at no point flatly declares (or implies, for that matter) that all such *-ido* adjectives are outgrowths of *-ar* verbs.

The presence of participles in *-ado* and *-ido* alongside certain verbs in *-ar* led to a brief exchange between Hanssen and Lang. Hanssen's *Spanische Grammatik auf historischer Grundlage* (§ 33:2) merely directed the reader to § 121 of Menéndez Pidal's *Manual.* In his detailed review[29] of Hanssen's book, Lang displayed annoyance that the author had failed to cite his relevant observations at pp. 169–70 of the *Cancioneiro gallego-castelhano.* Lang then went on to urge scholars to reconsider this problem in light of the existence in the Romance languages of pairs of infinitives in *-are* and *-ire;* he noted that ten years earlier G. Cappuccini had listed nearly two hundred such pairs for Italian alone[30]. Lang added from his own files possible examples drawn from Old French, Old Provençal, and Old Spanish of what he labeled, following Cappuccini, "heteroclitous verbs". In his *Gramática histórica de la lengua castellana* Hanssen accepted Lang's analysis and provided references to both Lang's *Cancioneiro* and to the aforementioned book review (§ 265)[31].

Dana Nelson and Malkiel are the only scholars who have dealt recently with this particular problem. Nelson points out that *robido* and *condeníu* are found only in Asturo-Leonese; he then goes on to link *(d)esmaído* to OCat. *esma(h)it* (possibly a Provençalism of Germanic background) and to note that *amodorrido* predates by several centuries *amodorrar* and its *-ado* participle. As for the

---

[27] *Tratado de la formación de palabras en la lengua castellana* (Madrid, 1920) p. 77.

[28] *El lenguaje de Lucas Fernández: Estudio del dialecto sayagués* (Bogotá, 1973), p. 425, s.v. *desmaýdo.*

[29] *RR,* 2 (1911), 331–47.

[30] "L'eteroclisia in *-are* e *-ire*", *Scritti vari di filologia [in onore di Ernesto Monaci]* (Roma, 1901), pp. 311–23.

[31] Malkiel has discussed the intellectual relationship and contacts between Hanssen and Lang in his essay "Federico Hanssen y Henry R. Lang," *BFUCh,* 31 (1980–81 [-82]), 274–84 = *Homenaje a Ambrosio Rabanales;* on the *-ido* participles at issue here, see pp. 283f.

genesis of *robido* and *condeníu*[32], Nelson speaks vaguely of "analogy which plays such a key role in the growth of the Western dialects" (293). In his aforecited essay on Hanssen and Lang, Malkiel places these *-ido* participles in the wider context of the pseudo-participial adjectives in *-ido* Malkiel's aforementioned study of *bellido* marks the first attempt to view these adjectives as a derivational series. This piece was planned as an etymological study of *bell-, vell-ido* and of *melindre* 'fritter', both of which the author traces to the family of MELE 'honey'. Two excursuses follow the body of the article; the first "The Hispanic Suffixes *-ido, -edo*" contains a subsection "The Adjectival Suffix *-ido*" (302–09), an alphabetically-ordered sampler of fifty-six *-ido* adjectives with references to medieval and Golden Age sources together with concise linguistic commentary. Malkiel noted the absence of cognates outside Hispano-Romance and stressed that, semantically, these adjectives centered around the notion of privation. He recognized that some of these *-ido* adjectives could be related to a recorded *-er* or *-ir* verb, but suggestes that in certain instances the adjective may have paved the way for the backformation of a corresponding verb (a phenomenon he had discussed twice in 1941)[33]. On the explicative side Malkiel hinted at the possible model furnished by the *-ido* participles which hung on as the sole survivors of those de-adjectival verbs in *-ir* which had been displaced by their *-ecer* counterparts (e.g., *enloquido* < *enloquir,* ousted by *enloquecer;* for leisurely discussion here, see Chap. three). Malkiel's later analysis of *amodorrido* threw no additional light on the *-ido* adjectives as a whole[34].

In a printed version of a 1964 short lecture series delivered at Indiana University, Malkiel outlined the first (and to date only) genetic explanation of what he now labelled "Spanish *-ido* indicative of inadequacy"[35]. Prior to the fourteenth century, Old Spanish had employed a threeway system of suffix-stressed past participles in *-ado, -ido,* and *-udo.* The language had also inherited a series of denominal adjectives in *-ado* and *-udo* which presupposed no intervenient verb. Malkiel suggested that the model of past participial *-ado, -ido, -udo* may have induced speakers to complete a triadic set of pseudo-participial denominal adjectives in *-ado, -udo,* and *-ido* by coining a set of

[32] *Condeníu* 'expletive applied to a person who has done something bad' is recorded in Braulio Vigón, *Vocabulario dialectológico del Concejo de Colunga,* ed. Anna María Vigón Sánchez, *RFE* Suppl. 63 (1955), p. 122, and María Josefa Canellada, *El Bable de Cabranes,* p. 149. Leo Spitzer, *Lexikalisches aus dem Katalanischen und den übrigen iberoromanischen Sprachen* (Genève, 1921), p. 42 explains *condeníu* as a blend of *condenado* and *jodido;* Corominas, *DCE,* s.v. *daño,* suggests the influence of *maldecido* on *condenado.*

[33] "The *amulatado* Type in Spanish," *RR,* 32 (1941), 278–95; "A Lexicographic Mirage," *MLN,* 56 (1941), 34–42.

[34] "Español *morir,* portugués *morrer* (con un examen de *esmirriado, morriña,* y *modorra*)," *BH,* 57 (1955), 84–128.

[35] "Genetic Analysis of Word Formation," *Current Trends in Linguistics,* ed. Thomas A. Sebeok, III: *Theoretical Foundations* (The Hague-London-Paris, 1966), pp. 305–64, esp. 333–36.

adjectives with *-ido*. Whereas *-ado* adjectives were semantically neutral, the *-udo* items denoted exuberant growth or excess of a given (usually physical) quality. Consequently the creation of denominal *-ido* adjectives indicative of the opposite property, namely inadequacy, would at one blow round out a derivational pattern and fill a semantic hole. As this avowedly tentative analysis constitutes the starting point for my own novel hypothesis concerning the genesis of the derivational series under study, I shall reserve further discussion until Chap. four. Malkiel's later analysis of *desfamn-, desfambr-ido*[36] and my own papers on *sencido, garrido*[37], and *tollido*[38] concentrate on the origin and vicissitudes of those individual items rather than on broader issues of derivational morphology.

I have already hinted that the major diachronic problem to be faced in these pages is the genesis of the denominal adjectives which comprise Group I. In order to understand how these formations came into being, the history of all pseudo-participial *-ido* adjectives must be scrutinized. In what follows I shall claim that the pertinent adjectives which have been set apart in Groups II and III provided the formal model (though not the semantic/functional impetus) for the minting of the pseudo-participial denominal *-ido* adjectives. Consequently, the history and discussion of the members of Groups II and III will here precede the detailed analysis of the Group I formations.

The number of attested denominal adjectives in *-ido* is small; indeed, many of these formations failed to outlive the Middle Ages. As a means of creating denominal adjectives, *-ido* did not come close to enjoying the productivity of *-ado* and *-udo*. For the most part, diachronically-slanted suffix studies have concentrated on the semantic growth and diffusion through the lexicon of the chosen element. In addition to its other tasks, this inquiry will have to determine the factors which stunted the growth of *-ido* as a marker of denominal adjectives.

This monograph has a two-fold purpose. Its immediate and most narrowly circumscribed goal is a cogent explanation of the creation within Spanish of a given series of adjectives. On the side of method and of diachronic theory, this study will seek to illustrate the crucial role of etymology, understood as word-history, as an essential analytical tool in diachronic derivational morphology, which has been a much neglected facet of Romance historical grammar. Around the turn of the century two master etymologists, Hugo Schuchardt and Jules Gilliéron, declared that each word has its own history. So too does each derivational affix, both as a member of a morpheme class and as an element of the lexical item in whose genesis it has played a role.

[36] "Studies in Luso-Hispanic Lexical Osmosis: Old Spanish *famn-, fambr-iento, (des)-fambrido,* Portuguese *fam-into, es-fom-eado* 'hungry', and the Growth of the Suffix *-(i)ento* < -(UL)ENTU," *HR,* 45 (1977), 235–67; on *desfamnido* see 261–62.

[37] "Older Luso-Hispanic *garrido* (a) 'silly, foolish', (b) 'handsome, beautiful': One Source or Two Sources?," *RPh,* 34:2 (1980), 195–205.

[38] "The Fragmentation of the Latin Verb TOLLERE in Hispano- (including Luso-) Romance," *RPh,* 37:2 (1983), 166–74.

CHAPTER TWO

The *-ido* Adjectives of Group III: A Study in Polygenesis

In the first chapter of this monograph I offered a tripartite categorization of the corpus of pseudo-participial adjectives under study here. The principle problem to be examined and, I hope, solved in these pages is the genesis of the adjectives in *-ido* derived from nouns, i.e. *adolorido, amodorrido, asombríu, desabrido, descolorido, desertido, desfacido, desmedrido, despavorido, esbaforido, enganíu, entenebrido.* In what follows I shall argue that the formal and semantic model for the creation of these adjectives was provided by the presence in the medieval language of those adjectives which I relegated for analytic purposes to Groups II (the lexicalized past participles of OSp. deadjectival verbs in *-ir,* to be discussed in Chapter Three), and III. Consequently, it will be necessary to scrutinize the history of the individual members of these two pre-existing groups as a prelude to my analysis of the denominal adjectives in *-ido.*

The series of lexical vignettes will begin with Group III, which contains the largest contingent of relevant *-ido* adjectives. I have already noted that, with regard to their origin, these adjectives are a heterogeneous lot, consisting of (a) the reflexes of Latin adjectival bases in -ĪTU, (b) the surviving past participles of OSp. *-er* and *-ir* verbs which fell early into disuse, and (c) the adaptations to Spanish morphophonological conditions of OFr. adjectives in *-i* and OProv. and/or OCat. formations in *-it/-ida.* As a result of such genetic diversity, the adjectives of Group III illustrate the workings of polygenesis and multiple causation understood as convergence in the creation of a formal pattern.

The lexical vignettes presented in this chapter follow the etymological breakdown of Group III just outlined. Within each subgroup, the word studies are in alphabetical order. Each one is self contained and explores the genesis of the *-ido* adjective at issue. In the case of some items which have been controversial for a long time in Spanish etymology (e.g., *aterido, desvaído, garrido, sencido, vellido*), I advocate an etymology for the given adjective; but in other instances the vignettes merely summarize the current state of knowledge concerning the word's history and how it came to function in Spanish as an independent adjective in *-ido* which speakers did not necessarily associate with a corresponding verb in *-er* or *-ir.*

Group III (a)

Three of these adjectives – *bell-, vell-ido, sencido,* and *transido* – continue documented prototypes in -ĪTU: MELLĪTU ← MEL, SANCĪTU ← SANCĪRE, and TRĀNSĪTU ← TRĀNSIRE. While most scholars do operate with a base ending in -ĪTU not all accept the etymologies here endorsed for *bell-, vell-ido* and *sencido;* though etymologically transparent in regard to its Latin background, *transido* may require further elaboration concerning its precise status within Hispano-Romance.

bell-, vell-ido 'handsome, beautiful',

Until 1946 most Romanists linked *bell-, vell-ido* to *BELLĪTU[1], allegedly the past participle of a *BELLĪRE presumably derived from BELLU. Although many prestigious Romanists and Hispanists have associated themselves with this derivation, several valid objections can be raised. Latin offers no direct or indirect evidence for *BELLĪRE (a theoretically-possible de-adjectival verb); note also the absence of a corresponding stative verb in -ĒRE or an "inchoative" in -ĒSCERE; cf ALBUS 'white', ALBĒRE 'to be white' and ALBĒSCERE 'to become white'. The Romance languages quite simply do not support the reconstruction of *BELLĪRE; such verbs as Fr. *embellir,* It. *imbellire, Sp. embellecer* 'to make beautiful,' have long been recognized as independent Romance parasynthetic formations. Almost all thirteenth-century examples of the Spanish adjective culled from reliably edited texts display *v-*[2], as does consistently OPtg. *velido.* The pattern of OSp. *v- b-,* OPtg. *v-* presupposes an ancestral *v-*/w/, while the Portuguese and Spanish progeny of BELLU regularly show *b- (bello, belo).* Medieval examples of *bellido* are late and many may result form secondary association with *bello*[3].

[1] For a survey of earlier pronouncements on the etymology of this adjective, see Malkiel, "The Etymology of Hispanic *vel(l)ido* and *melindre*", *Lg,* 22 (1946), 284–316, esp. 284f.

[2] "Enclinó las manos la barba *velida*" (*CMC,* 274); "... e a vós, Cid, barba *velida*" (*CMC,* 2192); "Dios, commo es alegre la barba *velida*" (*CMC,* 930); "Cató a todas partes con su ojo *vellido*" (*Apol,* 315*b*); "con estos sus adobos que la fazen *vellida*" (*Apol,* 370*c;* Alvar alters here the MS reading to *bellida* in his critical edition of the poem); "En el siglo non sé yo tan *vellida*" (*Alex.,* 389*d*); "mucha barva *vellida*" (*Alex.* O, 1566*c;* P reads *bellido*). Is the one instance of *bellidas* in Berceo, *SOria 29d* a scribal replacement for original *vell-?* Although the adjective under study is absent from the Alfonsine corpus, the name of the assassin of Sancho II is regularly transcribed in the *EE* as *Vellid Adolffo.* The 14th-century *LM* records the toponyms *Val vellido* and *Val bellido* (ed. Seniff, p. 81).

[3] With regard to the choice of initial consonant, the history of *bellaco* 'wicked, roguish; cunning, sly' parallels that of *bellido.* In the *GCU, LBA* and in Pero Guillén de Segovia's 15th-c. rhyming dictionary *La Gaya Ciencia,* this adjective is written *vellaco;* note also the derivative *vellacada* in *Rimado de palacio,* 228*d*). Nebrija's *Vocabulario de romance en latín* (1516) records *vellaco* and *vellaquería.* The spelling *bellaco* is found in the Escorial Glossary no. 1538. Portuguese and Italian have borrowed the

The autochthonous status of *bello* in Hispano-Romance is itself open to some question. Unfettered oral transmission of BELLU should have yielded **biello*[4], which might later have been transmuted to **billo;* witness -ELLU > OSp. *-iello* > *-illo,* SELLA 'seat, chair, stool' > OSp. *siella* > *silla.* Cultural conditions do not rule out analysing *bello* as an adaptation of OProv. *bel* (cf. OSp. *beldad* < OProv. *beltat,* ousted by the Italianism *belleza),* although a cogent explanation of the *-ll-* of the Spanish adjective must be provided. Such anthroponyms found in old charters as *Bellitus, Vellita* do not necessarily point to an authentic cognomen BELLITUS of the type BONITUS, CARITUS; rather, they may represent a Latinization of the vernacular *vellido.* The use as family names of adjectives denoting 'handsome' is not uncommon in Hispano-Romance; witness *Bello, Garrido,* and *Lozano.*

Malkiel set out on his own by suggesting MELLĪTU 'sweet, honey-like' as the ultimate source of *bell- vell-ido.* To account for the phonological difficulties posed by this etymology he claimed that MELLĪTU was caught up in the sporadic permutation of initial labials, for which he adduced a string of Latin and Romance examples. He admitted that in Hispano-Romance this sporadic shift tended to go in the opposite direction *b-/v-* > *m-.* On the semantic side Malkiel repeated J. B. Hoffman's observation that in colloquial Latin MELLĪTUS was applied with the meaning 'venustus, iucundus' to people. Malkiel found particularly compelling such coincidences of phraseological detail as OCULĪ MELLĪTĪ and *ojos vellidos,* LABRA MELLĪTA and *fablar vellido* 'to speak softly, sweetly', and PATER MELLĪTISSIMUS, NUTRIX MELLĪTISSIMA and OPtg. *mia madre velida,* as well as the presence of the cognomen MELLĪTUS.

Malkiel's hypothesis found little support at the outset. While satisfied with the semantic analysis, Félix Lecoy[5] remained unconvinced by the treatment of the phonological issue. Joseph M. Piel was the most strident critic[6]. Although willing to concede the possibility of a sound shift *m-* > *b-/v-,* he found Malkiel's semantic argumentation ill-founded and refused to accept his view of *BELLĪTU as an improbable reconstruction. For once Malkiel received a measure of support from Corominas (*DCE,* s.v. *bellido*), who claimed that *BEL-

---

Spanish adjective as *velhaco* (first attested in the OPtg. translation of the *LBA*) and *vigliaco* respectively. Corominas first analysed *bellaco* as a backformation from the abstract noun *bellaquería,* itself a borrowing from OCat. *bacallaria* 'roguish deed'; see his "Problemas del 'Diccionario etimológico'," *PRh,* 1:1 (1947), at 31–34, and *DCE,* s.v. *bellaco.* However, the *v-* of OSp. *vellaco* may undermine this hypothesis. In the [3]*BDE* Corominas described *bellaco* as "de origen incierto" and listed *bellaquería* among the derivatives of *bellaco.*

4 A notarial document from Upper Aragon (*Partido de Huesca*) dated 10 June 1360 includes in an inventory of goods "un almendrac biello"; see Tomás Navarro Tomás, *Documentos lingüísticos del Alto Aragón* (Syracuse, 1957), no. 120, 11–12. Is *biello* a local reflex of BELLU or an orthographic variant of OArag *viello* 'old' (= Cast. *viejo*)? The context does not make clear whether a handsome or an old cushion is at issue.

5 *Ro.,* 70 (1948–49), 135f.

6 *RPF,* 2 (1948), 298–300, and *RF,* 53 (1951), 429.

LĪTU resulted from a blend of BELLU with MELLĪTU; he adduced as evidence the coexistence of the phrases CICERO BELLISSIMUS and MELLITUS CICERO in letters sent to Cicero. In the revised version of his dictionary (s. v. *bellido*) he operates with a blend involving BELLĀTU and MELLĪTU. The consistent use of *v-* in OPtg. *velido* as opposed to the initial consonant of *belo* casts doubt on both these proposals. Any hypothesis invoking a lexical blend would require a partner with *v-*. Vicente García de Diego's *DEEH* (1954) contains separate entries for *bellido* 'bello' (106*a*), linked to *BELLĪTU and *vellido* glossed as 'velloso' (547*a*), allegedly a Romance derivative of *vello*.

Critics failed to note or respond to one additional facet of Malkiel's proposal. He had observed that latent and sporadic sound shifts often require as a catalyst association with a word of similar form and/or meaning. He wondered whether the series *vellado, velludo, velloso* 'hairy, covered with hair' ← *vello* 'hair' may have influenced the local reflex of MELLĪTU. The candidacy of this word family merits further exploration. At first glance one may rightly ask what strange sense of esthetics would link hairiness with physical pulchritude, especially in regard to women. In medieval France excessive and even superfluous hair on any part of the body where one would not expect to find it was considered a characteristic of an ugly man or woman. According to Alice Colby, portraits of handsome individuals in twelfth-century French narrative poetry lay no stress on beards or moustaches; in contrast, the mention of facial hair increases a person's homeliness[7]. On the Spanish side, Juan Ruiz, an authority on the physical attractiveness of women, turns to *velloso* in contexts that refer to less than appealing women (see *LBA,* 448*a*, 1013*b*; also 1485*c*, the author's alleged selfportrait).

Nevertheless it seems feasible to operate with a Romance blend involving the local reflex of MELLĪTU, in all likelihood **mellido,* and the family of *vello*. The starting point may well lie in the use of these adjectives with specific parts of the body. The correspondence between OCULĪ MELLĪTĪ and *ojos vellidos* cannot be dismissed as mere coincidence. Though the literal rendition of the Latin phrase is 'sweet eyes', the meaning is clearly 'fair, beautiful eyes'. The syntagm *ojos *mellidos* probably preceded *ojos vellidos*. The conflation of **mellido* with *vello* (or with one of its derivatives) could not have occurred with reference to the eyes. Attention must shift to the phrase *barva vellida* which by the dawn of Old Spanish literature had become an epic epithet used frequently in the *Cantar de Mío Cid* to refer to the warrior hero. *Barva* could also combine with other adjectives to designate important males: the Cid is referred to as "el de la barba grant" and "el de la luenga barba". Alexander the Great is twice identified in the *Libro de Alexandre* with the phrase "de la barva honrrada" (828*a,* 1945*a*). In medieval Spain the beard was a symbol of virility, authority, and honor. The full-bearded epic hero must have cut an imposing physical

[7] *The Portrait in Twelfth-Century French Literature (An Example of the Stylistic Originality of Chrétien de Troyes)* (Geneva, 1965), pp. 76, 81, 85.

figure and was "handsome" by medieval standards. The medieval language could employ *vellado* 'hairy' in conjunction with *barva;* witness *barva vellada* in *SDom.,* 669*c.* Could the full beard interpreted as an attribute of male physical fairness have brought together **mellido* and *vellado?* Speakers may have perceived only dimly any relationship between **mellido* and *miel* 'honey'. The presence of *mellado* 'jagged, nicked, ragged', ← *mella* 'nick, notch', of obscure parentage, with its more common suffix, may have further weakened **mellido.* The relative isolation of **mellido* would have facilitated its attraction into the orbit of the family of *vello;* the resulting *vellido* would have received formal support from *vellado* and *velludo* (the latter denoting an excessive degree of hirsuteness). Consequently, *vellido* owes its initial consonant to the family of *vello* and its meaning, in the final analysis, to MELLĪTU. From the beard and the eyes *vellido* came to be used with the face (cf. OPtg. *face velida*) and eventually the person.

sencido 'intact, unploughed, virgin (field)'

Two bases – SINCĒRU 'pure, intact' and SANCĪTU, past participle of SANCĪRE 'to consecrate, make sacred or inviolable by a religious act; to forbid on pain of punishment' – have fought for recognition as the etymon of OSp. *sencido,* mod. (regional) *cencido*[8]. Although both Latin adjectives are semantically plausible sources, neither can immediately underlie *sencido.* Advocates of SINCĒRU must account for the transformation of -ĒRU to *-ido,* whereas supporters of SANCĪTU must cogently justify the pretonic vowel of *sencido.* My aforementioned study attempted to show how several independent causes have come together to raise the pretonic vowel of OSp. **sancido,* a form open to interpretation either as the immediate reflex of SANCĪTU or as a past participle of **sancir* < SANCĪRE. A tendential (free) variation between *CenC* and *CanC* of the type observable in OSp. *sandío* ~ *sendío* 'crazy' *sancenno* ~ *sencenno* 'pure, unmixed bread', reinforced by the model of more frequent *CerC* ~ *CarC,* coupled with the possible influence of OSp. *señero, senziello* 'alone, isolated, single, simple', may have acted in concert upon **sancido,* which occupied an isolated position in the Spanish lexicon. My earlier study overlooked the possible role in the genesis of *sencido* of (etymologically-controversial) OSp. *cęncenno* ~ *cencenno, sancenno* ~ *sencenno* 'unleavened bread, a bread free from any admixture'[9].

---

[8] The earliest advocate of SINCĒRU was Carolina Michaëlis de Vasconcelos; later supporters of this hypothesis include Vicente García de Diego, Wilhelm Meyer-Lübke, and Brian Dutton. The first proponent of SANCĪTU was Leo Spitzer, backed years later by Corominas who, nevertheless, attributed the *e* of *sencido* to the influence of SINCĒRU. For details, see my note "The Growth of Old Spanish *sencido:* A Study in Etymology and Multiple Causation," *RPh,* 33:1 (1979), 130–37.

[9] For two differing genetic analyses of *cenceño,* see Malkiel, "The Etymology of Spanish *cenceño,*" *StP.* 45 (1948), 37–49; and Thomas Montgomery, "Sobre la etimología de *cenceño* 'pan ázimo'," *NRFH,* 19 (1970), 101–05.

In response to my paper, Eric P. Hamp outlined an alternative solution, namely a base *SINCĪTU[10]. On the methodological side, Hamp's proposal illustrates how an accomplished specialist in Indo-European etymology might attack a narrow-gauged Romance problem. Hamp observed that in Imperial Latin SANCĪTU and *SINCĒRU were "very close to being synonyms" (29). He then went on to say "that in purely formal terms of vocalism SINCĒRUM has the appearance of being related to SANCĪTUM AS ATTINGERE is to TANGERE. Moreover, with a prefix, the vocalism of SINCĒRUM would carry the impression of being motivated" (30), i. e., of being a compound of SANCĪRE. Consequently SINCĒRUS stood in a close formal and semantic relationship to SANCĪTUM. He concludes that the conflation of these two items engendered *SINCĪTU, the base underlying *sencido*.

One facet of Hamp's argument raises questions. A propos of SINCĒRUM he declares: "As a non-initial element in a complex it appears like a formal equivalent of SANCĪTUM *differng only in suffix* (31); (emphasis added). I question whether there existed sufficient motivation in the form of a productive suffix -ĒRUS for speakers to segment the adjective as SINC-ĒRUS, as they justifiably did with SANC-ĪTUS. Would not SINCER- have been regarded as a monomorphemic root? If one can judge by the popular etymology found in Donatus, "ut mel sine cera"[11], naive speakers identified the first syllable of SINCERUS with the preposition SINE. Ernout and Meillet state "le SIN- est le même premier élément de composé que dans SIM-PLEX" (i. e., 'without folds'?). I conclude that Hamp's *SINCĪTU is an unnecessary reconstruction.

transido 'deceased'

Although specialists do not doubt a genetic connection between OSp. *transido* and the family of TRĀNSĪRE 'to go across', questions do arise concerning the immediate source of the Spanish adjective. It is reasonable to see in *transido* the local product of TRĀNSĪTU, past participle of TRĀNSĪRE. At least two scholars (Manuel Alvar[12]; Corominas, *DCE,* s. v. *ir*) chose to view *transido* as the past participle of a putative OSp. *transir*. Although TRĀNSĪRE has survived as a verb in Gallo- and Italo-Romance dialects, my research has unearthed in Old Spanish only one example of an inflected form which unequivocally points to an OSp. *transir*[13]. In recent years several Hispanists have dwelt on the close con-

[10] Old Spanish *sencido* Again", *RPh,* 36:1 (1982), 28–31, with dissenting Editorial Post-Script by Malkiel, 31–34.

[11] Quoted in ⁴*DÉLL,* s. v. SINCĒRUS.

[12] See his *Vida de Santa María Egipciaca: Estudios, vocabulario, edición de los textos,* II (Madrid, 1972), s. vv. *transida,* and *transir,* p. 317.

[13] ". . . deyuso de los cielos todo lo que está en la tierra *se transyrá*", Genesis 6:17, as preserved in Escorial MS 1–j–3, edited by Américo Castro, Agustín Millares Carlo and Angel J. Battistessa, *Biblia medieval romanceada,* I: *Pentateuco*. This MS was prepared from the Hebrew Bible by Jewish translators. The same passage in the Judeo-Spanish Ferrara Bible (1553) also employs *transir;* see L. Wiener, *MLN,* 11 (1896), col. 103.

nection between *-ir* verbs and high (front or back) stem vowels; Thomas Montgomery specifically noted the paucity of *-ir* verbs with *a* as stem vowel[14]. Although the pattern *a–ir* does not automatically doom a verb (witness such high-frequency verbs as *abrir* 'to open', *partir* 'to leave', *salir* 'to go out'), one may ask whether it could play a role in its demise if the language has at its disposal handy substitutes.

Oral transmission into Hispano-Romance of TRĀNS both as prefix and preposition yielded *tras*. The *-ns-* cluster of *transido* may bespeak the retarding influence of Church Latin, a reasonable supposition in regard to an adjective meaning 'dead' (cf. OSp. *tránsido* 'death' < TRĀNSITU). I should like to suggest here another possible element in the history of *transido*. Whereas only *transido* turns up as an independent adjective in Hispano-Romance, Old French and Old Provençal afford examples of inflected forms of *transir* 'to die'[15]. Might the greater vitality of this verb in Gallo-Romance indicate that *transido* represents an adaptation to Spanish morphophonological conditions of OFr. *transi?* Gallo-Romance reflexes of TRANSĪTU display a less inhibited phonological development and a livelier semantic evolution than their Spanish counterpart; cf. dial. *trezi* 'se dit des graines quand elles germent et que le blé commence à couvrir la terre' (see *FEW*, s. v. TRĀNSĪRE).

In the older language *transido* exclusively meant 'dead'[16]; so used, *transido* is absent from the dictionaries of Palencia and Nebrija and appears to have died out before the end of the Middle Ages. In the post-medieval language *transido* is limited to such set phrases as *transido de dolor* 'wracked with grief, pain', *transido de frío* 'pierced with cold', *transido de hambre* 'starved'. The *Diccionario de autoridades* defines this adjective as 'fatigado, congojado consumido de alguna penalidad, angustia o necesidad. Dícese particularmente del que padece hambre', and illustrates *transido de hambre* with passages from the writings of Fray Luis de Granada and Padre Juan de Torres. Fr. *transi* has undergone a parallel semantic evolution, being used especially in combination with *froid* 'cold' and *peur* 'fear'.

The Vulgate-based version of the Bible preserved in Escorial MS 1–j–4 (ed. J. Llamas) turns to *perescerá* in the passage at issue. The inf. *transir* is used at least once in the *Cantigas de Santa Maria:* "eu mia molher tiinna que ja queria *transir*" (ed. Mettman, no. 378.47). *Transsido* 'paralysed' appears in the OPtg. *Cantigas d'escarnho e de mal dizer;* see M. Rodrigues Lapa, *Vocabulário galego-português tirado da edição crítica das "Cantigas d'escarnho e de mal dizer"* (Vigo, 1965), p. 102.

[14] "Complementarity of Stem-Vowels in the Spanish Second and Third Conjugations," *RPh*, 29:3 (1976), 281–96. Montgomery also notes that most *a- -ir* verbs have stem final *-r-*.

[15] Tobler-Lommatzsch, *AFW*, vol. 10, s. v. *transir*, col. 528.

[16] See *Milg* 266*d; SOria*, 165*b; Apol*, 587*d;* and *CZif*, pp. 65.11, 182.26.

Group IIIb

A handful of the *-ido* adjectives at issue (Group IIIb) began life as the past participles of *-er* and *-ir* verbs. While these verbs fell into disuse with the passage of time, their past participles managed to cling to life as independent adjectives, sometimes semantically far-removed from the original verb.

aterido 'stiff with cold, shaking with cold'

This adjective has been a long-standing crux of Spanish etymology. In the medieval language all inflected forms flanking *aterido* go back to *aterecer*. Is *aterir,* first recorded in post-medieval dictionaries, a backformation from *aterido* or did OSp. *aterecer* displace a prior *aterir,* of which *aterido* served as the past participle? Two rival hypotheses have dominated discussion of the history of this formation. The first is based on onomatopoeia: in 1611, Covarrubias (*Tesoro,* s.v.) remarked that *aterido* imitated the sound of chattering teeth. Almost three hundred years later, in reviewing one of P. E. Guarnerio's "Postille sarde", Meyer-Lübke proposed an onomatopoetic origin for the Italian and Sardinian forms denoting 'to become stiff with cold, to chatter with cold' discussed therin, as well as for Sp. Cat. *ti(ti)ritar*[17]. In both eds. of the *REW,* § 8664, he set up the onomatopoetic bases TERIT*(s)* and TETER, whose putative descendants included Sp. *ater-ir, -ecer, tiritar,* Gal. *terecer,* Ptg. *inteiriçar,* and obs. It. *intirizzare* (mod. *-ire*). García de Diego operated at least four times with onomatopoetic TER ~ TIR as the source for these forms as well as for *entelerido,* Sal. *atelecerse,* OSp. *atelerido,* and Sant. *atenecerse*[18]. Unfortunately, he neglected to document the alleged *atelerido* or to justify with textual evidence the label "Old Aragonese" attached to *entelerido.* García de Diego conceded that this analysis assumed that *aterir* first meant 'to shiver with cold' rather than 'to be stiff with cold'; if the opposite were true, the onomatopoetic hypothesis would obviously fall.

F. Diez was the first to suggest a genetic link between the family of *ater-ir, -ecer* and INTEGRU 'whole, entire'[19]. He included among the Romance formations ultimately traceable to that Latin adjective Sp. *ateritar* 'to chatter with cold', Ptg. *inteiriço* 'solid, whole', *inteiriçar* 'to make solid, whole', and (obs.) It. *intirizzare* (mod. *-ire*) 'to become stiff, rigid'. In addition to accepting Diez's etymology, Rufino José Cuervo supplied numerous examples of *aterido* extracted from Spanish literary texts of all periods and attempted to account for the genesis of *a-ter-ir, -ecer*[20]. Starting from the verb *enterecer* (documented in

---

17 *ZRPh,* 28 (1904), 635; Guarnerio's piece appeared in *Ro.* 33 (1904), 50–70.

18 *Contribución al diccionario hispánico etimológico, RFE,* Suppl. II (1923), § 596; *DEEH,* § 6645; *BRAE,* 45 (1963), 231–40; also, *Diccionario de voces naturales* (Madrid, 1968), pp. 650f.

19 *EWRS,* Pt. I (Bonn, 1853), s.v. *intero.* This entry is repeated in *EWRS* (^{5}1887).

20 *DCR,* I (P., 1886), s.v. *aterir.*

G. Alonso de Herrera, *Libro de agricultura* [1513]), Cuervo derived *aterecer* through prefix alternation of the type observable in *em-, a-pestar* 'to smell', *en-, a-clarar* 'to make clear', *en-, a-fear* 'to make ugly'. He proposed that *aterir* sprang up alongside *aterecer* on the model of such pairs as *contecer* ~ *contir* 'to happen', *gradecer* ~ *gradir* 'to please'. Was Cuervo unaware that in most instances the *-ir* verb historically preceded its *-ecer* counterpart? Moreover, he neglected to explain the derivation of *enterecer* from *entero.* Gustav Körting, while including *inteir-iço, -içar* and *intirizzare* in his LRW_3 (s.v. INTEGER), omitted the Spanish forms under study. Malkiel has advocated on several occasions derivations from INTEGRU[21]; he also hypothesized that the lively semantic development of *ater-ir, -ecer, entelerido* vis-à-vis their proposed common source reflects contamination, at various stages, with Sp. *tericia* 'jaundice' *ictericia, (fiebre) terciana* 'tertian fever' and *tir(tir)-itar* 'to chatter with cold'.

Corominas (*DCE,* s.v. *aterir*) hesitatingly endorsed Cuervo's analysis. He devoted the bulk of this entry to refuting the alleged onomatopoetic origin of *aterir* and *inteiriçar,* but accepted such a solution for It. *intirizzire.* He also brought into the discussion OPtg. *enterido (Padres de Mérida)* 'stiff, paralyzed' and *enterimento (Mestre Giraldo)* which Corominas claims may have meant 'stiffness', despite C. Michaëlis de Vasconcelos's interpretation of that item as 'dysentery, enteritis'[22]. He viewed *entelerido* as some sort of "ampliación fonética" of **enterido.*

Several considerations rule out the onomatopoetic solution favored by Meyer-Lübke and García de Diego. Although Hispanists have long operated with onomatopoetic creations, sound symbolism, and expressive word formation, these notions have not been subjected until recently to a close scrutiny of their underlying operating principles. In a major contribution to Hispanic linguistics (with possible implications for general linguistics), David A. Pharies[23] claims that "expressive words are the products not of an arbitrary act of 'creation', but of a rational process of 'formation', which, like other types of word formation, operates with two elements already present in the language, a derivational pattern and a phonetic source or base" (347). Expressive formations in Spanish conform to a canonical shape which can be conveniently exemplified by *titiritar* 'to tremble' and *pipiritaña* 'cane flute'. Pharies also claims that Spanish expressive formations are united by a strong common semantic denominator, namely "levity in the sense 'frivolous, not serious'" (349). No such connotation can be found in the *aterir* ~ *aterecer* ~ *aterido* family.

---

21 "Lexical Notes on the Western Leonese Dialect of La Cabrera Alta", *Lg.,* 25 (1949), 437; also, *Lg.,* 42 (1966), 450f.

22 *RLu,* 8 (1910), 251*n*4; for *enterido,* see José Joaquim Nunes, "Contribuição para um dicionário da língua portuguesa arcaica", *ibid.,* 27 (1928–29), 34.

23 "Expressive Word-Formation in Spanish: The Cases of *titiritar* 'tremble', *pipiritaña* 'cane flute', etc.," *RPh,* 36:3 (1983), 347–365; also, "What is 'creación expresiva'?," *HR,* 52 (1984), 169–80.

The overwhelming majority of the fifty-nine Spanish formations which Pharies has analyzed are nouns; significantly, the few verbs (*cucurutiar,* 'to spy on', *fafarachar* 'to boast', *mamarrastrar* 'to drag a suckling around', *tataratiar* 'to founder, struggle, stutter' and *titiritar* 'to shake, tremble'), are all members of the *-ar* class. In the case of *titiritar* (orig. *tiritar*), viewed by some workers as a congener of *aterido* and *aterecer,* Pharies argues that it was cast off by *tiritaña* ~ *tiritaina* orig. 'rich fabric', which came to mean 'flimsy silk fabric', 'thing of little substance'. The Spanish noun goes back to OFr. *tiretaine* 'coarse wool material', a derivative of *tire* 'silk cloth' < TYRIU 'cloth from Tyre'. In Pharies' own words "The semantic step between these two meanings and 'tremble' is reasonable enough, since flimsy things are easily set into motion" (351). In short, *titiritar* and *aterido* are by this logic not genetically related.

One other consideration rules out an expressive origin for the words under study. The earliest recorded uses of *aterecer* and *aterido* clearly mean '(to be) stiff with cold', e.g.,

> Et como les daua en los oios [el granizo] cegaua los e esfriaua los el frío de guisa que los *ateresció,* tan grant era (*GE,* II:1, 301*b*22–25); e entról la friura por los poros del cuerpo e tomó luego friura a Alexandre e le *atereció* por los neruios ... (*GE,* IV, 215*c*); ... e del grant dolor las mis mexiellas, maguer que eran tiernas, pararon se me *ateridas* e muy enflaquidas ... (*GE,* II, 426*b*4–6); Con la nief con el viento e con la elada frida/estaua la culebra de frío amodorrida/el omne piadoso que la vido *aterida* (*LBA,* S, 1349*a–c*).

The rival derivation of *aterir/aterido* from INTEGRU deserves further consideration. I should like to suggest here one possible sequence of events. In order to avoid the possibly awkward repetition of the initial syllable, speakers opted for **enterir* rather than **enenterir* as a de-adjectival parasynthetic verb based on *entero.* Then, following the model provided by such verbs as OSp. *em-brav-ir, en-flaqu-ir, en-gord-ir,* some members of the speech community may have segmented **enterir* as *en-ter-ir.* Such a division would presuppose that **enterir* had semantically distanced itself from *entero;* cf. *entregar* 'to hand over' and *enterar* 'to find out, learn' vis-à-vis INTEGRĀRE and/or *entero.* If one allows at the early stages for a measure of flexibility in the choice of prefix in the genesis of parasynthetic de-adjectival verbs, one can suppose *a-ter-ir* could have sprung up alongside **en-ter-ir.*

The branch of the family represented by *entelerido* seems to have followed an independent course. The medieval record offers no examples of *entelerido.* Cervantes *(Baños de Argel)* and Lope *(Las Batuecas)* employed that adjective with the meaning 'shaking with fear'. The compilers of the *Diccionario de autoridades* so glossed *entelerido,* equated it with both Lat. STUPENS and HORRENS and labelled it "término rústico y bárbaro." In Andulsian and New World Spanish, *entelerido* denotes 'sickly, feeble'. The starting point for this phase of the word's semantic development may have been 'shaking with fever or with chills brought on by an illness', which could reflect, as Malkiel has suggested, association with *tericia* 'jaundice' and/or *(fiebre) terciana* 'tertian fever'. Possible confirmation of the contact between the word families is provided by *atericia* 'jaundice', and *atercia,* attested in the fifteenth century, vis-à-vis *ectericia, ytericia* < Lat. ICTERICIA.

The processes underlying the shift **enterido* > *entelerido* remain to be clarified. As noted above, Corominas viewed *entelerido* as a phonetic expansion of **enterido;* Malkiel operated here with a interfix *-el-;* i.e., *ent-el-erido.* Yet, as interfixes are usually inserted between the radical and the suffix, would one not expect **enter-el-ido?* To judge by the comment in the *Diccionario de autoridades* and by the use Cervantes and Lope made of this adjective, *entelerido* appears to have arisen in uninhibited lower-class speech. It is not unreasonable to suggest that the various lexical blends posited in this vignette gave rise to **entererido* which led, via dissimilation, to *entelerido.*

desvaído 'lank, gaunt, dull (of colors)'

A discussion of Sp. *desvaído* as the past participle of a **(d)esvaír* is in order. The absence of such a verb from the Spanish record combined with the post-medieval first documentation of *desvaído* induced Corominas (*DCE,* s.v. *desvaído*) to favor explaining this adjective as a borrowing and adaptation of Ptg. *esvaido* ← *esvair-se* 'to vanish, become weak, faint', ultimately traceable to the family of EVĀNĒSCERE (cf. Ptg. *esvaecer* 'to disappear') ← VĀNUS 'empty, void'. Corominas does not attempt to account for such a borrowing on linguistic or cultural grounds.

Few other scholars have concerned themselves in any way with the origin and history of *desvaído.* García de Diego[24] listed *desvaído* among the native reflexes of ĒVĀDERE 'to go out, escape', an analysis which I have supported in print[25]. Such a hypothesis presupposes a verb **(d)esvaír.* It is well known that compounds, both popular and learned, formed on primitives derived from Latin prototypes in -ĒRE, -ĔRE, and -ĪRE tended to join the *-ir* class in Hispano-Romance, e.g., *recebir, con-, per-cibir* as against *caber* < CAPERE, *adquirir, con-, re-querir* as against *querer* < QUAERERE. In some instances the original primitive vanished; note *a-, es-, per-, re-, sa-cudir,* and learned *discutir* vis-à-vis QUATERE 'move, shake; beat, strike', which would have yielded **cader.* Although forms of VADERE have survived as parts of the suppletive paradigm headed by *ir* 'to go', the original verb and its compounds have not fared well in Hispano-Romance. OSp. *embaír* 'to attack; to confuse, cheat, deceive' goes back to INVADERE 'to go into; to attack' (cf. OArag. *envadir, embadexer*). One wonders whether *sombaír,* preserved in Judeo-Spanish, continues *SUBVĀDERE (cf. SUBĪRE) or whether it is a Romance compound involving *so-* (< SUB) +

---

[24] *Contribución al diccionario hispánico etimológico, RFE,* Suppl. II (Madrid, 1923), and *DEEH,* s.v., ĒVĀDERE.

[25] "Two Etymological Cruxes: Spanish *engreír* and *embaír* (with an Afterthought on *desvaído*)," *RPh,* 31:2 (1977), 220–225, esp. 224f.

embaír. *(D)esvaír,* if authentic, would formally parallel *embaír* and *sombaír.* Before the loss of *desvaír, *desvaído* may well have become lexicalized as an adjective. The language contains several *-ido* adjectives semantically akin to *desvaído: anudrido* 'emaciated', *desleído* 'weak', *esperido* 'thin', its polar opposite *en-, re-gordido* 'fat', and the chromonyms *de-, re-negrido* 'black(ened)', *descolorido* 'pale', *repretido* 'very black', *reverdido* 'green'.

The semantic evolution of *desvaído* calls for a brief comment here. Used with non-animate subjects, ĒVĀDERE could signify 'pass, flow out of'. In Hispano- and Luso-Latin ĒVĀDERE may have come to be used exclusively with such implied or expressed subjects as strength, vigor, blood, etc. The passage from *desvaído* 'drained of strength, blood' (cf. Ptg. *esvair-se em sangue* 'to bleed profusely') > 'gaunt, lank' poses no insuperable problem. The occasional use of *desvaído* as a color term would then represent a secondary development, perhaps stemming from the appearance of the skin of a gaunt, sickly person. Specialists in Portuguese such as Cornu[26] and Nascentes[27] derive *esvair-se* from ĒVĀNĒSCERE. In light of the regular fall of -N- and -D- in Luso-Romance, it seems defensible to contend that the Portuguese verb could represent a blend of ĒVĀDERE and ĒVĀNĒSCERE (cf. It. *svanire,* OFr. *esvanir,* as against OProv. *esvanezir,* Ptg. *esvaecer,* Sp. *desvanecer,* all meaning 'to faint'). Given the rarity of OPtg. de-adjectival verbs in *-ir,* I would go so far as to suggest that Ptg. *esvair,* like Cat. *esvair,* is, on the formal level, the local reflex of ĒVĀDERE. If this suggestion is correct, the presence of *esvair* in Portuguese and Catalan renders more probable the existence at some point in Spanish of **(d)esvaír.*

The etymologist cannot rule out a possible Catalan origin for *desvaído.* The formal and semantic similarity of the Spanish adjective to Cat. *esvait* 'faint, weak', past participle of *esvair-se* 'to faint' cannot be dismissed as mere coincidence. Surprisingly Corominas, often a zealous advocate of Catalan bases for Spanish words of doubtful origin, rejected vehemently on several occasions a genetic link between *esvait* and *desvaído*[28]. Corominas argued that *esvair-se* reflects the influence of *esvanir* 'to disappear, become weak' on *esvair* < ĒVĀDERE. The late initial documentation of *desvaído* appears to favor the hypothesis of a borrowing. However, one may ask why speakers felt a need to borrow such an adjective. Moreover, few Catalan adjectives entered Spanish. On balance, I feel that the analysis of *desvaído* as the lexicalized past participle of **desvaír* represents the best solution to this etymological crux.

empedernido 'hardened (like stone); cruel, obdurate'

The genetic status of *empedernido,* traceable in the final analysis to PETRINU 'stony', requires some discussion. Whereas Nebrija records *empedernido* and

[26] "Die portugiesische Sprache" as in Gustav Gröber, *Grundriß der romanischen Philologie* (²1904–06), pp. 916–1037.

[27] *DELP* (Rio de Janeiro, 1932), s.v. *esvair.*

[28] *DCE* and *DCECH,* s.v. *desvaído; DECLC,* s.v. *esvair;* see also *Lleures i converses d'un filòleg* (Barcelona, 1971), p. 52.

empedernescer, empedernir first appears in seventeenth-century lexical compilations (Covarrubias 1611, Oudin 1616, and Franciosini 1620). In the light of this chronological gap and of *-ecer* verbs synchronically flanked by an *-ido* participle (historically the last vestige of the corresponding *-ir* verb, see Chapter Three), Malkiel linked *empedernido* directly to *empedernecer*[29]; he regarded *empedernir* as a later creation, running counter to the usual current illustrated by *aborrir* > *aborrecer* 'to hate' and *contir* > *(a)contecer* 'to happen'. However, another analysis is equally conceivable. *Empedernir* may well have preceded *empedernecer;* indeed it may first have taken the shape **empedrenir* (cf. Ptg. *empedrenir*), constructed on a base *pedren-* as in *pedrenal* 'stony area'. Under the influence of such metathesized formations as *pedernal,* **empedrenir* would have yielded **empedernir* which, unattested in earlier stages of the languages, was displaced by its *-ecer* counterpart. The *empedernir* recorded in post-Renaissance dictionaries may be merely the fanciful invention of lexicographers seeking a mate for the isolated *-ido* adjective.

esperido 'exhausted, thin'

This adjective poses a problem of genetic classification. Should *esperido* be viewed as the lexicalized past participle of a long-extinct **esperir,* the forerunner of *(d)esperecer* 'to perish' (cf. the replacement of OSp. *perir* by *perecer*), or is it the organic reflex (with a trivial prefix change) of DĒPERĪTU ← DĒPERĪRE 'to perish'[30]? The antiquity and vitality (if not the authenticity) of *esperido* is also open to some question. No medieval examples of this adjective are on record. The lone documentation is an entry *esperido* in the *Diccionario de autoridades* which merely glosses the adjective as 'flaco, atenuado, de carnes'; no textual citation is offered.

florido 'flowered, in bloom'

Although *florido* appears to be derived directly from *flor* 'flower', comparative Romance evidence clearly implies that it originally functioned as the past participle of OSp. **florir;* cf. Rum *înflorì,* It. *fiorire,* Log. *florire,* Fr. *fleurir,* Prov., Cat. *florir,* which presuppose *FLŌRĪRE alongside FLŌRĒRE 'to be in flower', and FLŌRĒSCERE 'to bloom'. Like numerous primary and most secondary *-ir* verbs in Hispano-Romance, **florir* is assumed to have been displaced by its counterpart in *-ecer.* Association with *flor* doubtless aided the survival of *florido* as an independent adjective, so used as early as the extant fragment of the 13th-

---

[29] "Los derivados ibero-románicos de PETRINUS," *Fil,* 3 (1951), 201–206, esp. 205.

[30] García de Diego, *Contribución al diccionario hispánico etimológico, RFE,* Suppl. II (Madrid, 1923), records *esperido* and *(d)esperecer* s.v. DĒPERĪRE, p. 62. The *DEEH* entry DĒPERĪRE lists only *esperido.*

century *Roncesvalles* epic. OPtg. *frolido* either presupposes an earlier **frolir* or results from the influence on *florido* of OPtg. *frol* 'flower'. Both *frol* and *frolido* extended their domain into Western Hispano-Romance, as shown by their presence in the comedies of the Extremaduran Bartolomé de Torres Naharro. Editors of the *LBA* have emended the *fror* of 1664*h* of MS S (G and T are lacunary here) to *flor*. John Lihani[31] registers *frol* in the *sayagués* of the dramatist Lucas Fernández (d. 1542) and calls attention to its sporadic use in the works of Lope de Vega and Diego Torres Villarroel. José Lamano y Beneite reports *frol* in the early twentieth-century speech of the province of Salamanca[32]. Unlike many of the adjectives under discussion here, *florido* carries with it no negative semantic connotations.

gracido 'grateful, thankful'

OSp. *gracido* turns up once in Berceo and once in the Alfonsine *Primera Partida*[33]. However, in Old Portuguese and Old Leonese the verb *gracir* and its *-ido* participle are abundantly recorded (*Cancioneiro de Ajuda, Cancioneiro da Vaticana, Demanda do Santo Graal, Cantigas de Escarnho e de mal dizer; Alexandre* 0, 38*b*, 119*c*, 1061d; the corresponding passages in P employ forms of *gradescer*). To the East and North of Castile one finds OCat. *grasir* ~ *grazir* ~ *grair* (mod. *agrair*), OProv. *grazir*, flanked by *grazimen* 'thanks, recognition', *grazida* 'thanks', *grazidor* 'thankful'.

The isolated instances of *gracido* in Berceo and in the Alfonsine corpus seem to represent the last vestiges of OSp. **gracir*. In the historical perspective this verb can best be understood as an adaptation of OProv. *grazir*. The canons of Spanish and Portuguese derivational morphology render highly improbable the creation of a verb in *-ir* derived from *gracia* and *graça*. The voiceless sibilant of *gracir* may betray the secondary influence of these nouns. García de Diego, *DEEH*, s. v. *GRĀTĪRE, had already recognized the Provençal origin of *gracir*[34]. Corominas, *DCE*, s. v. *grado* II, states "la forma *gracir* . . . está en relación con oc. *grazir*, cat. ant. *grair*, hoy *agrair:* se explica por influjo de GRĀTIA sobre el derivado romance *GRĀTĪRE." Among Lusists Carolina Michaëlis de Vasconcelos supported a Provençal origin for OPtg. *gracir*[35].

---

[31] *El lenguaje de Lucas Fernández* (Bogotá, 1973), p. 451.

[32] *El dialecto vulgar salmantino* (Salamanca, 1915), p. 465.

[33] Elli fuesse por ello *gracido* e loado (*SLor*, 19*d*); ca más *gracidos* deven seer a los omnes los servicios que fizieren a dios de su voluntad (*Primera partida*, fol. 61r36, as edited in John Nitti and Lloyd Kasten, *Concordances and Texts of the Royal Scriptorium Manuscripts of Alfonso X el Sabio* (Madison, 1978).

[34] Earlier García de Diego, *Contribución . . .*, s. v. *GRĀTĪRE had operated with a blend of *gradido* and *gradecido* to account for *gracir*.

[35] The norms of Provençal diachronic phonology rule out the immediate derivation of *grazir* from *GRĀTĪRE. Both Carolina Michaëlis de Vasconcelos, "Glosário do *Cancioneiro de Ajuda*," *RLu*, 23 (1920), s. v. *gracir*, p. 41, and Corominas, *DECLC* I, s. v.

manido 'spoiled, gamy (of meat)'

This adjective originally served as past participle of OSp. *maner* 'to remain, stay; dwell' < MANĒRE, a verb which failed to outlast the thirteenth century[36]. The fourteenth-century translation of the Vulgate Old Testament preserved in Escorial MS i-j-4 (ed. J. P. Llamas) contains such forms as *manid* (Gen. XIX:2), *maniremos* (XIX:3), *manirá* (Num. I:10) which point to an inf. *manir,* a variant favored in Eastern Hispano-Romance (cf. OArag. *romanir,* with rounding of the unstressed vowel of the first syllable). Although the reflexes of MANĒRE disappeared, leaving in their wake only *manido* and substantivized *manida* 'abode', the compounds PER-. RE-MANĒRE survived in inchoative garb as *permanecer,* OSp. *remanecer* (OArag. *ro-*) 'to remain'.

Paradigmatic complexity may have played a major role in the relatively rapid demise of *man-er, -ir.* Unimpeded oral transmission of MAN-EŌ, -ES, -ET would have yielded **maño, manes, mane.* Malkiel has argued that speakers of Hispano-Romance chose to avoid in the verbal paradigm the morphophonemic alternation /ɲ/~/n/; witness the genesis of *tengo* 'I have', *vengo* 'I come' rather than **teño,* **veño* < TENEŌ, VENIŌ (cf. Ptg. *tenho, venho*)[37]. Subj. *manga* indicates that some speakers must have employed the ind. paradigm **mango, manes* etc. (cf. It. *rimango* 'I remain'). Old Spanish wavered between the "etymological" strong preterit *ma(n)so* and the analogical *manió.* The future very likely showed the alternation **manré;* ~ **marné* ~ **mandré* ~ **marré* (cf. OPtg. *marrei*)[38]; however note unsyncopated *maneremos* in the Alfonsine *GE* cited in fn. 36. The tendential avoidance of *-ir* verbs with stem vowel *a* may have contributed in some small way to the elimination of *manir.*

Paradigmatic complexity by itself need not automatically doom a verb, a fact illustrated by the uninterrupted vitality of such high frequency verbs as *decir, hacer, tener, venir, poder, querer.* If, however, the language happens to contain semantically appropriate and morphologically regular substitutes, speakers may jettison once and for all the afflicted verb. The Old Spanish

---

agrair, pp. 72*b*–74*a* operate with a *GRĀTIĪRE = /gratjire/, presumably reflecting the influence of GRĀTIA(S). On the possible existence of a sound correspondence -T- > Prov. *-z-*, see Josef Brüch, "Gab es im Altprovenzalischen ein *z* aus lateinischem Intervok. T?," *Philologische Studien aus dem romanisch-germanischen Kulturkreise. Karl Voretzsch zum 60. Geburtstage* .. (Halle, 1927), pp. 214–238, and Gerhard Rohlfs' critical rejoinder, *ZRP,* 51 (1931), 299–303.

36 "Fue para la posada d'Estrangilo querido/el huespet con qui ovo la otra vez *manido*" (*Apol,* 328*cd*); "non lo faremos pero *maneremos* en la plaça" (*GE,* I, 130*b*12); "el puerco acogióse a una cueva do solié *maner*" (*EE,* 393*b*1).

37 "New Problems in Romance Interfixation (I): The Velar Insert in the Present Tense (with an Excursus on *-zer/-zir* Verbs)", *RPh,* 27:3 (1974), 304–55, esp. 329–32. A similar situation is found in Old Italian in which *tegno, vegno* and *rimagno* gave way to *tengo, vengo* and *rimango;* for details, see Berthold Wiese, *Altitalienisches Elementarbuch*$_2$ (Heidelberg, 1928), § 102, and Gerhard Rohlfs, *GSI,* II, §§ 534–535.

38 For the OPtg. paradigm of *mãer,* see Carolina Michaëlis de Vasconcelos, *RLu,* 3 (1893–94), 171.

speech community had recourse to *permanecer, quedar,* and *fincar* (cf. Ptg. *ficar*) to replace *man-er, -ir,* 'to remain', and to *ve-, vi-vir* and *morar* to fill in for *maner* 'to dwell, reside'[39].

Corominas (*DCE* s.v. *manido*) first documents *manido* as an independent adjective in the writings of A. Guevara (d. 1545) with the meaning of 'cooked, tender'. This meaning of *manido* represents a radical narrowing of the original semantic scope of *man-er, -ir.* Did this semantic change precede the loss of the original verb in the Middle Ages? Conceivably *man-er, -ir* acquired in hunting and culinary circles the meaning *'to hang or age meat', with the resulting creation of such a phrase as *carne manida* 'meat that has been stored', 'high meat' (i.e., 'meat that has been stored too long'). Such a concrete meaning may have spared *manido* at the time of the demise of *man-er, -ir.* The survival of *manido* as a relatively late independent adjective was aided by the presence in the lexicon of other pseudo-participial *-ido* adjectives which bore a negative semantic connotation. Although Covarrubias' *Tesoro* (1611) does not reserve a separate entry for *manido,* the verb *manirse* is defined as 'detenerse de un día para otro . . . como *carne manida,* la que no se come recién muerta, sino que se guarda de oy para mañana'. César Oudin's bilingual dictionary (1607) records the transitive *manir la carne* which he renders as 'faisander, mortifier, attendrir'. Is *manir,* so used, the reincarnation of OSp. *manir,* absent from written sources for some two centuries, or is mod. *manir* a backformation extracted from the adjective *manido?*

Potentially relevant to this problem is Cat. *amanir* 'to prepare; cook, season'[40]. Such authorities as Meyer-Lübke (^{3}*REW,* 5341), Ernst Gamillscheg, and Corominas see in the Catalan verb a cognate of It. *ammannire,* OProv. *amanoir, OFr. amanevir* 'prepare, make ready', all of which have been linked since the days of Diez to the family of Gothic MANWJAN 'to prepare'[41]. Corominas insists that the Mallorcan use of *amanir la vianda o la carn* 'prepare meat' is a Castilianism genetically unrelated to the native Cat. *amanir.* Yet in 1696 J. Lacavalleria's *Gazophylacium catalano-latinum* glosses *amanir lo dinar* as 'prandium curare' and *amanir lo menjar o les viandes* as 'cibos coquere, condire'. It does not seem reasonable to separate genetically the Spanish culinary term *manir* from the formally-similar and semantically-related Catalan verb. It is tempting to suggest that Sp. *manir* and *manido* as cooking terms are borrowed from Catalan and are unrelated to OSp. *man-er, -ir;* however the absence of the prefix *a-* in the Spanish forms militates against this solution.

---

[39] Reflexes of MANĒRE did not fare well in the Romance languages; in addition to OSp. *man-er, -ir,* OPtg. *mãer,* OFr. *manoir,* OIt. *manere,* and Rum. *mînea* fell into disuse. In Rhaeto-Romance, Sursilvan *maner* has survived with the meaning 'to spend the night'.

[40] For a detailed discussion of Cat. *amanir,* see Corominas, *DECLC,* I (Barcelona, 1980), s.v. *amanir.* Clovis Brunel's suggestion, *Ro.,* 61(1935), 216–18 that the verbs under discussion go back to *ADMĀNUĪRE ← MĀNU 'hand' has found no supporters.

[41] García de Diego, *DEEH,* s.v. MANĒRE declared Sp. *manir* to be a reflex of MANWJAN semantically influenced by MANĒRE.

tollido 'paralyzed, crippled; mad, crazy'

In like fashion, *tollido* outlasted its parent verb *toller* 'to take away, remove', the local descendant of TOLLERE 'to raise, lift up'. The verb is abundantly documented in Old Spanish until ca. 1350, when it dramatically gave way before *quitar*[42]. Nebrija's Latin-Spanish dictionary records only *tollido,* which he glosses as 'debilis aliquo membro'. Although both Covarrubias and the *Diccionario de autoridades* both list *toller,* they classify the verb as obsolete. I have argued elsewhere that a degree of paradigmatic complexity combined with the unique stem alternation /ʎ/~/lg/(*tuelle* vs. *tuelgo, tuelga, tolgamos*) may have sufficiently undermined *toller* so that speakers chose to generalize the semantic scope of *quitar,* orig. 'to remove a debt or obligation or the burden of sin', a verb free of paradigmatic anomalies[43]. Prior to the demise of *toller,* its participle *tollido* had already started to follow its own course, coming to denote by the thirteenth century 'paralyzed, maimed, crippled', a narrowing and concretization of its original meaning (cf. the later analogous case of *manido* vis-à-vis *man-er, -ir*). In some fourteenth-century texts traceable to the Western portion of the Spanish linguistic domain *tollido* is used in the sense of 'mad, crazy'; cf. (in my view) genetically related Ptg. *tolo,* 'mad, crazy'. The presence in the lexicon of a host of negatively-colored *-ido* adjectives doubtless strengthened *tollido* as its parent verb gradually fell into disuse. Indeed such a shrinkage in the semantic scope of a verb's past participle when used as an independent adjective appears to bespeak a weakening of the source verb's currency. An evolved variant of *toller,* namely *tullir* 'to maim, paralyze' managed to cling to life after the severe contraction of its semantic range.

The analyst can choose to place on the fringes of Group III(b) a number of additional *-ido* participles. To judge by the available evidence, the infinitive and past participle may have been the only forms of some *-ir* verbs known to and/or regularly employed by many speakers of Old Spanish. For some members of the speech community, the *-ido* participle of such verbs may have already become independent adjectives. A substantial proportion of these items carry negative semantic connotations: *atordido* 'stunned, dazed' ← *atordir* (mod. *aturdir*), *desleído* 'weak, feeble' ← *desleír, embaído* 'cheated, deceived' ← *embaír, engreído* 'conceited, stuck up' ← *engreír, escarnido* 'mocked, scorned' ← *escarnir, fallido* 'failed, deceased' ← *fallir, fenido* 'deceased' ← *fenir* (cf. learned *infinido* 'unfinished'), *sepelido* 'buried' ← *sepelir, traído* 'betrayed' ← *traír.* Let me hasten to point out that not all such participles were evaluatively negative; witness *guarido* 'cured' ← *guarir, guarnido* 'garnished, adorned' ← *guarnir.* The presence in the language of such formations may have

[42] Whereas OFr. *toldre* ~ *tollir* failed to survive the Middle Ages, It. *togliere* and Cat. *toldre* 'to take away, remove' continue to flourish.

[43] "The Fragmentation of the Latin Verb TOLLERE in Hispano- (including Luso-) Romance," *RPh,* 37:2 (1983), 166–74 (with Editorial Postscript by Malkiel).

contributed to the association by speakers of the segment *-ido* with negatively-tinged adjectives.

Group III c

The adaptation during the medieval period of some Old French adjectives in *-i* and similar Old Provençal or Catalan bases in *-it* (fem. *-ida*) to Spanish morphological conditions helped to swell the ranks of Group III pseudo-participial *-ido* adjectives. In several of the following instances it is difficult to determine whether the immediate conduit of transmission into Hispano-Romance was Gallo-Romance or Catalan: *ardido* ~ *fardido* (also *faldrido*) 'bold, daring; astute, clever' < OFr. *hardi; (d)esmaído* 'weak, faint' < Cat. *esmait; (des)marrido* 'sad' < OFr. *marri* or Cat. *marrit, escaldrido* 'clever' < OCat. *escaltrit; fornido* 'strong, robust' < OFr. *forni* or Cat. *fornit; garrido* 'handsome, beautiful' < Fr. *garni.* Though apparently of no diachronic significance on the Spanish side, it is worth noting that most experts assign the French or Catalan forms to a Germanic prototype.

ardido ~ *fardido* 'daring, bold, astute'

Until 1970 few scholars had questioned Diez' dictum (*EWRS* Pt. 1, s.v. *ardire*) that OFr. *hardi* derived ultimately from Frk. *HARTJAN 'to make hard'; such adjectives as OSp. *(f)ardido,* Ptg. *ardido,* It. *ardito,* Prov., Cat. *ardit,* Sard. *ardidu* were regarded as borrowings from medieval Northern Gallo-Romance. Diez saw in Sp. *ardido* 'bold, daring' the semantic influence of *arder* 'to burn'. Josef Brüch contended that *HARTJAN had entered the Latin of the late Empire[44]. Menéndez Pidal claimed that *HARTJAN had given off a native verb **ardir,* of which *ardido* is the sole attested relic. In a footnote he lists the variant *fardido* as a Gallicism[45]. Corominas (*DCE,* s.v. *ardido*) correctly operated with two routes of transmission. Whereas the *f-* of *fardido* indicates, against the background of the contemporaneous shift *f-* > *h-*, an adaptation of OFr. *hardi* (with its aspirated inital consonant), *ardido* goes back to Provençal or Catalan *ardit* (note especially the OSp. variant *ardit;* rare OSp. *fardit* is a short-lived compromise form).

Arthur Greive devoted to *hardi* and its Romance congeners one of the eleven lexical vignettes included in his Bonn Habilitationsschrift on the origin of French '*h* aspiré'[46]. Two considerations led this scholar to reject the Ger-

[44] *Der Einfluß der germanischen Sprachen auf das Vulgärlatein* (Heidelberg, 1913), p. 47.

[45] *Cantar de Mío Cid: Texto, gramática y vocabulario,* vol. II (Madrid, 1911), s.v. *ardido,* p. 471; see also Vol. I, p. 174, where Menéndez Pidal labels *fardido* a Gallicism. In like fashion Bloch-Wartburg, [5]*DELF,* s.v. *hardi* operate with a lost **hardir* < HARTJAN.

[46] *Etymologische Untersuchungen zum französischen "h aspiré",* Romanische Etymologien 8 (Heidelberg, 1970), pp. 161–187.

manic origin of *hardi:* the presence of cognates in all Romance languages except Rumanian and its abstract meaning, as opposed to the concrete and practical nature of most Germanic loan words in Romance. Moreover, he claims to have found no parallels for the supposed semantic shift from 'hard, stiff' to 'bold, daring, intrepid'. Greive chose to trace the Romance formations at issue back to the family of ARDĒRE 'to burn', a possibility suggested for It. *ardito* 'courageous, daring' ← *ardire* 'to have the courage to' by O. Ferrari as long ago as 1676, and specifically rejected by Diez. The *h-* of *hardi* is explained by Greive (as are all instances of so-called '*h* aspiré') as a syntagmatically motivated anti-hiatic device.

With regard to the Spanish branch of this word family, Greive declared *ardido* to be the sole Hispanic product of *ARDĪTU; he dismissed *fardido* as a seldom-used "literary reminiscence" of OFr. *hardi.* The absence of derivatives with *f-* clearly demonstrates for Greive the non-native status of *fardido.* The medieval record, however, gives the lie to both statements: *fardido* and *faldrido* are amply documented in Old Spanish (especially in the thirteenth century). One also finds, albeit rarely, such derivatives as *fardidez(a),* and *enfardimiento.* The instance of *fardido* in the fourteenth-century Galician *Crónica troyana* is in all likelihood a Hispanism. One may suppose that use of *fardido* in the sixteenth-century chivalric novel *Palmerín de Oliva* reflects a deliberate archaism.

Although Greive does indeed present attractive semantic evidence in support of ARDĒRE, abundantly recorded OSp. *ardit* 'bold, daring' can in no way be explained as an autochthonous reflex of *ARDĪTU; *-ido* participles were not subject to apocope (with subsequent devoicing of the final dental); rather, adjectival *ardit* must be seen as an unadapted borrowing from OProv. *ardit.* Spanish furnishes no independent evidence for Hispano-Latin *ARDĪTU; Sp. *asar* 'to roast', Ptg. *assar* 'id.' < *ARSĀRE ← ARSU bespeak the presence of the strong past participle of ARDĒRE in spoken Hispano- and Luso-Latin (cf. OFr. *ars* alongside *ardre* ~ *ardoir*). One might argue that *ardido,* the Romance-created participle of *arder* 'to burn' may have had at best a secondary influence through formal resemblance on the semantic evolution of *(f)ardido.*

The circumstances surrounding the genesis of thirteenth-century *faldrido* (accompanied by *faldrimiento*) are far from clear. Texts show that this adjective, frequently used together with *sabio* and *sabidor,* meant 'astute, wise, skilled'[47]. Except for Arnald Steiger[48], who posited an Arabic base, the few specialists who have commented on this adjective view it as a variant of *fardido.*

---

[47] Some examples: Ambos eran eguales e en mannas *faldridos* (*Alex.* O 1944*c;* this verse is absent from P and rejected by Nelson in his critical reconstruction); El que era más *faldrido*/era aquell el su amigo (*SME,* vv. 183(-184); ca el omne *faldrido* e sabio e manso . . . (*CeD,* MS. A. l. 817; The corresponding passage in B reads . . . omne sabido e manso e sabio); mas como era *faldrido* en las otras cosas . . . (*GE,* I, 691*b*13); como era omne *faldrido* e muy sabidor (*GE,* IV, fol. 73*b*).

[48] "Aufmarschstraßen des morgenländischen Sprachgutes," *VR,* 10 (1949), 1–62 at 21f.

The semantic evolution from 'bold, daring' to 'wise' can be understood within the military context of the Reconquest. The transmutation of *fardido* into *faldrido* presents greater difficulties. Operating with a process he labelled "repercusión de líquidas," Corominas (*DCE,* s.v. *ardido*) assumed that *fardido* had cast off a **fardrido* which dissimilation subsequently converted to *faldrido.* He cited as a supposed parallel the case of *goldre* 'quiver' < *GORD(R)E < CŌRYTU, an equation about which he was more circumspect elsewhere (in the *DCE,* s.v. *goldre*). It is noteworthy that such a process never transmuted *ardido* to **aldrido.*

At first glance it seems reasonable to study *faldrido* jointly with its synonym *escaldrido.* However, doubts arise concerning the vitality (if not the authenticity) of *escaldrido* in medieval Castilian. Chapter 22 of Manuscript A of the late thirteenth-century *Castigos y documentos* ends with the passage "Yo destroiré la sabidoría de los sabios e la prudencia de los *escaldridos* e la fortaleza de los fuertes del mundo." The work's first editor, Pascual Gayangos (*BAE,* vol. 51) dismissed *escaldrido* as a corruption of *esclarecido* (Glossary, 604*c*). The passage at issue is not found however, in the original version of the *Castigos* (as edited in 1952 by Agapito Rey); but rather it occurs in the interpolated material taken from Juan de Castrojeriz's fourteenth-century *Regimiento de príncipes,* itself a translation and gloss of Egidius Romanus, *De Regimine Principum.* This example is the sole instance of *escaldrido* that I have encountered to the west of the Catalan-Aragonese linguistic domain. Three instances of *(e)scaltrido* turn up in the writings prepared under the direction (or at the behest) of Juan Fernández de Heredia[49]. In light of Cat. *escaltrit* (fem. *-ida*), one may wonder whether Heredia's form represents a borrowing from the East or a native Aragonese form. Cat. *escaltrit* is clearly a cognate of It. *scaltrito* 'astute, sharp, cunning' (cf. *scaltrire* and postverbal *scaltro*) and of OProv. *escautrit, escautrimen(t).* Italian etymological dictionaries have accepted Leo Spitzer's derivation[50] of *scaltrire* from CAUTERĪRE 'to burn, brand' ← CAUTERIU, as has Corominas with regard to OCat. *escaltrit,* mod. *escoterit* ~ *escotorit*[51]. A propos of *escaldrido,* clearly a cognate of the Provençal and Italian forms, Malkiel tentatively suggested that CALLIDU 'sly, cunning', was altered in its development by *faldrido*[52]. Though appealing enough on the semantic side, this solution could not account for the Italian and Catalan cognates. Corominas (*DCE,* s.v. *escaldrido*) laid at the doorstep of *faldrido* the change in Castilian territory of Cat. *escaltrit* into *escaldrido.* It seems safe to conclude that the rare OSp. *escaldrido* represents a short-lived foreignism which could not have played a role in the genesis of *faldrido* or exerted much influence in the creation of pseudo-participial *-ido* adjectives.

---

49 See John Nitti and Lloyd Kasten, *Concordances and Texts of the Fourteenth-Century Aragonese Manuscripts of Juan Fernández de Heredia* (Madison, 1982).

50 *AR,* 6 (1922), 164–165, and 7 (1923), 393.

51 *DECLC,* II, s.v. *caustic,* pp. 645*b*–646*a.*

52 *Lg.,* 22 (1946), 307.

desmaído 'feeble, exhausted'

The presence of *desmaído* 'feeble, exhausted' alongside *desmayar* 'to faint' and its own past participle *desmayado* has given rise to an exchange of scholarly opinions. I noted in Chapter One that Menéndez Pidal had included *desmayar* among that handful of *-ar* verbs which somehow had developed an *-ido* past-participle. Corominas (s.v. *desmayar*) suggested the possibility of a blend with semantically-akin *desvaído,* apparently forgetting that he had categorized *desvaído* as a Lusism first documented in the *Guzmán de Alfarache* (1607), whereas *desmaído* is amply attested in the thirteenth century. Nearly thirty years later Corominas[53] classed *desmaído* and Cat. *esmait* as heteroclitic modifications resulting from secondary influences[54]. D. A. Nelson[55] has identified the most convincing immediate source for *desmaído,* namely, OCat. *esmahit* ← *esma(h)ir,* which itself may have crossed the Pryenees from Gallo-Romance (cf. OProv. *esmair* ~ *esmaiar* ~ *esmagar*).

Romanists operate with as etymon *EXMAGĀRE, based on Gmc. MAGAN 'to have strength, power', to account for OFr. *esmaiier* 'to trouble, worry', the aforementioned OProv. forms, Ptg. *esmagar* 'to crush, squash, overpower', and OIt. *smagare.* The *-y-* of Sp. *desmayar* vis-a-vis the *g* of *EXMAGARE points to the non-native origin of this verb (cf. Salm. *esmagar* 'to crush, squash').

Some speakers of medieval Spanish apparently sensed a referential kinship between *desmaído* 'feeble' and *desmarrido* 'sad'. Whereas MS S of Berceo's *SDom.* reads *desmarrido* at 303*b,* MSS H and E here offer *desmaído* and *desmayado* respectively. MS P of the *Alex* thrice employs *desmarrido* in passage where O uses *desmaído* (246*d,* 746*d,* 2215*c*). In all three cases Nelson chooses the reading of P in his critical reconstruction of the poem. At 874*c* P matches the *desmaído* of O with *desmedido* which Nelson emends to *desmedrido* 'downcast' (discussed in Chapter Four). Paul Bénichou reports *desmaído* has clung to life in the *hakitía* (Judeo-Spanish) of Morocco[56].

(des)marrido 'sad, downcast'

To the best of my knowledge, no scholar has challenged the Germanic origin of OSp. *(des)marrido,* but the exact route which this adjective followed into His-

---

[53] *DECLC.* III, s.v. *desmaiar,* pp. 88*a*–89*a,* esp. 89*a.*

[54] Cynthia R. Crews, *VR,* 13 (1953), 207, commenting on the one instance of *desmaído* in the *CBaena,* suggested "This adjective may represent a new formation from the verb *desmayar* and not its past participle."

[55] "The Domain of the Old Spanish *-er* and *-ir* Verbs: . . .," *RPh,* 26:2 (1972), 293f.

[56] The ballad *El sevillano* preserved among the Sephardic Jews of Morocco contains the verse "Me volví a mi caza/muerta y *dezmayida*" (vv. 31–32). Another version of the same ballad uses *desvalida;* see "Romances judeo-españoles de Marruecos," *RFH,* 6 (1944), 69–70.

pano-Romance has generated some debate. Menéndez Pidal[57] viewed *marrido* as the past participle of a lost verb **marrir,* cognate to OFr. *marrir* 'to lose one's way; to lose one's spirit, to lose one's mind; to afflict, anger, offend; (refl.) to become sad, afflicted', < Gmc. *MARRJAN. It is unclear whether Menéndez Pidal means here to imply that the Germanic verb had already entered the vocabulary of the late Empire or whether he is tacitly operating with the subsequent Visigothic stratum of the Spanish lexicon (cf. Gothic MARZJAN 'to vex, anger, upset'). Ernst Gamillscheg labelled *MARRJAN an old Germanic loanword reflecting the loneliness and depression experienced by the Germanic soldiers dwelling in the Empire[58]. Few Romanists agreed with Gamillscheg on this point. The absence of cognates in Portuguese and Rumanian, the geographic outposts of the Romania, casts doubt on the early dating implied in such an analysis. Rum. *amărí* 'to embitter' more likely goes back to AMĀRU 'bitter' than to *MARRJAN as Gamillscheg had suggested. Unless other examples of *esmarrido* come to light in medieval Galician-Portuguese, the two instances of this adjective in the *Cantigas de Santa Maria*[59] should be classed as mere Hispanisms attributable to Alfonso X or his collaborators. Corominas (*DCE,* s.v. *marrar*) too, assumed that *marrido* originated as past participle of **marrir;* following Brüch and Meyer-Lübke, he attributed the rare Sp. verb *marrar* 'to lack, fail, err' to a blend of the supposed **marrir* with *errar* 'to wander'[60]. However, Spanish offers no independent evidence for the existence of **marrir* in the medieval language. The verb *desmarrir* recorded in Palet 1604, Oudin 1607, and Franciosini 1620 is clearly a backformation from *desmarrido*[61].

Such specialists as T. Braune[62], Josef Brüch[63], John B. de Forest[64], Walther von Wartburg (*FEW,* 16, 534*b*–536*b*), and Eugen Lerch[65] saw in *marrido* a borrowing from Gallo-Romance. Meyer-Lübke (*REW*$_3$ 5373) preferred Cat. *marrit* as the immediate source of the Spanish adjective, as did the compilers of the *Tentative Dictionary of Medieval Spanish* (1946). The Catalan form itself is

---

57 *Cantar de Mío Cid,* II, s.v. *maridas.* p. 749.

58 *Romania Germanica,* ^{2}1 (Berlin, 1970), § 21.

59 Ed. Mettmann, Nos. 145, v. 31 and 195, v. 80.

60 Both Fernández de Oviedo, *Las Quinquágenas,* I, 279, and Covarrubias, *Tesoro* considered *marrar* to be archaic; see Joseph Gillet, *Propalladia and Other Works of Bartolomé de Torres Naharro,* III: *Notes* (Bryn Mawr, 1951), p. 308.

61 The one example of transitive *esmarrir* 'to lose, misplace', found in an Eclogue attributed to Juan del Encina, represents in all likelihood a backformation from *esmarrido:* "Ca debes Fileno haber esmarrido/Cabrito o cordero o res madrigada," see *Teatro completo de Juan del Encina,* ed. Francisco Asenjo Barbieri (Madrid, 1893), p. 199.

62 "Neue Beiträge zur Kenntniß einiger romanischer Wörter deutscher Herkunft", *ZRPh,* 21 (1897), 213–224, at 214.

63 *Der Einfluß der germanischen Sprachen . . .,* p. 28.

64 "Old French Borrowed Words in the Old Spanish of the Twelfth and Thirteenth Centuries", *RR,* 7 (1916), 369–413, at 400.

65 "Germanische Wörter in Vulgärlatein?", *RF,* 60 (1947–48), 647–684, esp. 665–673.

regarded as a trans-Pyrenean importation. Johannes Terlingen[66] derived Sp. *marrido* from It. *smarrito* 'lost, confused'; but the frequent use of the Spanish adjective in thirteenth-century sources, as well as the semantic differences between *marrido* and *smarrito,* rule out this hypothesis.

The earliest texts which record *marrido* employ it in the sense of 'sad, downcast, disconsolate'[67]. The narrow range of meaning of the Spanish adjective contrasts with the wider semantic scope of the family of OFr. *marrir.* Lerch contends that 'sad' is a later stage in the evolution of OFr. *marrir* and that Spanish must have borrowed *marri* only after the French adjective had acquired this new meaning; in contrast, It. *smarrito* was itself borrowed at an earlier stage from Gallo-Romance[68], Although *marrido* appears to have enjoyed considerable vitality in medieval Hispano-Romance, it failed to produce such adjectival abstracts as **marridez(a)* or **marridura.* Before the end of the Middle Ages speakers of Hispano-Romance reinforced the negative connotation of *marrido* by prefixing *des-;* cf. It. *smarrito* and OCat. *esmarrit.*

The form *esmarnido* which turns up once in the Leonese-flavored *Cuento del Emperador Otas* (ed. Baird, p. 58:7) merits a brief comment here. The editor suggests hesitatingly a blend of *escarnir* and *esmarrir* (197). One must not discount the possibility of a scribal error. If *esmarnido* is linguistically authentic, it deserves analysis within the context of the proposed equation *garni* > Sp. *garrido* (see below p. 37).

favorido 'favored'

One newcomer from abroad joined the ranks of non-participial *-ido* adjectives as late as the sixteenth century. The route followed by *favorido* 'favored' on its way to the Iberian Peninsula remains unclear. This adjective may be a direct borrowing of It. *favorito,* first attested, according to Cortelazzo-Zolli[69], in the fourteenth-century *Bibbia volgare,* or an adaptation of Middle Fr. *favori(t),* itself a recent Italianism first documented in the first half of the sixteenth century (*DELF,* s.v.). Terlingen does not list *favorido* in his catalogue of Span-

---

[66] *Los italianismos en español desde la formación del idioma hasta principios del siglo XVII* (Amsterdam, 1943), p. 361. As early as 1705 Captain John Stevens' *A New Spanish and English Dictionary* had derived *desmarrido* from *smarrito;* see Samuel Gili Gaya, *Tesoro lexicográfico,* s.v. *desmarrido.*

[67] E.g., *FGonz,* 318*c, SLor,* 16*d, SDom,* 303*b, CeD,* 35.574, *EE,* 206r54. Should this adjective be interpreted as 'lost' or 'downcast' in *Apol* 316*b*?

Ruego.t dixo al metge- que la havié guarida
que me digas do seyo que mal so *desmarrida*
Véyome de mis gentes de mi logar partida
Si Dios no me valiere tengo que so perdida

[68] In his aforecited article Lerch suggested that OFr. *marri* had been influenced on the semantic side by the family of MAERĒRE 'to be sad'. The failure of this verb to survive in Gallo-Romance renders this hypothesis highly unlikely.

[69] *Dizionario etimologico della lingua italiana,* II (Bologna, 1980), s.v. *favore.*

ish Italianisms. The verb *favorecer,* found in the late fifteenth-century *Ysopete historiado* and in Nebrija's *Vocabulario* does not necessarily presuppose a prior **favorir;* in all likelihood, it was coined directly from *favor,* itself attested in one MS of the *Castigos y documentos.* The use of *favorido* by Torres Naharro, who spent many years in Italy, speaks for classifying this adjective as an Italianism[70]. In the first half of the eighteenth century, the *Diccionario de autoridades* characterized *favorido* as "lo mismo que *favorecido,* aunque de menos uso."

fornido 'strong, robust'

Despite disagreements about the shape of the base and its precise filiation, Romanists have long classified OFr. *fornir* (mod. *fournir*) as a Germanic loan[71]. Most etymologists have also regarded the French verb as the source of It. *fornire,* Prov. Cat. OSp. Ptg. *fornir.* In Hispano-Romance *fornir* and *fornido* are both attested in fourteenth-century Old Aragonese sources (in an inventory, in the translation of Guido della Colonna's *Historia Destructionis Troiae,* and in the writings of Juan Fernández de Heredia)[72], a fact which strengthens Corominas's contention (s.v. *fornir*) that Cat. *fornir* immediately underlies the Spanish verb. Like many verbs in *-ir, fornir* was quickly replaced in Spanish and Portuguese by its *-ecer* counterpart. While retaining its meaning, *fornido* found a place in the slang of the criminal element of Spanish society, as evidenced by its inclusion in Juan Hidalgo's *Vocabulario de germanía* (1609)[73]. The adjective *fornido* 'strong, robust', which lives on in the modern language, lends itself to analysis either as the sole survivor of short-lived *fornir* or as a direct adaptation of Cat. *fornit.* The example of *fornido* 'finished', encountered in Bartolomé de Torres Naharro's *Comedia Tinellaria* is an outright Italianism; cf. It. *fornito* 'finished'[74].

---

[70] For additional examples of *favorido* extracted from Golden Age sources see Gillet, *Propalladia,* III, p. 524.

[71] I note Harri Meier's unconvincing attempt to link Ofr. *fornir* and its cognates to a Lat. *FRUNĪRE ~ *FRUNISCERE; see his chapter "Frz. *fournir* Ital. *fornire,* Span.-Port. *fornecer*", *Neue lateinisch-romanische Etymologien* RVV 53 (Bonn, 1980), pp. 302–307.

[72] See Bernard Pottier, "Étude lexicologique sur les inventaires aragonais," *VR,* 10 (1949), 87–219, at 156; Evangeline V. Parker, "The Aragonese Version of Guido Delle Colonne's *Historia destructionis Troiae:* A Critical Text and Classified Vocabulary," Diss., Indiana University (1971), p. 152, 1.6. (I have not had access to the published version [Silver City, New Mexico, 1977]); and Nitti-Kasten, *Concordances and Texts . . . Heredia.*

[73] For further examples of *fornido* in fifteenth- and sixteenth-century sources, see Joseph Gillet, *Propalladia . . .,* III, p. 538. In some speech communities *fornir* and *fornido* were caught up in the shift of the stem vowel *o* > *u* in *-ir* verbs. I have come across one example of *furnir* (alongside *fornecer*) in those sections of the Arcipreste de Talavera's *Atalaya de las corónicas,* as edited by Inocencio Bombín, Diss., University of Toronto (1976), p. 244, l. 173; Gillet cites an example of pres. ind. *furne* from the *Comedia soldadesca* of Torres Naharro.

[74] Fernando González Ollé, *Textos lingüísticos navarros* (Pamplona, 1970) records *fornido* 'cumplido' in a document from 1491 from Puente la Reina; ". . . *fornido* e complescido este mi testamento . . ." (p. 191).

garrido 'handsome, beautiful'

Diez (*EWRS,* Pt. II b, s.v. *garrido*) analyzed *garrido* as a hybrid composed of an Arabic base GARÎ, which he glossed as 'schön, artig', plus the Romance suffix *-ido* as in *florido.* Lack of a more persuasive solution led a procession of Hispanists to accept unquestioningly this etymology. Ironically, leading Hispano-Arabists (A. Dozy, W. H. Engelmann, L. Eguilaz y Yanguas, and A. Steiger) pointedly omitted *garrido* from their catalogues of Spanish Arabisms. The first note of dissent came from Corominas (s.v. *garrido*), who genetically equated this adjective with OSp. OPtg. *garrido* 'noisy, silly, foolish', which he properly linked to the family of GARRĪRE 'to chatter'; cf. rare OSp. *garrir, garrimiento, garridencia.*

I have argued at length elsewhere that $garrido_1$ 'silly, foolish' and $garrido_2$ 'handsome, beautiful' represent genetically distinct homonyms. That study presents phonological, morphological, semantic, and cultural evidence to support the conjecture that $garrido_2$ is an adaptation to Spanish structural canons of OFr. *garni* in the meaning 'richly adorned, well dressed'. This equation presupposes that the *-rn-* of the proposed French base was transformed to *-rr* in Spanish *garrido.* Such a sound change does not regularly occur in the history of Spanish. In my aforementioned study I claim that lexical rather than phonological pressures (specifically an attempt by speakers to differentiate **garnido* < *garni* from *guarnido* 'furnished, equipped', the lexicalized past participle of *guarnir*) may have triggered here the switch from *-rn-* to *-rr-;* for details, the *historique du problème,* and pertinent bibliography, I refer the reader to *RPh,* 34:2 (1980), 195–205, followed by Malkiel's Editorial Post-Script, 205f. *Garrido* is one of the few pseudo-participial adjectives in *-ido* which has no negative nuance.

Two short-lived Gallicisms probably merit inclusion in the corpus of Group III(c) formations[75]. One adjective, *desanchalido* 'careless, negligent', flanked by *desanchalamiento* 'negligence' turns up once in the fifteenth-century *Confisión del amante,* a prose version of John Gower's Middle English verse *Confessio Amantis,* rendered into Spanish by one Juan de Cuenca "natural de Huete" from a lost intermediate Portuguese translation allegedly prepared by Robert Payn, a native of England who served as a Canon of the Cathedral of Lisbon. The adjective appears in a passage in which a young man is advised "de no ser peresoso *desanchalido* en los casos de amar" (ed. Knust and Hirschfeld, p. 173). The *-chal-* segment clearly indicates the genetic relationship of *desanchalido* to OFr. *chaloir* 'to be important, to matter', *nonchaloir* 'not to matter,

[75] Jeannie K. Bartha, "Four Lexical Notes on Berceo's *Milagros de Nuestra Señora*", *RPh,* 37:1 (1983), 56–62 has suggested that OSp. *descosido* as used at st. 418*c* is genetically distinct from mod. *descosido* 'disconnected, disjointed; talkative' ← *descoser* 'to unstitch'. She glosses Berceo's *descosido* as 'vile' and views it as an adaptation of OProv. *descauzit* 'gross, vile' ← *descauzir* 'to insult'.

to neglect', traceable in the final analysis to CALĒRE 'to be warm'. On Spanish soil this verb gave *caler* 'to be concerned about, to matter', used frequently as an impersonal in the medieval language. The immediate source of *desanchalido* may be Middle French *annonchali* 'indifferent, negligent ← *s'anonchalir* 'to lose courage, become indifferent'. The prefix *des-* was added in Hispano-Romance to emphasize the negative semantic content of the neologism. I have encountered no other instances of *desanchalido* in Old Spanish. The analyst cannot even attempt to determine with any degree of certainty whether Juan de Cuenca is responsible for the use of *desanchalido* in the *Confisión* or whether the Portuguese text furnished the model. I am unaware of OPtg. reflexes of CALĒRE with *ch-;* M. Rodrigues Lapa[76] views such OPtg. phrases as *non m'en cal, non lh'en cal* 'it doesn't matter (to me, to him)' as imitations of their Provençal counterparts.

Desanchalido may have been accompanied in the medieval language by a verb *desanchalar(se)* and the corresponding *-ado* participle/adjective. J. Benoliel documents in the Judeo-Spanish of Morocco *(hakitía) desanchalarse* "traer el cuerpo como descoyuntado y la ropa mal vestida, mal abotonada o cogida," and lists the *-ado* adjective and the deverbal *-amiento* abstract[77] found in the OSp. *Confisión.*

The other short-lived adjective *malbaylido* 'poorly cared for, neglected', an adaptation of OFr. *mal-, maubailli,* past participle of *mal-, maubaillir* 'to mistreat, neglect', calls for little comment. The notable scarcity of attestations in medieval sources suggests that this adjective enjoyed little vitality and may have been unknown to many speakers[78].

This chapter has sketched lexical vignettes of the *-ido* adjectives assigned in the opening chapter to Group III. In these adjectives the terminal sequence *-ido* has not functioned on the diachronic plane as a derivational suffix which has altered the form class and/or meaning of the base to which it is affixed. Genetically, the adjectives of Group III variously represent (a) the progeny of Latin participles in -ĪTU (b) lexicalized past participles of obsolescent Sp. *-er* or *-ir* verbs, and (c) the adaptation to Spanish morphophonological conditions of some foreign adjectives. In the cases of *esperido, transido* and *desvaído* some question arises as to their precise historical classification. With a few exceptions (*empedernido, escaldrido, esperido,* and a few late borrowings such as *favorido* and *fornido*), these adjectives are documented in early thirteenth-century sources and most are in all likelihood long-standing members of the Spanish

[76] *Vocabulário galego-português tirado da edição das "Cantigas d'escarnho e de mal dizer"* (Vigo, 1965), s.v. *cal,* p. 18.

[77] *BRAE,* 15 (1928), 55*a.*

[78] Sacrifica connusco, cambia essi sentido/Si non en ora eres que serás *mal bailido* (*SLor.* 42*d*); veredes que dapno les yo faré que más de quarenta yarán *mal vaylidos* (*Otas,* p. 33, l. 20–21). For examples of OFr. *mal-maubailli(r),* see Tobler-Lommatzsch, *AWF,* 5, cols. 1278–1280.

lexicon. Significantly, a sizeable proportion of these adjectives display a negative semantic connotation: *aterido, (d)esmaído, (des)marrido, desvaído, empedernido, esperido, manido, malbaylido, tollido,* and *transido.*

The analyst cannot, I repeat, speak of a derivational suffix *-ido* in the genesis of these adjectives. Faced with these formations as synchronic reality, speakers could begin to peel off an element *-ido* (with which they were highly familiar from the verbal system). The presence in the early Hispano-Romance lexicon of these items of diverse provenience must have played a role in attuning the linguistic consciousness of the speech community to a pattern of *-ido* adjectives which could not be immediately associated with a corresponding verb. Semantically, the content of the adjectives of this group must have helped to sow the seeds for the connection of pseudo-participial *-ido* with clearly negative overtones of meaning.

Surely it is significant that some of the semantically positive adjectives of Group III – *bell-, vell-ido, (f)ardido, gracido,* and *sencido* – have for all intents and purposes fallen into disuse. Indeed, it seems highly possible that the negative connotations of so many pseudo-participial *-ido* adjectives led to the elimination of those *-ido* adjectives which did not denote negative qualities or features. Confirmation of this supposition must await an examination of the *-ido* adjectives placed in Groups II and I.

CHAPTER THREE

The *-ido* Adjectives of Group II: A Study in Lexicalization

Although *-ido* is attached to a clearly identifiable adjectival base in those formations which comprise Group II, the parasynthetic nature of these derivatives and their passive semantic content disclose that for the most part they must have originated as the past participles of de-adjectival verbs in *-ir* which had been dislodged by their counterparts in *-ecer*. Despite the typological correspondence of these adjectives with the items set apart in Group IIIb, their separate treatment here is justifiable. Whereas the adjectives of Group IIIb represent the lexicalized past participles of primary verbs which had fallen into disuse, the items gathered together here continue the participles of secondary verbs in *-ir* derived from adjectival bases. Speakers would have experienced no trouble in connecting such items as *denegrido, enflaquido, enloquido* with *negro, flaco, loco* after the loss of the intervenient *-ir* verb. For the purposes of the analyses which follow, the following adjectives constitute the core of Group II:

> *amortido* 'dead', *denegrido* 'blackened', *de-, re-sequido* 'very dry', *des-, em-blanquido* 'whitened', OSp. *empobrido* 'poor, impoverished', OSp. *endurido* 'hardened, obdurate', OSp. *enflaquido* 'weakend', *en-, re-gordido* 'swollen, excessively fat', OSp. *enloquido* 'mad', OSp. *enralido* 'rendered sparse', OSp. *ensangostido* 'narrowed down', OSp. *renegrido* 'very black', OSp. *repretido* 'id', *revejido* 'prematurely aged', *reverdido* 'green'.

The available record indicates that these *-ido* adjectives outlived (or at least displayed greater vitality than) their parent verbs. Other documented *-ido* participles of de-adjectival verbs in *-ir* appear to have perished along with the original verb, e.g., *enfortido* ← *enfortir* 'to strengthen' ← *fuerte* 'strong', *enfranquido* ← *enfranquir* 'to free' ← *franco* 'free', *esclarido* ←*esclarir* 'to make clear' ← *claro* 'clear', *enrequido* ← *enrequir* 'to make rich' ← *rico* 'rich', and *establido* ← *establir* 'to make stable, firm' ← *estable* 'stable, firm'[1]. These adjectives are not of immediate concern here.

The medieval record furnishes little direct or indirect evidence for the vitality of the verbs in *-ir* underlying the adjectives at issue here. I have found no present indicative or subjunctive forms reflecting *amortir, denegrir, desequir,*

---

[1] One may legitimately question the inclusion here of *establir,* the forerunner of *establecer*. In all likelihood *establir* is a reflex of STABILĪRE 'to render firm' ← STABILE 'firm' rather than a local offshoot of *estable*. However, on the synchronic plane speakers of Old Spanish may well have perceived the *-ir* verb as a derivative of *estable*.

empobrir, endurir, enflaquir, engordir, enloquir, enralir, ensangostir, envegir, renegrir, repretir, revejir, reverdir. Examples of the infinitives themselves are rare. MS P of the *Alexandre* offers *enflaquir* at 537*a*, 690*b*, and 2259*c:* O responds with *enflaquecer, enflaquecir,* and *enflaquir* respectively. One instance of *reverdir* turns up as late as 1438 (*Corbacho,* ed. González Muela, p. 189). The short-lived verbal abstracts *endurimiento* (*GE,* I, 164*r*45) and *enloquimiento* (*GE,* I, 175*b*76) may well bespeak *endurir* and *enloquir.* The Old Aragonese law code *Vidal Mayor* uses the infinitive *ennegrir* 'to blacken'. Although both MSS of the *Libro de Alexandre* employ *enloqueció,* Nelson reconstructs pret. *enloquió* at 170*c*. In like fashion, he reconstructs *enraliendo* (which presupposes *enralir*) at 1028*d*; the respective MSS readings are *aclarexiendo* (P), *raleando* (O). At 2645 both MSS read *engordiendo* (without the expected metaphony) ← *engordir*. Although *engordar* had long since displaced both *engordir* and OSp. *engordescer,* P. Sánchez Sevilla reported inf. *engurdir* in the Leonese subdialect of Cespedosa de Tormes[2]. The imperfect *ensordién* in *Alexandre,* P 873*d* is matched in O by *ensordecién*; consistent with his editorial practices, Nelson chooses the shorter form in his critical reconstruction of this verse.

In the medieval period those *-ido* adjective which derive from de-adjectival verbs in *-ir* flourish primarily in texts composed or copied in the East of the Hispano-Romance linguistic domain. Berceo's writings include *amortido, empobrido, endurido, enloquido, esclarido,* and *establido*; interestingly, he chose *desecado,* and *denegrado* over *desequido* and *denegrido.* In the Eastern-colored MS P of the *Alexandre* the reader finds *amortido* (710*b*, 715*b*), *embravido* (217*a*), *encarido* (2525*c*), *enflaquido* (1867*c*, 2250*c*), *enfortido* (774*c*, 980*b*), *enloquido* (522*d*, 994*b*, 2439*c*, 1390*d*), *ensordido* (1003*b*), and *establido* (1560*b*, 1865*c*). The Leonese-flavored MS O contains *endurido* (350*b*; P-*estordido*), *enralido* (1415*a*; P-*enraído*). The thirteenth-century *Libro de Apolonio,* preserved in a fifteenth-century Castilianized copy of an Eastern original, contains instances of *amortido* (43*d*, 271*a*), *denegrido* (43*a*) and *endurido* (439*d*). *Denegrido* also turns up in the *Vida de Santa María Egipciaca* (731, 756) and in the Spanish translation of the Vulgate preserved in Escorial MS i. j. 8., a text whose dialect may well have been Old Navarrese[3]. Medieval Navarro-Aragonese *fueros* and notarial documents furnish occasional instances of *enfortido, enfranquido, enrequido,* and *establido*[4].

---

[2] "El habla de Cespedosa de Tormes", *RFE,* 15 (1928), 161.

[3] For a discussion of this problem see Mark Littlefield "The Riojan Provenience of Escorial Biblical Manuscript i. j. 8.," *RPh* 31 : 2 (1977), 225–34.

[4] See the respective Glossaries appended to Gunnar Tilander's editions of the *FAragón* and *VMayor,* to Max Gorosch's edition of the *FTeruel,* and to Fernando González Ollé's *Textos lingüísticos navarros* (Pamplona, 1970). José Yanguas y Miranda, *Diccionario de las palabras anticuadas que contienen los documentos existentes en los archivos generales y municipales de Navarra* ... (Pamplona, 1854) cites from unspecified sources *abonir* 'to make good', *embravir, endurido,* and *enfranquir.*

I have unearthed no examples of such *-ido* adjectives for Western and Central areas in original Asturo-Leonese sources or in pre-Alfonsine Castilian literary monuments and documents. The immense Alfonsine corpus contains isolated examples of *(en)durido, enflaquido, engordido, desequido, emblanquido, enloquido, envegido, establido* and *oscurido*[5]. In contrast, Catalan, following Eastern habits, matches the formation under study here with *amortit, desnerit, embravit, encarit, enflaquit, enfortit, engordit, enrarit, ensordit, envellit, establit, reverdit.* Against this background, it seems reasonable to suggest that the model provided by the Catalan adjectives may have strengthened the position of the corresponding *-ido* adjectives in Eastern Hispano-Romance while the *-ir* verbs to which they had originally been attached were being ruthlessly eliminated by their *-ecer* rivals. The few relevant formations in the Alfonsine texts are far outnumbered by adjectives in *-e(s)cido.* The few *-ido* forms in that corpus may simply reflect the influence of an Eastern copyist.

Instances of such *-ido* adjectives become distinctly rare after ca. 1300 as Castilian extends its linguistic prongs eastward. *Desequido* is attested in the Classical period; *resequido* lives on in modern Leonese. J. García Soriano[6] registers *revejido* in the popular speech of contemporary Murcia. A composition by Ruy Páez de Ribera included in the *Cancionero de Baena* (ed. Azáceta, no. 290) contains an instance of *engordido* (v. 65). The anonymous poet responsible for the *Coplas de Mingo Revulgo* (fifteenth-c.) turned at least once to *regordido.* Both *de-* and *re-negrido* have come down into the modern language; I have encountered one example of *repretido* from the writings of Diego Sánchez de Badajoz (1525–1549). Although *enloquido* appears not to have outlived the thirteenth century, *reloquido* turns up in a composition of Juan Alfonso de Baena (*CBaena,* ed. Azáceta, no. 395, v. 26). The Heredian corpus contains instances of *aflaquido, (a)franquido, (en)fortido, engordido, enrequido, esmortido,* all flanked by more numerous instances of *-e(s)cido*[7].

Attention must now turn to a question of pivotal importance: Why did the de-adjectival verbs in *-ir,* the source of most of the *-ido* adjectives of concern in this chapter, succumb before the onslaught of their *-ecer* counterparts? Numerous Old Spanish primary verbs in *-ir* were also eventually displaced by an *– ecer* doublet (e. g., *bastir* 'to furnish', *contir* 'to happen', *guarir* 'to cure', *padir* 'to suffer', ousted by *[a]bastecer, contecer, guarecer,* and *padecer* respectively). Most Romance languages have, to varying degrees, inserted an increment traceable to Lat. ĒSC-/ISC in selected parts of the paradigms of many of their *-ir(e)* verbs[8]. Spanish and Portuguese (and to a lesser extent, some Southern

[5] See John Nitti and Lloyd Kasten, *Concordances and Texts of the Royal Scriptorium Manuscripts of Alfonso X el Sabio* (Madison, 1978).

[6] *Vocabulario del dialecto murciano* (Madrid, 1932), p. 113*a*.

[7] John Nitti and Lloyd Kasten, *Corcordances and Texts of the Fourteenth Century Aragonese Manuscripts of Juan Fernández de Heredia* (Madison, 1982).

[8] The spread of the so-called "inchoative" element has attracted scholarly attention of late. See especially Andrew S. Allen's Berkeley dissertation (1980) "The Develop-

Italian dialects and the Campidanese variety of Sardinian) have gone the furthest by extending this element to all finite and non-finite forms of the affected verbs, which led in Iberia to the conjugation class shift of *-ir* to *-ecer*. Spanish thereby stressed this element's role as a derivational formative. Although Catalan preserved the *-ir* infinitive, the "inchoative" interfix was added to the rhizotonic forms of the present indicative and subjunctive of almost all *-ir* verbs[9]. Thus, whereas Cat. *establir* formally contrasts with Sp. *establecer, estableixo* matches *establezco*. Catalan and Spanish part company with respect to certain verbs; note Sp. *parto* ← *partir* 'to leave' vis-a-vis Cat. *parteixo* ← *partir*, Sp. *sirvo* and Cat. *serveix* ← *servir* 'to serve', *sigo* alongside Cat. *segueixo* ← *seguir* 'to follow' (cf. ONav. *seguecer*). In some instances speakers of Catalan may employ or omit *-eix*, as in *mento*~ *menteixo* ← *mentir* 'to lie' (vs. Sp. *miento*). As in Gallo-Romance, the interfix failed to spread into the past-participle in Catalan.

Genetically, OSp. *-ir* verbs fall into two categories: primary verbs (of Latin or Germanic background) and secondary verbs derived within Spanish from nominal and adjectival stems. Although the replacement of *-ir* verbs by their *-ecer* counterparts seems to have occurred slowly over the medieval period, secondary *-ir* verbs succumbed with greater rapidity. I have already demonstrated that de-adjectival *-ir* verbs are rare even in the earliest texts. On the other hand, a relatively late work such as Pero López de Ayala's *Libro rimado de palacio* (ca. 1400) continues to harbor such items as *aborrir* 'to abhor, hate, shun' (replaced in this meaning by *aborrecer*), *fallir* and *guarir* (flanked in the text by *fallecer* and *guarecer*), and *guarnir* (finally ousted by *guarnecer*). A substantial number of primary verbs in *-ir* successfully warded off the possible encroachment of *-ecer*, e. g., *abrir, partir, ceñir, costrenir, mentir, pedir, recibir, repetir, seguir, sentir,* and *servir.*

An *-ir* verb's status as a primary formation or as a derivative may have determined the speed with which *-ecer* spread through its paradigm. Why was one class of verbs more prone to rapid replacement by their *-ecer* doublets than the other? I contend it is no mere coincidence that the medieval record fails to document rhizotonic present indicative and subjunctive forms of de-adjectival verbs in *-ir*. In Spanish *-ir* verbs (whether of popular or learned origin), the stressed stem vowels *e* and *o* were subject to various morphophonemic alterna-

---

ment of the Inchoative Suffix in Latin and Romance"; of the various papers by Allen which preceded and followed the filing of this dissertation, the following are immediately relevant to this study: "The Interfix *e/esc* in Catalan and Rumanian," *RPh,* 31:2 (1977), 203–11; and "The Development of Prefixal and Parasynthetic Verbs in Latin and Romance," *Ibid.,* 35:1 (1981), 79–88; also, Curtis Blaylock, "The Romance Development of the Latin Verbal Augment -SK-," *Ibid.,* 28:4 (1975), 434–44; and Blair A. Rudes, "The Functional Development of the Verbal Suffix *-esc-* in Romance," in Jacek Fisiak, ed. *Historical Morphology* (The Hague, 1980), pp. 327–48.

[9] Old Catalan possessed such items as *envaneixerse* 'to behave vainly', and *reverdeixer* 'to become green again'. Should such items be interpreted as native derivatives or as thinly disguised adaptations of OProv. verbs in *-ezir?*

tions[10] brought about by the combined action of metaphony and the diphthongization of Spoken Latin open E and O[11]. One may well posit that such verbs as, say, *reverdir* and *engordir* were conjugated as follows in the present indicative and subjunctive:

**revirdo*	**engurdo*
**revirdes*	**engurdes*
**revirde*	**engurde*
**reverdimos*	**engordimos*
**reverdides*	**engordides*
**revirden*	**engurden*
**revirda*	**engurda*
**revirdas*	**engurdas*
**revirda*	**engurda*
**revirdamos*	**engurdamos*
**revirdades*	**engurdades*
**revirdan*	**engurdan*

Moreover, in the Old Spanish preterit the /j/ of the desinences *-ió, -iemos, -iestes, -ieron* would have generated high stem vowel in such forms as **revirdió*, **engurdió*, etc. (cf. *sintió* ← *sentir*, and *durmió* ← *dormir*). In like fashion the /j/ present in the Old Spanish imperfect endings *-iés, -ié, -iémos, -iédes, -ién* might have generated **revirdiés*, **enguirdiés*, etc. (witness *dizié* ← *dezir*, *murié* ← *morir*). Conceivably, some speakers might have already started to generalize the high vowel (especially the high back vowel) to all finite and non-finite members of the paradigm (as was to manifest itself in texts toward the close of the Middle Ages in such forms as *cubrir* 'to cover', *subir* 'to go up', older *cobrir, sobir*). The presence and spread of the high vowel sufficed to impair, if not obliterate, the vital formal connection between the adjectival base and its verbal offshoot: **revirdo* but *verde*, **engurdo* but *gordo*.

The insertion of the inchoative interfix into the paradigm of *-ir* verbs brought with it immediate advantages. Several linguists have already noted that the use of this element led to the transfer of the word stress from the stem to the syllable immediately following the verbal root in all three persons of the singular and in the third person plural of the present indicative and subjunctive. This displacement of the accent created columnar stress, i. e., in all six persons of the present indicative and subjunctive the stress now fell on the verbal suffix.[12] This accentual schema has prevailed in Catalan and Rumanian and in

[10] The one modern exception is *oír* 'to hear', but, cf. OSp. *udir*, pret. *udí, udió, udieron*, impf. *udié*, subj. *udades*, all in Berceo.

[11] For two different interpretations of these complex processes, see Malkiel, "Diphthongization, Monophthongization, Metaphony: Studies in their Interaction in the Paradigm of the Old Spanish *-ir* Verbs," *Lg.*, 42 (1966), 430–72; and, from the viewpoint of orthodox generative phonology, James W. Harris, "Diphthongization, Monophthongization, Metaphony Revisited," *Diachronic Studies in Romance Linguistics*, ed. Mario Saltarelli and Dieter Wanner (The Hague, 1975), pp. 85–97.

[12] For pertinent bibliography see Allen, "The Interfix *i/esc* ..." and Rudes (esp. with regard to Rumanian). Cf. the accent shift in OSp. *amáuamos* 'we used to love' <

all likelihood represents the original pattern in Old Spanish prior to the generalization of the *-e(s)c-* interfix to the first and second persons plural and eventually to the rest of the paradigm; witness Cat. *padir > pateix(o), pateixes, pateix, patim, patiu, pateixen;* OSp. *padir > padesco, padesces, padesce, *padimos, *padides, padescen.*[13] The result was that the stem vowels were freed from the various stress-governed morphophonemic alternations to which they were subject. By avoiding in this way root allomorphy, speakers were able to preserve the formal link between primitive and derivative and at the same time assert the relationship between adjectival primitive and derived verb. Throughout the history of Spanish, the addition of a prefix or of a derivational suffix has tended not to alter the shape of the base form; consequently there developed in the linguistic consciousness of the speech community a sense of formal continuity between base and derivative[14].

In all likelihood, speakers first resorted to the inchoative interfix in those *-ir* de-adjectival verbs with stem vowels *e, o*. Only a handful of the documented de-adjectival *-ir* verbs continued to display mid stem vowels. Since verbs with the root vowels *a i u* escaped the effects of metaphony, speakers would have had no trouble in preserving the formal and semantic connections between *flaco, duro,* and the paradigms of *enflaquir* and *endurir*. Such verbs probably ended up acquiring the interfix on the model of the many other secondary verbs in *-ecer* coined in Hispano-Romance or inherited from Latin. One may wonder whether a segment of the speech community ever attempted to re-establish the formal link between the adjectival base and its derived verb by generalizing throughout the verbal paradigm the stem vowel of the adjective in a type of recomposition familiar from the genesis of such verbs as OSp. *atañer* 'to touch', *refazer* 'to do again' ← *tañer,* 'to touch', *fazer* 'to do, make' vis-a-vis Lat. ATTINGERE, REFICERE, ← TANGERE, FACERE. In this context, recall unmetaphonized *engordiendo* in both MSS of the *Alexandre*. But it seems that the strength of the metaphonic vowel raising in *-ir* verbs and the iconic association which had developed gradually in the linguistic consciousness of the speech community between high stem vowels and this conjugation class blocked any such effort to remake the verb on the model of the adjectival primitive[15].

AMABĀMUS and *amáuades* 'you (pl.) used to love' < AMABĀTIS, which led to columnar stress in all six persons of the imperfect indicative.

13 Within one *tirada* of the *Cid* poem the reader will find pres. ind. *gradesce* (2853), *gradescen* (2856), *gradimos* (2860), and imper. *gradid* (2861). Theodore H. Maurer, Jr., posited such a "mixed" paradigm for denominal and de-adjectival verbs at the Spoken Latin level, e.g., GRANDĒSCŌ, GRANDĒSCIS, GRANDĒSCIT, *GRANDĪMUS, *GRANDĪTIS, GRANDĒSCUNT; subj. GRANDĒSCAM, GRANDĒSCAS, ... vs. *GRAND(I)ĀMUS, GRAND(I)ĀTIS; see his study "The Romance Conjugation in *ēsco* (*-isco*) *-īre:* Its Origin in Vulgar Latin," *Lg.*, 27 (1951), 136–45, esp. 139.

14 The addition of a suffix to an oxytonic base could lead to syncope: witness *sabroso* 'tasty' ← *sabor,* OSp. *descoraznado* 'downhearted' ← *corazón*.

15 In the seventies, three Romanists working independently observed and commented on the correlation of the high stem vowels /i/ /u/ with *-ir* verbs and of the mid stem vowels /e/ /o/ with the *-er* group; see Knud Togeby, "L'apophonie des verbes espagnols et

Old Spanish denominal verbs seem to have fared somewhat better than their de-adjectival counterparts. A handful of the former verbs have survived the Middle Ages and come down into the modern language. The speech community apparently was willing to tolerate a greater semantic gap between a substantival primitive and its verbal offshoot than between an adjective and the corresponding verbal derivative. In some cases the verb took as its starting point an extended meaning of the underlying noun. The verbs at issue (presented here in their Old Spanish garb) are *asir* 'to seize, grasp' ← *asa* 'handle', *atordir* (var. *estordir*) 'to stun' ← *tordo* 'thrush', *embotir* 'stuff, squeeze into' ← *boto* 'jug', and *engullir* 'to gobble, gulp down' via older **engolir* (preserved in Old Portuguese and Catalan) ← *gola* (mod. *gula*) 'throat'. One may wonder whether even at the Old Spanish stage speakers still perceived the conceptual link between *asir* and *asa, atordir* and *tordo. Asir* was further separated from *asa* by the insertion of the velar interfix: *asgo* 'I seize', subj. *asga.* The last formal vestiges of such a connection were jettisoned toward the end of the Middle Ages when the diffusion of the high back vowel throughout the entire paradigm transformed the aforementioned verbs into mod. *aturdir, embutir,* and *engullir*[16].

Portuguese, like its Eastern neighbor, generalized the inchoative element throughout the paradigm of affected verbs. In contrast to Medieval Hispano-Romance, Old Portuguese displays no vestiges whatever of de-adjectival verbs in *-ir.* Portuguese possesses no cognates of the Group II *-ido* adjectives. Conceivably, such items as, say, *empobrecer* 'to make poor; (refl.) to become poor' ← *pobre* 'poor', or *envelhecer* 'to grow old' ← *velho* 'old' were preceded by **empobrir* and **envelhir.* In Medieval Portuguese, primary *-ir* verbs were subject to morphophonemic alternations caused by the metaphonic raising of the mid vowel in some rhizotonic members of the paradigm: ind. *servo,* subj. *serva, servas, serva, servam,* with /e/, ind. *serves, serve, servem* with /ɛ/; ind. *dormo,* subj. *dorma, dormas, dorma, dormam,* with /o/, *dormes, dorme, dormem,* with /ɔ/. By the end of the Middle Ages the /e/ and /o/ had been further raised to /i/ /u/. It is possible that in the early medieval language *e* and *o* had not yet become /ə/ and /u/ in the arrhizotonic forms. A similar pattern could have been operative in such secondary verbs as **empobrir* and **envelhir.* The speech community may have found such alternations difficult or unacceptable vis-a-vis the stable vowel of the underlying adjective. The insertion of the inchoative interfix would have removed the word stress from the verb root and consequently eliminated the potentially troublesome root allomorphy. If unstressed vowels had not yet undergone reduction, the *o* of *empobrecer* and the *e* of

portugais en *-ir,*" *RPh,* 26:2 (1972), 256–64; Ralph J. Penny, "Verb-Class as a Determiner of Stem Vowel in the Historical Morphology of Spanish Verbs," *RLiR,* 36 (1972), 343–59; and Thomas Montgomery, "Complementarity of Stem Vowels in the Spanish Second and Third Conjugations," *RPh,* 29:3 (1976), 281–96.

[16] For further disucssion of this issue see my article "From *-ir* to *-ecer:* The Loss of Old Spanish *-ir* De-Adjectival Verbs," to appear in *HR*, 53 (1985).

envelhecer would have been phonetically identical with the stressed vowels of *pobre* and *velho* respectively. As a result, the speech community came to prefer to fashion de-adjectival verbs in *-ecer* as a way of avoiding alternations in the stem vowel and of preserving the formal connection between adjective and verb. Latin provided numerous examples of de-adjectival and denominal verbs in -ĒSCERE as a starting point for the wholesale minting of de-adjectival verbs in *-ecer*.

The predominance of -ĒSCERE (as opposed to -ĀSCERE/-ĪSCERE) in the formation of Latin de-adjectival verbs mirrors the original close association between the Latin inchoatives and the corresponding stative or essive de-adjectival verb in -ĒRE. Alongside ALBUS 'white' Latin offers ALBĒRE 'to be white' and ALBĒSCERE 'to become white'. Eventually speakers felt they could derive a verb in -ĒSCERE directly from the adjectival primitive[17]. In like fashion, as de-adjectival verbs in *-ecer* evicted their *-ir* predecessors at a relatively early stage in the history of Spanish, new de-adjectival verbs in *-ecer* were coined directly on the pertinent adjectival base. The model afforded by Latin verbs in -ĒSCERE must have played a major role in this process. Spanish *esvanecer* 'to vanish' ← *vano, endurecer* 'to render hard' ← *duro, engrandecer* 'to make big' ← *grande, engravecer* 'to make serious' ← *grave, enflaquecer* 'to weaken' ← *flaco, en-, a-fortalecer* 'to strengthen', ← *fuerte, enternecer* 'to make soft' ← *tierno, enralecer* 'to make scarce' ← *ralo/raro, ensordecer* 'to deafen' ← *sordo, esclarecer* 'to clarify' ← *claro, ennegrecer* 'to blacken' ← *negro, enverdecer* 'to make green' ← *verde* echo Lat. VĀNĒSCERE, DŪRĒSCERE, GRANDĒSCERE, GRAVĒSCERE, (var. -ĀSCERE), FLACCĒSCERE, FORTĒSCERE, TENERĒSCERE (var. -ĀSCERE), RĀRĒSCERE, SURDĒSCERE, CLĀRESCERE, NIGRĒSCERE, VIRIDĒSCERE.

Unlike Latin, Spanish makes extensive use of prefixes, in combination with verbal suffixes, to derive verbs from underlying adjectives (and nouns)[18]. Although *en-* (var. *em-*) was for a long time the favored parasynthetic pattern, older stages of the language document *es–ecer (esblandecer* 'to soften' ← *blando*), *a–ecer (aflaquecer* 'to weaken' ← *flaco*), *es–ir* (*esclarir* 'to clarify' ← *claro*), and *en–ar* (*engordar* 'to fatten' ← *gordo, ensanchar* 'to widen' ← *ancho, entercar* 'to make stubborn' ← *terco*)[19]. The Alfonsine *General Estoria,* Part IV, contains a single instance each of two of the *-ido* adjectives at issue without a prefix: *negrido* and *oscurido*.

---

[17] For a thorough discussion of Latin denominal and de-adjectival verbs, see Xavier Mignot, *Les Verbes dénominatifs latins* (Paris, 1968), passim.

[18] For comparative statistics, examples, and discussion regarding the use of prefixes, see Allen, "The Development of Prefixal and Parasynthetic Verbs . . ."

[19] Allen claims in his dissertation (p. 150) that the popularity of parasynthetic formations in *-ecer* as a device to coin neologisms began to wane after 1500. He also offers two novel suggestions: (1) speakers of Spanish favored the prefix *en-* in such verbs in order to create vowel harmony between prefix and suffix; (2) the stressed vowel of the nominal abstract suffixes *-eza* < ITIA and *-ez* < -ITIE reinforced the position of *e(s)cer* in the derivational structure of Old Spanish.

The Spanish record offers no evidence of an *-ecer* (much less an *-ir*) verb alongside *de-, re-sequido, renegrido, repretido,* and *ensangostido.* From SICCUS 'dry' Latin had spun off SICCĒSCERE 'to become dry' and SICCĀRE 'to make dry; to be dry', flanked by compounds in DE- and EX-. The presence in Old Spanish of the inherited verb *(de)secar* may have obviated the need to mint **ensequ-ir, -ecer.* My research has uncovered only one medieval example of *desequido* (*GE,* I, 282v12) alongside more frequent *desecado* (Berceo, *Duelo,* 38*c;* López de Ayala, *Libro rimado de palacio*). The model furnished by those *-ido* adjectives in Group II which carry a negative semantic connotation (see below) may have led to the coinage of *desequido* alongside *desecado.* The emphatic nature of the adjective is underscored by the prefix in the variant *resequido* (cf., *reseco* 'very dry, parched'; note *de-, re-negrido* and *repretido*). Indeed, *renegrido* may have furnished the model for *repretido* 'very black', of which the earliest example I have unearthed appears in the writings of Diego Sánchez de Badajoz; note also Judeo-Spanish *empretecer,* which need not presuppose a prior **empretir.*

One may account in like fashion for the genesis of *ensangostido* 'narrowed down' ← *angosto* 'narrow' ← ANGUSTU. Thus it is unnecessary to posit with Corominas (s.v. *angosto*) an *EXANGUSTĀRE to explain *ensangostar* alongside older *angostar.* One may justifiably invoke here the influence on *angosto* through lexical polarization of *ensanchar* 'to widen' derived from *esanchar* through nasal insertion in anticipation of the nasal in the root morpheme; note also *ensangostar* mirroring *enanchar.* There exists no independent evidence for **ensangost-ir, -ecer.* In the same way that *desequido* sprang up alongside *desecado,* so *ensangostido* may have come into being next to *ensangostado* ← *ensangostar.*

It seems safe to conclude that most of the *-ido* adjectives of Group II originally came into being as the past participles of de-adjectival *-ir* verbs. These participles managed to outlive the rest of the paradigm with which they had been associated. While Latin and most of the Romance languages limited the inchoative interfix to the infectum, Spanish and Portuguese, as has been noted, allowed it to diffuse through the entire paradigm. The interfix worked its way only gradually into the Old Spanish preterite and past participle; witness OSp. *connuvo* 'he knew' (Cl. COGNOVIT) alongside OSp. *conoscer,* and past participle *nado* (< NĀTU) flanking OSp. *nascer* 'to be born'. Conceivably such forms as *enloquido* and *empobrido* served, albeit briefly, as the past participles of *enloquecer* and *empobrecer* after these verbs had ousted their *-ir* predecessors. As the interfix wedged itself into the past participle, the shorter variant became lexicalized as an independent adjective in *-ido,* alongside which there no longer existed for many speakers a corresponding *-ir* verb.

Most (though I hasten to add, not all) of these adjectives carry a markedly negative semantic connotation:

amortido	ovo en un ratiello la memoria perdida/e la fuerça del cuerpo fue toda *amortida* (*SDom,* 426*cd*) toda la gente andaba *amortida* (*Apol,* 43*d*)

denegrido	la boca era empelecida / e derredor muy *denegrida* (*SME,* vv. 730–31)
	No es maravilla se es *denegrida* / fembra que mantiene tal vida (Ibid., vv. 755–56).
	El fuese su vía, dexónos con duelo / con mucha mansilla todo *denegridos* (*CBaena,* No. 36, vv. 25–26)
desequido	... e como estava allí *dessequidos* e las almas secas (*GE,* I, fol. 282v12).
empobrido	facienda tan granada es tanto *empobrida* / abés pueden tres monges aver en ella vida (*SDom,* 202*cd*).
	Entiendié gelo todos que era *empobrido* (*Milg,* 631*a*).
endurido	Avié el mesquiniello los braços encorvados / teniélos *enduridos* a los pechos plegados (*SDom,* 550*ab*)
	que tan mala colpada el nunca recibió parósse *endurida,* la cabeça primió (*Apol,* 439*cd*)
	...e tan cochas que semeiassen cortezas *enduridas* (*GE,* I, 458 *a* 7–8)
enflaquido	Bien a ora de viésperas el sol *enflaquido* (*Milg,* 464*a*).
	quando de todo en todo fueron ya *enflaquidos* / cayeron antel Rey todos piedes tendidos (*Alex,* p 1767*cd*)
	Del estudio que lieva es tanto *enflaquida* / que es de la flaqueza mal enferma caída (*Apol,* 208*ab*)
engordido	los dientes terrosos, la lengua *engordida* / color amarillo, los ojos jaldados (*CBaena,* no. 290, vv. 65–66)
	... assi se tornó despues del parto como en cosa *engordida* e vellosa e fea (*GE,* I, 272v10–12)
enloquido	Tenién alguantos dellos que era *enloquido*; dizién los otros non, mas era decebido (*SDom,* 509*bc*)
	assy estaua Ydus que andaua esmarrido / con rrauja del hermano andaua *enloquido* (*Alex,* P 522*cd*)
enralido	ouieron los alarues la carrera a dar / ca eran *enrralidos* non los podién durar (*Alex,* P 1390 *cd*)
	Los poderes de Dario eran fuerte *enralidos* / los unos eran muertos e los otros feridos (*Alex,* O 1415*ab*)
envegido	Ca de guisa era ya affechos allí. Los unos porque nasciera y como dixiemos los otros porque eran y *envegidos* (*GE,* IV, 121v69)
regordido	Los pechos tienen somidos/los ijares *regordidos*/ que non se pueden mover *(Coplas de Mingo Revulgo)*[20]
repretido	[Pablo] Este es blanco o es teñido? [Juan] Es prieto y muy *repretido* (Diego Sánchez de Badajoz, *Recopilación en metro,* II, p. 38)

B. Vigón defines *renegríu* (=*renegrido*) as used in the Asturian subdialect of Colunga as 'color amortado o denegrido que toma alguna parte del cuerpo por efecto de un golpe u otras causas'[21]. On the other hand, the examples of OSp. *emblanquido* and *reverdido* seem to convey no negative message, whereas mod. And. *desblanquido* is glossed 'desblanquecido, pálido, principalmente del rostro'[22]; cf. Sal. *desblanquinado* 'pálido, lívido'[23]. I wish to suggest that the nega-

[20] As in Julio Rodríguez-Puértolas, *Poesía de protesta en la Edad Media castellana* (Madrid, 1968), p. 211.

[21] *Vocabulario dialectológico del Concejo de Colunga, RFE,* Suppl. 63 (1955), p. 397.

[22] Antonio Alcalá Venceslada, *Vocabulario anduluz* (Madrid 1951), p. 217*b*.

[23] José Lamano y Beneite, *El dialecto vulgar salmantino* (Salamanca, 1915), p. 385.

tive semantic content of most of Group II *-ido* adjectives was perceived as a thread which links these formations and which played a significant role in their survival after the elimination of the parent *-ir* verb. In contrast, the *-ido* participles of semantically positive de-adjectival verbs in *-ir* seem to have died along with the verb; witness the fate of short-lived *enfortido* 'strengthened', *enfranquido* 'freed', *esclarido,* and *establido.*

In this chapter I have sought to demonstrate that those *-ido* adjectives which at first glance seem to rest directly on a primary adjective are in reality the lexicalized past participles of de-adjectival verbs in *-ir* which had given way to their *-ecer* counterparts[24]. In genetic terms, *-ido* is here not a derivational suffix but rather a true participial marker. After the demise of the source verb in *-ir,* speakers would have had no trouble in peeling off *-ido* as a recognizable morpheme. With time the speech community came to interpret such items as, say, *enflaquido, engordido, enloquido* as the immediate derivatives of *flaco, gordo,* and *loco.* Such a situation would have further strengthened in the linguistic consciousness of the Old Spanish speech community the growing status of *-ido* as a derivational suffix to be used in extracting adjectives directly from non-verbal bases. I shall return in the next chapter to the importance of the negative semantic connotations carried by most of these adjectives.

[24] At least two formations which I have placed in Group I may lend themselves to inclusion in Group II if genetically they are the lexicalized past participles of denominal *-ir* verbs. Does the prefix of OSp. *enlexido* and *entenebrido* indicate that these negatively-colored adjectives are past participles of **enlexir* and **entenebrir* rather than direct offshoots of OSp. *lixo* (mod. *lijo*) and *ten-, tin-iebras* (mod. *tinieblas*)?

CHAPTER FOUR

The History of Denominal Adjectives in *-ido*

The denominal *-ido* adjectives gathered together in Group I pose a series of problems for the historian of the Spanish language. Although isolated instances of such formations turn up in other Romance languages (OPtg. *doorido, escoorido,* It. *saporito,* Sard. *lanidu*), only Spanish has developed any sort of adjectival series coined by affixing *-ido* to a nominal base. Such formations presumably represent an Hispanic innovation rather than the continuation of a Latin prototype lost elsewhere. Although the parent language did coin some -ĪTUS adjectives based on third-declension -Ī- stem nouns, not one of these adjectives came into Spanish through vernacular transmission. Whereas such Latin adjectives remained semantically neutral, the Spanish denominal adjectives in *-ido* all carry a markedly negative connotation. With the exception of *modorra* (of non-Latin background), all the nominal bases underlying the adjectives discussed here are etymologically transparent. A short historical sketch of each denominal *-ido* adjective (presented in alphabetical order) will precede the analysis of these formations as a derivational pattern. Citations from relevant passages of Old Spanish texts are gathered together in an Appendix at the end of this chapter.

(a)dolorido 'saddened, afflicted, grieved'

This adjective is abundantly documented since the thirteenth century. In the medieval language *dolorido* usually turns up without the prefix and is frequently coupled in synonymic iteration with *triste* 'sad'. Whereas *doloroso* describes the presence and abundance of pain, sorrow, or grief, *dolorido* stresses the effect or result of a prior action or event (i.e., 'struck by grief, afflicted'). The prefix *a*-may betray the influence of *adolescer* 'to suffer' and/or *adolorar* 'to cause pain', while the one instance of *endolorido* in the Alfonsine *Judizio de las estrellas* (ed. Hilty, p. 12*b*37) displays in its choice of prefix the influence of the *en- -ido* adjectives which constitute Group II. In light of the absence of a series of denominal *-ido* adjectives from Luso-Romance, *doorido* may represent a local adaptation or imitation of the Spanish cognate; cf. the correspondence of OPtg. *door* (Mod. *dor*) to Sp. *dolor.* Portuguese speakers did not hesitate to borrow the unadjusted Spanish form *dolorido.*

Dolor has given rise to various verbal derivatives worthy of mention here. The single example of pret. *dolorí* from the *Fazienda de Ultra Mar* (ed. M.

Lazar, p. 183.3) hardly authorizes the analyst to view *dolorido* as the lexicalized past participle of a OSp. **dolorir*. One student of this text[1] has chosen reasonably to class *dolorir* as a Catalanism (OCat. *dolorir*)[2] due in all likelihood to the Eastern scribe responsible for the sole extant copy of this text. Alternatively, one may consider the possibility that *dolorido* spawned an early and short-lived backformation in *-ir*. Texts written by exiled Spanish Jews offer instances of *adoloriar*[3] (reflecting the diffusion of *-iar* in denominal and deadjectival verbs). Rare OSp. *doloriento* seems to stress the ongoing nature of the condition: "fue el sol levantado triste e *doloriento*" (*Alex,* 2606*a*). Such a use of an *-iento* adjective betrays the influence on *-iento* < (UL)ENTU of present participles in *-iente* < -ENTE. For the most part Spanish affixes *-iento* to concrete nouns usually confined to the less elegant sections of the lexicon, e.g., *grasiento* 'greasy, grimy, oily' ← *grasa, harapiento* 'ragged, tattered' ← *harapo, piojento* 'louse-infested, moth-eaten' ← *piojo, sangriento* 'bloody' ← *sangre*[4]. The conjoining of *-iento* to an abstract noun is a much rarer occurrence. The choice (if not the genesis) of *doloriento* in this passage from the *Alexandre* may have been determined by the exigencies of rhyme.

amodorrido 'sleepy, drowsy'

Amodorrido is the only denominal *-ido* adjective in which the suffix is appended to a non-Latin base (to judge by the *-orra-* segment of *modorra*)[5]. The adjective displays a clear passive coloration, 'overcome by drowsiness, lethargy'. Unlike *(a)dolorido, amodorrido* usually appears in Old Spanish with its prefix. The record shows that *amodorrido* enjoyed considerable vitality from the time of Berceo through the sixteenth century; by 1611 Covarrubias had labelled it as antiquated and rustic. Gradually *(a)modorrado,* first attested

---

[1] Albert G. Ganansia, "Morfología, aspectos dialectales y vocabulario de *La Fazienda de Ultra Mar",* Diss., The Ohio State University (1971), p. 145.

[2] Medieval documentation is offered by Alcover-Moll, *DCVB,* IV, s.v. *dolorir,* p. 541, and Corominas, *DECLC,* III, p. 166*a.*

[3] Examples are presented by Leo Wiener, "The Ferrara Bible", *MLN,* 11 (1896), col. 32, and Richard D. Abraham, "The Vocabulary of the Old Judeo-Spanish Translation of the Canticles and their Chaldean Paraphrase", *HR,* 41 (1973), 2.

[4] On the formal and semantic evolution of *-iento* < -ULENTU, see Malkiel, "Studies in Luso-Hispanic Lexical Osmosis . . .", *HR,* 45 (1977), 235–67.

[5] Unanimity does not reign with regard to the etymology of *modorra.* Diez, [5]*EWRS,* p. 496, s.v. *modorra* took Basque *modorra* 'trunk' as his starting point. Meyer-Lübke included this derivation in the body of [1]*REW* s.v. *modorro,* 5631, but in a footnote on p. 929 of the Word Index he classed *modorro* as a hybrid involving Lat. MUTILU 'mutilated, shorn' and the Basque suffix *-orro.* The word family at issue was omitted from [3]*REW.* Corominas, *DCE,* s.v. *modorro* linked this family with Basque *mutur* 'angered, inconvenienced', which, in turn, might be an adaptation of Lat. MUTILU. Jules Cornu had linked Ptg. *modôrro* to VETERNU 'somnolence, lethargy' (*Grundriß,* 2. Aufl., I, p. 767, § 28); García de Diego accepted this solution for Sp. *modorra, DEEH,* § 7144c.

(without the prefix) in the *Coplas de Mingo Revulgo* (mid-fifteenth century), displaced its *-ido* counterpart; the sixteenth-century *amodorriado* possibly mirrors the transition from the *-ido* to the *-ado* adjective (unless it is the participle of an unattested denominal *-iar* verb). The Aragonese variant *esmodorrido* may presuppose an earlier **desmodorrido* which fits the favored parasynthetic pattern for denominal *-ido* adjectives. The loss of *-d-* with subsequent, if not immediate contraction of the contiguous identical vowels led to the coining of *amorrido* (1517); cf. Salm. *amorrarse,* And. *morro,* Cespedosa de Tormes *amorriao*[6] = St. *amodorrarse, amodorro,* and *amodorriado.* The coining of *amodorrecer* 'to become drowsy' and the abstract *amodorrimiento* 'drowsiness' postdates *amodorrido* by a wide margin. Although *amodorrimiento* may not require the presence of an underlying *-ir* verb, its genesis discloses the verbal qualities felt by speakers to be inherent in the independent adjective *amodorrido.* Oudin's *Tesoro* includes *amodorrido* in the entry for *amodorriado.* The *Diccionario de autoriadades* equates *amodorrido* with *amodorrado* and notes that the *-ido* variant is "de poco uso". Ptg. Cat. *modorra* are not accompanied by a corresponding *-ido/-it* adjective.

asombríu 'pale as a result of growing in the shade'

María Josefa Canellada unearthed *asombríu* (with *-íu* as the local equivalent of *-ido*) in the Asturian subdialect of Cabranes[7]. The analyst today can only speculate whether *asombríu* is a formation of long standing fortuitously unattested in the early records, or a relatively recent local coinage. Perhaps one can invoke the retention of the residual adverbial usage of genetically-related Ast. *solombra* in Cabraniego as indirect evidence that *asombríu* also constitutes a relic. A. Alcalá Venceslada reports that And. *asombrar(se)* has retained the etymological meaning 'to grow, to be in the shade'[8], which semantically contrasts sharply with Berceo's *desombrado* (*Milg* 743a) 'deprived of one's shadow'. No evidence points to the existence of **desombrido,* a theoretically feasible formation.

desab(o)rido 'insipid, tasteless; unpleasant'

In all likelihood, *desab(o)rido* is built directly on *sabor* 'taste' (although the presence in the language of *desabor* 'tastelessness, unpleasantness' may have prompted speakers to coin this adjective). The shortened variant displays a tendential syncope triggered within Old Spanish by the welding of a stress-bearing inflectional or derivational suffix to an oxytonic root (cf. *sabroso* 'tasty,

[6] These forms are extracted from Malkiel, "Español *morir,* portugués *morrer* ...", *BHi,* 57 (1955), 118–20.

[7] *El Bable de Cabranes, RFE,* Suppl. 31 (1946), p. 106.

[8] *Vocabulario andaluz* (Madrid, [2]1951), p. 64*a*.

flavorful' ← *sabor*[9], *fedroso* 'stinking' ← *fedor, descoraznado* 'discouraged' ← *corazón* 'heart', see also OSp. syncopated futures and conditionals of many *-er* and *-ir* verbs). In contrast, the longer form (which lives on in And. *esaborío,* Sal. *desaborido*)[10] reflects an attempt by some speakers to preserve the original shape of the underlying primitive; cf. *saboroso, fedoroso. Desab(o)rido* is the only denominal *-ido* adjective which is flanked by a semantically positive counterpart shorn of the negative prefix *des-,* namely *sab(o)rido* 'tasty, pleasant, agreeable', analysable either as an apheresized backformation from *desab(o)rido* or as an immediate derivative from *sabor.* The first possibility fits better the known facts; since all other Spanish denominal adjectives in *-ido* involve the interplay of a suffix and a prefix, one might have expected a semantically positive derivative from *sabor* to turn up as **a-, *en-sabor-ido* (if not *-ado*). Italian formally matches *sab(o)rido* with *saporito* but possesses no equivalent of *desab(o)rido.* Although Battisti-Alessio (*DEI,* s.v. *saporire*) document *saporito* two centuries earlier than *saporire,* the adjective may still have originated as the participle of the *-ire* verb (which seems to have fallen into disuse). To complicate the Hispanic picture even further, thirteenth-century sources also document *(de)sabor(g)ado* (whose *-g-* is ultimately traceable to ICĀRE) as an apparent synonym of *desab(o)rido*; note, however, the absence from the language of **desabrado* alongside *desabrido.*

These adjectives based on *sabor* appear to have enjoyed considerable vitality in the pre-Alfonsine period. The text tradition of the *Calila e Digna* shows one case of outright rivalry between the *-ado* and *ido* variants. The phrase "la melezina *desaborida*" of MS A (ed. Keller and Linker, p. 127:1895) is matched in the later MS B by "la melezina *desaborada*" (p. 127:2183); yet in another passage both MSS agree on "*desabrida* vida" (p. 36:646 and 697).

To judge by their absence from the writings of Alfonso the Wise, of don Juan Manuel, of Juan Ruiz, the Heredian corpus, the *Poema de Alfonso XI,* and *El Corbacho, desab(o)rido* experienced a temporary setback while *sabrido* and the variants in *-(g)ado* fell into oblivion. Alfonso de Palencia turned to *desabrido* in glossing Lat. INCONDITUM; Nebrixa defined *dessabrido* as 'insulsus, fatuus, insipidus' and accorded two separate entries to *dessabrimiento* (1) 'insulsitas, fatuitas', and (2) 'morositas'. The adjective turns up once in the 1499 edition of *La Celestina* (90r24). In addition to *desabrido* such post-Renaissance lexicographers as Covarrubias, Palet, Oudin, Minsheu, and Franciosini register *desabrir* and *desabrimiento* 'tastelessness'; the compilers themselves may have extrapolated on their own the *-ir* verb from the *-ido* adjective. Conceivably, the association of *-ido* with negatively-flavored denominal adjectives condemned semantically positive *sab(o)rido* to an early death.

---

[9] The analyst might choose to trace *sabroso* directly back to LLat. SAPORŌSU (with syncope of the intertonic vowel).

[10] Alcalá Venceslada, p. 253*b*; Lamano y Beneite, p. 383.

desanguido 'anemic'

Desanguido is reported but once in the writings of Salvador Jacinto Polo de Medina (1609–1679)[11]. It is absent from the Spanish dictionaries compiled between 1492 and 1726 which Samuel Gili Gaya surveyed for his *Tesoro lexicográfico.* This adjective if authentic stands apart from most derivatives of *sangre* by taking as its core a more Latinate form of the base (cf. Ptg. *sangue* and OSp. *sanguino* 'blood-colored', employed, if not minted and introduced, by Alfonso X). Old Spanish adjectives referring to the absence of a part of the body or of an associated quality usually involve parasynthetic formations in *des- -ado*; witness *descabezado* 'headless', *descarnado* 'scrawny, emaciated'[12], *descoraznado* 'discouraged', *desdentado* 'toothless', *desmembrado* 'limbless', and, especially in the present context *desangrado* 'bled dry' alongside *desangrar.* Theoretically conceivable **desangrido* appears never to have materialized. One could argue that *desanguido* was coined (as a nonce formation) on the model of pre-existing denominal *-ido* adjectives, especially semantically-akin *descolorido* 'pale'.

There is good reason, however, to believe that *desanguido* is a ghost word which has crept into the corpus of denominal adjectives in *-ido.* It seems that Rodríguez Marín either misread his source or was led astray by a misprint. In their respective editions of the *Fábula burlesca de Apolo y Dafne,* Adolfo de Castro[13] and Angel Valbuena Prat[14] have both printed *deslanguido,* which does make sense in the context[15]. Valbuena states that for the *Fábula* he followed the edition of 1634 published in Murcia. I have had the opportunity to examine the poem at issue as printed at fols. 25r–35v of Polo de Medina's *Universidad de amor y escuelas de interés. . . .* (Zaragoza, 1664); the reading is clearly *deslanguido* (fol. 35v).

---

[11] See Francisco Rodríguez Marín, *Dos mil quinientas voces castizas y bien autorizadas que piden lugar en nuestro léxico* (Madrid, 1922), p. 116, who extracted *desanguido* from Polo de Medina, *Obras en prosa y verso* (Zaragoza, 1664), p. 234.

[12] A propos of *descarnado,* another medieval formation calls for a brief comment here. At 2372*c* of the *Alex,* Luxuria is described in MS. P as "suzia, *descarnida,* más ardiente que leral". MS. O reads "suzia e *escarnida* más ardiente que cal." Clearly *escarnida* 'scorned' makes no sense here. Assuming *descarnida* to be a mere variant of *escarnida* (witness the well known wavering of *des-* and *es-*), Nelson chooses to reconstruct *descarnada* 'of dessicated flesh' as the original reading. Let me raise here the possibility that *descarnido* is a linguistically authentic (though ephemeral) denominal adjective based on *carne.* Only the discovery of additional examples of *descarnido* can resolve this question.

[13] *Poetas líricos de los siglos XVI y XVII,* BAE, 42 (Madrid, 1875), pp. 207–10.

[14] *Obras completas de Salvador Jacinto Polo de Medina* (Murcia, 1948), pp. 211–24.

[15] Con las voces muy flacas y en los huesos,/tono convaleciente y *deslanguido*/a no estar en ayunas el gemido.

(d)esbaforido ~ (d)esbafarido ~ (d)esbaharido
'breathless, confused, stunned'

The variants in *es-* predominate in the two medieval texts which preserve this derivative from OSp. *bafo ~ baho* 'breath, vapor' (a word of onomatopoetic origin). I have encountered this adjective in the *GE* (Part IV) and in the fourtheenth-century *Cuento del Emperador Otas,* a work of Leonese backround based on an Old French original. Further west, one finds OPtg. *esboforido* 'breathless' (with the *a* of *bafo* labialized by the consonants on either side of it; cf. Ptg. *fome* 'hunger' vs. OPtg. *fame*). The *-r-* wedged between the stem and suffix proper betokens the influence of *vapor,* a medieval Latinism which contemporary men of learning regarded as the etymon of *bafo*; witness *vafor* 'steam' (*Lucidario,* ed. Kinkade, 100:10). This false etymology led the Spanish Academy, centuries later, to advocate the spelling *vaho* for the modern descendant of *bafo*. The verbal coloring of the OSp. adjectives at issue is disclosed by the presence in the *GE* (Part IV) of *esbaharimiento* and of *esbaharamiento*. The same text contains forms reflecting *esbafar-, esbahar-ecer*. The *-ido* adjectives may have been flanked by a variant in *-ado*; note *desbaforadu* 'breathless' reported in the Judeo-Spanish of Bosnia[16].

descolorido 'colorless, pale'

Descolorido turns up infrequently in medieval sources (*Alex,* P 31*a*; [O is lacunary here]; and in the fourteenth-century Aragonese translation of Guido della Colonna, *Historia Destructionis Troiae*). The Alfonsine *Cantigas de Santa Maria* contain *escoorido* (ed. Mettmann, 255.49) which may well represent the adaptation to Galician-Portuguese of central *descolorido* on the model of *color : coor : descolorido :* X. Old Spanish seems to have favored *descolorado* (*Milg* 743*b, Apol* 387*a, GE,* I, 567*b*40) to denote paleness or the absence of color. Preference for the *-ado* adjective may have been supported to no small degree by the OSp. triad *colorado ~ codrado ~ corlado*[17] 'having color; flowery, adorned'. Although OSp. *colorado* could denote 'reddened' as early as the Alfonsine period (*GE,* II, 444*b*20; 343*b*8; *GE,* IV 187*a*), it acquired only toward the end of the medieval period the meaning 'red', a hue which Old Spanish had designated with *bermejo* and *roxo*. This semantic narrowing of the scope of *colorado,* combined with the arrival on the scene from Italy of *colorito,* whence *colorido,* may have breathed new life into *descolorido* at the expense of *descolorado*. Cervantes had recourse to *descolorido* on at least four occasions. Lope de Vega not only employed *descolorido,* but went so far as to coin *descoloridita* (used in rhyme with *enfermita*) and *descoloridillo* (alongside *en-*

---

[16] Kalmi Baruch, "El judeoespañol de Bosnia", *RFE,* 17 (1930), 133.

[17] Whereas *colorado* may derive directly from *color,* the syncopated OSp. variants represent oral transmission with secondary adjustments of COLŌRĀTU.

fermillo). Lope's writings also supply examples of the inf. *descolorir* and of *descolorido* used with *haber* in compound past tenses[18].

desertido 'abandoned, deserted, unpopulated'

My initial analysis of *desertido* (see Chapter One) as an offshoot of *desierto* possibly requires a degree of nuancing. The adjective appears to have enjoyed only a restricted circulation; no examples turn up outside the historical writings of Alfonso X. The noun *desierto* goes back without question to DĒSERTU which began life as the past participle of DĒSERERE 'to separate from, to leave behind, abandon' a verb formed on the model of and as a pendant to CONSERERE 'to join together' ([4]*DELL,* s.v. SERŌ). Promptly DĒSERTU acquired independent status as an adjective denoting 'deserted, abandoned'. In the language of the Church the adjective became substantivized with the meaning 'a deserted or abandoned place' (following the model of Gk. ÉRĒMOS). Medieval Spanish employed *desierto* almost exclusively as a noun. Instances of clear-cut adjectival use are rare. In the Old Spanish rendering of the Vulgate preserved in Escorial MS i-j-6 the feminine singular *desierta* in "muchos fijos son de la *desierta*" (Galatians 4:27; Vulg. "filii desertae") carries the substantival meaning 'the deserted wife'. Berceo's *Sacrificio de la Misa* offers one example of adjectival *desierto:* "tabla maravilosa non de obra desierta" (12*d*)[19]; also "la su tierra *desierta*" (*GE,* IV, 77*r*6).

As the nominal use of *desierto* was clearly gaining the upper hand, some speakers may have attempted to preserve and set off the now vestigial adjectival status of the reflex of DĒSERTU[20]. The passive component of the adjective's syntactico-semantic scope called for a formation in *-do*. Some members of the speech community may have grafted on the base *desert-* a neologism in *-ido* suggested by other semantically-negative models in *des- -ido* and the similar connotation of the suffix. Speakers presumably had no difficulty associating *desertido* with *desierto* on the synchronic plane. The Old Spanish family headed by *desierto* also includes *desert-ar, -amiento* and at least one instance of *desertimiento*[21].

Identical in structure to and synonymous with *desertido* is Balkan Judeo-Spanish *(d)eskampido*[22]. My research has uncovered no traces of this adjective

[18] Carlos Fernández Gómez, *Vocabulario de Cervantes* (Madrid, 1966), s.v. *descolorido,* and *Vocabulario completo de Lope de Vega,* I (Madrid, 1971), s.vv.

[19] In the Vocabulary accompanying his edition of the *Sacrificio,* Claudio García Turza glosses *desierto* 'abandonado, desamparado' (246).

[20] For medieval examples of OSp. *desierto,* see Emanuel S. Georges, *Studies in Romance Nouns Extracted from Past Participles,* revised by Jerry R. Craddock and Yakov Malkiel, UCPL, 63 (Berkeley, Los Angeles, and London, 1970), p. 118.

[21] Did there exist a short-lived OSp. verb *desertir*? Witness "*desertit* vos puertas del cielo fuerte mientre", *GE,* IV, 76*v*101.

[22] This adjective has been reported by Cynthia M. Crews, *Recherches sur le judéo-espagnol dans les pays balkaniques* (Paris, 1935), p. 298; and Joseph Nehama (with the collaboration of Jesús Cantera), *Dictionnaire du judéo-espagnol* (Madrid, 1977), s.vv. *deskampido* and *eskampido,* pp. 166 and 187.

in medieval sources or in modern Peninsular rural dialects. Unless *(d)eskampido* is a local creation of the Balkan communities, it must have had medieval antecedents which happen to remain undocumented. *(D)eskampido* was substantivized with the meaning 'uninhabited place' (cf. the parallel evolution of DĒSERTU; note also *deskampado* 'open space, clearing') which coexists with *eskampino* 'id' alongside *(d)eskampido*. It *scampare,* 'to free', *scampato* 'freed' confirm the chronological priority in Spanish of the *-ado* adjective over its *-ido* counterpart.

desfacido 'furious'

The one recorded instance of this adjective occurs in *Alex,* P, 547*d* in rhyme position; the corresponding verse in O offers *porfazido.* Julia Keller[23] and, later, Louis F. Sas[24], define *desfacido* as 'angered, enraged'; on the other hand, the family of *por-, pro-, pos-façar* denotes 'slander, insult'[25], Nelson reconstructs here *desfazido,* adducing the example of *desfecho* in *SDom,* 547*d.* Does the invocation of *desfecho* imply that Nelson holds *desfazido* to be a regularized past participle of *desfazer* rather than a denominal offshoot of OSp. *faz* 'face'? Medieval adjectival derivatives from *faz* include *desfazado* 'brazen' (*EE,* 711*b*32) and *desfaç(i)ado* 'with the face destroyed' (*CZif,* ed. González Muela, pp. 207 and 254).

One may ask whether the exigencies of rhyme determined the use in *Alex* 547*d* of *desfacido/porfazido* instead of the more frequent *-ado* variants. In such a case, what degree of linguistic authenticity did the poet or scribe attribute to *desfacido* or *porfazido?* Both *-ido* adjectives can possibly be viewed as nonce formations which speakers would have had no difficulty in interpreting as variants of *desfaçado* and *porfaçado.*

desmed(r)ido 'scared, downhearted'

Although there is no need to doubt the long-accepted link between *desmed(r)ido* and *miedo* 'fear', the genesis of this short-lived adjective raises two questions: What is the origin of the *-r-* between the base and the suffix? What is the relationship of this adjective to the OSp. verb *desmed(r)ir* (SMill, 202*b, Alex* O, 2302*d*)? The anaptyctic *r* is not limited to the above-cited forms or, for that matter, to Hispano-Romance; witness *medroso* 'fearful', its derivative *medrosía* 'fearfulness', and the verbs *amedrentar* (alongside rare *amedrecer*) 'scare, intimidate', *esmedrecer* 'to become fearful', and *esmedrear* 'to infuse fear', as well as Ptg. *med(o)roso* and Gal. *medroña* vis-a-vis *medo* 'fear'.

[23] *Contribución al vocabulario del "Poema de Alixandre"* (Madrid, 1932), s.v. *desfacido.*

[24] *Vocabulario del "Libro de Alexandre", BRAE,* Suppl. 34 (1976), s.v. *desfacido.*

[25] On the history of this verb family and its relation to the local progeny of FACIE 'face', see Malkiel "The Ancient Hispanic Verbs *posfaçar, porfaçar, profaçar:* A Study in Etymology and Word-Formation," *RPh,* 3: 1 (1949), 27–72.

Corominas (*DCE,* s.v. *miedo*) sees as the leader word in the diffusion of this *-r-* *med(o)roso* which he claims continues a Hispano-Latin *METORŌSU, allegedly generated on the model of *PAVŌRŌSU ← PAVŌRE 'fear'. This hypothesis rests on a string of hypothetical (though possible) formations. Years earlier García de Diego had posited a *METŌRE created alongside METU on the model of synonymous PAVŌRE, TIMŌRE, TREMŌRE; one might also invoke HORRŌRE, TERRŌRE[26]. Neither Portuguese or Spanish display any traces of **medor* beside *miedo.*

Med(o)roso is perhaps not the sole starting point for the spread of this *-r-* in the family of *miedo.* Speakers may have wished to distinguish with the utmost clarity between *desmedido*$_1$ 'scared, downhearted' and *desmedido*$_2$ 'wild, unbridled', the latter an offshoot of *medir* 'to measure'. The medieval record discloses some confusion between these two items. In *SMill* 202*b* the manuscript tradition records both *desmedir* and *desmedrir*; the context calls for the meaning 'to dishearten'[27]. The same sense is required in *Alex* P, 874*c* and 1081*b,* where the MS reads *desmedido.* In both instances Nelson reconstructs *desmedrido.* A crucial role may have been played by *desmedrar* 'to spoil, ruin' and *desmedrado* 'spoiled, ruined', members of the word family headed by *medrar* 'to improve, better' < MELIORĀRE. Indeed, it is possible that the presence of the pair *desmedrar* ~ *desmedrado* may have led to the minting of *desmedrir* alongside denominal *desmedrido. Desmedrido* seems not to have survived the thirteenth century; speakers apparently preferred synonymous *despavorido* ← *pavor* (see below). Ironically, formal and referential association with the family of *desmedrar* may have finally doomed *desmedrido.* Speakers may have no longer connected this adjective with *miedo* and may have viewed it as a morphologically anomalous (if not gratuitous) offshoot of *desmedrar.* In one passage of the *EE,* the base MS followed by Menéndez Pidal reads *esmedrida* (p. 312*a*29–31); four other MSS offer *desmedrada,* which better fits the context. The canons of diachronic phonology clearly indicate that Ptg. *desmedrar* is borrowed from Hispano-Romance[28].

(d)espavorido 'frightened, scared'

The medieval record consistently offers the form *espavorido* (flanked by occasional instances of apheresized OArag. *spavorido,* and one case of prefixless *pavorido* [*CBaena,* 94v60]). The initial consonant of the modern form reflects the later confusion of the prefixes *des-* < DIS- and *es-* < EX-. The adjective enjoyed considerable currency in the medieval language (especially in the Alfonsine and Heredian corpora); indeed, its vogue may have contributed to the elimination of quasi-synonymous *(d)esmedrido.* At first glance it seems that

[26] *Contribución* . . . § 403, s.v. *METOR: also, *DEEH,* § 4321.

[27] Dutton prints *desmedrir* in his edition of the poem.

[28] According to José Pedro Machado, the Portuguese verb is not documented prior to the sixteenth century, [2]*DELP,* s.v. *medrar,* p. 1530. For bibliographic clues to earlier pronouncements on *medrar,* see Antenor Nascentes, *DELP,* s.v. *medrar.*

espavorido rests on OSp. *pavor* 'fear'. The verb *espavorecer* 'to frighten, get frightened' does not necessarily presuppose an earlier *-ir-* verb, of which *espavorido* would be the lexicalized past participle. Lat. (EX)PAVĒSCERE may have provided a sufficient formal model for the creation of an *-ecer* verb from *pavor*. Unlike the pair *desfambrido* ~ *enfambrecer,* here both the *-ecer* verb and the *-ido* adjective derived from *pavor* share a prefix. The sole medieval example of *espavorir* known to me invites some comment. In the Bible translation preserved in Escorial MS i-j-8, Deuteronomy 20:8 reads: "Quál es medroso e de flaco corazón? Vaya e tórnese a su casa, por que no faga *espavorir* los coraçones de sus hermanos, assi como es *espavorido.*" The infinitive here translates PAVĒRE of the Vulgate; in Deut. 31:6 and 8, this same Latin verb is rendered by *espavorescer.* The presence of *espavorido* in the source from which i-j-8 was copied, may have spurred on the scribe or translator (who, to judge by the text's linguistic traits, may well have been an Easterner) to coin *espavorir* (cf. Cat. *espavor[d]ir.*) Given the lack of vitality displayed in Old Spanish by *espavorir,* it seems safe to state that the medieval speech community perceived a direct link between *espavorido* and *pavor.* Mod. *despavorir,* a distinctly later creation, is absent from Covarrubias' *Tesoro* (1611), but found its way into the dictionaries of Oudin (1607) and Franciosini (1620); the latter comments on this verb's rarity. Sobrino (1705) records *espavorir* and the corresponding *-ido* adjective. The *Diccionario de autoridades* includes *despavorir,* supported by a citation from the *Mýstica ciudad de Dios* of Madre María de Jesús de Agreda (1602–65)[29]

enganíu 'hungry'

This adjective today is found only in the same Asturian subdialect (Cabraniego) that has preserved *asombríu.* The presence of possible congeners in Southern France, Portuguese dialects, Catalan, and far-off Sardinia may bespeak an originally wider diffusion in Hispano-Romance of an adjectival *-ido* offshoot of *gana(s)* 'avid desire', ultimately of Gothic origin[30]. Wartburg (*FEW,* s.v. GAINÔN) reports for various Southern French dialects *agani(t)* ~ *ogoni(t)* 'starved, weakened, thin, exhausted (by hunger or fatigue); poor quality (of harvests, plants, fruits, trees)'. In Portugal *enganido* 'withered, weak, sickly (of grains and vegetables)' turns up in Tras-os-Montes[31]; farther north, the Galician subdialect spoken at Límia employs *enganido* in the sense 'para-

---

[29] Kelvin M. Parker, *Vocabulario clasificado de los folios gallegos de la "Historia troyana"* (Normal, IL., 1975), p. 67 cites two instances of OGal. *espavorado.*

[30] The latest statement on the prehistory of *gana* and its genetic relationship to Sp. *ganar,* Ptg. *ganhar* 'gain, win', appears in Malkiel, "Between Monogenesis and Polygenesis," *Papers from the Third International Conference on Historical Linquistics,* eds. J. Peter Maher et al. (Amsterdam, 1982), pp. 235–72, esp. 243–50.

[31] Augusto C. Moreno, "Vocabulário trasmontano (Mogadouro e Lagoaça)," *RLu,* 5 (1897–99), p. 46.

lyzed' (cf. referentially and formally similar OSp. *tollido,* mod. *tullido)*[32]. Catalan contains *aganit* ~ *aganyit* 'thin, very weak, sickly' beside the corresponding *-ir* verb. Sardinian offers *agganidu, inganidu* 'hungry' flanked (in Logudorese) by *inganare* 'to arouse desire' and *(d)isganare* 'to lack desire'. Although *gana* reflects the Spanish-Catalan layer of the Sardinian lexicon, it is unclear whether the local adjectives also represent borrowings or are native derivatives of *gana.*

There is no need to question the analysis of *enganíu* as an offshoot of *gana(s).* Corominas seeks to segregate from this family the aforecited Portuguese and Catalan forms, arguing that the *-n-* of the former and the *-ny-* [ɲ] of *aganyit* presuppose an ancestral *-nn-*. The Asturian adjective does not enter into his discussion of *gana.* The quest for an appropriate etymon led him to CANNA 'reed', the source of Cat. *escanyolit* 'weak, thin' (orig. 'thin as a reed'); he attributed the *g* to sporadic voicing of *c-* (cf. his derivation of *engreír* from *encreer*)[33].

Yet the formal similarities and referential overlap of Ast. *enganíu* and the Southern French, Portuguese, and Catalan forms strongly suggest common origin or some point of contact. Corominas has no qualms about joining his colleagues in classifying Ptg. *ganas* as an Hispanism. He is even willing, though with great reluctance, to view Cat. *gana* as an early borrowing from the center of the Peninsula. Wartburg views the Gallo-Romance forms as echoes (without any intermediate *-ir* verb) of GAINÔN and Occ. *gana* as a backformation from *aganit.* He claims that this analysis also holds for the relevant Catalan and Galician forms. Conceivably the adjective now apparently restricted to Cabraniego enjoyed greater currency in medieval Hispano-Romance and found its way, alongside *gana,* into Portuguese and Catalan. It seems unlikely that Catalan coined on its own initiative an adjectival derivative in *-it-* from the Hispan ism *gana.* As for the palatal nasal of Cat. *aganyit,* one might see here the influence of synonymous *escanyolit* upon *aganit*[34].

entenebrido 'dimmed'

This short-lived adjective turns up once in the thirteenth-century metrical version of the *Vida de Santa María Egipciaca* and once in the *General Estoria.* In both instances it qualifies *ojos* 'eyes'. The adjective could either be an immediate derivative from OSp. *ten-, tin-iebras* 'fog, mist; blindness' or the lexicalized

---

32 H. Schneider, "Studien zum galizischen des Limiabecken (Orense-Spanien)," *VKR,* 11 (1938), 265*a.* In Evora the phrase *andar enganido* is glossed as 'stiff with cold' in Manuel Gomes Fradinho, "Maneiras de dizer alentejanas," *RLu,* 31 (1933), 99. In contrast Tavares Texeira reports that in parts of Tras-os-Montes *aganar* means 'oppressed by the heat'; see "Vocabulário trasmontano (colhido no concelho de Moncorvo)," *RLu,* 13 (1910), 110.

33 This equation is criticized in my note, "Two Etymological Cruxes . . .," 221.

34 Corominas surveys the multibranched family of Cat. *canya* in his *DECLC,* II, s.v. *canya,* pp. 494*b*-501*a.*

past participle of **entenebrir,* ousted before long by *entenebrecer*. The choice of the prefix *-en-,* used so frequently in parasynthetic denominal and de-adjectival verbs, militates in favor of the latter hypothesis (without automatically ruling out the alternative solution). On the other hand, one must bear in mind the rarity in Old Spanish of denominal verbs in *-ir*.

quellotrido

Marginal to the corpus of denominal *-ido* adjectives is the jocose formation *quellotrido,* a member of the family headed by *(a)quell-, quill-otro,* a compound of *aquell(o)* and *otro*; it is defined in the sixteenth century by Juan de Valdés as "arrimadero para los que no sabían o no se acordavan del vocablo de la cosa que querían decir"[35]. John Lihani explains *quellotro* as a "muletilla sin significado especial pero que adopta cualquier sentido requerido por el texto."[36] *Quillotro* is first attested in the theater of Juan del Encina; the corresponding *-ar* verb first appears in the *Vita Christi* (1482) of Fray Íñigo de Mendoza. The single instance of *quellotrido* of which I am aware is found in the stage *sayagués* (a medium conducive to jocular lexical creations) of the Extremaduran dramatist Lucas Fernández (1474–1542)[37]. It is unnecessary to follow Lihani (who glosses this adjective as 'perfecto' [532]) in reconstructing such a Latin monstrosity as *ECCE ILLU ALTERĪTU. *Quellotrido* is conceivably an ephemeral offshoot of *quellotro* which some speakers may have regarded as an anomalous, and for that matter, superfluous past participle flanking *(a)quellotrar*.

Denominal Adjectives in *-ido:* Formal and Semantic Considerations

Without exception the denominal adjectives in *-ido* carry a decidedly negative connotation, denoting some form of physical deprivation or emotional discomfiture. On the semantic plane, the underlying nominal primitives fall into two groups: (a) a handful of positive or neutral bases (*bafo* 'breath', *color* 'color', *sabor* 'taste', and *faz* 'face', assuming *desfazido* is an offshoot of this noun) and (b) a larger group of nouns with negative connotations (*dolor* 'pain, grief', *desierto* 'deserted or abandoned place', *famne* ~ *fambre* 'hunger', *ganas* 'avid desire', *miedo* 'fear', *modorra* 'drowsiness, stupor', *pavor* 'fear', *sombra* 'shade', *tiniebras* 'darkness'). Only in *desbaforido, descolorido, desabrido* (and

---

[35] *Diálogo de la lengua,* ed. José F. Montesinos (Madrid, 1928), p. 116.

[36] *EL lenguaje de Lucás Fernández,* p. 533.

[37] Abundant documentation of this word family is offered by Miguel Romera-Navarro, "*Quillotro* y sus variantes," *HR,* 2 (1934), 217–25, and Gillet, *Propalladia,* III, pp. 239–55. Lamano y Beneite, p. 592, reports *quillotro* in the speech of Ciudad Rodrigo.

possibly in *desfazido)* does the adjective explicitly indicate that its referent lacks or suffers from a dearth of the (positive) qualities associated with *bafo, color, sabor* (and perhaps *faz*). However, the suffix *-ido* does not by itself convey the negative message (witness the positive semantic value of OSp. *sab[o]rido*); rather, it is the prefix *(d)es-*[38] which principally determines the negative reading of *desbaforido, descolorido,* and *desabrido*. With negatively-valued bases, *(d)es-* serves to intensify the meaning of the underlying noun, whereas *a-* and *en-* seem to convey the notion of entering into the undesirable state or condition at issue. Both *a-* and *en-* function here as interchangeable variants in much the same way as they did in serving speakers to coin OSp. secondary verbs in *a-, en- -ecer*. We recall from the lexical vignettes that *adolorido* acquired its prefix at a relatively late date (perhaps following the model of *adolecer* and/or *adoloriar),* and that Aragonese matched *amodorrido* with *esmodorrido*. For many speakers **desombrido* may have come to mean the opposite of the notion which speakers wished to express with *asombríu*; cf. *desombrado* 'deprived of shade'.

Most of the nominal bases to which *-ido* has been affixed share certain semantic and formal features. All are abstract nouns denoting physical or emotional states and/or qualities. Once again *desfazido,* provided it is an authentic derivative from *faz,* seems to constitute an exception; however, this adjective denotes an abstract quality, 'furious, angry'. On the formal side, most of the underlying primitives are disyllabic and display stem-final *-r* or a consonant cluster with *r* as the final element. In the majority of relevant formations, the *-r* is preceded by tonic *o*. In *desmedrido* and *esbaforido,* the *-r-* preceding the suffix did not originally form part of the base noun. Speakers may have come to associate denominal *-ido* with stem final *-r,* to the extent of supplying an interfix *-(o)r-* where needed. The two exceptions are *desfazido* and *enganíu*. I wonder whether the deviation of *desfazido* on several counts from the general pattern explains its brief lifespan (if it was indeed more than a scribal nonce). Similar considerations may explain the restriction to a single conservative Asturian subdialect of a once more widely spread **enganido*. Whereas *desanguido,* if genuine, appears to be a late nonce formation, a **desangrido* ← *sangre* would have smoothly fitted the predominant formal pattern.

By no means was *-ido* the only suffix available in Old Spanish to derive verbally-colored parasynthetic denominal adjectives with negative semantic content. Several of the *-ido* adjectives under study faced competition from

---

[38] Medieval Hispano-Romance displays early conflation of the prefixes *des-* < DIS- and *es-* < EX-. Jesús Neira Martínez has claimed that in Leonese and Aragonese *des-* originally served to create antonyms (e.g., *deshacer* 'to undo, destroy' ← *hacer; desamor* 'coolness, dislike' ← *amor* 'love'), while *es-* served to coin denominal and deadjectival verbs (e.g., *esclar-ir, -ecer* 'to make clear' ← *claro* 'clear'); see his "El prefijo /des/ en la lengua gallego-portuguesa," *Verba,* 3 (1976–[77]), 309–18. The history of these prefixes is also examined by Mercedes Brea, "Prefijos formadores de antónimos negativos en español medieval," *Verba,* 3, 319–41.

rivals in *-ado: desabor(g)ado* vs. *desabrido, descolorado* vs. *descolorido, asombrado* vs. *asombrido, desbaforado* vs. *desbaforido, desfazado* vs. *desfazido.* Denominal adjectives denoting loss of body parts (or of associated faculties) clearly favored *des- -ado: descabellado, descarnado, descoraznado, desdentado, desflorado, desmembrado* (vs. *membrudo*). Except for problematic *desfazido,* speakers seem to have shown no inclination toward developing denominal *-ido* adjectives from anatomical primitives. All in all, the small corpus of *-ido* adjectives gives the impression of representing a stunted derivational pattern even within the confines of the early medieval language.

At this juncture a brief return to the *-ido* adjectives of Groups II and III is in order. I noted above (Chapter Three) that, with the exception of *(d)esblanguido* and *reverdido,* all the Group II *-ido* adjectives (originally fossilized participles, for the most part, of obsolescent de-adjectival verbs in *-ir*) have a decidedly negative flavor. In all cases the adjective underlying the derived verb can lend itself to a negative or unfavorable interperetation: *angosto, duro, flaco, gordo, muerto, negro, pobre, ralo, seco, viejo.* In this group the base itself furnishes the negative reading of the derived adjective. I observed in Chapter Two that most of the Group III *-ido* adjectives describe undesireable states or conditions: *aterido, desvaído, (d)esmarrido, (d)esmaído, entelerido, esperido, malbaylido, manido, transido.* It seems safe to declare that the negative semantic reading of any of the pertinent *-ido* adjectives derives from the base itself or from the combination of the prefix *des-* and base rather than solely from *-ido.*

A crucial distinction between the denominal adjectives of Group I and the formations placed in Groups II and III must now be drawn. Only in Group I does *-ido* behave like a true derivational suffix, an element purposely welded to a base in an effort to generate a new lexical item which belongs to another form class or which is equipped with a meaning different from that of the underlying primitive. When a derivational suffix is found to be so employed, clearly speakers have already endowed it with a specific meaning or at least associated it with a given, often broad, connotation. In Groups II and III, *-ido* is not genetically or functionally a derivational morpheme. In Group II, *-ido* started out as the inflectional suffix used to create the past participle of de-adjectival verbs in *-ir,* while in Group III, *-ido* originated as (a) the reflex of Latin adjectives or participles in -ĪTU, (b) as the participial suffix of obsolescent primary verbs in *-er* and *-ir* and (c) as the adaptation to Spanish morphophonological conditions of OFr. adjectives in *-i* and OProv. OCat. formations in *-it/-ida.* I wish to suggest at this juncture that *-ido* acquired its negative meaning through use with the semantically negative bases which underlie the negative adjectives in Groups II and III. Thus *-ido* became secondarily tinged with negative force. In short, the *-ido* adjectives of these two groups provided the formal model and the semantic foundation for the use of *-ido* as a genuine derivational suffix in the coining of those denominal adjectives which comprise Group I.

The history of the Old French nominal abstract suffix *-ise* furnishes a noteworthy parallel to the semantic trajectory posited here for Sp. denominal

-ido. Controversy surrounds the origin of *-ise*, especially as regards its genetic filiation with -ITIA, the source of the OFr. abstract suffix *-ece*. The latest thinking holds that *-ise* crystallized through contamination of two semantically related items, namely IŪSTITIA 'justice', whence OFr. *justise*, and IŪDICIU 'judgment', the source of OFr. *juise*. Speakers would have segmented *justise* into a base *just-* and a grammatical morpheme *-ise*. At the outset *-ise* served to coin semantically neutral nominal abstracts from substantival, adjectival, and verbal bases (in competition with *-ece, -erie, -ie*, and *-oise*). On the formal side, *-ise* found itself attracted almost exclusively to bases with a stem-final dental occlusive. Many such nouns in Old French displayed a markedly pejorative semantic overtone, e.g., *bastard* 'bastard', *beste* 'beast, fool', *couard* 'coward', *sot* 'idiot'. As a result *-ise* came to acquire a sharply negative overtone[39].

The verbal component of the semantic makeup of the Spanish adjectives in *-ido* is essential to an understanding of their genesis. The denominal *-ido* adjectives under study convey a passive message and display a perfective aspect. Thus *dolorido* does not merely signify 'sad', but rather 'saddened, grief-stricken'; it is not just an outright equivalent of *triste* 'sad' (with which it is often coupled in medieval texts). *Amodorrido* denotes 'rendered drowsy, stunned' rather than 'drowsy, sleepy'; *desfambrido* means 'deprived of food, starved' rather than 'starving'; *asombríu* brings forth the idea of 'covered with shade, shaded' not 'shady'; *desabrido, descolorido*, and *desbaforido* indicate 'deprived of taste', 'devoid of color', and 'short of breath' respectively, not just 'tasteless', 'colorless', 'breathless'. The presence of the prefixes *a-, des-, en-* heightens the verbal element: The conditions or states denoted by these adjectives result from a prior action. They do not express any inherent, temporally unlimited characteristic of the noun modified and they are often joined to their referent by such (semi-) auxiliaries usually associated with the passive voice in Old Spanish as *andar, estar, fincar, seer*, and *yazer;* witness:

Como oso rravioso que *anda desfanbrido* (*Alex*, P, 529*d*)

Estava la culebra medio *amodorrida* (*LBA*, 1349*b*)

Lo que tu tanto temes e *estás desmedrida* (*SOria*, 106*a*)

Estava trabajada, pensativa e muy *dolorida* (*Corbacho*, p. 252)

Los que bien lo amavan *fincavan doloridos* (*SDom*, 104*c*)

Tu entrar en tal casa, yo *fincar desfamnido* (*SLorenzo*, 67*b*)

El infant con la quexa *se[d]ié descolorido* (*Alex*, 31*a*)

Perdí toda la sangre *yogui amodorrido* (*Duelo*, 17*b*)

---

39 The history of *-ise* has been studied in considerable detail by Margaret S. Breslin, "The Old French Abstract Suffix *-ise:* Studies in its Rise, Internal Diffusion, External Spread, and Retrenchment," *RPh*, 22:4 (1969), 408–20; also Malkiel, "Genetic Analysis of Word Formation," pp. 343–45.

The Genesis of Denominal Adjectives in *-ido*

Attention must now turn to two crucial questions. The OSp. denominal adjectives in *-ido* represent, I repeat, an internal creation of medieval Hispano-Romance rather than the continuation of an inherited Latin prototype. Not one of these adjectives descends directly or indirectly from a Latin denominal in -ĪTU whose reflex might have functioned as a leader word. Why did speakers bother to coin these denominal adjectives? If these formations filled some need perceived by a segment of the speech community, why did only a handful of nouns end up generating *-ido* adjectives?

Medieval Spanish adjectives can be divided into two structural-genetic types: primary adjectives, for the most part disyllabic and tending toward the canonical shape CVC(C)V[40], inherited from Latin (with some later additions from Visigothic, Arabic, and Gallo-Romance) and secondary adjectives extracted from underlying nouns, verbs, and primary adjectives. Although secondary adjectives in the modern language outnumber primary adjectives (in terms of sheer quantity though not necessarily of frequency), the reverse situation seems to hold true in the early medieval language. Medieval writers tended to eschew prolix adjectivization; often they linked adjectives to their referent by means of a copula verb or a preposition[41]. To judge by the learned shape of the suffix or the relatively late first appearance of the formation, many secondary adjectives were purposefully minted on classical models by late medieval and Siglo de Oro Latinate writers. Borrowings from Italian added *-esco* to the inventory of adjectival suffixes. Significantly, both *-ado* and *-udo* figure together with *-ano, -ino,* and *-uno,* among the few vernacular suffixes employed from the outset to coin denominal adjectives.

Over the years, students of Romance derivational morphology have come to realize that speakers may coin a derivational suffix to expand or round out a series of affixes sharing a common consonantal pillar. Such a view of the genesis of certain suffixes may save the analyst a desperate (and often fruitless) search for a formal prototype in some source language. Diez' treatment of derivational morphology discloses as early as 1838 incipient awareness of this derivational mechanism[42]. Paul Foerster laconically stated: "Neue Suffixe sind durch Abänderung des Vokals gewonnen z.B. *-ocho, -ucho* aus *-acho, -icho;*

---

[40] Malkiel has suggested recently that the disyllabicity of primary adjectives was a goal which the medieval Spanish speech community strove to attain; see his essay "Semantically-Marked Root Morphemes in Diachronic Morphology," *Perspectives on Historical Linguistics,* eds. Winfred P. Lehmann and Yakov Malkiel (Amsterdam, 1982), pp. 133–243, esp. 149–61.

[41] Observations on adjectivization in Medieval Spanish can be found in María Rosa Lida de Malkiel, *Juan de Mena, poeta del prerrenacimiento* (Mexico, 1950), pp. 251–83; and Chap. VIII, "El epíteto medieval: Berceo, Ruiz, Mena" of Gonzalo Sobejano, *El epíteto en la lírica española* (Madrid, 1956), pp. 181–215.

[42] *GRS,* II: *Formenlehre,* p. 276.

-uno aus *-ano, -ino; -asco, -esco, -usco* aus *-isco*"[43]. Credit for first throwing adequate light on this process perhaps should go to the Lusist Carolina Michaëlis de Vasconcelos who declared in her Coimbra lectures of 1911–12 and 1912–13 (posthumously published in 1946): "Um modo especial de multiplicar os sufixos heredados consiste na tendência de alterar a sua vogal tónica criando *gamas vocálicas* (original emphasis) perfeitas ou imperfeitas[44]." She exemplified these vocalic gamuts with such Latin series as -ĀCEUS, -ĪCEUS, -ŌCEUS, -ŪCEUS; -AGO, -IGO, -UGO; -ĀMEN, -ĪMEN, -ŪMEN; -ĀNUS, -ĪNUS, -ŪNUS; and with the Portuguese sets *-aço, -iço, -oço, -uço,* and *-agem, -igem, -ugem.* Michaëlis de Vasconcelos followed Diez and Foerster in suggesting a tendential iconic correlation between the choice of tonic vowel in a suffix and a general meaning: /i/ and /e/ carried out a "diminutive" function, whereas /o/ and /u/ bore augmentative-pejorative value respectively; /a/ often served as a phonic embellishment. Her contemporary, Federico Hanssen, operated with a similar phonosymbolic interpretation of the stressed vowels in Spanish suffixes[45]. In the Thirties, Gerhard Rohlfs observed that the dialects of Southwestern France were disposed favorably to creating entire suffix series by varying the tonic vowel which preceded the consonantal pillar. He presented by way of example the sets *-as. -is, -os, -us; -ac, -ec, -oc, -uc; -arru, -orru, -urru;* and *-at, -et, -it, -ot,* matched, he stressed, in Hispano-Romance by *-azo, -izo, -uzo; -aco, -eco, -ico, -ueco, -uco; -arro, -orro-, -urro;* and *-ato, -ete, -ito,* and *-ote*[46]. Bengt Hasselrot was not unaware of this means of suffix creation. In his discussion of the -TT- diminutive suffixes (in his view, of Celtic background), he stated: "En principe on pourrait s'attendre à trouver tous les phonèmes vocaliques représentés devant -TT-, comme cela est arrivé pour d'autres suffixes, et cela soit par *génération spontanée* (emphasis added), si j'ose dire, soit par analogie avec des suffixes de sens voisin, par croisement[47]."

In 1970 Malkiel made the first attempt to use systematically consonantal pillars and vocalic gamuts as a means of classifying synchronically the derivational suffixes of a selected Hispano-Romance dialect[48]. In the nominal and adjectival suffixes, he identified seventeen pillars which entered into vocalic gamuts containing from two to five vowels. Malkiel himself questioned the authenticity or vitality of several of the suffix series he had posited. Adopting the terminology of the Prague School, he labelled as "integrated" those suffixes which participated in vocalic gamuts, and as "unintegrated" those suffixes which stood alone. One major conclusion of Malkiel's descriptively-slanted

[43] *Spanische Sprachlehre,* § 245, p. 195.

[44] *Lições de filologia portuguesa . . . Curso de 1911–12* (Lisboa, 1946), pp. 73f.

[45] *GHLC,* § 270.

[46] "Beiträge zur Kenntnis der Pyrenäenmundarten", *RLiR,* 7 (1931), 119–69, esp. 123f.

[47] *Études sur la formation diminutive dans les langues romanes, UUA,* 11 (1957), p. 130. Nyrop (*Grammaire historique,* III, § 220), had made a similar observation anent the creation of -ĪTTUS, -ĀTTUS, and -ŌTTUS alongside -ĪTTUS.

[48] *Patterns of Derivational Affixation in the Cabraniego Dialect of East-Central Asturian,* UCPL 64 (1970).

monograph has clear diachronic implications: "Since this kind of patterning is a living force, there is a constant latent challenge for speakers to fill 'empty pigeonholes' in the shorter gamuts, to press into service suitable new pillars . . . and to nuance the semantic load of each unit . . ." (58). Malkiel had applied earlier the notion of vocalic gamuts to the diachronic study of selected suffixes. The second installment of his history of denominal adjectives in *-uno* considered this suffix in relation to *-ano* and *-ino* against the background of the Latin triad -ĀNU, -ĪNU, and -ŪNU[49]. On a later occasion he suggested that the existence of three-way gamuts in Spanish such as *-ado, -ido, -udo; -ano, -ino, -uno; -acho, -icho, -ucho; -azo, -izo, -uzo* may have been an analogical model for the reduction of the Latin quadripartite system of infinitives to the tripartite pattern of Spanish[50].

Latin suffixes transmitted orally into Hispano-Romance tend to yield disyllabic stress-bearing morphemes containing a single medial consonant. The consonantal pillar may indeed constitute the phonic core of the suffix. Atonicity and the early loss of -D- may have combined to doom -IDU as a productive derivational morpheme in Hispano-Romance[51], whereas the presence of the tonic accent may have saved *ío* < ĪVU (as in *donadío* 'gift' < DŌNĀTĪVU, *poderío* 'power') and *-ía* despite the absence of a consonantal pillar. Spanish displays a "drift" toward organizing derivational and inflectional suffixes into vocalic triads and tetrads. Suffixal triads involving the vocalic gamut *-a-, -i-, -u-* were particularly successful. Some such gamuts continue similar series in the ancestral language, e.g., *-ano, -ino, -uno* < -ĀNU, -ĪNU, -ŪNU, participial *-ado, -ido* (OSp.) *-udo* < -ĀTU, -ĪTU, -ŪTU, infinitival *-ar, -er, -ir* < -ĀRE, -ĒRE, -ĪRE; others are genetically heterogeneous, composed of the reflexes of substratal, Latin, and imported derivational morphemes as well as suffixes coined by the speech community, e.g., *-án, -én, -ín, -ón; -asco, -esco, -isco, -usco; -arro, -orro, -urro; -ete, -ito, -ote.* Although most Spanish suffixes do enter into such gamuts, some of the most frequently employed suffixes stand alone; e.g., *-ero, -ista, -or, -oso,* and *-ura.* Most adjectival suffixes have remained aloof from vocalic gamuts; witness *-iento, -iondo, -oso; -able* is accompanied only by *-ible.*

Malkiel's analysis of denominal *-ido* adjectives within the framework of the genesis of suffixal vocalic gamuts identifies the morphological hole filled by these formations. Prior to 1350, Old Spanish regularly employed a tripartite pattern of suffix-stressed (the so-called "weak") past participles: *-ado, -ido,*

---

[49] "Nuevas aportaciones para el estudio del sufijo *-uno*", *NRFH,* 13 (1959), 241–60, esp. 256–58.

[50] Infinitive Endings, Conjugation Classes, Nominal Derivational Suffixes, and Vocalic Gamuts in Romance", *ALH,* 17 (1982), 15–48 [submitted in 1976].

[51] The vicissitudes of -IDU in the Iberian Peninsula have been examined in Josep Gulsoy, "L'evolució de la terminació adjectival -IDUS en català i castellà", *Homenatge a Josep M. de Casacuberta,* II (Montserrat, 1981), pp. 25–42; and in my piece "Derivational Transparency and Sound Change: The Two-Pronged Growth of -IDU in Hispano-Romance", *RPh,* 31:4 (1978), 605–17.

-udo matching *-ar, -ir,* and *-er* verbs respectively. While still associated with their parent verb, many of these participles acquired quasi-autonomous existence as independent adjectives. Spanish had also inherited from Latin models in -ĀTU and -ŪTU the ability to coin denominal adjectives in *-ado* and *-udo* which diachronically and functionally were independent of underlying *-ar* and *-er* verbs; in contrast, the few Latin denominal adjectives in -ĪTU had left no traces in Hispano-Romance. Sensitized by the past-participles to a triadic system of adjectival elements in *-ado, -ido,* and *-udo,* some segments of the speech community set out on their own and attached the terminal segment *-ido* to selected nominal stems for the purpose of rounding out a vocalic gamut of denominal adjectives in *-ado, -ido,* and *-udo.* I repeat here my suggestion that the presence in the early medieval language of the *-ido* adjectives of Groups II and III, which many speakers must have already perceived as elements unassociated with any *-ir* verb, acted on the formal level as a model in the further formation of denominal *-ido* adjectives which displayed no link to an identifiable source verb. I shall return below to the semantic impact of the *-ido* formations in Groups II and III upon the genesis of these adjectives.

The need to round out a vocalic gamut was not felt with equal intensity in all languages which offer the same basic structural conditions. Like Old Spanish, Medieval Portuguese (though not the modern language), Old Provençal, and, to this day, Catalan and Italian show a tripartite "weak" past participle pattern: OPtg. *-ado, -ido, -udo,* OProv. and Cat. *-at, -it, -ut,* It. *-ato, -ito, -uto.* These languages also contain well-developed series of denominal adjectives in *-ado, -udo; -at, -ut; -ato, -uto.* Yet only in Hispano-Romance did speakers make a significant effort to round out with a third member this denominal set. Old Spanish also possessed a series of nouns in *-ado* indicative of social and political institutions (e.g., *condado* 'county' ← *conde* 'count', *reinado* 'reign' ← *reino* 'kingdom') and another string in *-ido* designating sounds and noises (e.g., *balido* 'bleating', *ladrido* 'barking'). On the other hand, Spanish shows no secondary nouns in *-udo.* Speakers apparently felt no need to complete the vocalic gamut in derived nominals. Isolated items such as It. *crinito, saporito* on one side and OPtg. *doorido, escoorido* on the other (which, I suspect, represent adaptations to local conditions of their Castilian counterparts) do not bespeak Italian or Portuguese denominal series in *-ito* and *-ido,* respectively. It is worth noting that Portuguese, Catalan, and Italian lack for the most part independent non-verbal formations comparable to the Spanish *-ido* adjectives of Groups II and III. Italian adjectives of the type *imbellito* 'improved in looks, beautified' are clearly linked by the speech community to the corresponding *-ire* verb *(imbellire).* Such Catalan adjectives as *amortit, desnerit, empobrit, endurit, enflaquit, engordit, enrarit, revellit, reverdit,* cognates of the OSp. adjectives of Group II, were each accompanied by a corresponding *-ir* verb (in which the *-eix-* interfix had penetrated only into the rhizotonic forms of the present indicative and subjunctive).

Did the new use of *-ido* to coin denominal adjectives serve any function beyond the morphological role of filling out a neatly balanced *(-a-, -i-, -u-)* suffixal vocalic gamut? To the best of my knowledge Malkiel is once again the only scholar who has proposed a tentative answer to this question, suggesting in 1966 that *-ido* so used also filled a semantic gap. Malkiel labelled this suffix "Spanish *-ido* indicative of inadequacy." He classed *-ado* as a semantically neutral marker which denoted resemblance (appearance, shape, color, size) or some other kind of objective relation between the derived adjective and the underlying noun. On the other hand, *-udo* denoted an excess, abundance, plethora, with special reference to overdeveloped parts of the body (or related physical and psychic qualities)[52]. Malkiel concluded by describing denominal *-ido* as "an effective marker of sparseness and inadequacy ... filling, at the same time, a formal gap in the suffixal inventory of Spanish and a semantic lacuna" (333).

One must now ask whether these adjectives as a group do in fact connote 'sparseness, inadequacy, lack'. Do speakers interpret negative adjectives in terms of the lack of the corresponding positive quality? Of the adjectives at issue, only *(d)esbaforido, descolorido,* and *desabrido* signal specifically the absence of the traits primarily or secondarily associated with the substantival base. However in these three items the idea of 'absence, lack' is conveyed by the prefix *des-* rather than by the suffix *-ido.* In the remaining *-ido* adjectives, the base already carries a negative message. In such items as (a) *adolorido, amodorrido, asombríu, desfamnido, (d)esmedrido, (d)espavorido, enganíu, entenebrido;* (b) *amortido, denegrido, empobrido, endurido, enflaquido, engordido, enloquido, enralido, ensangostido, revejido,* the derived adjective does not indicate the absence or attenuated presence of the underlying base or of any qualities associated with it.

The sequences of sounds which come together to form a derivational morpheme have no inherent meaning; it is speakers who endow them with a given content. The positive or negative reading of a denominal *-ado* adjective depends on the meaning(s) and connotation(s) of the base. The choice of a suffix genetically identical with the participial suffix adds a passive slant and perfective aspect to the resulting adjective. There seem to exist no formal or semantic constraints on the nature of the nominal base to which *-ado* is affixed. On the other hand, *-udo* does indeed bring a specific shading to the denominal adjec-

[52] In the last decade at least three scholars have had occasion to concern themselves actively with the fate of -ŪTU in Romance: Malkiel, "Ancien français *fau, fëu, malostru.* A la recherce de -ŪCUS, suffixe latin et paléo-roman de la 'mauvaise fortune'", *TLL,* 11:1 (1973), 177–90 = *Mélanges Paul Imbs;* "Primary, Secondary, and Tertiary Etymologies: The Three Lexical Kernels of Hispanic *saña, ensañar, sañudo", HR,* 42 (1974), 1–31, esp. 15–27; Thomas J. Walsh, "Two Problems in Gallo-Romance Etymology, II: Affixation as a Clue to Etymology: The Case of Old Prov. *faduc,* Old Fr. *(mal-, dur-) fëu", RPh,* 35:1 (1981), 99–104; and Otto Gsell, "*FĀTŪCUS, *ASTRŪCUS und die Herkunft von lateinisch-romanisch -ŪCUS," *RPh,* 36:3 (1983), 391–93. The papers by Malkiel and Walsh beautifully illustrate the importance for sophisticated etymological research of examining derivational patterns.

tives in whose coinage it participates. It was attached at first only to nouns which designated a specific part of the anatomy or which were associated in some obvious way with the human body and mind. The resulting adjective denoted 'oversize, excessiveness, abundance (to the point of grotesqueness)' and often had to be interpreted in a negative fashion. In such adjectives as *barbudo* 'heavily bearded' (cf. *barbado* 'bearded'), *corpudo* 'fleshy, corpulent', *orejudo* 'long-eared' (cf. Lat. AURĪTUS), the suffix *-udo* is the formal element which conveys the meaning of excess in the new adjective vis-à-vis underlying *barba, cuerpo, oreja.* No need for any prefix was felt in the genesis of denominal *-udo* adjectives.

The lexical analyses presented throughout this monograph have led me to conclude that speakers had not endowed the terminal segment *-ido* with the meanings 'lack, dearth, inadequacy'. Through the use of the suffix with the genetically heterogeneous negatively-flavored adjectives that comprise the bulk of Groups II and III, the speech community came to associate pseudo-participial *-ido* with formations bearing negative overtones. I repeat once more that the majority of denominal *-ido* adjectives rest on evaluatively-negative bases. Only in these adjectives did *-ido* function as a true derivational suffix. In so doing, it served two functions: on the formal plane, it completed a three-way suffixal vocalic gamut; on the semantic level, it served to hypercharacterize the negative content of the newly-minted adjective and to stress its passive and perfective slant.

Hypercharacterization is a means of causing a distinctive linguistic feature or category to stand out more sharply. It often takes the form of a double or multiple morphological marking of the trait in question (e.g. gender, number, mood, tense, voice)[53]. If my analysis is correct, the *-ido* suffix in such items as *desabrido* and *descolorido* repeats the negative reading furnished to the adjective by the prefix *des-;* in such derivatives as *desmedrido, despavorido, -ido* reinforces the negative message already jointly transmitted by prefix and base; in *adolorido, amodorrido, asombríu,* and *entenebrido,* the suffix reiterates the negative semantic content of the base. A derivational suffix usually adds semantic and grammatical information not contained in the base to which it is attached. Spanish tends not to use derivational suffixes regularly as a redundant morphological marker of information found elsewhere in the derived lexical item.

Failure of a Derivational Pattern

The relatively small corpus of denominal *-ido* adjectives indicates that this suffix failed to strike root as a productive derivational morpheme. Several of

[53] For a detailed examination of this phenomenon (with special regard to the marking of gender) see Malkiel, "Diachronic Hypercharacterization in Romance", *ArL,* 9 (1957), 79–113, and 10 (1958), 1–36.

these adjectives were short-lived; post thirteenth-century examples are lacking for *(d)esbaforido, desertido, (d)esmedrido, desfazido,* and *entenebrido.* I suspect that speakers may have coined denominal adjectives in *-ido* primarily to complete the triadic denominal series *-ado, -ido, -udo.* Although denominal *-ido* may have plugged a hole in the derivational system, it filled no crying semantic need. The speech community could just as easily coin an evaluatively negative denominal adjective with *-ado* (and an appropriate prefix if necessary). Speakers felt no compelling urge to hypercharacterize by means of a specialized affix a given adjective's negative semantic flavor; if they had felt such an urge, one might expect to find traces of such experiments as **desdentido,* **desmembrido,* **desvergonçido* rather than only the recorded *-ado* counterparts. Most of the denominal *-ido* adjectives eventually faced competition from *-ado* rivals (unsuccessful for the most part) cf. *adolorado, amodorrado* (both recorded, if not created, distinctly later than their *-ido* counterpart), *a-, de-sombrado, desabor(g)ado, descolorado* (more in vogue than *descolorido* until the shrinkage of *colorado*'s semantic range), *desfazado,* and *entenebrado.* The present-day analyst has no way of knowing if the speech community experimented with other denominal *-ido* adjectives which found no place in the extant medieval corpus. Such experimentation would constitute a sign of the suffix's vitality. Note that *asombríu* and *enganíu* are known only from a modern conservative Asturian subdialect; the use of *deskampido* (see above, s. v. *desertido*) in Balkan Judeo-Spanish may, but need not, bespeak its presence in the medieval language. Although perhaps esthetically pleasing on the formal level, these new *-ido* formations contributed in no way to the economy or tightening of the language's derivational resources. The suffix appears not to have had a strong emotional impact on speakers. For a goodly portion of the speech community, this new role of *-ido* may have constituted excess derivational baggage.

The important role of *-ido* as a past participle suffix, increased after its ouster of *-udo* in the mid-fourteenth century, may have stunted the potential for its growth as a derivational suffix. Malkiel has recently suggested that the growing use of /i/ as a key vowel in verbal desinences associated with the *-er* and *-ir* classes may have played the main role in the expansion of participial *-ido* at the expense of *-udo*[54]. The close association of *-ido* with the domain of verbal inflection may have doomed its use as an adjectival suffix. In contrast, denominal *-udo* expanded and flourished after the retreat of *-udo* as a participial marker. The uninterrupted vitality of inflectional and derivational *-ado* reflects the continued strength of the *-ar* conjugation class.

---

[54] "In Search of Coefficients in Diachronic Morphological Analysis: /i/ as an Increasingly Dominant Vowel in Spanish Inflectional Morphemes", *Proceedings of the Eighth Annual Meeting of the Berkeley Linguistics Society* (1982), pp. 36–78; on *-ido,* see esp. pp. 48–53. In his paper "Infinitive Endings, Conjugation Classes . . .", 42–45, Malkiel suggested as another factor in the elimination of participial *-udo* the marked difference between the tonic vowels in the set *-er:-udo* vis-à-vis the vocalic compatibility in *-ar: -ado* and *-ir:-ido.*

The trajectories followed in Hispano-Romance by the individual members of the Latin denominal triads -ĀNU, -ĪNU, -ŪNU, and -ĀTU, ĪTU, ŪTU display some striking parallels. Spanish denominal adjectives in *-ado* and *-ano* are semantically neutral. In contrast, *-uno* and *-udo,* while enjoying a high degree of productivity, acquired specialized meanings. Starting from such Latin adjectives as APRŪ(G)NU 'pertaining to the boar', and CAPRŪNU 'related to the goat', *-uno* was attached to zoonyms to form relational adjectives, e.g., *abejuno* ← *abeja* 'bee', *asnuno* ← *asno* 'ass', *cabruno* ← *cabra* 'goat', *perruno* ← *perro* 'dog'. We have seen above that adjectives such as CORNŪTU 'horned', NĀSŪTU 'with a big nose' provided the foundation from which Sp. *-udo* became associated with anatomical primitives and formed adjectives denoting 'large size, excessive (to the point of grotesqueness)'. On the other hand, the local reflexes of -ĪNU and -ĪTU did not fare nearly so well. The former was ousted by *-uno* as a marker of relational adjectives pertaining to animals. The diminutive function which *-ino* acquired in Romance may have scotched its vitality as an adjectival formant (except for its occasional use in such items as *granadino* 'from Granada', *tunecino* 'from Tunis' [vs. *tunecí*], *alfonsino* 'Alfonsine' [vs. *alfonsí*]). Starting in the fifteenth century, denominal *-ino* enjoyed a brief comeback in Latinate formations, e.g., *canino* 'dog-like', *caprino* 'goat-like', *cavallino* 'horse-like', *leprino* 'hare-like'.

One wonders whether it is mere coincidence that in these two sets the suffix with tonic /i/ failed to strike root as a productive formative of denominal adjectives. As already mentioned, such Romanists as Diez, Foerster, Hanssen, and Michaëlis de Vasconcelos joined together the high front vowel and the idea of diminutiveness. Most Spanish diminutive suffixes bear a stressed *i;* witness *-ico, -illo* (< older *-iello*), *-ino,* and *-ito*. The stressed vowel might have had something to do with the acquisition by *-ino* of its new status as a marker of the diminutive. The gradual connection of disyllabic suffixes containing stressed /i/ with the several notions subsumed under the label "diminutive" might have been yet another factor in the stunted growth of Spanish denominal adjectives in *-ido*.

A summary of this chapter's findings is now in order. The denominal adjectives in *-ido* are entirely a local creation of Hispano-Romance; in no way do they continue the handful of Latin denominal adjectives in -ĪTU. Several independent forces converged to give rise to the Spanish adjectives. Conditioned by the three-way system of past participles in *-ado, -udo,* and *-ido* (corresponding to verbs in *-ar, -er,* and *-ir* respectively), speakers of Old Spanish attempted to round out the series of denominal adjectives in *-ado* and *-udo* which represented a pattern inherited from Latin and expanded in Hispano-Romance. This desire to fill a formal hole in a derivational series reflected a drift observable in Spanish toward the creation of sets of suffixal vocalic gamuts each dominated by a consonantal pillar. The presence in the language of the *-ido* adjectives which I have placed in Groups II and III had attuned the linguistic consciousness of the speech community to the existence of adjectives in *-ido* which could not be identified synchronically with corresponding *-ir* verbs. In like fashion many of the denominal *-ado* and all the denominal *-udo* adjectives were not accompanied by an *-ar* or *-er* verb.

At no time in the history of Spanish did the denominal adjectives in *-ido* come close to attaining the popularity of their *-ado* and *-udo* counterparts. The adjectives in *-ido* give the impression of an aborted or stunted derivational series. The overwhelming majority of the other pseudo-participial *-ido* formations carry negative semantic readings, as do all the denominal adjectives in *-ido,* most of which spring from semantically negative bases. Consequently, speakers came to see *-ido* as a means of hypercharacterizing an adjective's negative semantic message, which had already been conveyed through the choice of prefix or through the base noun itself. Although *-ido* neatly completed a three-way vocalic gamut, it filled no semantic need. Denominal *-ido* was in fact a derivational morpheme. Its range of applicability seems to have been limited to nouns denoting undersirable physical conditions or emotional states. Such functional restrictions did not favor its rapid growth. In addition, the strengthening of *-ido*'s role as a past participle marker and the tendential iconic association of disyllabic suffixes, involving stressed /i/ with the category of diminution may have stifled any further productivity of *-ido* as a denominal adjectival formative.

APPENDIX

(a)dolorido

Ixó del monesterio el señor amidos;
despidióse de todos los sus fraires queridos;
los que bien lo amavan fincavan *doloridos;*
los que lo bastecieron ya eran repentidos.
(Berceo, *SDom,* 104)

Vio cosa mal puesta, ciudat tan denegrida,
pueblo tan desmayado la gent tan *dolorida;*
demandó esta cuita porqu'era hi venida,
Por qué toda la gente andava amortida;
(*Apol,* 43)

Espídete agora con lo que as oído,
aqueste lugar pobre non eches en olvido,
fallarás el tu pueblo triste e *dolorido,*
faziendo lloro e llanto, metiendo apellido.
(*FGonz,* 241)

E vio a ellos todos rotos e *doloridos* . . .
(*GE,* I, fol. 106v15)

En sus pechos feriendo, a Dios manos alçando,
sospiros *doloridos* e triste sospirando,

signos de penitencia de los ojos llorando;
do más fazer non pueda, la cabeça enclinando
(*LBA,* G, 1139, S *dolorosos*)

amodorrido

Tan afincadamientre fizo su oración,
que le udió la madre plena de bendición;
com qui *amodorrida* vio grant visión
tal que devié en omne fer edificación.
(Berceo, *Milg,* 528)

Con esta sobrevienta que nos era venida,
perdí toda la sangre, yogui *amodorrida:*
quería seer muerta más que sofrir tal vida,
si muerta me oviessen, oviéranme guarida
(Berceo, *Duelo,* 17)

Todos *amodorridos* fueron a la pelea;
pusieron las sus azes, ninguno non pletea
la compaña del mar las sus armas menea;
veniéronse ferir, deziendo todos: "Ea".
(*LBA,* 1101)

Con la nief' e con el viento e con la elada frida,
estava la culuebra de frío *amodorrida;*
el omne piadoso que la vido aterida
dolióse mucho d'ella e quísole dar la vida.
(*LBA,* 1349)

(de)sab(o)rido

Teniendo que su dicho non li serié creído,
delante muchos omnes tollióse el vestido,
demostrólis un fierro qe traié escondido,
cinto a la carona correón *desabrido*
(Berceo, *Milg,* 407)

Fizo poner el cuerpo en el suelo barrido,
en una riqua colcha d'almatraque batido.
Puso.l sobre la cara la manga del vestido,
ca es pora la cara el fuego *dessabrido*
(*Apol,* 307)

. . . asy commo el que fuerça su talente e tomar la melezina *desaborida* con esperança que fará pro.
(*CeD,* MS A, p. 127, ll. 1895–96)

E quanto ha andado en este mundo torna viejo e a escosa e *desabrida* vida
(*CeD,* p. 36, l. 646)

Veno a su monesterio el bon abad benito,
fo de sus compañeros mucho bien recebido,
dixo él: "Benedicite" en voz muy bien *sabrido,*
dixieron ellos: "Dominus" en son bono complido.
(Berceo, *SDom,* 277)

descolorido

El infante con la quexa seyé *descolorido,*
triste e destenprado de todo sabor exido;
commo si lo ouies alguno por ventura ferido,
o si algunas malas ouiese entendido
(*Alex,* P 31)

Se tornó *descolorido* por la rauia del furor.
(*CTroyana,* p. 43.13)

desertido

. . . et maguer que las cibdades et las pueblas dichas auién yazido yermas e *desertidas* . . .
(*EE,* 652*a*41)

. . . e muestra la tu faz sobrel to santuario que es tornado *dessertido.*
(*GE,* IV, 67r71–72)

Estas cosas dize el sennor dios: *desertida* será toda la tierra, mas pero non la acabará.
(*GE,* IV, 78r51–52)

Ca será la tierra assolada e tornada *desertida.*
(*GE,* IV, 80r10–11)

desfamn-, desfambr-ido

Seráte santo padre, por grand yerro tenido,
tú entrar en tal cena, yo fincar *desfamnido.*
(*SLor,* 67*ab*)

Quando syntió Diómedes que lo avién ferido,
commo non sopo quién era, touos' por escarnido;
ovo tan fiera ira e fue tan encendido,
commo osso ravioso que anda *desfanbrido.*
(*Alex,* P, 529; O-*defamido*)

Andauan estos anbos entre los enemigos
commo unos leones que andan *desfanbridos*
(*Alex,* P, 1012*ab;* O-*defamidos*)

. . . o muriessen a guisa de buenos por armas e no de *hambridos*
(*EE,* p. 30*a*44–45)

Andava ý un milano volando *desfambrido*
(*LBA,* 413*a*)

(d)esmedrido

Si.l pessó o si.l plogo, triste e *desmedrido,*
ovo del pleito todo a venir connocido,
elli con sus conpannas fo luego convertido,
murió enna fe buena, de la mala tollido.
(Berceo, *Milg* 696)

Lo que tú tanto temes e estás *desmedrida,*
que los Cielos son altos, enfiesta la subida,
Yo te los faré llanos, la mi fija querida,
que non abrás embargo en toda tu venida.
(Berceo, *SOria,* 106)

Quando fue lo del campo todo bien várrido,
tornaron a las duennas pueblo *desmedrido;*
fueron luego robadas de todo su vestido
et de quantos adobos con sigo avién traído
(*Alex,* O 1081; P-*desmedido*)

Queriénlo muchas veces los malos escarnir,
facién malas figuras por a el *desmedrir;*
(Berceo, *SMill,* 202*ab;* var. *desmedir*)

Con todas estas nuevas e todo el ruydo
iva el Rey Dario fiera ment esmarrido,
que la muerte de Menona le avié *desmedido,*
que avié por verdat estraño braço perdido.
(*Alex,* P 874)

... bibda e dessolada de sus fijos, coffonduda de los bárbaros, *esmedrida* por la llaga, fallida de fortaleza ...
(*EE,* p. 312*a*28–30; MSS var *desmedrada*)

(d)espavorido

... espertó luego muy *espavorido* e fue triste mucho por ello.
(*GE,* IV, 21*r*20)

Jheremias ... falló la yerma toda e fue ende muy *espavorido* e fuesse dend.
(*GE,* IV, 45v89–91)

Aquí podemos ver si perfeto e conplido
fue este inocente, después qu'el su gemido
[..........] fincó así *espavorido*
en el temor de Dios, e por Él escogido
(López de Ayala, *Libro rimado,* 2004)

que vos me digades que nombre avedes,
o qu'es la razón por qué así tenedes
vos, linda, fermosa, la fas *pavorida*
(Ruy Paéz de Ribera, *CBaena,*
no. 288, vv. 22–24)

Díxele que non dormía
mas qu'estava *espavorido*.
(Ruy Paéz de Ribera, *CBaena,*
no. 295, vv. 11–12)

entenebrido

Las sus orejas que eran albas,
mucho eran negras e pegadas,
entenebridos avié los ojos
perdidos avié los mencojos.
(*SME,* vv. 726–729)

Ay de nós, ca pecamos. Por ende es fecho triste el nuestro coraçón. Por ende son *entenebridos* los nuestros ojos.
(*GE,* IV, 103*r*98)

esbaf-, esbah-arido

E ellos quando oyeron aquellas palabras, pararon se *esbaharidos* cada uno catando cada uno contr' al qui seyé cerca él.
(*GE,* IV, 93*r*3–5)

Quando el esto oyó, fue todo *esbafarido,* ca él non osava fablar por miedo de su señor, Terrín.
(*Otas,* p. 123.16–17)

E qué fazedes aquí, gente *esbafarida?*
(*Otas,* p. 26.6)

Pues, id me vos allá – dixo Garsir – e sed bien razonado, e contadle todo este pleito, que non seades *esbafarido*
(*Otas,* p. 72.20–21)

Conclusion

In this monograph I have sought to account for the genesis of a compact series of adjectives coined in Old Spanish through the affixation of the suffix *-ido* to noun bases. The creation of these adjectives has been depicted against the background of those preexisting Old Spanish adjectives in *-ido* which were, for many speakers, free from any synchronic association with a verb in *-er* or *-ir* (I label such formations "pseudo-participial adjectives in *-ido*"). Genetically these pseudo-participial adjectives continue such diverse sources as (1) Latin adjectives and participles in -ĪTU; (2) past participles of Old Spanish primary verbs in *-er* and *-ir;* (3) past participles of Old Spanish de-adjectival verbs in *-ir;* (4) borrowed Old French adjectives in *-i,* Old Provençal and Old Catalan adjectives in *-it* (fem. *-ida*), and Italian adjectives in *-ito.* By studying the history of each relevant lexical item I have been able to identify the diverse sources from which these adjectives sprung and how they came to function as pseudo-participial adjectives in *-ido.* In like fashion a scrutiny of the history of each and every denominal adjective in *-ido* has been a necessary prelude to the analysis of these adjectives as part of a derivational pattern.

For the most part previous diachronically-slanted suffix studies have concentrated on the rise of a given formation, its spread through the lexicon, and its evolution. The factors which led to the erosion of a given suffix's role as a productive derivational element have hardly received systematic attention[55]. In this study I have attempted to identify the reasons why *-ido* attained no degree of currency as a device for creating denominal adjectives. Unlike *-udo, -ido* so used did not carry a clear semantic message; rather it served to hypercharacterize the negative semantic reading of the new adjective into whose formation it had entered. True, denominal *-ado* did not bear a specific meaning either, but its association with the ever-productive class of verbs in *-ar,* and the survival of numerous reflexes of Latin denominal adjectives in -ĀTU, assured the vitality in Spanish of the denominal adjectives in *-ado.* Although some speakers may have found the completion of the series of denominal adjectives in *-ado, -udo,* and *-ido* aesthetically satisfying, the lack of a sharply defined function for *-ido* probably worked against its continued productivity as a suffix employed to create new denominal adjectives. Any such potential role for *-ido* may have been further doomed by the vigorous expansion of inflectional *-ido* as the past participial suffix for verbs in *-er* and *-ir.*

The history of a suffix is inextricably linked to the history of the lexical items in whose formation it has played a role. The student of derivational morphology cannot afford to ignore the findings of etymological research. Thanks to the efforts of Hugo Schuchardt, Jakob Jud, Walther von Wartburg, Yakov Malkiel, and Kurt Baldinger, etymology in the twentieth century has come to be understood as the study of the complete history of an individual lexical item or of an entire word family, i.e., of the circumstances attendant upon its birth, growth, spread, and, if relevant, demise. In like fashion I have attempted to explain how *-ido* came in Spanish to be tried in the coining of denominal adjectives and why it failed to become productive in this role. Etymology has traditionally been limited in its purview to the history of the root morphemes, but I contend etymologists must expand the scope of their discipline to include the history of the derivational morphemes as well. Students of derivational morphology must learn to consult the history of each lexical item which bears the element under study. The analytic techniques of sophisticated etymological research are applicable to the study of intricate problems of diachronic derivational morphology; indeed, I contend that etymology and diachronic derivational morphology appear to be but two sides of the same coin.

[55] Many valuable insights on suffix loss can be found throughout Anita Katz Levy's unpublished University of Pennsylvania dissertation (1969), "Factors in the Distribution of Suffixes in the Romance Languages".

Bibliography
Books, Monographs, and Articles

Abraham, Richard. "The Vocabulary of the Old Judeo-Spanish Translation of the Canticles and their Chaldean Paraphrase." *HR,* 41 (1973), 1–5.

Adams, Edward L. *Word Formation in Provençal.* New York and London: Macmillan, 1913, University of Michigan Studies, Humanistic Series, Vol. 2.

Alcalá Venceslada, Antonio. *Vocabulario andaluz.* 2nd ed. Madrid: Real Academia Española, 1951. Rpt. Madrid: Gredos, 1980.

Alcover, Antoni M. and Francesc de B. Moll. *Diccionari català-valencià-balear.* 10 vols. Palma de Mallorca, 1926–1962.

Alemany y Bolufer, José. *Tratado de la formación de palabras en la lengua castellana.* Madrid: Suárez, 1920. Orig. in *BRAE,* 4 (1917), and 5 (1918).

Allen, Andrew S. "The Development of the Inchoative Suffix in Latin and Romance." Dissertation, University of California, Berkeley, 1980.

–. "The Development of Prefixal and Parasynthetic Verbs in Latin and Romance." *RPh,* 35:1 (1981), 79–88.

–. "The Interfix *i/esc* in Catalan and Rumanian." *RPh,* 31:2 (1977), 203–211.

Allen, Jr., Joseph, H. D. *Portuguese Word-Formation with Suffixes.* Language Dissertation, No. 33. Baltimore: LSA, 1941.

Bartha, Jeannie K. "Four Lexical Notes on Berceo's *Milagros de Nuestra Señora." RPh,* 37:1 (1983), 56–62.

Baruch, Kalmi. "El judeoespañol de Bosnia." *RFE,* 17 (1930), 113–154.

Battisti, Carlo, and Giovanni Alessio. *Dizionario etimologico italiano.* 5 vols. Florence: Barbera, 1950–57.

Bénichou, Paul. *Romances judeo-españoles de Marruecos.* Madrid: Castalia, 1968. Orig. in *RFH,* 6 (1944).

Benoliel, José. "Dialecto judeo-hispano-marroquí o hakitía." *BRAE,* 15 (1928), 47–61. Other installments in *BRAE,* 13–15.

Blaylock, Curtis. "The Romance Development of the Latin Verbal Augment -SK-." *RPh,* 28:4 (1975), 434–444.

Bloch, Oscar, and Walther von Wartburg. *Dictionnaire étymologique de la langue française.* 5th ed. Paris: PUF, 1968.

Boggs, Ralph Steele et al. *Tentative Dictionary of Medieval Spanish.* Chapel Hill: University of North Carolina Press, 1946.

Braune, T. "Neue Beiträge zur Kenntnis einiger romanischer Wörter deutscher Herkunft." *ZRP,* 21, (1897), 213–224.

Brea, Mercedes. "Prefijos formadores de antónimos negativos en español medieval." *Verba,* 3 (1976), 319–341.

Breslin, Margaret S. "The Old French Abstract Suffix *-ise:* Studies in its Rise, Internal Diffusion, External Spread, and Retrenchment." *RPh,* 22:4 (1969), 408–420.

Brüch, Josef. *Der Einfluß der germanischen Sprachen auf das Vulgärlatein.* Heidelberg: Winter, 1913.

–. "Gab es im Altprovenzalischen ein *z* aus lateinischen Intervok. *t?.*" in *Philologische Studien aus dem romanisch-germanischen Kulturkreise: Karl Voretzsch zum 60. Geburtstage.* Halle: Niemeyer, 1927, pp. 214–238.

Brunel, Clovis. "Le Traitement du groupe NU̯: A propos de Provençal *marvier,* français *manivelle* et *amanevi.*" *Ro.,* 61 (1935), 210–219.

Canellada, María Josefa. *El bable de Cabranes.* Supplement 31 to *RFE.* Madrid, 1944.

Cappucini, G. "L'eteroclisia in *-are* e *-ire.*" In *Scritti vari di filologia [in onore di Ernesto Monaci].* Rome: Forzani 1901, pp. 311–323.

Castro, Adolfo de. *Poetas líricos de los siglos XVI y XVII.* BAE, 42. Madrid. Rivadeneyra, 1875.

Colby, Alice. *The Portrait in Twelfth-Century French Literature (An Example of the Stylistic Originality of Chrétien de Troyes).* Geneva: Droz, 1965.

Cornu, Jules. "Die portugiesische Sprache." in Gustav Gröber, *Grundriß der romanischen Philologie.* 2nd et. Strassbourg: Trübner, 1904–06, pp. 916–1037.

Corominas [Coromines], Juan [Joan]. *Breve diccionario etimológico de la lengua castellana.* 3rd ed. Madrid: Gredos, 1976.

–. *Diccionario crítico etimológico de la lengua castellana.* 4 vols. Berne: Francke, and Madrid: Gredos, 1954–57.

–. *Lleures i converses d'un filòleg.* Barcelona: Club, 1971.

–. "Problemas del diccionario etimológico, I." *RPh* 1:1 (1947), 23–28.

– and José A. Pascual. *Diccionario crítico etimológico castellano e hispánico.* Vols. 1–4. Madrid: Gredos, 1980–81.

–, Joseph Gulsoy and Max Cahner. *Diccionari etimològic i complimentari de la llengua catalana.* Vols 1–3. Barcelona: Curial, 1980–.

Cortelazzo, Manlio and Paolo Zolli. *Dizionario etimologico della lingua italiana.* Bologna: Zanichelli, 1979–.

Covarrubias Orozco, Sebastian. *Tesoro de la lengua castellana o española.* Madrid, 1611. Ed. by Martín de Riquer. Barcelona: Horta, 1943.

Craddock, Jerry R. and Emanuel S. Georges. "The Hispanic Sound Suffix *-ido.*" *RPh,* 17:1 (1963), 87–107.

Crews, Cynthia M. *Recherches sur le judéo-espagnol dans les pays balkaniques.* Paris: Droz, 1935.

–. Review of Walter Schmid, *Der Wortschatz des "Cancionero de Baena".* in *VR,* 13 (1953), 206–209.

Cuervo, Rufino José. *Diccionario de construcción y régimen de la lengua castellana.* Vol. I. Paris, 1886; rpt. Bogotá: Instituto Caro y Cuervo, 1953.

Diez, Friedrich. *Etymologisches Wörterbuch der romanischen Sprachen.* Bonn: Adolph Marcus, 1853. 5th ed. Bonn 1887.

–. *Grammatik der romanischen Sprachen,* II. Bonn: Weber 1838. 3rd ed. Bonn, 1871.

Dworkin, Steven N. "Derivational Transparency and Sound Change: The Two-Pronged Growth of -IDU in Hispano-Romance." *RPh,* 31:4 (1978), 605–617.

–. "The Fragmentation of the Latin Verb TOLLERE in Hispano- (including Luso-) Romance." *RPh,* 37:2 (1983), 166–174 (with Editorial Post-Script, 174f.).

–. "From *-ir* to *-ecer:* The Loss of Old Spanish De-adjectival *-ir* verbs." To appear in *HR,* 53 (1985).

–. The Genesis of OSp. *sencido:* A Study in Etymology and Multiple Causation." *RPh,* 33:1 (1979), 130–137.

–. "Older Luso-Hispanic *garrido* (a) 'silly, foolish' (b) 'handsome, beautiful': One Source or Two Sources?" *RPh,* 34:2 (1980), 195–205 (with Editorial Post-Script, 205f.)

–. "Two Etymological Cruxes: Spanish *engreír* and *embaír* (with an Afterthought on *desvaído*)." *RPh,* 31:2 (1977), 220–225.

Ernout, Alfred, and Antoine Meillet. *Dictionnaire étymologique de la langue latine*. 4th ed. Paris: Klincksieck, 1959.

Fernández Gómez, Carlos. *Vocabulario completo de Lope de Vega*. 3 vols. Madrid: Real Academia Española, 1971.

–. *Vocabulario de Cervantes*. Madrid: Real Academia Española, 1962.

Fleischman, Suzanne. *Cultural and Linguistic Factors in Word Formation: An Integrated Approach to the Development of the Suffix -age*. UCPL 86. Berkeley, Los Angeles, and London: University of California Press, 1977.

–. "Factores operantes en la historia de un sufijo: El caso de *-azgo*." In *Estudios ofrecidos a Emilio Alarcos Llorach,* III. Oviedo: Universidad de Oviedo, 1978, pp. 75–85.

Foerster, Paul. *Spanische Sprachlehre*. Berlin: Weidmannsche Buchhandlung, 1880.

Forest, John B. de. "Old French Borrowed Words in the Old Spanish of the Twelfth and Thirteenth Centuries." *RR,* 7 (1916), 369–413.

Gamillscheg, Ernst. *Romania Germanica. Sprach- und Siedlungsgeschichte der Germanen auf dem Boden des alten Römerreichs*. Vol I. 2nd ed. Berlin: de Gruyter, 1970.

Ganansia, Albert G. "Morforlogía, aspectos dialectales y vocabulario de *La Fazienda de Ultra Mar*." Dissertation, The Ohio State University, 1971.

García de Diego, Vicente. *Contribución al diccionario hispánico etimológico*. Supplement 2 to *RFE*. Madrid, 1923.

–. *Diccionario de voces naturales*. Madrid, 1968.

–. *Diccionario etimológico español e hispánico*. Madrid: S.A.E.T.A. [1955].

–. *Elementos de gramática histórica castellana*. Burgos: El Monte Carmelo, 1914.

–. "Etimologías españolas." *BRAE,* 43 (1963), 217–248.

–. *Gramática histórica española*. Madrid: Gredos, 1951.

García Soriano, Justo. *Vocabulario del dialecto murciano*. Madrid: Bermejo, 1932.

Georges, Emanuel S. *Studies in Romance Nouns Extracted from Past Participles*. Revised by Jerry R. Craddock and Yakov Malkiel. UCPL, 63. Berkeley, Los Angeles, and London, 1970.

Gili Gaya, Samuel. *Tesoro lexicográfico*. I. *A–E*. Madrid: CSIC, 1960.

Gillet, Joseph. *Propalladia and Other Works of Bartolomé de Torres Naharro*. Vol. III. *Notes*. Bryn Mawr, 1951.

Godefroy, Frédéric. *Dictionnaire de l'ancienne langue française et de tous ses dialectes*. 10 vols. Paris: F. Vieweg, 1881–1902.

Gomes Fradinho, Manuel. "Maneiras de dizer alentejanas." *RLu,* 31 (1933), 99–137.

González Ollé, Fernando. *Textos lingüísticos navarros*. Pamplona: Diputación foral de Navarra, 1970.

Greive, Arthur. *Etymologische Untersuchungen zum französischen "h aspiré"*. Romanische Etymologien 8. Heidelberg: Winter, 1970.

Gsell, Otto. "*FATŪCUS, *ASTRŪCUS und die Herkunft von lateinisch-romanisch -ŪCUS." *RPh,* 36:3 (1983), 391–393.

Gröber, Gustav. *Grundriß der romanischen Philologie*. 2nd ed. Strassbourg: Trübner, 1904–06.

Guarnerio, Pier Enea. "Postille sarde." *Ro.,* 33 (1904), 50–70.

Gulsoy, Josep. "L'evolució de la terminació adjectival -ĬDUS en català i castellà." *Homenatge a Josep M. de Casacuberta.* Vol. II. Montserrat, 1981, pp. 25–42.

Hamp, Eric P. "Old Spanish *sencido* again." *RPh,* 36:1 (1982), 28–31.

Hanssen, Federico. *Gramática histórica de la lengua castellana.* Halle: Niemeyer, 1913.

–. *Spanische Grammatik auf historische Grundlage.* Halle: Niemeyer, 1910.

Harris, James. W. "Diphthongization, Monophthongization, Metaphony Revisited." In *Diachronic Studies in Romance Linguistics.* Eds. Mario Saltarelli and Dieter Wanner. The Hague: Mouton, 1975, pp. 85–97.

Hasselrot, Bengt. *Études sur la formation diminutive dans les langues romanes.* UUA 11. Uppsala, 1957.

Keller, Julia. *Contribución al vocabulario del "Poema de Alixandre".* Madrid: Tipografía de la *Revista de archivos, bibliotecas y museos,* 1932.

Körting, Gustav. Lateinisch-romanisches Wörterbuch, 3rd ed. Paderborn: Schöningh, 1907.

Lamano y Beneite, José. *El dialecto vulgar salmantino.* Salamanca: Real Academia Española, 1915.

Lang, Henry R. *Cancioneiro gallego-castelhano: The Extant Galician Poems of the Gallego-Castilian Lyric School (1350–1450).* New York: Scribner's Sons, and London: Edward Arnold, 1902.

–. Review of Federico Hanssen, *Spanische Grammatik auf historische Grundlage.* RR, 2 (1911), 331–347.

Lapa, M. Rodrigues. *Vocabulário galego-português tirado da edição crítica das "Cantigas d'escarnho e de mal dizer".* Vigo: Galaxia, 1965.

Lecoy, Felix. Review of Malkiel, "The Etymology of Hispanic *vel(l)ido* and *melindre".* *Ro.,* 70 (1948–49), 135–136.

Lerch, Eugen. "Germanische Wörter in Vulgärlatein?." *RF,* 60 (1948–49), 647–684.

Levy, Anita Katz. "Factors in the Distribution of Suffixes in the Romance Languages." Dissertation, University of Pennsylvania, 1969.

Lida de Malkiel, María Rosa. *Juan de Mena, poeta del prerrenacimiento.* Mexico, D.F.: Colegio de Mexico, 1950.

Lihani, John. *El lenguaje de Lucas Fernández: Estudio del dialecto sayagués.* Bogotá: Instituto Caro y Cuervo, 1973.

Littlefield, Mark G. "The Riojan Provenience of Escorial Biblical Manuscript i.j.8." *RPh,* 31:2 (1977), 225–234.

Machado, José Pedro. *Dicionário etimológico da língua portuguesa.* 2nd ed. Lisbon. Confluência, 1967.

Malkiel, Yakov. "The *amulatado* type in Spanish." *RR,* 32 (1941), 278–295.

–. "Ancien français *fäu, fëu, malostru.* À la recherche de -ŪCUS, suffixe latin et paléoroman de la 'mauvaise fortune'." *TLL,* 11:1 (1973), 177–190 = *Mélanges Paul Imbs.*

–. *"The Ancient Hispanic Verbs posfaçar, porfaçar, profaçar:* A Study in Etymology and Word-Formation." *RPh,* 3:1 (1949), 27–72.

–. "Between Monogenesis and Polygenesis." *Papers from the Third International Conference on Historical Linguistics.* Eds. J. Peter Maher et al. Amsterdam: Benjamin, 1982, pp. 235–272.

–. "Los derivados ibero-románicos de PETRINUS." *Fil,* 3 (1951), 201–206.

–. "Diachronic Hypercharacterization in Romance." *ArL,* 9 (1957), 79–113, and 10 (1958), 1–36.

–. "Diphthongization, Monophthongization, Metaphony: Studies in their Interaction in the Paradigm of the Old Spanish *-ir* Verbs." *Lg.*, 42, (1966), 430–472.
–. "Español *morir,* portugués *morrer* (con un examen de *esmirriado, morriña* y *modorra*)." *BH,* 57 (1955), 84–128.
–. "Etymology: New Thoughts and Possibilities for its Rejuvenation." *Scritti linguistici in onore di Giovan Battista Pellegrini.* Vol. I. Pisa: Pacini Editore, n.d. [1983], pp. 589–624.
–. "Etymology and the Structure of Word Families." *Word,* 10 (1954), 265–274.
–. "Etymology as a Challenge to Phonology: The Case of Romance Linguistics." *Lautgeschichte und Etymologie: Akten der VI. Fachtagung der indogermanischen Gesellschaft, Wien, 24–29 September 1978.* Wiesbaden: Reichert, 1980, pp. 260–286.
–. "The Etymology of Hispanic *vel(l)ido* and *melindre.*" *Lg.*, 22 (1946), 284–316.
–. "The Etymology of Spanish *cenceño.*" *StP,* 45 (1948), 37–49.
–. "Federico Hanssen y Henry R. Lang." *BFUCh,* 31 (1980–81 [82]), 274–284 = *Homenaje a Ambrosio Rabanales.*
–. "Genetic Analysis of Word Formation." *Current Trends in Linguistics,* III: *Theoretical Foundations.* The Hague-London-Paris, 1966, pp. 305–364.
–. "On Hierarchizing the Components of Multiple Causation." *Studies in Language,* 1 (1977), 81–107.
–. The Hispanic Suffix *-(i)ego: A Morphological and Lexical Study Based on Historical and Dialectal Sources.* UCPL, 4:3. Berkeley and Los Angeles, 1951, pp. 111–214.
–. "Infinitive Endings, Conjugational Classes, Nominal Derivational Suffixes, and Vocalic Gamuts in Romance." *ALH,* 17 (1982), 15–48. [Submitted in 1976.].
–. "Interlocking of Etymology and Historical Grammar Exemplified with the Analysis of Spanish *desleír.*" *Proceedings of the Second International Conference on Historical Linguistics.* Ed. William M. Christie, Jr. Amsterdam: North Holland, 1976, pp. 285–310. (With discussants' remarks at pp. 310–312.)
–. "The Latin Background of the Spanish Suffix *-uno:* Studies in the Genesis of a Romance Formative." *RPh,* 4:1 (1950), 17–45.
–. "Lexical Notes on the Western Leonese Dialect of La Cabrera Alta." *Lg.*, 25 (1949), 437–446.
–. "A Lexicographic Mirage." *MLN,* 56 (1941), 34–42.
–. "Lexis and Grammar — Necrological Essay on Émile Benveniste (1902–1976)." *RPh,* 34:2 (1980), 160–194.
–. "Multiple versus Simple Causation in Linguistic Change." *To Honor Roman Jakobson: Essays on the Occasion of his Seventieth Birthday.* Vol. II. The Hague-Paris: Mouton, 1967, pp. 1228–1246.
–. "New Problems in Romance Interfixation (I): The Velar Insert in the Present Tense (with an Excursus on *-zer, -zir* Verbs)." *RPh,* 27:3 (1974), 304–355.
–. "Nuevas aportaciones para el estudio del sufijo *-uno.*" *NRFH,* 13 (1959), 241–290.
–. "The Pan-European Suffix *-esco, -esque* in Stratigraphic Projection." *Papers in Linguistics and Phonetics to the Memory of Pierre Delattre.* Ed. Albert Valdmann. The Hague: Mouton, 1973, pp. 357–387.
–. *Patterns of Derivational Affixation in the Cabraniego Dialect of East-Central Asturian.* UCPL 64. Berkeley, Los Angeles, and London, 1970.
–. "Perspectives d'un renouvellement de l'étymologie romane." *Actes du XIIIè congrès international de linguistique et philologie romanes (Québec, 1971).* Vol. I. Quebec City: Presses de l'Université Laval, 1976, pp. 967–986.

–. "Primary, Secondary, and Tertiary Etymologies: The Three Lexical Kernels of Hispanic *saña, ensañar, sañudo.*" *HR,* 42, (1974), 1–31.
–. "In Search of Coefficients in Diachronic Morphological Analysis: /i/ as an Increasingly Dominant Vowel in Spanish Inflectional Morphemes." *Proceedings of the Eighth Annual Meeting of the Berkeley Linguistics Society.* Eds. Orrin Gensler et al. Berkeley, 1982, pp. 36–78.
–. "Semantically-Marked Root Morphemes in Diachronic Morphology." *Perspectives on Historical Linguistics.* Eds. Winfred P. Lehmann and Yakov Malkiel. Amsterdam: Benjamins, 1982, pp. 133–243.
–. "Studies in Luso-Hispanic Lexical Osmosis: Old Spanish *famn-, fambr-iento, (des) fambrido,* Portuguese *faminto, es-fom-eado* 'hungry', and the Growth of the Suffix *-(i)ento* ← -(UL)ENTU." *HR,* 45 (1977), 235–267.
Maurer, Theodore H. "The Romance Conjugation in -ĒSCO (-ĪSCO) -ĪRE: Its Origin in Vulgar Latin." *Lg.,* 27 (1951), 136–145.
Meier, Harri. *Neue lateinisch-romanische Etymologien.* RVV 53. Bonn, 1980.
Menéndez Pidal, Ramón. "Etimologías españolas." *Ro.,* 29 (1900), 334–379.
–. *Manual de gramática histórica española.* 6th ed. Madrid: Espasa Calpe, 1941.
–. "Notas para el léxico románico." *RFE,* 7 (1920), 1–36.
–. *Orígenes del español: Estado lingüístico de la Península Ibérica hasta el siglo XI.* 3rd. ed. Madrid: Espasa Calpe, 1950.
Meyer-Lübke, Wilhelm. *Grammatik der romanischen Sprachen,* II. *Formenlehre.* Leipzig: Fues, 1892.
–. *Romanisches etymologisches Wörterbuch.* Heidelberg: Winter, 1911–20. 3rd. ed. Heidelberg: Winter, 1930–35.
–. Review of P. E. Guarnerio, "Postille sarde". *ZRP,* 28 (1904), 635.
Michaëlis de Vasconcelos, Carolina. "Glossário do *Cancioneiro da Ajuda.*" *RLu,* 23 (1920), 1–95.
–. *Lições de filologia portuguesa.* Lisbon: Revista de Portugal, 1946.
–. "Fragmentos etimológicos." *RLu,* 3 (1893–94), 129–190.
–. "Mestre Giraldo e os seus tratados de Alveitaria e Cetraria: Parte II. Estudos etimológicos: Contribuições para o futuro dicionário etimológico das linguas românicas peninsulares.", *RLu,* 13 (1910), 222–432.
Mignot, Xavier. *Les Verbes dénominatifs latins.* Paris: Klincksieck, 1968.
Montgomery, Thomas. "Complementarity of Stem Vowels in the Spanish Second and Third Conjugations." *RPh,* 29:3 (1976), 281–296.
–. "Sobre la etimología de *cenceño* 'pan ázimo'." *NRFH,* 19 (1970), 101–105.
Moreno, Augusto C. "Vocabulário trasmontano (Mogadouro e Lagoaça)." *RLu,* 5 (1897–99), 22–51, 88–114.
Nascentes, Antenor. *Dicionário etimológico da língua portuguesa.* Rio de Janeiro, 1932.
Navarro Tomás, Tomás. *Documentos lingüísticos del Alto Aragón.* Syracuse: Syracuse University Press, 1957.
Nebrija, Antonio de. *Gramática de la lengua castellana.* Ed. Antonio Quilis. Madrid: Nacional, 1980.
–. *Vocabulario de romance en latín.* Ed. Gerald Macdonald. Philadelphia: Temple University Press, 1973.
Nehama, Joseph (with the collaboration of Jesús Cantera). *Dictionnaire du judéoespagnol.* Madrid: CSIC, 1977.
Neira Martínez Jesús. "El prefijo /des/ en la lengua gallegoportuguesa." *Verba,* 3 (1976), 309–318.

Nelson, Dana A. "The Domain of the Old Spanish *-er* and *-ir* Verbs: A Clue to the Provenience of the *Alexandre*." *RPh,* 26:2 (1972), 265–303.

Nitti, John, and Lloyd Kasten. *Concordances and Texts of the Fourteenth-Century Aragonese Manuscripts of Juan Fernández de Heredia.* Madison: Hispanic Seminary of Medieval Studies, 1982. [Microfiches].

–. *Concordances and Texts of the Royal Scriptorium Manuscripts of Alfonso X el Sabio.* Madison: Hispanic Seminary of Medieval Studies, 1978. [Microfiches].

Nunes, José J. "Contribuição para um dicionário da língua portuguesa arcaica." *RLu,* 27 (1928–29), 5–79.

Nyrop, Kristoffer. *Grammaire historique de la langue française.* III. *Formation des mots.* Copenhagen: Gydendalske Boghandel, 1908.

Paucker, C. V. "Materialen zur lateinischen Wörterbildungsgeschichte." *ZVS,* 26 (1883), 409–423.

Penny, Ralph J. "Verb-Class as a Determiner of Stem Vowel in the Historical Morphology of Spanish Verbs." *RLiR,* 36 (1972), 343–359.

Pharies, David A. "Expressive Word Formation in Spanish: The Cases of *titiritar* 'tremble', *pipiritaña* 'cane flute', etc." *RPh,* 36:3 (1983), 347–365.

–. "What is 'creación expresiva'?" *HR,* 52 (1984), 169–180.

Piel, Joseph M. Review of Malkiel, "The Etymology of Hispanic *vel(l)ido* and *melindre.*" *RPF,* 2 (1948), 298–300.

Pottier, Bernard. "Étude lexicologique sur les inventaires aragonais." *VR,* 10 (1949), 87–219.

Raynouard, François J. M. *Lexique roman.* 6 vols. Paris, 1844.

Real Academia Española de la Lengua. *Diccionario de autoridades.* 6 vols. Madrid, 1726–1739. Facsimile, ed. Madrid: Gredos, 1964.

Rodríguez Marín, Francisco. *Dos mil quinientas voces castizas y bien autorizadas que piden lugar en nuestro léxico.* Madrid: Tipografía de la *RABM,* 1922.

Rohlfs, Gerhard. "Beiträge zur Kenntnis der Pyrenäenmundarten." *RLiR,* 7 (1931), 119–169.

–. *Grammatica storica della lingua italiana e dei suoi dialetti,* II: Morfologia. Tr. Temistocle Franceschi. Turin: Einaudi, 1968.

–. "Provenz. *-z-* aus intervokalischen *-t-*." *ZRP,* 51 (1931), 299–303.

Romera Navarro, Miguel. "*Quillotro* y sus variantes." *HR,* 2 (1934), 217–225.

Rudes, Blair A. "The Functional Development of the Verbal Suffix *-esc-* in Romance." In *Historical Morphology,* ed. Jacek Fisiak. The Hague: Mouton, 1980, pp. 327–348.

Sánchez Sevilla, P. "El habla de Cespedosa de Tormes." *RFE,* 15 (1928), 131–172, 244–282.

Sas, Louis F. *Vocabulario del "Libro de Alexandre".* Supplement 34 to *BRAE.* Madrid, 1976.

Schneider, H. "Studien zum galizischen des Limiabecken (Orense-Spanien)." *VKR,* 11 (1938), 69–145, 193–281.

Sobejano, Gonzalo. *El epíteto en la lírica española.* Madrid: Gredos, 1956.

Spitzer, Leo. "Ital. *Scaltrire*". *AR,* 6 (1922), 164–165, and *AR,* 7 (1923), 393.

–. *Lexikalisches aus dem Katalanischen und den übrigen iberoromanischen Sprachen.* Geneva, 1921.

Steiger, Arnald. "Aufmarschstraßen des morgenländischen Sprachgutes." *VR,* 10, (1949), 1–62.

Terlingen, Johannes. *Los italianismos en español desde la formación del idioma hasta principios del siglo XVII.* Amsterdam: N. V. Noord, Hollandsche Uitgevers Maatschappu, 1943.

Texeira, Tavares. "Vocabulário trasmontano (colhido no concelho de Moncorvo)." *RLu,* 13 (1910), 110–126.

Tobler, Adolf, and Erhard Lommatzsch. *Altfranzösisches Wörterbuch.* Berlin: Weidmannsche, 1925–1936, and Wiesbaden: Steiner, 1954-.

Togeby, Knud. "L'apophonie des verbes espagnols et portugais en *-ir.*" *RPh,* 26:2 (1972), 256–264.

Valbuena Prat, Angel. *Obras completas de Salvador Jacinto Polo de Medina.* Murcia: Academia de Las Letras, 1948.

Vigón, Braulio. *Vocabulario dialectológico del Concejo de Colunga.* Ed. Ana María Vigón Sánchez. Supplement 63 to *RFE.* Madrid, 1955. Orig. 1886.

Wagner, Max Leopold. *Dizionario etimologico sardo.* 3 vols. Heidelberg: Winter, 1957–62.

–. *Historische Wortbildungslehre des Sardischen.* Romanica Helvetica, 39. Berne, 1952.

Walsh, Thomas J. "Two Contrastable Approaches to Suffixal Derivation: The Case of Romance *-esco -esque.*" *RPh,* 33:4 (1980), 489–496.

–. "Two Problems in Gallo-Romance Etymology." *RPh.* 35:1 (Aug. 1981), 89–104.

Wartburg, Walther von. *Französisches etymologisches Wörterbuch: Eine Darstellung des galloromanischen Sprachschatzes.* Vol I. Leipzig: Klopp: later volumes Basel: Helbing and Lichtenhahn, 1922–.

Wiener, Leo. "The Ferrara Bible." *MLN,* 11 (1896), 12–21, 42–53.

Wiese, Berthold. *Altitalienisches Elementarbuch.* 2nd ed. Heidelberg: Winter, 1928.

Yanguas y Miranda, José. *Diccionario de las palabras anticuadas que contienen los documentos existentes en los archivos generales y municipales de Navarra.* Pamplona, 1854.

Editions of Medieval Texts

Alfonso X

Cantigas de Santa Maria. Ed. Walter Mettmann. 4 vols. Coimbra: Acta Universitatis Conimbrigensis, 1959–72.

Concordances and Texts of the Royal Scriptorium Manuscripts of Alfonso X el Sabio. By John Nitti and Lloyd Kasten. Madison: Hispanic Seminary of Medieval Studies, 1978.

General Estoria. Vol. I. Ed. Antonio García Solalinde. Madrid: Centro de Estudios Históricos, 1930. Vol. 2, Parts I and II. Ed. Antonio García Solalinde, Lloyd A. Kasten, and Victor R. B. Oelschläger. Madrid: CSIC, 1957–1961.

Judizio de las estrellas. Ed. Gerold Hilty. Madrid: Real Academia Española, 1954.

Primera crónica general. Ed. Ramón Menéndez Pidal. 2 vols. Madrid: Gredos, 1955.

Berceo

El duelo de la Virgen. Los himnos. Los loores de Nuestra Señora. Los signos del juicio final. Ed. Brian Dutton. London: Tamesis, 1975.

Los milagros de Nuestra Señora. Ed. Brian Dutton. London: Tamesis, 1971.

Poema de Santa Oria. Ed. Isabel Uria Maqua. Madrid: Castalia, 1981.

Sacrificio de la Misa. Ed. Claudio García Turza in his *La tradición manuscrita de Berceo*

con un estudio filológico particular del MS 1533 de la Biblioteca Nacional de Madrid Logroño: CSIC, 1979.
La vida de San Millán de la Cogolla. Ed. Brian Dutton. London: Tamesis, 1967.
La vida de Santo Domingo de Silos. Ed. Brian Dutton. London: Tamesis, 1978.
–. Ed. Teresa Labarta de Chaves. Madrid: Castalia, 1973.

Bibles

Biblia medieval romanceada judío-cristiana. Ed. José Llamas. Madrid: CSIC, 1950.
Biblia medieval romanceada, I: *Pentateuco según los manuscritos escurialenses i-j-3, i-j-8 y i-j-6.* Eds. Américo Castro, Augustín Millares Carlo and Angel J. Battistessa. Buenos Aires: Instituto de Filología, 1927.
Biblia medieval romanceada l.i.8. The 13th-Century Spanish Bible Contained in Escorial MS 1.1.8. Ed. Mark G. Littlefield. Madison: Hispanic Seminary of Medieval Studies, 1983.
El Nuevo Testamento según el manuscrito escurialense 1.1.6. Del Evangelio de San Marcos al Apocalipsis. Versión castellana de hacia 1260. Eds. Thomas Montgomery and Spurgeon W. Baldwin. Suppl. 22 to *BRAE,* 1970.

Caballero Zifar

Libro del caballero Zifar. Ed. Joaquín González Muela. Madrid: Castalia, 1982.

Calila e Digna

El libro de Calila e Digna. Eds. John E. Keller and Robert White Linker. Madrid: CSIC, 1967.

Cancionero de Baena

El cancionero de Juan Alfonso de Baena. Ed. José María Azaceta. 3 vols. Madrid: CSIC, 1966.

Cantar de mío Cid

Cantar de mío Cid. Texto, gramática y vocabulario. Ed. Ramón Menéndez Pidal. 3 vols. Madrid: Espasa Calpe, 1944–46. Orig. 1908–11.
Poema de mío Cid. Ed. Colin Smith. Madrid: Cátedra, 1979.

Castigos y documentos

Castigos e documentos para bien vivir ordenados por el rey don Sancho IV. Ed. Agapito Rey. Indiana University Publications, Humanities Series, 24. Bloomington, 1952.

Celestina

Facsimile ed. of 1499 ed. prepared by the Hispanic Society of America. New York

Confisión del amante

Confisión del amante por Joan Goer. Spanische Übersetzung von John Gowers "Confessio Amantis". Eds. Hermann Knust and Adolf Birch-Hirschfeld. Leipzig: Dr. Steele and Co., 1909.

Coplas de Mingo Revulgo

Extracts as in Julio Rodríguez Puértolas, *Poesía de protesta en la Edad Media castellana.* Madrid: Gredos, 1968.

Crónica troyana

"The Aragonese Version of Guido Delle Colonne's *Historia destructionis Troiae:* A Critical Text and Classified Vocabulary." Ed. Evangeline Viola Parker. Dissertation, Indiana University, 1971.

Fazienda de Ultra Mar

La Fazienda de Ultra Mar. Biblia romanceada et itinéraire biblique en prose castillane du XIIe *siècle.* Acta Salmanticensia, Filosofía y letras, 18:2. Salamanca, 1965.

Fernández de Heredia, Juan

Concordances and Texts of the Fourteenth-Century Aragonese Manuscripts of Juan Fernández de Heredia. By John Nitti and Lloyd Kasten. Madison: Hispanic Seminary of Medieval Studies, 1982.

Fueros

El Fuero de Teruel según los mss 1–4 de la Sociedad Económica Turolense de Amigos del Pais y 802 de la Biblioteca Nacional de Madrid. Ed. Max Gorosch. LHMA, 1. Stockholm: Almkvist Wiksells, 1950.

Los Fueros de Aragón según el manuscrito 458 de la Biblioteca Nacional de Madrid. Ed. Gunnar Tilander. Lund: Gleerup, 1937.

Vidal Mayor: Traducción aragonesa de la obra "in excelsis Dei thesauris" de Vidal de Canellas. Ed. Gunnar Tilander. 3 vols. LHMA 4–6. Lund: Ohlsson, 1956.

Gaya Ciencia

La Gaya Ciencia de P[edro] Guillén de Segovia. Ed. José M. Casas Homs. 2 vols. Madrid: CSIC, 1962.

Gran conquista de Ultramar

La gran conquista de Ultramar. Ed. Louis Cooper. 4 vols. Bogotá: Instituto Caro y Cuervo, 1979.

Juan del Encina

Teatro completo de Juan del Encina. Ed. Francisco Asenjo Barbieri. Madrid: Real Academia Española, 1893.

Libro de Alexandre

El Libro de Alexandre: Texts of the Paris and Madrid Manuscripts, Prefaced with an Introduction. Ed. Raymond S. Willis, Jr. Elliott Monographs 32. Princeton, 1934.

Libro de Alixandre: Reconstrucción crítica. Ed. Dana A. Nelson. Madrid: Gredos, 1978.

Libro de Apolonio

Libro de Apolonio: Estudios, ediciones, concordancias. Ed. Manuel Alvar López. 3 vols. Madrid: Fundación Juan March, 1976.

Libro de buen amor

Libro de buen amor: Edición crítica. Eds. Manuel Criado de Val and Eric W. Naylor. Madrid: CSIC, 1965.

Libro de la montería

Alfonso XI, Libro de la montería Based on Escorial MS y.ii.19. Ed. Dennis P. Seniff. Madison: Hispanic Seminary of Medieval Studies, 1983.

Lucidarios

Los lucidarios españolas. Ed. Richard P. Kinkade. Madrid: Gredos, 1968.

Martínez de Toledo, Alfonso

Arcipreste de Talavera o Corbacho. Ed. Joaquín González Muela [and Mario Penna]. Madrid: Castalia, 1970.

"*La Atalaya de las Corónicas* del Arcipreste de Talavera: Edición crítica de parte del texto con un estudio introductorio y vocabulario." Ed. Inocencio Bombín. Dissertation, University of Toronto, 1976.

Otas de Roma

Análisis lingüístico y filológico de Otas de Roma. Ed. Herbert L. Baird, Jr. Supplement 33 to *BRAE,* 1976.

Poema de Fernán González

Poema de Fernán González: Texto crítico con introducción, notas y glosario. Ed. C. Carroll Marden. Baltimore: Johns Hopkins University Press, 1904.

Poema de Fernán González. Ed. Juan Victorio. Madrid: Cátedra, 1981.

Rimado de Palacio

Pero López de Ayala, Libro rimado de palacio. Ed. Jacques Joset. 2 vols. Madrid: Alhambra, 1978.

Vida de Santa María Egipciaca

Vida de Santa María Egipciaca. Estudios, vocabulario, edición de los textos. Ed. Manuel Alvar López. 2 vols. Madrid: CSIC, 1970–72.

Abbreviations
Books, Journals, Monograph Series

AFW	*Altfranzösisches Wörterbuch* by Adolf Tobler and Erhard Lommatzsch
ALH	*Acta Linguistica Hafniensia*
AR	*Archivum Romanicum*
ArL	*Archivum Linguistcum*
BAE	*Biblioteca de Autores Españoles*
BDE	*Breve diccionario etimológico* by Juan Corominas
BFUCh	*Boletín de filología de la Universidad de Chile*
BH	*Bulletin Hispanique*
BRAE	*Boletín de la Real Academia Española*
DCE	*Diccionario crítico etimológico de la lengua castellana* by Juan Corominas
DCECH	*Diccionario crítico etimológico castellano e hispánico* by Juan Corominas and José A. Pascual
DCR	*Diccionario de construcción y régimen* by Rufino José Cuervo
DECLC	*Diccionari etimològic i complimentari de la llengua catalana* by Joan Coromines et al.
DEEH	*Diccionario etimológico español e hispánico* by Vicente García de Diego.
DELF	*Dictionnaire étymologique de la langue française* by Oscar Bloch and Walther von Wartburg.
DELL	*Dictionnaire étymologique de la langue latine* by A. Ernout and A. Meillet
DELP	*Dicionário etimológico da lingua portuguesa* by José Pedro Machado
EWRS	*Etymologisches Wörterbuch der romanischen Sprachen* by Friedrich Diez
FEW	*Französisches etymologisches Wörterbuch* by Walther von Wartburg
Fi	*Filología*
HR	*Hispanic Review*
Lg	*Language*
LHMA	*Leges Hispaniae Medii Aevi*
LRW	*Lateinisch-romanisches Wörterbuch* by Gustav Körting
MLN	*Modern Language Notes*
NRFH	*Nueva Revista de Filología Hispánica*
REW	*Romanisches etymologisches Wörterbuch* by Wilhelm Meyer-Lübke
RF	*Romanische Forschungen*
RFE	*Revista de Filología Española*
RLu	*Revista Lusitana*
RLiR	*Revue de linguistique romane*
Ro	*Romania*
RPF	*Revista Portugesa de Filologia*
RPh	*Romance Philology*
RR	*Romanic Review*

RVV	*Romanistische Versuche und Vorarbeiten*
StP	*Studies in Philology*
UCPL	University of California Publications in Linguistics
UUA	Uppsala Universitets Årsskrift
VR	*Vox Romanica*
ZRP	*Zeitschrift für romanische Philologie*
ZVS	*Zeitschrift für vergleichende Sprachforschung*

Medieval Texts

Alex	*Libro de Alexandre*
Apol	*Libro de Apolonio*
CBaena	*Cancionero de Baena*
CeD	*Calila e Digna*
CMC	*Cantar de mío Cid*
CTroyana	*Crónica troyana*
CZif	*Caballero Zifar*
EE	*Estoria de España*
FAragón	*Fueros de Aragón*
FGonz	*Poema de Fernán González*
FTeruel	*Fuero de Teruel*
GCU	*Gran conquista de Ultramar*
GE	*General Estoria*
LBA	*Libro de buen amor*
LM	*Libro de la montería*
Milg.	*Milagros de Nuestra Señora*
SDom	*Vida de Santo Domingo de Silos*
SLor	*Vida de San Lorenzo*
SME	*Vida de Santa María Egipciaca*
SMill	*Vida de San Millán de la Cogolla*
SOria	*Vida de Santa Oria*
VMayor	*Vidal Mayor*

Word Index

WESTFIELD
UNIV.
LONDON
COLLEGE